ZNIPER

A SNIPER'S JOURNEY THROUGH THE APOCALYPSE

By C. Ward 3

© 2019 by C. Ward III

All rights reserved. This book or any portion thereof may not be reproduced or used in any manner whatsoever without the express written permission of the publisher except for the use of brief quotations in a book review.

ISBN: 9781980597131

www.MarksmanshipTrainingCenter.com

www.GunfighterSeries.com

I dedicate this book to...

My family, my children, and the love of my life, aka FreckledFox1, the crusher of overconfident Halo gamers.

Also to my good friend Kevin the Tactical Leprechaun; Raymond with his superior craftsmanship of Gundo Holsters; my old friend Crazy Chad, who can talk himself into—or out of—any situation; all my Marksmanship Training Center cadre, clients, and friends, whom I've learned so much from; my past, present, and future overseas deployment brothers-in-arms from all walks of life who share the common blood of patriots.

And to all of those who suffered through the rough draft, chapter by chapter, yet still encouraged me to continue the story. Special thanks to the editors: Sidekick, Michelle, and Elite Authors.

CONTENTS

FOREWORD
ACKNOWLEDGMENTS
    PRELUDE
STAGE ZERO
    PANDORA
    SHADOWS
    THROWING BRICS
    PANDORA'S PITHOS
    TRIGGERNOMETRY
    PANDORA'S EVIL
STAGE ONE
    SMALL TOWN, USA
    PLOUTONION OPENED
    THE ROAD NOT TAKEN
    MONSTERS
STAGE TWO
    UMBRA
    UNWANTED GUESTS
    SHACKING UP
STAGE THREE
    ADVERSARIES
    PAYMENT PLAN
    INTEL
    THE WALL
    WOLF PACK
    PREGAME

STAGE FOUR
- *GAME TIME*
- *GAME OVER*
- *Баба-Яга*
- *HOMECOMING*
- *SILK ROAD*
- *COTERIE*
- *KILL OR BE KILLED*
- *SNAKE EATERS*

STAGE FIVE
- *VISITING NEIGHBORS*
- *COMMAND AND CONTROL*
- *EPILOGUE*

AFTER PARTY
- *THE HUNT*
- *Z FIGHTER*

Foreword

CW3 depicts this as a work of fiction. Is it? I found myself floundering, fiction or nonfiction? All too often relatable with parallels of life.

Blind corpses walking the earth, infected and multiplying. Are we fiction or nonfiction?

Maybe one of these days, the emergency broadcast system will not be a test....

When all is lost, and daylight ends, I'll carry you and we will live forever,

Your FreckledFox

The world will never be the same. ZNIPER is an excellent science fiction novel, end of the world, biological accident turning people into twisted humanoid monsters. Ward has always impressed me with his all-encompassing zombie knowledge, and he introduces his vast military and tactical knowledge into the story as well. This will make the arm-chair quarter back military combat arms fan base very happy and won't keep them up at night pondering if they should write a letter to the author, asking him to make a change they suggest. For other people, they may learn something interesting.

The ZNIPER prelude starts out a couple of months into the zombie apocalypse, then jumps back into the start of the bio-disaster event of the century. Ward weaves the story through different lives involving story characters based on the personalities of real people, who's unique skill sets, talents and social traits make for an interesting dynamic. As you read, you will be able to relate to the personalities and emotional situations that the characters face in this fantastic tale and as they navigate their unique situations. As I read the chapters as Ward made them up, I couldn't wait to see what was going to happen next. It's that type of read. With the story bounding from *one life story to another, you are interested in seeing what's happening to one person or set of people but can't wait to see what the other people are experiencing. I couldn't wait to read what was next and thoroughly enjoyed the story. I know you will also.*

Kevin Lippert – The Tactical Leprechaun

Gunfighter, LLC Cofounder

Acknowledgments

This story has numerous zombie–horror pop cultural references hidden within that were inspired by a long list of great authors, screenwriters, and film producers. I am in no way associated with, nor am I taking credit for, the creative works listed in the back of this book. The references in my story do not take away or add value to the original creative work; furthermore, this story would read the exact same without the references.

Half the fun of this story is stumbling into—or hunting for—the hidden zombie-culture Easter eggs. For this reason, the full acknowledgment treasure map is located at the end of the story. No peeking! That would spoil the surprises.

PRELUDE

Kickoff

It's all fun and games until...

Over the past couple of months, their living conditions had deteriorated horribly. He was always hungry. He was always tired. And he hadn't played video games in months. The everyday stress levels were far worse than any school exam ever taken before the world went dark. Long story short: this sucked.

Today was another one of those stressful days. They'd never needed an Eradication Team and Survivor Rescue Team to work simultaneously. This refugee-recovery op must be awfully important for the town.

Recently there'd been an increasing amount of threat activity around the area; perhaps the Rescue Team was losing their nerve and wanted them for backup. Highly doubtful. The guys on the Rescue Team would heroically attempt the impossible, just to ensure their little town remains a beacon of light for anyone left in the darkness.

Typically his dad, Victor, would lead the Eradication Team, but Michael guessed that he and his brother had graduated up the ranks to go solo. Today's mission would be difficult to screw up, since they were essentially on clean-up duty. But those new guys they had brought along—who couldn't seem to sit still, constantly shifting their position—were making him nervous and were going to get them all compromised.

Wiping the layer of grime off his watch, he saw they had ten very long minutes until kickoff. It seemed like they have been there for an eternity already. Of course, waking up at 0200 to sneak out under the cloak of darkness didn't help. He would rather be actively engaging targets; the waiting really sucked.

His earbud crackled to life. "ERT this is SRT. Ten minutes."

He pushed the button on the side of his yellow handheld radio. "This is ERT. We're ready."

"Range card made with TRPs?"

"Affirmative," he replied.

"Roger that, bud; stick to the plan. If things go sour, use the planned escape route we went over."

"OK, Dad. Looks like we're good, though. They're totally going for the bait again."

"Roger that; don't let your guard down. Don't get sloppy. And keep an eye on those new guys. See you after the show. Out."

Michael had no clue how he, a thirteen-year-old, had been elected to lead the Eradication Team on this day. He wasn't nervous about the mission, for he knew exactly what to do, and this was an easy task compared to what the town had been through as of late. Nonetheless, he didn't want to disappoint his dad, and keeping his kid brother safe was a heavy weight to bear.

Zavier, his eight-year-old brother, had the best ears in town. No joke. He could hear someone whispering in the next house, especially if they were discussing cookies. Not only did his kid brother have a good sense of hearing but Zavier was also almost as good of a shot as he was. Almost.

Looking over his shoulder, he could now see the outlines of Grumpy and Deuce on the backside of the roof. They both turned to face him after he tossed a small piece of the roof gravel at them to get their attention. Michael pointed at his watch, then held up both hands with fingers spread to signal ten minutes. They nervously nodded and turned back around to watch their sectors. *Noobs*, he thought.

Normally, those guys would be safely guarding the wall along with the rest of the town security detail. Michael wasn't too sure how they came to be part of his team today. His dad had told him in private to keep them safe, but if this mission got too hot, he was to protect his brother first. And that's exactly what he would do.

He glanced at Zavier, who was lying right next to him, drawing circles in the roof gravel. "Z, after the party starts, you take the closer ones from here to the bait; I'll get the farther ones beyond the bait, OK?"

"I bet I get more than you," Zavier teased.

"Is that a bet? What are we betting on?" Michael asked.

Zavier thought about it for a while. "I get your dessert tonight."

"Ha. Only if you win—which you won't. And then *I* will get *your* dessert tonight."

"We'll see." Zavier grinned with a twinkle in his eye.

"You good on your come-ups?" Michael quizzed.

"Yes, Michael. This is too easy. I'll dial up after I've cleared halfway to the bait, right around that blue car."

"What's your lead?"

"Leading edge at most on the farther faster ones. Too easy."

"Easy huh? Maybe we should switch sides and you take the far ones? There isn't much of a breeze this morning…Maybe it *will* be easy," Michael thought out loud.

At the same time, they shouldered their rifles, staring through their scopes, preparing for the kickoff. From the rooftop of the Three Sisters Bridal & Occasion store, with the morning sun now rising over the trees directly behind them, they could easily survey the street in front of them, and there were plenty of targets to be had. Strangely, neither he nor his brother were bothered by the Grays anymore. They still gave him the creeps, and he completely respected their lethality, but eradicating them had become an average everyday chore.

Those *things* out there were absolutely disgusting, and he didn't want to look directly at them. He could still see traces of human as they crept forward on muscular legs or when they squatted in the dark. He knew they were no longer human; almost everyone had accepted the fact—the infected were incurable.

Their tumorous bodies were covered in large, bulbous pus boils and thick scabs. If one were close enough to them—or using the high-powered zoom of a scope—they'd see the horrid diseased insides through their tight transparent skin. The Grays' thick blood was full of the infection that gave their hairless, muscular body a grayish color.

There were some theories on the cause and effects of the infection, but no one in their town really knew for sure. The only thing they did know was that the Grays were deadly, especially in large numbers like the horde before them now, and more so during the day than at night. The Grays' thick leathery skin was hard to puncture with an average knife and easily deflected small-caliber bullets like the .22 rimfires his brothers had practiced with before the world went dark. Destroying enough of the organs would eventually kill a Gray, but a center mass hit to the brain would put them down immediately.

Mrs. Cloud, the town's high school biology teacher, had become obsessed with the Grays' anatomy, which in turn had made Michael's eradication job much easier. She'd discovered that the Grays had pinpoint pupils, which made them practically blind (but still very deadly) at night. And…there was a rumor she had used a hand saw to cut open a Gray's skull! *That's so disgusting!* Michael thought to himself, recalling the story.

She'd found that only a small portion of the brain's center was still healthy; the rest of the outer tissue had been, for the most part, destroyed by the infection, which is why, they all knew now, they could not be cured.

He looked at his watch again. "Z, two minutes to get ready. Do you remember all the plan?"

"Yes, Michael...we went over it like a million times already."

"OK, just making sure. If we mess this up, Dad could get hurt out there."

"Yeah, there are quite a bit more Grays today than before."

Michael agreed silently as he watched the horde pushing in toward the center of the street, drawn to the bait that his older brother, Curtis, had so cleverly crafted. Michael was kind of surprised the bait was still alive after being out there all night. They had tried this technique before, but never with this kind of success. The Grays must have been creeping there all night just to rock out to Hollywood Undead—which was what was being played at full volume down the street.

Curtis had been able to charge a car battery using a solar panel, somehow he salvaged parts to make a car radio work, and then programmed it to play his favorite rock band on repeat all night long. Michael's brother liked to eradicate in bulk, which is why the radio's timer had been set to ignite the fuse at exactly 0700.

Their bait hung out of the upstairs window of the Other Side of the Moon gift shop. The fuse was an electronic igniter for a model-rocket motor the Scavenge Teams had found in a craft store in the next town over. The rocket motor was jammed into a road flare, which would create a nice windproof flame. The propane tanks hung directly below the radio. The tanks needed to be "opened" remotely at the time of ignition, which is where Michael had come into play.

Thirty seconds on his watch. He tossed another pebble at his rear security guys. His thumbs-up was returned with a nod. He pressed the talk button on the yellow handheld radio. "ERT going loud in ten seconds."

"Copy; SRT standing by."

"Z, get ready. This is going to be louder than the other ones. You should cover your ears. Remember all the fundamentals; don't get trigger-happy wasting ammo trying to beat my count."

Z nodded without taking his cheek off the stock. Michael grinned, knowing his little brother was about to rack up a record kill count by cleaning up the horde of Grays.

Michael rolled his own cheek onto his rifle stock like he had done countless times before. He found the large propane tank in his scope and quartered the target with his reticle. Closed his eyes, took a deep breath, and exhaled, flattening his body against the roof, feeling the gravel grind into his rib cage. Slowly, relaxed, he opened his eyes. Still on target, his natural point of aim was right on. Keeping his cheek welded to the stock, he looked over his scope's eyepiece. The top turret was dialed to his three-hundred-yard elevation setting, windage knob on the side, was on zero.

Inhale…exhale…He watched the reticle effortlessly climb up the gift shop facade as he slowly breathed out, stopping perfectly on the propane tank as the road flare popped to life, jetting out a bright-red flame with a thin trail of drifting smoke. Rifle flicked off safe. Finger found the cold, smooth curve of the trigger.

"On target," Michael whispered.

"Send it," his little brother commanded.

The explosion rocked the entire street, sending a shockwave and deadly debris missiles through the air. The building they were on trembled and groaned violently as it was engulfed in a pungent dust cloud. And that…was when the entire plan went south…

STAGE ZERO

PANDORA

The giver of gifts.

Anesidora startled awake to an ear-piercing *bwhaaaaa, bwhaaaaa, bwhaaaaa*. Sluggishly gaining her bearings, she leaned over and slapped the snooze on her alarm, knowing in seven minutes, the same torture would occur again. *I really need a new alarm clock*, she thought, sticking her head under the pillow. Maybe one of those softly waking clocks that simulate the morning sun, slowly illuminating the room. Sunrise: that mysterious celestial event she hadn't had the pleasure of witnessing for many months now.

Deciding she would skip the few extra blissful moments of comfort under her almost-too-heavy down blanket, she got up and turned off the electronic torture device on the nightstand. In a sleep-drunk stupor, she made her way down the short hallway into the kitchen, finding the teakettle exactly where she'd left it daily for the past two years.

She sat heavily in one of the not-so-comfortable chairs with matching kitchen table, pressing the remote button without picking it up, and turned on the TV in the adjacent room. "Let's see what they are selling us today," she said out loud as the twenty-four-hour news channel came to life. Some perfectly manicured talking-head commentator, who appeared overly exasperated, was going on and on about some sort of civil unrest in the Milwaukee Riverwalk area while a too-fast-to-read text crawler ran across the bottom of the screen, telegraphing something about an upcoming BRICS Summit meeting somewhere Anny didn't care about.

She filled the French press from the whistling teakettle, slowly pushed the plunger down with much precision and practice, as she watched the gourmet coffee grinds magically transform the hot water into the nectar of the gods.

Smelling the aroma and feeling the hot liquid spreading through her immediately brought her to life. Standing up from the rigid chair, rotating her neck, flopping her arms around while bouncing on the balls of her feet, she was ready to get the day started. She killed the TV while pulling her long black hair into a ponytail; those modern infomercial "news" stations only upset her anyway.

Turning on her favorite internet radio station a little too loudly for this early in the morning, she began her daily wake-up/workout routine, starting with a few jumping jacks to get the caffeinated blood flowing through her body.

After that, she showered, dressed, and was out the door of her small and simple two-bedroom condo located in the smaller-size city of Berkley, just on the northern outskirts of Detroit, Michigan. She'd bought the place because it was close enough for an easy drive to work yet far enough to shield her from the negative energy of the big city.

Every day she asked herself why she didn't buy a bigger place with the piles of money she made, but the truth was she was still in the giant hole called "student debt"; and besides, living here alone, she was more than comfortable. She wasn't really a materialistic-type person who needed to keep up with the Joneses with a trendy McMansion. Someday, if things worked out, maybe she'd entertain the topic of moving in with her boyfriend.

As her garage door opened, the dashboard clock turned to 4:00 AM—just in time to check for the daily travel instruction. Her employer, customer—*whoever it was*—had a ridiculous security protocol that required her to get to work differently each and every day. "For your security and ours," they'd said when briefing her at new-hire orientation.

Her phone chimed, right on time, and a text read "696-10." This meant she was to meet the shuttle at the Park and Ride carpool lot at exit 10 off highway 696.

Perfect, she thought while grinning to herself. It was the closest of the five pick-up locations, and there was a drive-through coffee shop right there. She'd have plenty of time, but just in case, she pushed down the accelerator of the aging yet reliable car. Again, she could afford to drive a nicer luxury car, but she didn't for a couple of reasons. One: she didn't want the hassle of it getting stolen or broken into as it sat unattended at the Park and Ride. And two: her employer "recommended" that they drive an inconspicuous but dependable automobile to and from work. Once they were at home, they could drive whatever they desired.

Sitting in the Park and Ride lot, she reclined back, listening to a morning talk show with a comedian doing a hilarious bit about Hot Pockets—yesterday's show, actually, because the rest of society was still snuggled in bed. After scanning through new emails on her phone, she read a message from her boyfriend asking if she would like to meet at the lake cottage this weekend. *That sounds amazing, especially after last month's project*, she thought.

She saw her ride just as she was bringing her nuclear hot and oh-so-delightful chai tea latte to her mouth. A white shuttle bus with miscellaneous hotel advertisements plastered on the side and a big "Private Party" sign lit up above the front windshield pulled in, did a loop, and stopped, facing the lot entrance.

"Let's go save the world," she said to herself, trying to find enthusiasm as she turned to lock her car.

Standing next to the shuttle's open side door was an elderly man dressed casually in a pair of jeans and a long-sleeve sweater holding a clipboard and a pen, marking off names. As Anesidora approached, she overheard the conversation between the next passenger and the keeper of the clipboard.

"Sorry, Betty, you are not on this shuttle today."

"But my instructions were"—the flustered woman pulled out her phone to show Mr. Clipboard, and the look on her face went from triumph to defeat—"Shit! Wrong location!"

"Call your supervisor for instructions. They may send another shuttle for you, *or* you might get the day off work," he said sternly.

"I'm already here, though, can't I just..." The woman's begging trailed off.

He looked at her blankly because they both knew—they all knew—that the mere suggestion of breaking security protocol could lead to harsh reprimands. The act of actually breaking security protocols could bring termination, extreme fines, or even incarceration, or all the above! This was all part of the same new-hire orientation, which every person—from the janitors to the executives—attended. With this brief came a phone book–sized packet that required no fewer than ten thousand signatures and initials, resulting in writer's cramp for a week.

Betty turned and walked back to her car without another word.

"Name?"

Anesidora's answer of "Anny" was awarded with a nod as she stepped past Mr. Clipboard and up the shuttle stairs. Even though this shuttle bus could fit a couple dozen passengers, it typically only transported about half that, and she wondered if the other shuttles throughout the city were jammed full of workers or if this spacious ride was a perk of her position.

Small talk about sports, weather, and upcoming vacations could be overheard as she took her seat next to a window. She nodded to the young man sitting across the aisle from her. Without taking out his earbuds, he smiled and said, "Morning." A couple of years ago, when she'd first stepped onto a similar shuttle, she thought everyone was being rude and insolent to the new girl, but now she understood the invisible wall of privacy that everyone respected.

She was known by her nickname, Anny. Even after the two years on this project, she only associated with a handful of individuals which she's still clueless to anyone's real or full names. Another part of the ridiculous security protocol that she often believed an overkill. But for every rule, there is a reason. Not only did anyone not know her real name but there was also absolutely no way to legally trace her association to this employer, customer, *whoever it was*.

Technically she was self-employed, a 1099 contractor, responsible for her own taxes, health insurance, etc. etc. etc. She was even coached on how to create a fictitious company and open a business checking account so she could get paid without direct association from her employer, customer, *whoever it was*. She was recruited before she had even finished her second doctorate from Perdue University. A recruiter from a company called GENUTEK had given her just enough information to pique her interest. The job description seemed to be molded perfectly for her, and the pay...well, the pay was way more than any new graduate could possibly expect. Of course, there was the risk of becoming clinically antisocial. Even though in her new career she would be creating scientific breakthroughs daily, she would receive no publicity, nil credit, and their work would go completely unnoticed by the rest of the world.

As time went on, she started piecing together that GENUTEK was only the HR department and a headhunter for whoever really owned this project. Her hypothesis—based on zero facts,—was a US federal agency, probably CDC, Biodefense, or DARPA. There were no GENUTEK business cards, no GENUTEK name tags on lab coats, not even a nice shiny GENUTEK sign in the lobby. Anny didn't know if all the employees at the Detroit facility were part of GENUTEK or the actual "customer" for whom the research was. As far as she was aware, GENUTEK sold no products, held no patents or copyrights so their only source of funding could come from selling research information or government funding.

Realizing she had already found the bottom of her latte, she frowned as the shuttle turned down the uneven and pothole-damaged Vernor Highway. She didn't care for this section of the city; it was terribly depressing and made her sick to her stomach—literally, the smell of raw sewer caused her to dry heave. The SL4 biocontainment lab coming into view was perfectly camouflaged in plain sight, right smack in the middle of Detroit Metro.

The huge eighteen-story, 500,000-square-foot Michigan Central Station building had been abandoned many years ago and left to crumble, with every entrance covered in graffiti-painted plywood and chain-wrapped doors. That was the camouflage, which brilliantly matched the surrounding buildings on this stretch of deserted street. Some unknown transportation company is the official owner of the building, which may or may not be true. Their "customer" either owns them, too, or is paying them a handsome rental fee for this one-hundred-plus-year-old rotting corpse of an historic building.

Anny often wondered how the building had been retrofitted for the "customer's" needs without the public's knowledge. Being directly on the train track probably helped with material deliveries and construction noise. The building was an eyesore for sure, and whenever the neighbors complained about it, a promise was made by the city and the current owners to clean it up or add replacement windows to the tower. Truthfully, neither the city nor the owners cared about the building's condition, because they had a well-paying, tight-lipped long-term tenant.

She overheard the driver talk into the handset of the dash-mounted radio, "Six-nine-six-ten, one Mike out."

The radio's volume was turned down too low to decipher what the response was.

They passed the building, rounded the corner, and then slowly turned into a driveway behind the super structure. The driver made a sharp turn at the rear of the building, putting them on a sloping ramp leading into an underground parking deck.

At the base of the ramp was an automated garage door that was activated by the driver's ID card and a wave to the not-so-hidden surveillance camera. The door rolled up; then the bus slowly entered what appeared to be a shadowy, small single-car garage.

The door rolled back down with a bang. Anny and everyone else on the bus were half-blinded as bright halogen lights flickered on, not only on the ceiling but in the floor as well. The vehicle-inspection process always seemed to take forever but was finished in less than a minute. Soon, a second heavy solid-metal gate to the front of the vehicle slid to the right to allow them into the parking deck.

The entire commute from home to here was only about thirty-five minutes. Traffic was light this early in the morning, meaning faster drive time and lower risk of exposure.

The parking garage, which only accommodated the shuttle buses, was in a similar condition to the rest of the building: dark and damp, with a smell to match the decor. Everyone swiftly exited the shuttle with a smile or nod to Mr. Clipboard, then made their way to a single steel entrance door along the wall, where a fairly large but very fit woman (probably a CrossFitter) with another clipboard stood.

"Six-nine-six-ten, check in here please!" she half shouted.

All the passengers, including Anny, passed Ms. Clipboard in the same routine as before: Name? Nod. Next. And through the door they went. Maybe this was to make sure the shuttle didn't pick up any hitchhikers along the route here? Inside the parking lot exterior door was a singular long, well-lit, very clean (compared to the outside) room with a dozen matching steel doors that had a green and red light above each one.

Anny walked over to a door with an illuminated green light, opened it, stepped inside, and shut the door behind her. One entire wall of this cramped closet-size space was made up of several lockers, like the kind found in a train or bus station. She opened a locker, grabbed a basket, and started getting undressed. Everything she brought into the building stayed in the basket: clothes, jewelry, watch, phone, everything except her driver's license. After slipping on the provided hospital-style scrubs, she slid the basket back into the locker and pulled the key, securing the door.

Exiting the opposite side of the sterilization room, she passed through a metal detector on her way to a caged window, handing her locker key and her driver's license to a uniformed guard inside. Without a smile, a nod, or a "screw you," he simply handed back her issued access ID badge, which she quickly clipped to her breast pocket. "Badges must be visible at all times," she had been told, several times.

The guard pushed a button, and the large metal door to her left made a loud *click*, which meant the magnetic lock had disengaged for her to enter.

"Time to save the world," Anny said to herself again, breathing out heavily, trying to find motivation to start the workday.

SHADOWS

Rifle Setup

Michael closed his eyes, inhaling a deep breath through his nose and slowly out his mouth. He relaxed completely, letting his body flatten and mold to the grassy hill. With his eyes closed, he could feel the warm breeze push against his cheek while tousling his perfectly groomed light-brown hair.

He opened his eyes and could see a perfect clear image though the lens. Only one problem: he wasn't centered on the target. He could easily just lean into the rifle stock to center the reticle, but his dad, who was lying right beside and slightly behind him, would probably smack him. Even his little brother would heckle him for such a newbie mistake.

He dug in his toes, lifted his belly up off the ground, and shifted to the right just a smidge, realigning his entire body behind the rifle. He closed his eyes again, relaxing, and reopened them to check his natural point of aim. Perfect. He flicked the safety off and felt the smooth curve of the trigger on his index finger.

"On target," Michael said.

"Send it," said his dad.

He exhaled smoothly one last time. As his chest flattened against the ground, he watched the reticle naturally move from the ground, trail up the post, and stop center on his intended aiming point. Michael slowly squeezed the trigger. The .22 caliber rimfire with a suppressor makes a barely audible *pffffffff* sound when fired.

"Call your shot," his dad said, sounding irritated.

"Left eye," Michael said. His dad slapped him on the shoulder kind of hard, surprising him. "What?" he asked, looking back at his dad, who wore a great big proud smile.

"Great shot! Eject that round, leave the bolt up, and put it on safe. Let's walk down to inspect the targets." He looked at Curtis, the oldest brother, who nodded his head with a surprised look of approval.

"My turn, my turn," Michael's younger brother, Zavier, begged.

"Not yet. Let's go check the targets first; then you can have another go." His dad glanced at the rifles as they started the walk downrange to ensure they were all on safe. "Michael, why did you call left eye?"

"I was centered on the head, but as I was squeezing the trigger, I watched the crosshairs shift slightly to the left side of the head. I couldn't actually make out the eyes from that far away."

"That's good. Most shooters don't have the discipline or skill to call their shots. It's very important when you miss that we know why you missed. That way, the second shot can be quickly corrected for a center-mass hit. We'll practice with that later when Curtis and I shoot the bigger guns. If you notice the reticle keep shifting left all the time, that means you have too much finger on the trigger."

As they got closer to the target boards, they could see the holes in the zombie-themed playing cards. Michael's ten of hearts card had a cartoon zombie fisherman with a small hole where the left side of his head should have been. He smiled to himself as his dad put his arm around him.

"Zavier! High five, bud! Look here, you hit almost all your cards."

"Yeah, but I missed some, and not all are in the center," Zavier said to his dad.

"No worries, buddy. We can work on it. Question for you: When you are looking through the scope, are the edges nice, sharp, and clean or a little fuzzy?"

"A little fuzzy, but usually only a little on one side."

"OK, gather around," Victor said to all three of them. He grabbed a stick and drew an almost perfectly round circle in the dirt, then scribbled on one side of the circle's edge. "All right, this is called *sight alignment*. You don't need to remember that, just what the effects are. When the scope is fuzzy, we call that *shadow*. If the entire edge has shadow or is fuzzy, then we need to adjust the scope either closer or farther to your eye to clear that up. Your problem, Z, is that you only have shadow on one side like this, right?"

Zavier nodded.

"What happens is if you have shadow on the right side, then your bullet is going to impact on the left side of the target. Same with up, down, left, and right. The bullet will always impact on the opposite side of the shadow. You need to be sure you have absolutely no shadow. The hard part is: How do we achieve good sight alignment while being completely relaxed? Michael, how do you do it?"

"I don't know, I'm just relaxed. I don't have to move my head at all; the cheek thingy is in the right position, I guess."

"Exactly. We need to adjust Zavier's cheek thingy, also known as the *comb*, so he's not straining and moving his neck around like a wild turkey. Let's do that now, and we'll check Curtis's rifle too. After that, let's take a break to set up camp."

■■■

Victor pulled a small toolbox out of his rifle bag.

"OK, Zavier, lie down behind your gun and relax. Open the bolt and make sure it's on safe. OK, close your eyes, take a deep breath, let it out, and then open your eyes without moving your head. Can you see through the scope?"

Zavier said, "No, I'm too low."

Curtis said, "I have to push my face closer to the scope to get a full picture."

"All right, Zavier, let's fix your comb first." His dad had cut some of their sleeping-mat foam into small squares. He bent one piece over the top of the rifle stock and secured it with some camouflage-skull-pattern tape. Zavier smiled. "Try that, bud. Same drill. Close eyes, relax, and then open eyes.

"Hey, that foam feels soft on my cheek!"

"How's the picture? Still fuzzy? If so, we can add some more foam to raise your cheek up."

"No, I think it's good," Zavier said.

"Hold on, stay in position. I'm going to look through the other side of your scope. Just to double-check, when I look through the objective lens side, I can barely see the reticle, but your eyeball is huge! The reticle is perfectly centered on your pupil. I'd say this gun is good for you now. So…if you miss the zombie cards now, it's all your fault and not the guns. Capisce? You want to see a giant eyeball? Look at Curtis's.

"Curtis, you're up." His dad started unscrewing all the little screws in the scope rings. "I'm going to slide the entire scope back a bit. Staying relaxed and comfortable, tell me when you get a full clear picture."

"Now!" Curtis said.

"Alrighty, then, I'm going to tighten these back down. Let me put a bubble level on it first to make sure it's married up with the gun. We don't want the reticle to be lopsided."

His dad put a level on the gun and one on the top of the scope. Then he grabbed a weird-looking screwdriver. "This is a torque wrench. These tiny screws have fine threads that can strip out easily. If we over tighten the rings around the scope, we could literally crush the inside of the it. And we all know how superhuman strong I am, this torque wrench will protect the goods."

Curtis just smirked and shook his head at his father's lame joke.

"What? You don't think I'm strong? Let's unload the Jeep now; then we can go throw a few rounds downrange."

THROWING BRICS

A global coup d'état

"The US and her allies have bullied their way into a global position of authority using aggressive policies for over two hundred years. We are all in agreement: the time has come for a new global power. One that is fair, one that can work collectively to produce a better future—not for just one region, but for the entire planet."

President Putin didn't have to sell the idea of creating a new governing global super power. No, that decision had been made long ago; it's why they had been meeting annually for the past decade.

The whole world could see the US dropping the ball; they were practically relinquishing the keys to the kingdom voluntarily. They had recklessly spent themselves into the deepest unsustainable debt in history while lecturing the UN council on resource management at the same time. The current president's foreign policy had laid the foundation for the rebuilding of the Ottoman Empire, which had been successfully dismantled during WWII. Vladimir shook his head. He believed there were more non-Americans living in America than loyal citizens—the Americans were just handing over generations of hard work and astonishing achievements.

Vladimir sat up straight in the plush black leather chair, straightened the sleeves of his custom-tailored Kiton suit, and leaned forward, folding his hands on the large oak table. He didn't need to raise his voice to be heard; this was a small, discreet, private meeting with no press, no spectators, not even personal advisors. "The time has come. We have successfully accomplished and surpassed all our goals over the past five years with ease. The Westerners simply cannot see the world falling apart around them. If we do not push them off the edge, they will fall on their own when we are least prepared to handle the fallout."

President Xi Jinping, China's head of State, stood up and started to pace the small room. "President Putin, I am not exactly clear on your intentions at this time. But I agree with your assessment. The US has simply become too big to exist. Any new laws of theirs have a rippling economic effect that creates tsunamis of damaged currency around the world. This summit, we together, are now in position to challenge the US and their World Bank creation. Our combined purchasing power parity is now double that of the US. This will only grow as other developing nations drop the US dollar as a trading currency in exchange for the BRIC."

"The universities in the US are in shambles. They used to create the smartest and brightest innovators on the planet. It seems now that political science has overwhelmed the education curriculum with liberal arts." Prime Minister Narendra Modi lowered his head sadly. "It really is a shame. They are producing the next generation of takers. They will only continue the foreign policy of looting the globe for their own gain. Hell, they are even looting each other. They can't seem to help it. The majority of our top grads are taking the top-tier professional positions in the US with ease. It seems they must import talented labor as well as goods and commodities. Our universities in India are now producing professional talent surpassing the US educational system."

Putin listened, but he already knew what they were saying. Frustration was being felt around the world. It truly was the time to act. The rest of the world wanted the US gone and they knew it; they just wouldn't tell the bully it was time to go home. Russia had retaken USSR territory with only sharp words as a retaliation. The US president was too weak to fight back. Russia had basically kicked the US and their clown-shoe rebels out of Syria. His short Chinese friend here had almost sunk a US battleship last week in the South China Sea with nothing more than a twenty-second media clip before a story about an overdosed sports player. The Great America was already gone. They may as well make it official.

"The time has come for the change of power. It's time to pull the plug on the old dying empire. The time is now to initiate the final phase." President Putin announced.

"I agree with what has been said, but I do not feel that Brazil is ready to take on the great empire to the north. We cannot sustain a military engagement with NATO and allies, even if Russia and China are doing the heavy lifting," said President Dilma Rousseff.

"Nor can South Africa," said President Jacob Zuma. "Any sort of direct action against the US, militarily or economically, the US military could go rogue by taking retaliatory action on their own without orders from their bureaucratic government. Even if BRICS controls four times the land area than the US, they still have military technology superiority without question. They could launch a drone war on us without ever leaving home."

Putin leaned back in his chair. "Let's play the 'What If' game. What if the United States was no longer a threat or a concern, if they simply stumble and fall peacefully?"

"We would still have her allies to contend with," said President Rousseff.

"They're too weak," said Putin. "The European Union politicians and IMF World Bank are so self-centered, they are destroying Europe from within just as fast as the Americans. After the fall, we the BRICS will be the governing power of global stability. Yes, they will resist our terms at first. Then we will cripple them with military and trade sanctions, just as they have implemented over the past one hundred years. Once they have destroyed themselves with pride and greed, they will seek our help, which we will assist."

"Canada and Australia?" asked President Rousseff.

"Canada, without the safety blanket of the US, will take no part in global matters. Australia may do the same, but they will need to be monitored."

"What of the Persians?" asked Prime Minister Modi.

"I fear they will be the ones to take down Europe. The Europeans will already be in shambles without the support of the US and market instability. They will need to be dealt with in time. I'm sure we can all agree there will be no room in the New World for their caveman religious extremism or their barbaric culture. I do not understand the US supporting contribution with the Arab Spring Uprising. These past few years have put the entire world in danger of an Ottoman reconstruction. It's just another signal for us to make the final preparations for a global changeover."

"President Putin, we can play the 'What If' game all day," said President Xi Jinping. "The fact is the United States is still a global superpower with an unmatchable military industrial complex, along with a vast network of allies. Any sort of hostile action we take against them will be a stalemated mutual destruction scenario or worse. Perhaps we wait until after their next presidential election; they might just hang themselves."

"Of course they will hang themselves! Have you been watching their candidate-selection process? They care more about someone's gender, ethnicity or age, or grooming appearances, or how much the population can loot from the very people who make their country great. Yes, they have already been hanging themselves for a long time. We just need to kick the chair out from under them to make it a clean transition."

Putin got up and walked over to the window, where he stood for a good long minute. Then, turning to face the group, he said, "Let me tell you how."

PANDORA'S PITHOS

Good intentions and all that stuff...

The elevator lobby was another clean, well-lit, and not-too-spacious room. As Anny debated taking the elevator or the stairs, she overheard the two guards who were nonchalantly holding up the wall, rifles casually slung across their backs.

"How many?" the taller of the two said.

"Four last night," the shorter, stockier man said. "That means you owe me a beer."

"I think you're lying. You've won three times this week. I want to see the report!"

Anny stepped closer. "I'm sorry to butt in, but what are you talking about?"

"Nothing really," the shorter guard said as he stood more upright. "We have a running bet on how many transients the night shift has to shoo away throughout the night."

"Oh...any of them ever get in?" she asked curiously.

"No, night shift has some sort of reward when they catch one lurking; it's like a game to them," the tall guard said. "The daytime ones are more trouble. They try to sneak into the building to vandalize and be destructive."

"Does your shift offer a reward?" Anny asked.

The two guards look at each other and grinned childishly. "Yeah, sort of," the tall one said.

"All right, say no more. Off to work for me. My name is Anny, by the way."

"Leprechaun," said the short man with closely cut red hair, extending his hand. "This is Dan."

"Nice to meet you. Don't work too hard. I'll buy you lunch sometime if I see you there," she said, turning for the stairs.

"You got it!" they said, almost in sync.

Anny was used to men stumbling and stuttering in her presence. She didn't think of herself as a supermodel, but she had always had a giddy-making effect on men. Maybe it was her athletic build or maybe her light complexion due to her Mediterranean ancestry. As much as she appreciated the attention, she was very happy with the relationship she was in.

For most of the workers here, this career was a total social buzzkill. They had a very strict no fraternization policy at work. Outside of work, how was she supposed to have a relationship with someone with whom she was forbidden to share the most exciting parts of her life? Back when she was dating, she'd tried using the 'Health Inspector' cover story she'd been made to memorize, but telling someone a fake story made her extremely uncomfortable. Luckily, her boyfriend was a security contractor for an unknown employer in an unknown location. His career secrecy matched her own, and so they shared a mutual understanding: don't ask too many work-related questions.

Stairs it is, she thought. The caffeine-blood mixture needed a stir, and besides, going down was easier than going up. She'd take the elevator up at the end of shift.

She would have thought retrofitting the upper levels of this old building would have been easier and more cost beneficial to the customer. But the risk of a squatter accidentally compromising the lab was too great, and keeping the lab subterranean increased containment protocols tremendously. Retrofitting the substructure probably wasn't all that difficult anyway, since the infrastructure was already in place.

In its prime, this old building had serviced up to four thousand train passengers a day and held over three thousand office workers. Most of the daily seven thousand Michigan Central Station visitors were unaware they were sitting on top of a 150,000-square-foot munitions bunker. This station had been a major supply-staging area for the Michigan war industry during WWI. Everything from bullets to tanks had been stored under this building.

There were five sub levels: Sublevel One (SL1) was for administrative- and building-logistics staff. Having been here for two years, Anny had yet to go to SL1. Any and all personal admin problems (which she almost never had) were handled though her immediate supervisor.

Sublevel Two (SL2) held a luxurious cafeteria, comfy lounge, decent exercise room, and even sleeping accommodations for the workaholics or in case of emergency mandatory overtime—which also never happened.

SL3–SL5 were where the real science happened. Most new hires started on SL3, where teams would find ways to destroy every harmful virus, parasite, pathogen, bacteria, and fungus known to man—and many unknown to man as well. Being on SL3 was very exciting and rewarding work, although it was a bit easy. Most of these Nasties (a generic blanket term used for all the harmful microscopies) were simple organisms that, once introduced to a certain compound, shriveled up and died. All the scientists needed to do was go through their arsenal and catalog what worked and what didn't.

If a scientist was really good at their job on SL3, they would eventually get promoted to either a team supervisor position or to SL4 depending on personality. Some people were natural leaders and possessed the passion for killing the Nasties—those were the team supervisors. Others, like Anny, were promoted to SL4, where "cures" were investigated.

After she'd first been promoted, she would reach for the SL3 stairwell door out of habit and swipe her badge while looking into the facial- and voice-recognition system. Of course, she no longer had access to that floor, which prompted an ugly, annoying tone from the access-control box. Do this a few times and the facilities security team would come out of nowhere and throw a bag over your head, dragging you into a dark room from questioning.

SL4 was the meat and potatoes of the entire project. SL4 was where practical science was pioneered. Once the Nasties found a host, how did they kill the Nasties without harming the host? Seemed easy enough, but one Nasty may take years to beat. Even with all the advanced technology in this lab that made her Perdue University–tech look like children's toys. Very rewarding, yet extremely frustrating work. Hence the sleeper pods on SL2—some of the scientists would get so wrapped up in finding the cure that they refused to go home. Not Anny, though; she did her best work while fully rested and not stressed.

SL5 was the cream-of-the-crop mad scientists. Once in a great while, a new specimen would be delivered to SL3 that must first be identified, cataloged by the kill teams, and then cured by SL4. The "new specimen" was exactly that: new to the world. Created downstairs in the SL5 dungeon. There were rumors once of a new Nasty that SL5 had received from NASA—but again, there were zero facts to back up any rumors of a Space Nasty. Anny had no desire to ever get promoted to that subfloor. In her mind, there were plenty of Nasties on this planet already. No need to create more. But the scientists on SL3 and SL4 looked forward to conquering whatever SL5 threw at them next.

Successfully opening the stairway-access door to her subfloor, she was greeted by the bright lights, white walls, and freshly shined floor of the SL4 lobby. Not really a lobby—more like a foyer, with a conference room to the right and, to the left, a small kitchen with forever-brewing gourmet coffee and snacks. Straight ahead was a singular long hallway, with one door on each side and a door to the supply locker at the end. Cure Team Alpha on one side of the hallway and Cure Team Bravo on the other. These two teams did not interact with each other. In fact, they were in some sort of constant competitive battle. When SL4 had a new project, each team would race to the cure. Whoever won usually received a nice pay bonus and extended vacation—but, more importantly, the bragging rights were a big morale booster.

There had been several occasions when her team was ordered to end research on a Nasty. Sometimes this was a relief because no progress had been made whatsoever; other times it was infuriating because they were 99.9% completed with their cure project. Someone once let it slip that a facility in another city had beat them to a cure. That caused some questions to arise: Which city? How many other facilities like this were there? Of course, those questions were never answered, and Mr. Loose Lips was immediately terminated.

Swiping her badge and looking into the facial- and voice scanner, she said, "Anny, three-eight-six-nine." The door made a familiar *click*, and she opened the door to "A TEAM."

TRIGGERNOMETRY

1.5 Up, 3 Left

After setting up their tents a safe distance from the firepit, the boys grabbed their rifles and equipment, then walked to a different part of the rifle range.

"Oh my gosh, I can't even see the targets all the way down there. How far is that?" asked Zavier.

"Well, we have some paper targets up close at one hundred yards that we will use to ensure the scopes are sighted in properly. Then we are going to hit those white steel targets. The closest one is at three hundred yards, the farthest one is about 1050 yards."

"That's insane!" said Michael.

"That," his dad, said smiling, "is mastering the science and shooting fundamentals we have been practicing all day. And a whole lot of bragging rights. Hitting that farthest target is no different from hitting that zombie in the head earlier. The only difference is that we have to compensate for things like gravity, air drag on the bullet, and wind effects. A couple other things, too, but those are the biggies."

Curtis took three shots on a paper target at one hundred yards. The three holes almost touched each other. "How come they didn't hit center?" he asked.

"Because we monkeyed with your scope. No problem, though; we can adjust it," his dad said while still looking through a big spotting scope that looked like it could easily spot people on Mars. "Can you see your holes? How far from center would you estimate you are off?"

"Maybe an inch and half low and three inches right—ish."

"Math lesson for all: pay attention boys," Victor said, pulling them all in closer. "If you look though the spotting scope, you can see Curtis's shots are off-center, so we are going to adjust his crosshairs to impact where he is aiming.

"Scopes come in two different measurement types: MOA (Minute of Angle) or Mil (Mil Radian). Same principle on both, just different units of measurement. All ours are in MOA. One full MOA adjustment at this one hundred–yard target will move the bullet about one inch. So...Curtis needs to move his bullet left three inches. How does he do that?"

Zavier shrugged.

"Three inches would equal three MOA, correct?" Michael said, kind of unsure of himself.

"Correct. And how do we do that, exactly? The top knob on the scope moves the reticle up and down for elevation adjustments. The one on the right side here, that is for windage adjustments, which moves it left and right. Curtis, go ahead and adjust it three full MOA to the left. Use the top to go up how many?"

"One and a half?"

"Yup, one and half MOA to move it an inch and a half at this distance. Do that, then send three more good shots. Michael and Zavier, use the spotting scope to see if they hit center this time."

"Another math test: These are obviously not laser guns—which would be a whole lot cooler if they were. But instead, they shoot out these metal bullets. Even though they are going extremely fast, they start falling to the ground as soon as they leave the muzzle. The farther they go, the longer they are in the air, and the longer gravity pulls it down.

"Remember how many inches one MOA represents at one hundred yards? Yup, one inch. Here's the tricky part: MOA and Mils are actually an angular unit of measurement. Don't worry about the big scary word—all that means is that it spreads out the farther away it gets. Example: One MOA at one hundred yards is about one inch. Easy, right? The same one MOA at two hundred yards equals two inches. At three hundred yards, the same one MOA equals three inches. So what do you think one MOA at five hundred yards equals?"

"Five inches," the three brothers said together.

Victor smiled. "You didn't know you were going to do math this weekend, did you? This is fun math, though."

Zavier fell back and spread his arms on the ground. "I don't like math."

"OK, smarty pants. For the time it takes the bullet to get from here to the three-hundred-yard target, gravity will pull the bullet down about twelve inches…it's actually a little less than that, but let's say twelve for this exercise. We need to adjust for that twelve inches of drop. At three hundred yards, how many MOA is twelve inches?"

"Four," said Curtis.

"Do you agree, Michael?"

"Yeah, because at three hundred yards, one MOA equals three inches. The twelve inch drop divided by three inches equals four MOA."

"Well, let's see if your answer is correct. Curtis, dial four full MOA on the elevation turret, and then give me one good shot, center mass, on the three-hundred-yard target. Zavier, watch through the spotting scope and tell us where it hits."

Dad watched Curtis as he relaxed, took the gun off safe, and gently squeezed the trigger.

Thwack was the sound the bullet made as it hit the steel target.

"Awww, that was sweet!" said Zavier. "There's a big black mark where the bullet hit."

"Congratulations, you passed Sniper Math 101. The bullet blasted the paint off the steel target. Pretty convenient, because we wouldn't be able to see the hole in a paper target from here. Where did you hit?"

"A little high from where I was actually aiming," Curtis said.

"How high?"

"About an inch and a half, maybe."

"All right, sniper-math grads, figure it out. What is the MOA correction to move the bullet down one and a half inches at this three-hundred-yard target?'

"One MOA is three inches, so half of that."

"I agree. Curtis dial down half an MOA, and give me a headshot on that same target."

"On target."

"Zavier, are you watching through the spotting scope? Tell him you are ready to watch the impact by saying 'send it.'"

"Send it!" Zavier shouted loudly, as he always did when wearing the hearing-protection muffs.

Thwack. Right in the middle of the head. "One dead zombie, right there. Great shot. That was easy, huh? Next drill: dial the elevation turret back down to zero, and look for the five-hundred-yard target designated with a red triangle off to the side."

"OK, I found it."

"Go ahead and refix your position; your body is all off to the side of the rifle. If you are not directly behind the rifle, your body will not absorb the recoil properly, causing the rifle to jump all over the place; then you'll have a hard time finding the target again after the shot.

"OK, math quiz: For a five-hundred-yard target, our bullet will drop forty-five inches. How much do we need to come up?"

"Nine!" Michael and Curtis said at the same time.

"Nine what? Are we talking MOA, inches, clicks, chicks, cookies, or what?"

"Nine MOA," said Curtis as he reached up to spin the top turret.

"Michael, move the spotting scope to the five-hundred-yard target. When he shoots, see if you can see the bullet fly through the air. It will look like the bubble trails in the movie *The Matrix*, like there is a smudge or bug on the lens."

"On target."

"Curtis, see how the wind flag is flopping from right to left? At this distance, we are going to have to shoot into the wind, OK? Go ahead and aim at the right armpit."

"OK, on target."

"Send it!" screamed Michael, mocking his little brother.

About half a second later, the rewarding *thwack* was heard. "Great shot, Curtis!"

"I saw it; I really saw it. I actually saw the bullet in the spotting scope. Only for a split second, though," said Michael, grinning. "That was cool!"

"That it is. Sometimes when the sun is just right, you can see the sun shining off the bullet while it's in flight. That is really cool," said Victor. "Curtis, how did that feel?"

"Pretty good, but if I wouldn't have aimed at the armpit, I probably would have missed, right? How did you know how much the wind would move it?"

"Practice. Lots and lots of practice. There are math formulas and ballistic programs to calculate the wind drift. But truthfully, observing the wind speed and direction is the real skill involved in distance shooting."

"That was fun. Can we try farther out?"

"We can, but later. This sun is getting hot, and I hear the ice-cream shop in town calling our name. We'll shoot some more this evening after it cools off some, and maybe the wind will die down a little to make it easier for you. Let's pack up our gear and grab our swimsuits before we take off."

PANDORA'S EVIL

Only hope remains.

Anny strolled into the lab, expecting an easy day of wrapping up a project report that her team had just triumphantly concluded. As the rest of Team A filtered into the lab one by one, all wearing cheerful smiles, Anny noticed Alice Krippin, her team leader, pacing near the door.

As the last of her coworkers entered through the door, Alice said in a loud, stern voice, "Everyone, follow me into the war room. Now."

The mood in the room went from cheerful over their recent project victory to timid. Unaccustomed to hearing Alice in such a serious tone, they quickly stood, stools screeching across the freshly polished floor, and then fast-stepped into the strategy room.

Quickly finding a seat around the long conference table, they all stared at Alice, who was pacing in front of a whiteboard-covered wall. "We have a new Nasty to battle. Dr. Mercer, I want you to finish the report on the cure of SYD-398 as soon as you can, then regroup with us. Team, we are now on mandatory overtime."

Immediately, everyone looked around the room at each other with questioning looks.

Anny was the first to speak. "What is it, Dr. Krippin? What are we up against?"

Alice continued to pace back and forth. "The organization's leadership is breaking all protocols on this. Teams A and B will be working together instead of in competition. Level Three labs are having a hard time with this one and have yet to effectively destroy the Nasty. To keep the study completely blind, we normally start building information from the ground up with no input, but time is of utmost importance. Also, breaking protocol, Level Five has announced this hybrid Nasty is not one of their creations. Origin's completely unknown."

"What do we know about it?" asked Sayeed as he and everyone else uncapped their pens to take notes.

"Just a few hours ago, we received this report, courtesy of Dr. Jenner." As Alice dimmed the lights, a bright Center of Disease Control logo appeared on the whiteboard with the words "Top Secret–Sensitive Compartmented Information." She clicked on the first image displaying the top view of a patient's head surgically cut open with the brain in view. "What's wrong with this brain?"

"Other than the fact that the top of the skull is missing?" asked Will while reaching for a pitcher of water.

Doug, sitting next to Anny, quickly answered, "The tissue has black spots, almost like small burn marks. First diagnosis would be a prion protein. If the spots were on top of the brain tissue, I would say a form of cancer."

Alice looked at the group. "Prion is the forerunning hypothesis as of now."

Anny said, "Prion isn't anything new. In humans, the protein can be passed down from parent to offspring. In nature, the prion lingers in clay and other minerals from the decay of urine, saliva and other bodily fluids of dead animals. Animals are known to be infected though environmental ingestion."

Sayeed added, "The prion is mostly found in India and Mexico. Where did this patient reside? Are we looking at a mutation of sorts, like FFI or Mad Cow?"

"I'll come back to the location of this patient shortly. This prion has most certainly mutated, which we will touch on again shortly." Alice took a long, deep breath, as if not knowing what to say.

Looking at each scientist in the room, she clicked on the next set of photos. "We all know what this is, but please refresh our memories."

Sitting at the far end of the table, Dr. Mercer stopped typing up his report to add to the conversation. "Picture on the left is a parasite. The look of a sperm wearing a dunce hat suggests the flesh-eating disease Leishmania. The image of the patient on the right covered in massive lesions and scabbing would strengthen my hypothesis."

"Transmission methods?" asked Alice, glancing around the room.

"Sand-fly bites," said Anny. "Again, not common to the USA. Thankfully, because it's difficult to treat with our strict drug-importation laws. Dr. Krippin, what country did this patient live in?"

Ignoring the question, Alice clicked on the next slide, bringing up a magnified image of a spore that looked like a medieval mace–type weapon—a gray orb with several protruding spikes. Alice turned to look at the room.

Will said, "It's a fungus, ascomycota division. Can you give us another clue?"

"I will give you a hint: most commonly found to grow on insects, this specific one on—or should I say *in*—ants. Discovered by Tom Petch in 1931."

"The zombie spore..." Sayeed trailed off as a new image came up on the screen.

Doug stood up and walked closer to the board to examine the picture of the next patient.

Anny also stood up. "I don't understand. The Ophiocordyceps unilateralis targets ants strictly. It digs into the host's brain and nervous system, takes control of the host to direct it to the most beneficial environment for reproducing, usually high in trees. As it matures, the host grows a spore-filled tumor out of its head until it pops, raining new spores across the jungle floor. But this here...it can't be."

Alice also stared at the images. "The Ophiocordyceps genus has 140 species that grow on insects. There has never been a case involving mammals."

The room fell silent for several minutes. The image on the board that held their breathless attention was that of a human patient with a large gray growth the size of a cantaloupe protruding from the side of his or her disfigured neck.

Dr. Mercer, who had abandoned his report, asked, "So what does the prion and Leishmania have to do with the zombie spore?"

Alice turned to face her staff with pain in her face, a look of devastation. In a fearful whisper, she said, "These images are all of the same patient. One patient—out of about two dozen—the CDC has quarantined in the United States, all of them with the exact same single source of infection. Transmission, incubation period, contagiousness have not been verified as of now, but we believe it to be casual human-to-human contact."

"So...does this mean Fourth of July is canceled?" asked Will to no one in particular

"As stated before, A and B teams will be working together on this project. Full information sharing. Let's get started. Night crew prepped the tissue samples provided by the CDC. They are in the vault. Primate patients have already been introduced to the new Nasty; begin data collection on infection symptoms and results." Alice said, talking quickly.

"I'll pull the tissue samples from the vault," said Anny.

"Sayeed, can you gather a blood sample from the primate?"

"On it!" he said, already heading for the door.

■■

Over the next several hours, the entire substructure was a beehive of activity. People were scrambling up and down the stairwell, in and out of corridors, from one lab to another. The clerks in SL1 were bringing fresh coffee pots and snacks to SL3–SL5. Even the janitorial staff was running paperwork from one subfloor to another. Anny had never witnessed anything like it.

By lunchtime, SL3 had completed their initial testing. They had gone through their entire arsenal to kill the Nasty. The problem was they could only destroy one piece at a time—not the entire contagion at once. In fact, when one portion was destroyed, the other two seemed to duplicate faster. The mad scientists in SL5 were unsuccessfully dissecting genetic code, looking for clues of its origin.

Zero progress had been made other than understanding the absolute bizarre nature of this parasite/fungi/prion hybrid. In fact, it seemed as they were further behind than before as frustration started setting in.

This organization housed the most brilliant bioscientists on earth; each individual piece of this puzzle typically would be an easy task. But whatever this hybrid was, it stopped them dead in their tracks.

Soon, each staffer was given a piece of paper that offered a scripted generic excuse about a citywide salmonella outbreak they were to notify their loved ones with on why they would be working late today and possibly days or weeks to come.

"Guess the health inspector is pulling double duty for a while," Will said to himself, putting his face back into the microscope.

Anny needed to let her boyfriend know she wouldn't make it to the lake cottage for the weekend. She exhaled loudly while slumping her shoulders forward at the thought of missing out on another much-needed relaxing weekend. Since all employee cell phones were in the storage lockers at the security check-in station, she got up to make her way up to the SL2 cafeteria area, where there was a bank of secure phones they could use for personal use. Her shoes squeaked on the tile floor as she rounded the end of her well-lit workstation. She was just reaching out to open the lab door when the entire building went pitch black.

STAGE ONE

SMALL TOWN, USA

The Greatest Fourth in the North

"Dad, is Erica coming up this weekend?" asked Zavier as they drove into town.

Victor shouted over the loud wind rushing over the topless Jeep and oversize tires rumbling down the road, "She is. She'll be up sometime tomorrow. She had some important meetings today she couldn't sneak out of. I think she's bringing us some extra camping chow too."

Victor enjoyed his weekend getaways with his boys. Camping, shooting, small-town fun in the "Great Up North," as everyone called vacationing in northern Michigan. Unplugging from the busy rat race for a long weekend is just what he needed, especially after this hectic past year.

"Should we get ice cream before or after the beach?"

"Before!" they all said in unison.

"Curtis, park us in the first spot you see. Being a holiday, the streets will be packed," Victor told his oldest son, who had just recently received his driver's license. "Or just pull this beast on top of the smallest car you see." The kids loved their dad's lifted Jeep. They also enjoyed watching people stare in envy as they cruised by.

They ended up circling the small downtown area three times before finding a spot in front of a local diner. "Good spot. Maybe we will eat here later before heading back to the range. We're going to have a bit of a walk to the beach, though."

They grabbed their beach towels and some beach toys and then headed across the street to the local ice-cream shop, which always had a ridiculous line out the door. As they found the end of the line, Victor asked if they were getting ice cream or shakes. As always, Zavier would get a cone that would be melted all over him by the time they reached the beach. Michael and Curtis got something new each time. Victor liked that they enjoyed being adventurous, even if it was only ice cream.

Zavier and Michael were still debating which flavors were better when they stepped into the line behind a short blonde lady. "Aby Van Helsing is it, with the Chamber of Commerce?" asked Victor.

The short lady turned around and said, "Yes, that's me. What can I do for you?"

"Just wondering what time the fireworks are tonight."

"Fireworks start just after nine thirty. It's the greatest Fourth in the north," she said with a smile and tilted head.

"So the banner says," he said, eyeing the banners and fliers plastered all over the town. "Thank you for the info."

She smiled and turned back around to catch her spot in line.

They finally made their way to the front of the line, got their cold deliciousness, and started walking toward the public beach. The sidewalks were packed, which made crossing the street a chore. As they stepped up to the last intersection, Victor noticed the town's sheriff was directing traffic.

"Sheriff Bohner," said Victor as he stepped up to the crosswalk, holding Zavier's hand. "Don't you have deputies for traffic control?"

"They're too busy chasing kids on quads through town and drunk boaters. Besides, I like to see who all's in my town, and this is the best spot to do it," said the sheriff.

The small town of Lake City housed approximately 850 permanent residents. On the weekends, especially this weekend, the town's population quadrupled in size with vacationers like Victor from the metro areas of lower Michigan.

"That it is. Good luck this weekend with the crazies, and be safe on the roads. The kids and I are camping at the rifle range, so if you're up that way, feel free to stop by for a s'more," said Victor as they crossed the road, knowing the sheriff would be too busy with drunken tourists tonight.

Strolling halfway down the boardwalk, they finally found an open patch of beach to claim. As expected, Zavier had a stream of melted double chocolate running from his hand, down his arm, and then dripping off his elbow.

"Well, at least you'll taste good for the fish in the lake," Victor told him with a smirk. By the time he could negotiate Zavier's shirt off without covering it in more chocolate, his brothers were already diving into the water.

Victor spread out a beach towel, took his shirt off to enjoy the summer sun, and then stacked their clothes on one end of the towel. Lying back on the stack of clothes, he decided to shut his eyes for a minute…

■■

Victor woke to the sound of metal crunching, glass shattering, and tires squealing. He sat up quickly, seeing his children in the water looking and pointing beyond the beach to the main road. Victor turned around just in time to see a small sedan hit the curb and go flying down the hill directly toward him. He dove left and rolled in the sand just as the front of the car slammed into his beach towel, bouncing violently, then continued into the lake with an enormous splash.

The car was still afloat but sinking fast. As Victor dove into the water, he could see the driver's face smashed against the steering wheel. His boys reached the car at the same time. "Curtis, try opening the passenger door!" Victor was shaking the door handle and pulling on the driver's side with no luck.

Curtis shook his head.

"Michael, toss me a fist-size rock from the beach!"

Michael made it to the shore in record time, found a big rock, and threw it to his dad. In one smooth motion, Victor caught the rock, palmed it, and then smashed the driver-side window. The car began filling with water as he reached in to unlock the door. He had to put his feet against the car and pull on the door with both hands to counter the resistance of the water flowing in.

The car went under water as everyone on the beach watched in horror. Victor surfaced with the driver a short time later. He pulled the driver to the shore using a lifeguarding sidestroke he had learned during Combat Water Safety Swimmer training in the Marine Corps.

"Someone call 911!" Victor yelled to the gathering crowd. Victor laid the driver out flat, then did a quick look over for bleeding. He tilted his chin back and put his own ear and cheek to the driver's mouth while looking at the driver's chest for signs of breathing.

"My phone's dead."

"Mine is too."

"Dad, my phone is dead too."

Looking beyond the crowd on the beach toward town, Victor could see a small pillar of black smoke drifting up. But there were no sirens, no other traffic noise, no nothing. He looked at his watch. Nothing on the screen. "You there! What time is it?"

"I don't know; my watch is dead too!"

Victor looked at his boys, who all wore a confused look. "Grab our stuff. Let's go."

"What about this guy?" said someone from the crowd, pointing to the driver.

"He'll be all right. Unconscious for now. Maybe a concussion. Carry him up the block to the fire department if you want. EMTs should be on duty," Victor said as he turned to leave.

"What's going on, Dad? Where are we going?"

"I have an idea. Let's go find the sheriff."

■■

The intersection where he found the sheriff was chaos. Cars were smashed into each other, some had crashed into buildings, some on the sidewalk, and others had stopped in the middle of the road.

"Sheriff Bohner, you realize what just happened? Do you know what an EMP is?"

Victor couldn't tell if the sheriff was in shock or if he was just that cool calm and collected. "Yeah, unfortunately I do. It's the worst of the doomsday scenarios. You think this is it?"

"I do. You probably know that we are in a major shitstorm here. This is your show, but I would try to gather as many of these people as you can find and explain what just happened. Tell them the truth. We don't know if it was a solar flare, a localized EMP attack or countrywide. Many of the tourists may want to make their way back south toward home. You and I know that's a bad idea, but I would let them go. There's four times the people in this town as normal because of the holiday, which means resources will be depleted within a few days. It's about to be the wild, wild west."

"What are you going to do?" asked the sheriff.

"My boys and I are going to go gather our camping gear. We'll be back in a couple of days. I'd recommend getting the city council together to begin coordinating emergency action plans. Whatever is left of this town when we get back, we'll help out anyway we can."

"Happy Independence Day," said Sheriff Bohner as he turned and headed up the street toward the center of town.

■■■

"Come on, boys. let's get our stuff out of the Jeep." Victor said to his boys. But when he looked back, all three of them were standing on the sidewalk with the same look of terror they had coming out of the haunted house last Halloween.

"Dad, what's an EMP? What's happening?" asked Curtis.

"OK, boys, this is going to be hard to wrap your head around. I'm not sure if I believe it just yet myself. An EMP is an Electromagnetic Pulse. Imagine a large tidal wave of electrical radiation rippling through the air. Every modern electronic has a solid-state microcircuit built to operate on a tiny amount of energy. An EMP's energy tsunami will overload and fry those tiny microcircuits."

"How do you know that is what happened?"

Victor held out his arms and spun around. "Look around. I knew it as soon as the cell phones and wristwatches were dead."

Michael asked, "What caused it?"

"That is a great question. The best-case scenario, this is a cosmic event. Maybe a large solar flare from the sun. It wouldn't be the first time in history. If it's solar, this might be an isolated incident and help could come sooner or later."

"Worst-case scenario?" asked Curtis.

"We are under attack. An enemy could have nuked us from high altitude, most likely a few of them across the country. If that's the case, life as we know it will never be the same. EMP is the worst kind of attack, because our society will collapse within days, citizens will start robbing and killing each other for food. People will freeze and starve to death during the winter without electricity and fuel. Then, when there is hardly anyone left, the enemy rolls in and conquers the land with little to no resistance."

"Nuked us? Won't we all die from radiated acid rain or something?" Michael asked, looking pale.

"No, you're talking about getting radiation sickness from fallout. That's caused by ground-burst nuclear weapons that kick up radioactive particles into the atmosphere, then fall back to earth. High-altitude weapons don't do that. I didn't even see a flash or a heat wave, did you? You know what also sucks? Even if our phones did survive, most likely the communication satellites overhead at the time probably got cooked, meaning we couldn't call anyone anyway."

"So where are we going now?"

"To grab our guns from the jeep and then to the grocery store on the way back to camp. I don't want us to be anywhere near population, even this town, over the next few days."

Zavier asked, "If the cars don't work, how are we getting back to camp?"

"We walk, son. We walk."

PLOUTONION OPENED

Unlocking the gates of Hades.

Every day was a leg workout day for Kevin and the other security staff who chose to climb the eighteen-story (plus sublevels) stairwell to the "Crow's Nest" overlooking Michigan Central Station's property and surrounding neighborhood. There was a secure elevator that could take him to the top, but that would be cheating. Starting his workout at the very bottom of the substructure stairwell, Kevin slung his M4 across his back, then started the incline hike slowly, taking two steps at a time, leaning into a deep lunge and straining his leg muscles with each lift. He typically made it ten floors before having to climb the stairs like a normal person.

It was right about then that the stairwell lights unexpectedly went out, causing him to stumble and crash into the darkness, landing heavily on his shoulder. After a few disorientating seconds of self-evaluation, painfully rotating his arm in wide circles, and wiggling his fingers, the emergency lighting flickered to life.

"The hell was that?" he muttered out loud. Expecting an eruption of chatter, he examined his radio to make sure it was powered on and dialed to the correct channel. It was.

"Base, Base, this is Leprechaun." Silence.

"Base, Base, this is Leprechaun. Power failure in the stairway to heaven, over." More silence.

That's not good, he thought. He unslung his rifle for better control and started bounding up the stairs as fast as his already-burning thighs would allow. Once he got to the top, he burst through the fire door to the Crow's Nest to find himself looking down the barrel of a rifle.

"Whoa, whoa, whoa, it's Leprechaun! What are you doing out here Fred? You better lower that thing before I beat you with it."

The guard dipped his muzzle slightly so he could see clearly over the sights. "Sorry. Something happened."

"Yeah, I know. The lights just went out in the stairway," Kevin said, clearly irate.

"No, I mean out there, man," Fred said, ignoring Kevin's anger and pointing toward the large northwest-facing windows. "Something's not right. It's like someone hit the pause button. Everything just stopped."

They both walked over to the artistically cracked windows matching all the others while also being mirrored so their surveillance activities wouldn't draw attention to the inconspicuous dilapidated building. Kevin immediately noticed the CCTV camera displays were off. He picked up one of the several pairs of binoculars sitting on the window ledge.

"Look at the highway," Fred instructed.

"Residual morning traffic?"

"Look closer, man!"

Kevin zoomed in, then focused on the closest stretch of highway, where cars where at a standstill. Instead of bumper to bumper as usual, they were stopped with abundant space between vehicles, and all the drivers were outside, wandering around on the road. Kevin scanned down a busy city street that held the same strange activities.

"You see?" Fred asked. "Do you hear that?"

Kevin shook his head while still observing, trying to understand the phenomenon.

"Exactly! Nothing! It's fucking quiet, man!"

Lowering the binos, he watched a thick black smoke column protruding swiftly from the downtown city center, darkening the would-be-clear sky. It appeared that Detroit proper was on fire.

"What happened there?" He tilted his chin toward the smoke.

"A damn plane fell out of the sky! Fell right into the city, man!"

"Your comms work? My radio is dead."

"Nah, man, I tried to call on the phone. Hard line is down too."

Kevin instructed Fred to run down to the Security Operation Center to report everything he had seen. He then unlocked the weapons cage, pulling out a large spotting scope and a .338 Lapua bolt-action rifle, then attempted to power on the Kestral weather meter with ballistics calculator—only to find the electronic device completely inoperable.

■■■

What was normally a one-hour observation post turned into an all-day standing. Today, he didn't mind. In fact, he preferred being up here, able to use his own two eyes to witness the events taking place in the city. Eventually, another security member came to replace him.

"Hell of a day, eh, Leprechaun?"

"You got that right."

"Tell me what you got here, then head down to the cafeteria. All-hands meeting from the head shed in fifteen minutes. That includes us, too, for a change."

Kevin gave a quick synopsis of what had happened throughout the day and handed over the detailed range card he had sketched with distances and elevation adjustments for several visual reference points. He doubted they would need it, but it had kept him busy and vigilant for the several hours he'd been up in the Crow's Nest.

■■

By the time he made it to the cafeteria, it was standing room only. Everyone was there: janitorial staff, kitchen staff, administrators, a bunch of suits, people in lab coats, and even the shuttle bus drivers. He squeezed in against the back wall, where he found a few of his coworkers.

A man dressed in slacks, an untucked button-up shirt, absent tie, and quarter-rolled sleeves climbed on top of a table near the front of the cafeteria. "Ladies and gentlemen, may I please have your attention? Please, please take a seat if you have one. For those who do not know me, my name is Dr. Neville, Project Operations Director of this facility. At approximately eleven thirty, the United States was attacked by several EMP weapons—"

Like kicking dirt on an anthill, the crowd quickly became agitated, buzzing with questions and erupting concerns.

"Please. Please. Let me tell you what we know as of now." Waiting for the crowd to settle, he paced the length of the long table, looking down, running his hand through his hair, looking like someone who'd had an all-night executive board meeting. "An EMP is an Electromagnetic Pulse weapon designed to destroy electronics. This is what caused our power failure this morning. Since then, we have been running on emergency generators. The bad news is this attack just crippled our nation. The way of life as we have known it is over. The good news is an EMP is a line-of-sight weapon, and the one that hit us was off the East Coast somewhere near southern Virginia. Anything out in the open was surely fried. But if underground or heavily shielded, there is a good chance electrical equipment could be salvageable. Being subterranean is why our emergency generators and equipment are still operational. I know that you all have a lot of questions and are concerned for your family's well-being, but first I'd like the Director of Security to make an announcement."

Holding his hand out, he helped Mr. Dellione step up onto the table. "Hello. Most of you know me or my security staff. What I am about to say may seem extreme or even fabricated, but please believe everything I am about to propose. As Dr. Neville has said, life as we all know it has changed. This crisis will not be fixed today, tomorrow, or even next week. You need to take the next couple of hours to reflect on this calmly and rationally. Anyone who wants to take a look at the city, which is now in a state of flaming chaos, you are welcome to accompany security to our eighteenth-floor observation post. Some of you may wish to remain secured in this building for the next three to five days until generator fuel is depleted. Most of you will probably want to get home as soon as possible. What we all need to understand is that all our shuttle vehicles, even after being in the garage, are inoperable except for two. But even those two are useless on the blocked roads. This means when we leave this building, two hours from now, we will be on foot, carrying only the clothes you are wearing and a small food satchel put together by our considerate cafeteria staff.

"My job is to not only protect this building, but also all of you. My security staff also wants to get home, and in doing so, will offer an armed escort through the city. Located on the wall behind you are four routes which we will be traveling. Write your name below the route you wish to take. The choice is up to you to either tag along with us, go on your own, or stay here. Good luck. May God grant you a safe travel. From this day forward, self-protection and perseverance are individual responsibilities. Keep your powder dry."

As Mr. Dellione stepped down, the room exploded in conversation and debates. Kevin quickly made his way to the door before a tidal wave of people would trample him in a stampede. As he rounded the corner, he ran directly into a familiar face.

"Anny, is it?"

She looked at him, clearly shaken, then instantly barraged him with an array of questions.

"Leprechaun? Ah, hi. Where are you going? What are you going to do? Are you leaving with the rest of them? This is bad. This is really bad!"

"I'm not sure yet. I have no reason to get home, so I might sit tight to formulate a semi-intelligent plan of action. You are right: this is bad. The next steps need to be smart. It's only day one, and the gunfire inside the city sounds like the Iraq invasion."

"I don't mean the EMP. Yeah, uh that's bad too. But something worse—much worse—has happened. You should come with me right now!"

Kevin was rational, quick thinking, and generally a good judge of character. He knew that knowledge is power, and she had high-level information that he did not. At that moment, he decided his short-term survival strategy was best fit for a well-balanced team, and hopefully he had just recruited his first member.

■■■

He leaned forward in the office chair with his elbows on the conference table, rubbing his temples with both hands, trying to soak in what Anny had just described to him as potentially a new plague. This wasn't his kind of battle—he preferred an enemy he could see and outmaneuver strategically. "You think they are related? The timing…EMP and this new pathogen?"

"I couldn't begin to speculate. In the big scheme of things, it doesn't matter," she said. "What does matter is that we lost power, lab cultures were compromised, the air filtration was down for over ten seconds. Contamination procedures were broken because of the crises topside. I've voiced my concerns already about the possibility of infected people running around inside this building, getting ready to march right out into the population!"

A shiver ran down his spine. This was really bad. An EMP doomsday event multiplied by a biological-containment breach. Over the next couple of hours, Anny and Kevin discussed short-term options and speculated on what was happening to the rest of the world.

In the parking garage a couple of hours later, the majority of the staff left their place of employment for the last time, never to return again. Kevin watched them as they walked with their heads hanging low in a single-file formation out of the parking garage, with only a couple of security guards for each large group. He said his goodbyes to a few close friends, carefully maintaining a safe hygienic distance brought on by thoughts of a virus crawling over all of them.

He swung open the door to the security office, surprised to see his partner doing the same thing he had come to do: pillage the equipment locker. Dan looked up at Kevin, then continued stuffing his backpack.

"Don't take it all; I'm getting in there too. Where you heading? You have a plan?" asked Kevin.

"Have a small cabin up north. Some of my family normally use it for the holidays. I'm going to fight my way through this city Rambo-style to the rural areas, then start patrolling north."

"I might have a better idea if you are interested…"

With arms full of equipment, Kevin and Dan crashed into the conference room. They unceremoniously dropped the pile of backpacks, gun belts, and rifles on the long, polished wooden table.

Kevin looked up. "Anny, do you remember Dan from this morning? He's going in our same direction. Who's this?"

A new pretty face, also dressed in a white lab coat, came around the table with an outstretched hand, offering a firm handshake. "I'm Stephan, SL4 tech on Bravo Team. I'm also heading in the same direction. Would you happen to have another one of those I could borrow, preferably with a red dot?" she asked, pointing to the M4 rifles piled on the table.

Dan gave Kevin a surprised look and shrugged. "Sure, we have plenty. More guns in the fight, the better."

A voice came over the intercom system: "Attention in the facility. Attention in the facility. All personnel must evacuate by midnight tonight. I say again, all personnel must evacuate the facility by midnight tonight. Pompeii Protocol initiated."

"What the hell is Pompeii Protocol?" asked Anny.

"Flipping the *oh-shit* switch. It sanitizes the sublevels with thermite, then collapses the superstructure into the hole. It's the worst-case scenario procedure that has been in place long before the labs were even operational. I guess they don't expect to reopen for business anytime soon," Dan stated.

"There goes the 'start fresh after a good night's sleep' plan," Kevin acknowledged.

"Traveling under the cover of darkness might be beneficial. Leprechaun and I will grab another set of gear for Stephan." Dan offered. "Can you grab some bottles of water and any packaged food you can find? If you have comfortable clothes and walking shoes, I recommend putting them on."

THE ROAD NOT TAKEN

is often a rough route.

"Are we ever going to go home? Do you think we'll ever find Erica?" asked Michael.

"I don't know. I can't say honestly. Erica knows that we are here, which is a lot safer than in the city. She's strong, smart, and resourceful. She knows that I would fight through hell to get her to safety, but neither of us would risk putting you boys in danger by traveling right now. She'll make her way to us—I'm certain of it. But the world is a lot bigger now," Victor commented, poking the campfire coals with a flimsy stick. "A few days ago, we could board a plane and fly anywhere in the world in less than a day. Now? It took us three days just to walk the ten miles back here from town."

"True, but we also didn't walk the road, which would have cut the time down drastically," Curtis noted.

"And I hope you all understand why we didn't. If not, I fear you soon will."

Victor knew that at the moment, these country roads were safe to travel, but he recognized they were in the calm before the storm. They did not walk the road—instead, he used this time to show them how to use roads as a "handrail" for navigation, to stay far enough away to remain hidden from dangers but close enough to observe. He taught them some basic patrolling formations, hand- and arm signals, how to avoid and cross open areas, how to avoid hilltops and look for environmental disturbances that could mean danger or dinner. They all took turns walking point in formation; even little Zavier walked the front, still armed with his .22 rimfire rifle, which had been used to harvest three squirrels.

To keep the condensation off while they slept, they built temporary lean-to shelters out of thick pine branches. The firepits were dug deep for a low-burning flame only high enough for cooking and comfort. When camp was made, Victor and the boys would circle the area, looking for anything worth foraging. They practiced making snare traps; set perimeter alarms made from string, stones, and empty soup cans; and Victor taught them how to camouflage the camp to avoid being seen from the road.

They finally made it back to the rifle range, where they were happy to find their tents and supplies still waiting for them, right where they had left them three days ago.

Being an active member who volunteered often to help with projects at the training center, Victor had a key to the metal-pole barn building and utility sheds used for storage and training classes. While the kids relaxed around the campfire, Victor searched the buildings for anything they could use. At first, he found the obvious useful hand tools, including a machete and small folding E-tool shovel. He grabbed a couple of coats and clean T-shirts off the apparel rack for the kids. Inside a filing cabinet in the classroom, he found a flashlight that surprised him when it came to life as he turned it on out of habit.

"Kids! Kids! Come here quick!"

They came piling through the door, breathing hard from the quick sprint—a competition to see who could get there first. Inside the dark room, Victor shined the flashlight into their eyes.

"Look what I found!"

"Yeah, we can see that," Michael said, shielding his eyes.

Victor turned it off. "This light—this flashlight—should not be working right now. But for some reason, it is!"

"Maybe the EMP couldn't penetrate the metal building?" Curtis said.

"Maybe..." Victor said, looking around, contemplating. "You might be right; the light was inside the metal filing cabinet. Maybe the building and the cabinet created enough insulation to protect it? Open all the doors and windows so we can get some sunlight in here and start searching for other electronics that work! This is great news! Maybe stuff in people's basements or garages will still work."

■■

Even though they encountered no resistance, it took them longer than expected to travel the seemingly short distance from the Michigan Central Station, down the railroad tracks, over a couple of streets to the east, then followed the river north a few blocks to the marina.

Downtown Detroit was unnervingly quiet and dark, shadowed by tall buildings illuminated only by the waning moon. The air was thick with rancid smoke that smelled of burning jet fuel and structure fires. They took their time performing a bounding overwatch technique, where Kevin and Anny would sit tight in a hidden position, watching and listening to the streets and their surroundings, while Stephan and Dan would walk forward a short distance to find a similar hidden spot. Then, Kevin and Anny would leapfrog past while the others kept watch. Doing this took a lot longer than a typical stroll through the city, but they all felt safer doing so.

At the marina, they searched for a suitable boat for the journey up the coast. One of the large luxury yachts would have been preferred, but with all the onboard computers being fried, they were as useless as the motionless cars on the freeways. They settled for a decent-size open-top bass boat with an outboard engine and a cute name: *Subtle Wave*. Kevin and Dan seemed to know the most about boat engines, so Anny and Stephan stood watch on the shoreline.

After cutting and splicing ignition wires, then passing a couple of blown fuses, the engine purred to life. At the gurgling sound of the engine, Stephan and Anny came running down the dock, carrying two small gas cans and a plastic bag of some sort.

"Look what we found: extra fuel and a vending machine full of snacks and soda!" said Stephan.

"This seems really strange, doesn't it? Taking all this stuff...I mean, it's theft," said Anny.

"I don't think we are hurting anyone. Tomorrow all the grocery stores will be empty, if they are not already. Think of this as scavenging or foraging in a retro hunter-gatherer sense," Dan noted.

"To tell you the truth, I'd do about anything to get out of this city before sunrise," Kevin added. "I'm not a fan of murder in cold blood, but the rules of day-to-day living changed today."

The four climbed on board the newly commandeered boat with all their belongings, untied from the dock, and slowly started trawling away from the marina, heading north. As the small boat approached the open water, the morning sky lit up with a flash, and an incredible peal of thunder rolled across as their former top-secret place of employment imploded into a pile of debris and rubble—a spectacular event that would never see a headline on any news outlet.

Before dawn, they spotted another marina on the northern side of Lake St. Clair. They felt like a Viking raiding party coming to shore to plunder. After acquiring more gas cans, a couple of empty coolers, a folding travel map, several fishing poles, and a tackle box, they continued on their aquatic journey.

By late morning, they had traveled halfway up the narrow St. Clair River, with Michigan off the portside and Canada off the starboard. They had only spotted one other boat, heading in the opposite direction and giving them a wide berth, and not a soul was to be seen on land.

They took turns taking the helm, checking fuel levels, and watching the shore, trying to track their location on the tourist map. Lying down across the backseat with a shirt over her head, Anny asked, "Could we stop for a while? I have a killer headache and am a little sick to my stomach."

"I concur; we should shore up for a little bit to rest," offered Dan.

"Sorry, I don't want to slow us down. I'm not sure if it's the entirety of the situation or motion sickness," Anny said.

"Or both. No problem. It's getting hot out, anyway. We should find some shade off the water. We could all use a rest," Dan replied.

They found a secluded cove with a nice sandy spot to anchor as close as they could to shore. They carried their gear up the small beach to make a little camp just inside the tree line for the best shade and breeze off the water.

The stress of yesterday's catastrophic events, night travel, and the brutal morning sun reflecting off the water took its toll. They had all passed out, sleeping heavily for several hours. Stephan was the first to wake. Lifting her ball cap off her face, she rubbed her eyes and was startled to see a large overweight man staring at her, holding a double-barrel shotgun.

"What are you assholes doing on my beach?" he asked loud enough to wake up the others.

"Sorry, sir, we didn't know this was private property. We'll leave right away," said Kevin, holding his hands up. "We meant no harm."

"Damn right you'll leave. You'll be leaving those backpacks and weapons as well," the big man, said lifting the shotgun over his protruding belly.

"Look, sir, we're not giving you our gear. But if you are in need, maybe we can barter," Dan said sternly.

"I don't think you dickheads understand! You're trespassing. I ought to burry you right here. In fact, I just might do that," he said, shouldering the shotgun and pointing it right at Dan.

"But that's our stuff!" Anny cried out. "We'll starve! You can't do that!"

"Well, maybe, little lady, I'll keep you right here with me. Just to help me out with some special chores for a couple long days," he said with a repulsive grin and a wink.

"Hold on. Hold on," said Stephan. "Here, take my bag. I'm tired of carrying it anyway." She held it out for the fat man to take.

With a triumphant smirk, he reached over to grab it, lowering his shotgun slightly. He took hold of his prize, and it swung down under the unexpected weight.

It was then that he saw the pistol, that she had held hidden.

With the bag out of the way, Stephan fired two quick shots into his abdomen, causing his stained cutoff sleeved shirt to turn crimson red. The look in his eyes went from shock to pain to rage as his shotgun swung toward Stephan. She was faster, taking a step to the right and angling away from his shotgun. Thrusting the pistol out in a two-handed grip, she rolled her shoulders forward slightly—and now, with the muzzle only an arm's length from his face, she didn't even need to aim.

Stephan didn't remember firing the first two shots, but the sound of the third shot seemed to linger forever as the pistol slide recoiled backward in slow motion, ejecting a smoking brass shell casing, chambering a fresh round as the slide sprung forward.

"Holy shit! You just murdered him!" Anny screamed.

"He was going to take all our supplies! He was about to kidnap you to do Lord knows what!" Stephan cried out.

"He wasn't going to kill us, though!" Anny yelled back.

"Same thing," Kevin said, calmly assessing the situation. "Takes our stuff now, we starve in a few days. Same as killing us here but slower. Where did you learn to handle a weapon like that?"

"I've taken a couple of classes and shot a few practical shooting competitions at a local gun club. I'm not the best, but I can handle a gun without hurting myself," said Stephan firmly.

Still stunned from the entire incident, they all stared at the mess of what used to be a man lying facedown in a pool of bloody sand. "I'm going to be sick," Anny said as she turned away and then heaved into the water.

"This could have been avoided," Kevin said. "We should have scouted around before setting up camp. We should have had a watch; not everyone passed out sleeping at the same time. We're actually kind of lucky he didn't rob or kill us in our sleep. We should get out of here. Soon. Like right now, we need to leave."

■■■

The four travelers continued northbound up the narrow St. Clair river crossing under the Blue Water Bridge right as the river spilled into the great Lake Huron. After much debate, they decided to continue slowly pushing north throughout the night, sticking close to shore for navigation and the occasional quick and cautious pit stop. As they reached the thumb of Michigan's mitten-shaped topography, they again debated at length to either cross the thirty-ish miles of rough open water or stick to following the shoreline of the Saginaw Bay, adding an additional one hundred miles to their boat trip. They opted to raid another marina for fuel and then to bravely, or foolishly, traverse the fourth largest lake in the world in a pitifully undersized boat.

Beat up and nauseated from heavy rolling swells, they finally made landfall near the preselected small coastal town of Tawas, which had a crescent-shaped bay that housed beautiful blue and green water. Near a lighthouse with a tall white tower and an attached bright-red home, they spotted a lone man along the shore, who, from a distance, appeared to be only armed with a couple of fishing poles. Giving the elder some distance, they drove the boat right at the beach until they hit sand.

"He looks harmless enough, and we have the numbers on him, but just in case...cover me," Dan advised.

"You should leave him be. He's probably the bait for a trap," Anny said under her breath.

Dan gave her a disregarding glance and dropped his weapons and equipment. Empty-handed, he strolled over to the fisherman with a casual swagger. After trading a handshake, some news about southern Michigan state of affairs, and one gently used, no-longer-needed fishing boat, Dan returned to the group with a bucket full of fresh fish and some disheartening information about the locals. Apparently small towns, such as this, were not immune to lawlessness in the absence of order.

A major waypoint had been reached in their journey, and the next leg was a straight shot west for ninety miles through lightly populated regions. The four-day boating expedition had shaved 110 miles of dense urban zones—and who knows how many walking days and other deadly complications—off their trip. Even though they were all ready to leave the boat behind, the waterborne transportation had been a brilliant idea.

Skirting the small town, ducking and weaving through patchworks of uninhabited areas, they were able to use binos and rifle scopes to observe the desolate town made up of boarded-up shops, broken store widows, and burnt-out shells of small businesses.

Just on the other side of town, they found the beginning of the landmark they needed: Route 55, running east-west parallel to Huron National Forest, which was where they would make camp.

MONSTERS

The veil of society is very thin.

"Come on, kids, we're almost there. No piggyback rides, so don't even think about it," Kate scolded her children, who'd started this trek by running ahead at a sprint down the road. Now they were constantly falling behind with relentless complaining.

Kate, with her young children—Max age eight and Tina age six—had been in Lake City, partying at her boyfriend's house on July 4th. After the lights had gone out, it didn't take long for all the beer and pizza to disappear, along with the snacks they had ready for the big fireworks party. Bags of chips don't last that long when they're had for breakfast, lunch, and dinner. After a couple of days of clogged toilets and sweaty armpits, tensions started to rise.

Kate's junkie boyfriend told her, "Make yourself useful and go find some grub. Take your little food consumers with you too. And don't you dare come back empty-handed." On her way to the town's only grocery store, she stopped at the corner gas station to find the doors chained shut.

"That's not fair! People have to get stuff! Just because the power's out…how are we supposed to get our smokes? This can't be legal," she shouted as she shook the doors violently. "Come on, brats, let's go to the stupid grocery store."

When she made it to Budgens' Grocery Store, she felt a welling desperation. Not only were their doors locked as well but she could also clearly see through the large windowpanes that the shelves and coolers were completely empty. She cursed and kicked the door in frustration. Her house was about five miles north of town, right on the main road. She'd rather walk home than go back to her belittling boyfriend, and besides, she had a couple days' worth of food in her kitchen pantry.

She was hot and tired. Her flip-flops were killing her feet. Her sweat-stained shirt was starting to chafe her armpits. She walked with her head down, only looking up to turn and yell at the kids to catch up. Turning forward again, looking through the heavy mirage boiling up from the asphalt, she spotted an old red pickup truck parked sideways across the road. Thinking nothing of it—in fact, excited by the possibility of finding some sodas, snacks, or, lord willing, a pack of cigarettes—she picked up her pace, flip-flopping down the road.

As she reached for the passenger-side door handle, a tall man holding a metal pipe rounded the front of the truck. "Well, well, well. What do we have here?"

It all happened so quickly. Two other men crawled out of the ditch, seizing Max and Tina. The tall man pushed Kate down, grabbed her by the hair, and then sadistically dragged her behind the truck.

"Shut your mouth, woman, or we'll gut your filthy kids," he snarled into her ear. Yet she still struggled under him, jerking and bucking until one of the other men open hand smacked her face, then pinned her hands to the painfully hot pavement.

The tall man laid on top of her, wrestling her legs apart. After walking all this way from town, she didn't have much strength to put up a fight. With little effort, he got to his knees, ready to claim his barbaric prize. With an evil, lustful laugh, he tilted his head back to the sky and howled like the wild animal he was.

His ritualistic howl was cut short by a .308 caliber, 175 gr boat tail hollow point bullet entering the back of his skull, sending energy waves through the soft brain tissue. The bullet remnants, along with secondary projectiles of skull fragments, exited his face to impact the stomach of the second man binding her hands. A second shot rang out before his heavy, bloody corpse landed on top of Kate.

She could hear her children's muffled screams. Kate didn't realize that she was also screaming hysterically while fighting frantically to get out from underneath the dead man that was covering her in warm, sticky fluid. She stood up in a daze. Max and Tina ran around the truck to her. Someone else was also running toward her. Shouting. Waving. Confusion.

"Move! Move! Get out of the way! Move!" He was running down the steep grassy embankment right toward her.

She was a petrified statue. The apparition bounded past her, swinging a very large rifle like a golf club, striking the moaning gut-shot man trying to crawl away. She heard a sickening wet crack as the bottom of the rifle struck the bastard who had slapped her face earlier.

Her hero strapped the rifle/club over his shoulder, then pulled a pistol off his hip, aiming it wildly here and there, circling the truck, aiming down in the ditches, going to each bloody mess lying on the pavement, kicking each one in the groin. None of the bodies moved.

"Are you OK?" he asked, looking at her, at the children, around them in the distance. "Are you hurt? Come here, sit on the tailgate. Here, drink this water. Hey, kiddos, are you OK? What are your names?"

"I'm Max, sir. My sister's name is Tina. This is my mom."

"Where are you heading? Why are you on the road?"

"Home, sir. We live just over there, around that next bend."

He patted them down quick. "No signs of holes. Looks like you're going to live." The man turned around to look toward the grassy knoll he'd come from. He put a hand straight up, then made several circle shapes in the air. Three people of different sizes stood from the top of the hill, then started walking toward them.

"My name is Victor. This is Curtis, my oldest son; Michael and Zavier. Curtis, check the truck for anything usable. You say you live just over there? You should get going now."

"You shouldn't walk on the roads anymore," Michael chastised.

"And you should have weapons to protect yourselves," Zavier added.

When Curtis opened the truck, it made a familiar *ding, ding, ding* sound. Everyone perked up. He reached in and turned the ignition key, starting a roaring engine. "Why does this truck work?"

"Old vehicle, no microchips. Carbureted, not electronic fuel injected. Maybe it was in a metal barn. That's about the extent of my mechanical knowledge."

Kate asked with a shaky voice, "Can we take the truck?"

"Not a chance. This truck is our good-deed savior fee. Although we will take it into town, where it'll be put to communal good use."

"There's nothing left in town. We just came from there. All the stores are empty. Can you give us a ride home?"

"Nope. You get to finish walking home while contemplating how lucky you are to be alive and how best to stay that way," Victor said flatly.

■■

"Good evening. This is Elizabeth Corrin bringing you today's BBN global news reports. EU and UN officials announced today that relief efforts inbound to the United States have again been postponed as a result of troubling international financial uncertainties. The Chinese government has guaranteed early emergency medical supplies and personnel, along with shipments of emergency food rations, to be delivered this week.

"Adding further fears to international financial crises, several Islamic Terrorist groups, who recently claimed responsibility for the

US attack, are now promising equally devastating attacks across Europe. UK parliament has ensured that all resources available are being used to bring these terrorists to justice, including full cooperation between NATO and Russian military forces now actively involved in antiterrorism campaigns in northern Africa, Yemen, and Pakistan.

"In other news, fuel-shortage easements are on the way as OPEC nations are prepared to resume oil production and distribution as the entire oil commodities market has now switched from the US dollar to the precious metals– and energy-backed BRICS credit.

"Next, we have a breaking World Health Organization report from Mexico—but first a commercial break…"

■ ■

Dan woke up early to a chill in the damp morning air. Stretching his arms out wide, rubbing his dry eyes, and rolling to his side, he noticed the pink color through the forest canopy on the eastern horizon. He rolled over with an exaggerated sigh, then stood up, stretching again.

"Anny, I thought you were going to wake us up for watch?" Dan said as he moved closer to the fire, kneeling down to add another log.

"Wasn't tired. Couldn't sleep anyway," she said, staring into the fire.

"I can understand that; this ground is unforgiving. But you must be exhausted. Are you feeling OK?" He warmed his hands next to the smoldering coals.

"What's it to you? You just want me to sleep defenseless so you can murder me like you did that fat guy on the way here."

"Whoa, Anny, hold on, there! What are you talking about? No one is going to hurt you. We're a team. I get it. What happened back there was quite traumatic and disturbing to say the least. But no one here is out to get you. Is that why you can't sleep?" he asked with concern.

"Forget it." She stood up and stormed off into the woods, out of sight.

He shook his head a bit out of confusion, then tossed a couple more logs onto the fire. He stirred the coals around and leaned down close to the base, expelling a full lung gust of air. The coals blew bright yellow, then ignited the smoldering kindling.

Dan set four cleaned-out soup cans on the rocks lining the firepit. After adding water from a nearby stream, he watched as the cups began to boil. It wasn't perfect, but boiling would kill most of the bacteria in the water. Between the sediment and the tin-can taste, the water was horrible, but he had a secret weapon. He sifted through the outside pocket of his backpack until he found the hidden treasure: instant coffee, powdered creamer, and sugar singles.

Using a rolled-up shirt as an oven mitt, he set down a can of coffee next to Kevin and Stephan, then gently nudged them awake. "Careful, the coffee is nuclear hot," he warned.

"Oh, man...where did you get this?" Kevin asked with a yawn.

"Security Office before we bailed out."

"Oh, Dan, I love you. You're a saint," Stephan said, struggling to get upright.

Dan grabbed the last can of coffee and headed out into the bush to find Anny. After several minutes of searching the area, he returned to camp, still holding the can of coffee.

"Where's Anny?" asked Kevin.

He shrugged. "I don't know. Maybe she's going number two. I don't think she's feeling all that well." Dan went on to describe the morning's strange dialogue between he and Anny. "I know we have a long way to go, but how about we stay here for the day? Maybe do a little hunting? Give everyone a hiking pause to clear our mind and rest the legs. Refocus?"

"The sooner we get to our destinations, the better. As each day goes on, good people will become hungry and desperate. Desperate people do desperate things. The veil of civilized society is very thin. It won't take long for violence to become the new societal norm," Kevin said.

"I agree with Dan. Let's take a rest day. We all want to get there as soon as possible, but if Anny is ill, it won't do us any good to keep pushing. And if we are just trudging along with our heads down, we'll likely get ourselves killed on the way," Stephan argued.

They stayed the day, each taking turns guarding camp. Dan spent time gathering more water from the nearby stream, straining and boiling the best he could, filling every available container. Kevin scouted around for small game, edible berries, mushrooms, or whatever he could find useful, which wasn't much. Stephan went downstream to rinse out her clothes and hung them on a branch to dry while she took a cold river bath.

At camp later in the afternoon, Dan and Stephan watched Kevin carefully skin a porcupine he'd knocked out of a tree earlier in the day. "I'm told that these are good eatin'. Too bad we don't have any potatoes and carrots and a big ol' pot to stew this in," Kevin said wistfully.

As they finished cleaning up and getting ready to spit their dinner over the fire, Anny walked around a tree, startling them all.

"Hey, Anny. Where have you been? We got worried. We went looking for you. We thought maybe you decided to stay in that town back there. We're about to cook dinner," Stephan said.

"I'm not hungry," Anny said flatly.

"Are you OK? You look kind of pale. You didn't have any fish last night. When's the last time you ate?" asked Kevin.

Anny stood there for a moment with glassy eyes, looking in their direction but not at them. As if she was looking past them, daydreaming.

"Anny?"

"That's not my name. Not my real name, anyway."

"Anny isn't your name? We all used aliases at work—protocol that doesn't really matter much now. Danial was my grandfather's name. He died in World War II. I took his name in his honor."

"My name is Kevin, went by Leprechaun for obvious heritage reasons. What's your real name Anny?"

"I don't remember. I can't remember. It's right there, at the front of my mind, but I can't grasp it," Anny said, staring at them blankly. "I'm having trouble recalling a lot of things. I can't remember where we're going. I know we have a destination. Someplace safe? I can't remember where, though..." she trailed off.

"Anny. Look, our world was tossed upside down. We've gone through some disturbing events. You haven't slept in how long? If you can stomach it, you really should try to eat something and lay down. It's safe here; we can stay as long as we need to," Stephan proposed.

Anny turned around without a word, stumbled over to tree, and sat down on the ground, leaning back against her backpack and slumping her head against the tree.

The sun had gone down hours ago. The three of them stood around the campfire, arguing.

"Look at her! She needs a doctor. Serious medical attention!" Dan said while pointing toward Anny, who had been restlessly tossing back and forth, moaning incoherently.

"Back in Tawas, where we made landfall, there was a Raven Medical Center where Route 55 dead-ends at the lake. I highly doubt it's still open. In fact, it was probably looted days ago, but maybe we ask around town for help. Surely doctors and nurses are still in the area," Kevin suggested.

"I don't know, but she's not healthy," Stephan said. "She's kind of scaring me. This is serious."

Right then, Anny materialized out of the darkness, standing opposite of the fire. Even in the dark, with only flickering campfire casting dancing shadows over her skin, she was ghostly pale. Her clothes were dirty from lying on the damp forest floor. Her dark hair was matted and hanging over her face. And the smell…that smell that came from a soiled baby diaper. "You're talking about me. Conspiring?" Anny said in a low, raspy voice, slowly rotating her stare. "You're going to kill me. Take my food and weapons."

Dan put up his hands. "Anny, we're worried about you. We are going to find you a—"

Without warning, Anny dove across the fire, tackling Dan to the ground, kicking up sparking logs and coals. Screaming. Punching. Clawing. Dan put his hands out, trying to block the relentless melee, searching for purchase to gain control. Reaching across his chest, he was able to trap her forearms. He lifted one knee and shifted his hips, positioning himself for a defensive roll.

She sat on top of him in full mount with the heels of her shoes locked behind his leg. Before Dan could engage his countermove, she arched back and shrieked a terrifying mix of agony and rage. Lunging back down with force that bypassed Dan's obstructing arm hold, she bit into his trapezius muscle, scraping teeth against his clavicle as he cursed in pain.

Kevin ran forward, lifted his knee to his chest, and then extended his leg with every muscle he had, planting his boot against Anny's shoulder and kicking her off Dan. She rolled twice and landed in a squat. She coiled, her face covered in wet blood. She screamed again and sprung into an attack toward Kevin.

In his peripheral vision, he could see Dan holding his shoulder with blood flowing through his fingers; he watched Stephan, wide-eyed, draw her holstered Glock; and he saw a feral looking Anny flying through the air with outstretched hands right toward him.

Kevin stepped back and caught his foot on a protruding tree root. He fell backward, snapping a small tree on his way down, and landed heavily on his back with a thud, knocking the air out of him. Anny landed at his feet, her hands grasping his boots, and she remained there, convulsing.

He quickly jumped to his feet in a defensive fighting stance, breathing heavily. Stephan ran to him with her pistol pointed down at Anny's twitching, twisted form. Blood sprayed upward like a mini geyser where the broken sapling tree had punctured right through the side of her neck.

"That bitch bit me!" Dan yelled from behind them.

"Oh, man. Oh, dear Lord. What did we do?" Kevin said with a quiver in his voice, leaning forward to administer some sort of first aid. He had to do something. As he bent down reaching for Anny's head, Stephan yanked him back, causing him to land on his butt. "Are you crazy? We have to stop that bleeding!" he shouted.

"Look!" Stephan said, kneeling down next to the large puddle of blood flowing into a low spot on the forest floor. She knelt carefully next to the growing pool, leaning left and right, then gazing back to Anny's still-twitching body.

"What is it?" Dan asked, holding onto a tree for support with his other hand while applying pressure to his shoulder wound.

She took the light off her pistol, holstered the gun, and then turned on the light shining it into the bloodstream. "Look at the blood. The black wisps swirling in it. That's not soil or debris," Stephan said, looking up at Dan's shoulder fearfully. "She was infected."

■■■

"Welcome back to BBN. This is Elizabeth Corrin bringing you a World Health Organization report out of Mexico. Authorities have reported an unidentified 'aggressively spreading' pathogen has plagued the small town of La Cabellera, located fifty miles south of the US–Mexico border. The WHO asks anyone in northern Mexico to report any persons with symptoms of prominent rashes and/or unusual paranoid hostility. Transmission methods are still being investigated.

"In local news, the highly anticipated football game between Barcelona and Manchester United has finally been rescheduled…"

STAGE TWO

UMBRA

The brightest light casts the darkest shadows.

Sheriff Bohner strolled up the sidewalk, assessing the damage from yesterday's fire. It supposedly had been started by accident when a makeshift moonshine still had been tipped over, igniting combustibles in a garage. The only available emergency response action had been to warn the neighbors, then sit back and watch house after house burn. Thirteen homes on this block, all reduced to smoldering piles of ash. Luckily, most of the structures were unoccupied vacation homes. The homes with permanent residents would need to be relocated.

He had just crossed Main Street, looking both ways for traffic out of habit and examining a still-smoking pile of wreckage that had been a house yesterday, when he caught a familiar sound far off in the distance. Second-guessing himself, he stood tall, rotating left and right, trying to catch the sound again.

He then watched an old red truck slowly negotiate a maze of stalled-out vehicles in the street and come to a casual stop in front of him. He recognized the driver of the old pickup right away. Without emotion—or mentioning the fact that the boys were riding in the bed of the truck with their rifles illegally—Sheriff Bohner asked, "That's not your truck, Victor. Where did you get it?"

"Three wannabe bandit rapists kindly donated it. We left them where they had set up a roadblock ambush about four miles north of town. We figured you or the town could use a cargo hauler."

The sheriff didn't bother asking for clarification on the incident. "A running truck is a high-value asset these days. Probably the most valuable. You're giving it to the town? Just like that?"

"Maybe more of a trade. We're in need of an empty residence here in town." Victor got out, looking around the charred destruction.

"If you have any still standing with a little less fire damage, that is. Preferably one close to downtown, on or near the lake for water, and with a working fireplace for heat. Assuming we survive until winter. As for the truck, my boys and I still get access to it as needed, with no questions asked. Other than that, it's all yours."

"I know just the place. Drive us down to the blue Victorian house next to the library," Sheriff Bohner said, climbing into the bed of the truck with Curtis and Michael.

They drove slowly, passing through the small town, taking in the ghostly appearance of what had recently been a thriving tourism community. Now the streets were vacant of people, stores were locked, windows dark or boarded up, loose paper littered the street, and abandoned vehicles clogged the road.

As they pulled up to the assigned blue two-story house across from the city beach, a sudden burst of emotion swelled inside Victor. Erica will love this house. He wondered if she was on her way, if she had made it out of the city, if she was still alive. "This is a wonderful home, Sheriff. It's empty? You know where the owners are?"

"Gone, like most of the other Fourth of July tourists. Once the store shelves went dry and their kitchens went empty, most decided to try their luck walking home. The town council and I pleaded for them to stay, to help rebuild here, lectured them about safety in numbers and all. They still left."

"Might be a blessing in disguise—vacationers don't have the same sense of communal ownership as your year-round residents who will look out for one another. Besides the fire, what other problems are you having?"

"You name it. A lot of fights broke out when the vacationers departed, residents tried making them leave their provisions behind. Tensions and desperation are starting to flare up. We've seen a lot of domestic violence and thieving complaints. A few dead from breaking into still-occupied cabins. Several elderly residents dependent on medical equipment have been found deceased; as medication runs out, we'll have more. Soccer mom on the south side had to go cold turkey off her antidepressants—went psycho, killing her entire family. We caught her walking down Main Street in a bloody nightgown. I only have three deputies now; the others have gone missing. Probably took off to find family. That's just the human problems—the city's entire infrastructure has collapsed. This place is borderline anarchy."

"Any community meetings lately? Try to get everyone on same sheet of music? Getting people to work on common goals of survival will help," Victor suggested.

"We've tried. Not many will show up, though. It's just too far to walk. Especially if we don't have any pertinent or useful information for them," the sheriff said, exhausted.

"I have an idea. See if you can spread the word for a town hall–type meeting down by the beach tomorrow evening at sundown. Get with city council; let's work out some immediate strategies for food production. Speaking of food, tell everyone there'll be BBQ—that will get their attention. Don't tell the local enviro-cops, but my boys and I are going out to poach a couple of deer." Victor handed Sheriff Bohner a handheld walkie-talkie. "Here, take this. We found these up at the training center. I'll give you a call tomorrow when the fur is downed. You can send the truck to pick us up."

■ ■

They had lost Dan a couple of days ago. His shoulder had showed signs of infection: thin black lines expanding away from the bite wound down his back and over his chest, indicating he was on borrowed time. Because of the pain, he could no longer carry his backpack, forcing Kevin and Stephan to spread load his heavier equipment, which later drew complaints fueled by the same conspiracy paranoia Anny had displayed. Even though they'd kept a watchful eye on his worsening condition, late into the sixth night, Dan simply disappeared, leaving everything behind.

They didn't know if Dan had slipped off into the wilderness to die in peace like a wounded animal, if paranoia drove him to escape, or if he'd vanished mercifully, knowing that he was quickly becoming a danger to Kevin and Stephan.

Because Kevin and Stephan were now carrying twice the weight in equipment, grimly donated to them by their fallen team members, their pace had decelerated dramatically. They took another short pause behind some thin bushes to observe the main road they had been following.

"Since workplace security protocols and disclosure agreements are probably no longer binding, can you fill me in?" asked Kevin. "Bring me up to speed at least to a basic understanding about this disease? Like where it came from?"

"From what we were told, when our lab first became aware, two dozen victims across the USA had been quarantined by the CDC, which is extremely odd considering the individual components of the hybrid pathogen are typically not found here. Where it originated exactly, we don't know—or, I should say, we were not told."

"Area up ahead looks clear. We should keep walking toward that large hill. We'll stick to the tree line. I noticed you writing on a notepad. Were you documenting Anny's and Dan's symptoms?"

"Yeah, I'm logging the similarities and time lapses from initial infection. Warning signs, indicators, per se. Poor Anny. She made her concerns about a possible contagion leak and the extreme carelessness of releasing all the staff workers known to all the lab's top administrators. Then, all the while it turns out, she was infected too. We don't know who or how many people were infected in our building, let alone what the CDC had been tracking. The more we can document, learn, and understand now, the better you and I will be. We're in a perfect pressure cooker for a plague outbreak. People are no longer isolated in their homes; they are out in groups. Poor hygiene and general sanitation. Lack of proper biohazard containment response assets, etcetera."

Kevin nodded, taking it in. "You're right about hygiene and sanitation. Power is out. That means water and sewer too. People will suffer from weaker immune systems caused by malnourishment. Many will starve to death. The deceased will not be properly buried. Deadly medieval-type diseases are going to return just from that."

"And that doesn't even include this new Nasty that doesn't discriminate between weak or strong. It doesn't care if you are armed or defenseless, how rich or poor you are. We were shown images of late-stage victims of this hybrid. This thing is cruel." Stephan shuddered.

Kevin grasped for understanding. "How does it work? What is it, exactly? What caused Dan and Anny to go crazy? Is it like Mad Cow Disease or something?"

"Yes, kind of, but that is only part of it. The Nasty is an unknown-origin hybrid of parasite, fungus, and prion that'll infect the body with slow-acting symptoms. The symptoms you and I witnessed were straightforward signs of FFI, which is the human mutation version of Mad Cow Disease. FFI stands for Fatal Familial Insomnia. Sounds familiar, right? Am I boring you, or do you want details?"

"I'm not going to remember the technical stuff, but yeah, keep going so I have a better understating of what we're up against. We'll have to change our tactics, our route, hell, maybe even the way we go on living when this thing spreads. Besides, we have a lot of time to kill and I'm curious."

"OK, since we're on topic of the FFI prion. Transmission in mammals is typically ingestion, but it is also transmitted via bodily fluids, including saliva and blood. Once in the body, it immediately targets brain tissue. Early signs include increasing insomnia, resulting in paranoia and phobias. Then come hallucinations and panic attacks triggered by long-term lack of sleep, followed by rapid weight loss. Late stages are dementia, during which the patient becomes unresponsive or mute. This primal regression process normally transpires in about thirty-six months. I'd say our hybrid Nasty has a fast track. The signs we need to look for are profuse sweating from natural infection fighting, pinpoint pupils from brain swelling, stiff neck and joints, elevated blood pressure and heart rate, and constipation is also common. Late-stage stuff will be obvious."

"That sounds horrible. I see why Dan may have taken off into the woods now," Kevin said thoughtfully.

"Yeah, and that's only one of the three parts of the hybrid. And we still do not understand what the combined capabilities of all three are."

Kevin paused and took a knee on a soft mossy spot of the forest floor overlooking a cow pasture. "Before you continue, I have an idea. You see that farmhouse over there, across this clearing? I see smoke coming out of the chimney—someone's home. I bet they have some freshly butchered livestock and harvested produce. Shall we take a chance and ask nicely?"

They waited for thirty minutes—standing, then sitting—on the driveway at a comfortably safe distance from the farmhouse. They thought that whoever was inside would spot them, see that they were not a threat, and then open up a dialogue to see what they wanted. After thirty minutes of waiting, Kevin changed tactics.

"Helloooooo! Hello there!" Kevin shouted toward the house, as if he was yelling from ship to shore. It worked. A window curtain fluttered a bit. They continued to wait in the driveway with the same strategy. Ten minutes later, the door cracked open, and out stepped a slightly older man clutching a shotgun.

"What do you want?" he yelled back to them.

"To barter, sir, for food and shelter for the night. The two of us are passing through, heading west. We have come a long way. We were in Detroit the day the lights went out."

"Come closer so I don't have to yell. Nice and slow. OK, stop there. What do you have to trade?"

"We lost a couple of our friends last week. We can give you some of their equipment, backpacks, and weapons."

"Yeah, we could work something out. Ma and I were getting dinner prepped; we'll add a bit more for you. How's a pot-roast stew sound?"

"How can we help?" Kevin asked, salivating at the thought of a warm meal and stepping up onto the porch with an outstretched hand. "This is Stephan. I'm Kevin. We're at your service, sir."

■■■

Not having much to carry in, it didn't take long for Victor and his sons to get settled in. They went through the house upstairs, in the attic, downstairs, in the basement, and garage, searching for anything useful. Later that night, they carried in buckets of lake water to take a stand-up bath in the tub. It wasn't the best, but it sure felt good to get cleaned up.

"Why can't we bathe out in the lake like we used to?" asked Zavier while struggling not to spill his bucket of water.

"Because until we set up rainwater collectors, we'll have to get drinking water from the lake too. It's going to taste bad enough without the soap."

Victor made a mental note to set up a tripod-style water filtration system he'd seen in an old survival manual. Suspended between the tripod legs would be three tiers of fabric: The top tier would hold a bunch of loose grass. The middle layer contained the cleanest sand you can find—beach sand would work great. And the bottom piece of fabric would hold large clumps of charcoal. Pour the water in the top, and let gravity do the work, straining it through all three layers and collecting it in a clean drip bucket at the bottom. He'd never actually attempted it, but he might as well try; the concept was an easy one.

They had been playing a board game while the sun was still up. Now the darkness forced all four of them into the living room, each of them reading a newfound book, huddled around the one candle Victor had limited them to.

Lost in thought and gazing at the candle flame, Victor's eyes shifted toward the fireplace. "Those tall trees out front," he said aloud but more to himself, "we should chop those down for firewood. After we come back tomorrow, let's start on that." Keeping everyone busy would be crucial to keeping a strong mind. The more individuals sit around contemplating new-world hardships, the worse it was on their souls. *We must stay busy*, he thought.

They woke up early as the summer sun came up. For breakfast, they only had leftover rations they had found at the rifle range and soda they had found in the basement. Supplies were running out.

"Grab your gear, boys. Let's head out before the sun gets too warm. I want you all to pay attention today, OK? Next time, only two of you will go hunting; the other two will stay here in town for other projects."

They took off eastward on foot, the shortest route toward the wooded rural area. As soon as they entered the forest, they were in stealth mode, patrolling in formation as they had been practicing, stopping often and searching for signs. Surprising even Victor, they quickly came across a freshly used runway. He asked the kids to look at the hoof marks in the mud to determine the direction of travel, which they followed to a hayfield.

As soon as Victor could see the forest thinning, he halted their patrol. "Use your rifle scopes or binos from here. Try to look through and beyond all this brush in front of us to observe the open field. Let me know what you can see. Take your time. Zoom in with your magnification power, then adjust the focal point so this close vegetation is blurry and the field is crisp and clear.

"Zavier, you too. Use this tree to hold up your rifle so your arms don't get tired." He showed him how to rest his nonfiring hand on the tree, then lay the rifle across his arm for support. "Scan slowly side to side. Start up close, then far. Look for target indicators. Movement is the easiest to pick up. Watch for deer to lift their head or flick their tail. Contrasting color will be difficult with tan deer in a hayfield, but look for different shades of brown. Look for shape and outline; this will also be difficult while looking through all this brush, but look for the horizontal outline of their backs. Smell is the last target indicator, which doesn't do us a lot of good right now, but keep it in mind as you are patrolling. Remember what we smelled like last night before taking a bath? I could smell you from across the yard."

"I've got one. Make that two or three," Michael said.

"Direction and distance?"

"Eleven o'clock. Maybe three hundred yards."

"OK, let's stalk closer. The best way to move is in the low ground or behind a hill for cover, which there are none here. So let's move nice and slow, sticking very low to the ground. Did you guys see our food supply this morning? If we screw this up, we're going hungry for a few days. Since there's no low ground to use, try to use shadows, and be sure to keep a thick tree or bush between you and the target to mask your movements, OK? Leave our packs here."

Victor took off his pack, quietly laid it on the ground, and then moved into a low crawl, slowly inching toward the hayfield, wishing he had his ghillie suit. It was a slow process. Stopping often, he looked for the most concealed route possible. He frequently glanced at a microcompass attached to his watchband, because when you're that low to the ground, it is easy to lose cardinal direction. Using the thick green vegetation, they could easily move faster in a high crawl or even a squat, but Victor used this as an opportunity to teach his children the stealthy art of patience. They continued forward, placing one hand in front of the other, moving dry sticks out of the way and carefully avoiding shaking large bushes that would flag their position.

Stalking closer to their final firing position, Victor fought the salivating daydreams of the best chopped venison stew Erica could make if she were here or the piles of sun-dried jerky he could begin curing tonight. They had made it twenty yards from the hayfield clearing, still far enough inside the wood line to use the natural shadows of the forest, when Victor halted his low-crawling convoy behind a large fallen cedar tree.

Observing from behind, under, or around concealment was the optimal method, but he didn't have much of a choice, and using the top of this cedar log would make for a nice strong rifle support.

Victor motioned his boys up to the log. "Zavier, you're going to spot for me. Michael, spot for Curtis. I'd have you guys shoot also, but your .22s are not the right tool for this job, so just spot for now, and let us know if the deer drops or which way they run. Curtis, pick a stationary deer on the far right; I will go far left. It's about three hundred yards to that lone oak tree they're grazing next to. Do you remember your bullet-drop adjustment from last week? Good, go ahead and dial it on your elevation turret now, then very slowly get into position.

"Zero wind deflection this morning, so aim for the heart, right behind the shoulder. To get two of them, we'll need to fire at the exact same time. Michael, I want you to count down from five. Curtis, as soon as you hear the *T* in *two*, you need to squeeze the trigger. We use the *T* in *two* for a couple reasons I'll explain later. For today, just roll with it. Are you ready? OK. Michael, on you."

All four were homed in on the small herd grazing in the open hayfield. "Five. Four. Three. T—"

Victor and Curtis shot in unison, scoring two good hits. By the time they recovered from the recoil and were back on target, all they could see were bounding deer retreating into the forest.

"I think they both fell," Zavier said, jumping to his feet.

"Sit back down, bud." Victor grabbed him. "If they are wounded out there, we want them to stay put and bleed out so we're not chasing them through the woods."

After several minutes of observing, ensuring their prey hadn't moved, they slowly walked back to retrieve their packs. The boys were excited, practically running out to the large oak tree to confirm a successful hunt. Victor remained vigilant, scanning the area for threats. Humans would soon be like hyenas, coming in packs to steal a fresh kill.

It was then, looking to the far side of the field, that Victor saw fast-moving fragments of what appeared to be an odd alien-like naked person sprinting through the tree line, disappearing into the shadowy forest.

■■■

Stephan and Kevin enjoyed dinner with Harry and Helen Cooper immensely. Trying hard to not rudely slurp down the heavy, warm meal too quickly, they shared information back and forth about current events in the local area and what it was like on their journey from Detroit, up the coast, and across the state. Kevin asked where they were exactly as he pulled out his map, confirming his navigation fears. They were far behind his original planned timeline.

They sorted through Anny and Dan's equipment, deciding what they could part with. They offered an M4 rifle, a Glock pistol with Gundo Holster, and a full P-Mag for each, a backpack, and a pair of Steiner binoculars. Kevin and Stephan spent a little time that evening coaching Harry on how to disassemble, clean, and operate the weapons.

Appreciatively accepting the equipment, Harry offered each a glass of warm bourbon as they sat around the kitchen table. Stephan decided to warn them about the looming biological outbreak. Being a former nurse, Helen was interested in the details and asked plenty of questions about the parasite.

"Well, the complex parasite portion of the new hybrid seems to be one of the twenty human contractible species of Leishmania."

Stephan informed their hosts. "What makes this parasite so peculiar is that to promote its survival in the host, it will modulate the immune response of the host, giving the parasite the most optimal breeding environment. It's a horrid flesh-eating disease that starts with small bumpy rashes, then grows into painful, large volcano-shaped ulcers, finally crusting over with thick scabby layers. Normally these skin lesions are isolated, but in the images I have seen, the patient was covered with them. Affected people in early stages usually have fever, weight loss, and swelling of the spleen and liver. Leishmania is normally transmitted by sand-fly bites, but with the hybrid? Who knows? Could be bodily fluid transfer or maybe casual skin-to-skin contact."

After more questions and answers about the parasite, Harry offered them a clean upstairs bedroom, which was gratefully accepted, although Kevin asked to sleep on the couch, closer to the front door.

When they woke in the early morning, the smell of eggs and ham filled the house. Stephan stumbled into the kitchen to see Kevin already at the table with a cup full of steaming black coffee and a childish grin.

After breakfast, they began to pack up to get an early start on the day's hike. With a stern warning about how it's considered rude to not accept a gift, Helen gave them each a brown paper bag with lunch and dinner to take. Stephan took it reluctantly, thanking her again for their generosity.

"I was thinking last night that our barter wasn't quite fair. The items you gave us are very valuable. I want to give you these two handheld HAM radios I had in the basement. Unbelievably, they still work! Before you say no, I have three more to spare. So don't worry about it." Harry took a few minutes to give them an impromptu communications class on their capabilities, program channels, and how to turn them on and scan.

"We are very appreciative, and thank you for your hospitality, Mr. Cooper. Be cautious who you let in next time, though; even healthy people who are not infected with this disease are going to start becoming forceful for basic human needs."

Kevin and Stephan shook hands with their hosts and set out across the farm field to continue their journey west.

■■

On the beach, a larger-than-normal crowd gathered around a blazing bonfire, finishing generous portions of venison BBQ graciously prepared by the local family diner. After the meat had been cooked, a load of wooden pallets from a nearby store were carried down to add some height to the fire.

As the city mayor stood on a picnic table and addressed the crowd, Victor scanned the townsfolk, noticing only a couple of people were openly armed, other than his family and the sheriff's department of four.

The mayor used Victor's discoveries as an example, asked everyone to search their basements, barns, and neighboring property for electronics that may still work. An electrician made a comment that if any operational gas-powered generators where found and brought into downtown, a small electrical grid could be managed.

An idea proposed to have a similar community dinner every night, to report project progress and disseminate information, was very well received. They understood that if they ate community food, they had to conduct community work. Seemed fair enough.

There were many topics addressed. Most topics were agreed upon, and others brought out complaints from the crowd. They all generally agreed that certain tasks needed to be quickly prioritized, and many people volunteered.

The resale thrift shop owner said they had several bicycles that could be donated to the town and a pile of scrap bikes that could be cannibalized if they could get some assistance. With a soft, saddened voice, one of the nursery owners offered to replace all the beautiful potted flowers with vegetable seeds. Several elderly ladies offered to help her. She mentioned starting a community compost pile; several local farmers agreed and discussed other agricultural solutions. Considering the population, almost all the men and half the women wanted to be on the hunter teams. An arrangement was made for designated groups to have specific days of the week, giving everyone time in the woods and time for other laborious projects.

The sheriff suggested to those residing in the countryside to relocate closer to the town's nucleus. He could not promise a rapid response—if any response at all—to the outer rural areas. Sheriff Bohner addressed the increase in violence and how any hostile situations would be swiftly dealt with if his department was to be involved. Self-protection was more critical now than ever before.

Victor offered marksmanship and weapons-handling classes to anyone interested. He recommended the homes who owned more firearms than people arm their neighbors who had none. "Individually, we are weak; as a working collective, we are strong. Violence is coming. The harder we work, the better we make our living conditions, the more others will want to take what you have worked hard to produce. They will do this out of desperation, greed, jealousy, or just plain evilness. All are basic to human nature."

A younger gentleman by the name of Nicholas announced that his boss at Andy's Gun Works located on the edge of town might have a mediocre inventory of hunting rifles and ammo. "He's a business man, so Andy won't just give it away. He'll expect a fair trade for sure," Nicholas concluded.

At the beginning of the meeting, most of the faces wore expressions of individual survival and sadness, but as they departed for the night, there was a sense of tribal strength. By the end of the evening, everyone seemed to have a sense of purpose again. Instead of gloomy desperation and fear, there was hope.

UNWANTED GUESTS

Party crashers are the worst.

A few days later, Stephan and Kevin attempted the previously successful room-and-board bartering trick again. But this time they only received unwelcomed profanity and threatening warning shots from the occupant.

Tonight, they made camp in a small wooded clearing. Just as they got somewhat comfortable around a low-burning campfire, the air became thick and stagnant. Shortly after evening dusk faded into darkness, there came the sound of a light drizzle pitter-pattering on the overhead forest canopy.

Visually assisted with only small flickers of a drowning fire, they quickly strung up rainwater collectors using empty trash bags and boot laces. Other trash bags were wrapped around their packs to help keep their equipment and spare clothes dry.

At first, the light rain was an uplifting refreshment that subdued the sweltering summer heat and chased away the maddening mosquito swarms. Hiding behind separate bushes, Kevin and Stephan stripped down naked, excited for a natural revitalizing shower, scrubbing and rinsing off weeks worth of sweat and grime while laughing like kids in a backyard water sprinkler.

They repeatedly tried and failed to find dry timber to keep the comforting campfire lit as the light sprinkle increased to a steady rainfall. It quickly became clear that in this section of the forest, there wasn't much material to make shelter out of, and it was now too dark to search farther out or relocate camp. There was no place dry enough to sit or sleep. Their lighthearted mood dissipated. It was going to be a long night.

Sometime later, the night sky erupted with a blinding flash and long-lasting angry rumbles. The rain turned into a full-on monsoon-style downpour. Stephan's soaking wet baseball cap fell off her face as she rolled over miserably, drenched and cold, disappointed to not see a warm, glowing fire or a morning sunrise. When an energy bolt lit up the sky with an instantaneous crack that vibrated through her, she looked directly into the wide, frightened eyes of Kevin, who was holding one finger over his mouth in the "hush" gesture while his other hand clenched his pistol close to his chest.

Surprised and startled, her body went stiff. Not daring to move an inch, she searched the blackness of the forest for any threatening signs. The rain was heavy, the wind was blowing, and her shivering muscles ached from lying in a soggy pile of leaves. Another violent explosion of lightning strobed the forest scenery.

There. Only a hundred feet away at most. Had she really seen it? She rapidly blinked the pooling rainwater out of her blurry eyes. In the flash, she had seen what looked like someone standing naked in the woods. Something with an alien-like sickly gray skin. Was it watching them? It was, just standing there in the rain, motionless, staring. Her pulse quickened; she could feel her heart thumping against her rib cage. She held her breath until she felt dizzy. The blackness was constricting, suffocating.

The night sky lit up with a long burst, sending streaking lightning bolts in all directions. Yes, it was there, still standing and staring at them—but it was not alone! Stephan sucked in sharply through clenched teeth as she counted three more of them squatting against trees, close to the first one. When the flash ebbed and the forest went dark again, she slowly slid her hand down across her body to her holster, where she found the grip that gave her comfort from the darkness closing in on her. Without a sound, she brought her pistol up to her chest just as Kevin had done.

In the next flash of light, her eyes quickly flickered from the horrifying group of statue-like intruders back to Kevin, who was very subtly shaking his head *no* while trying to mouth something unreadable. She took it as a signal to not spring to her feet and start shooting wildly into the night, which was exactly what she desperately wanted to do.

She lost track of time. She felt drained. Her entire body hurt. It seemed that these demonic creatures of the night had either not noticed them or were not interested. Each flash of lightning became less intense and further apart. The thunder was just a distant rumble now.

She kept her eyes locked in their direction, studying each time the forest lit up with a quick glimpse. The rain had slowed to a light drizzle again, but the wind was still strong, blowing leaves and branches wildly. She suppressed a scream when, without any warning, all four of the ghastly creatures were standing only ten feet away as the sky faintly glowed from the now-distant storm.

Then, without a sound, they were gone, like ghosts in the wind. The following morning, Kevin and Stephan both swore to never sleep in the open again.

■■

"Good morning. This is Elizabeth Corrin bringing you today's BBN global news reports. Europe has been rocked by a series of overnight attacks that EU officials have classified as the most extensive coordinated terrorist attack in world history. Explosions at parliament and transportation facilities in Paris, Madrid, Zurich, Warsaw, Frankfort, Amsterdam, Copenhagen, and even here in London.

"Unverified reports of the PLO, Hezbollah, the Islamic State and many others are all claiming responsibility for what is being declared the most devastating coordinated Islamic attack since 9/11.

"The EU financial markets, which were scheduled to reopen today, will remain closed until further notice. Here in the UK, all banks, schools, and nonemergency government services will be temporarily halted. All citizens are being asked to remain home from work today. This morning, the Ministry of Defense, along with other NATO forces in cooperation with Russian Military Intelligence, have launched a full-scale retaliation in what some are already labeling World War Three.

"In other troubling news, UN officials have stated that Chinese relief efforts in western America have had significant setbacks as major violent outbreaks are prohibiting aid distribution. We're getting reports of Chinese aid workers being attacked by desperate unarmed civilians who are fighting—even scratching and biting—for much-needed basic provisions.

"The deployment of the Admiral Kuznetsov aircraft carrier has been announced by Russian officials to assist Chinese relief in America. Russian officials claim security resources are being utilized for humanitarian efforts only. The same officials, however, would not comment if the standard armament, including twenty-four military helicopters and thirty-six airplanes, were on board.

"The curious question still remains: Where is the location of the United States's Atlantic and Pacific fleets? Some fear that commanders have gone rogue."

■■■

It had been a week since Victor had attended the first town meeting, and for the most part, he was quite pleased with how this small town was pulling together.

The minor inconveniences of not having internet, a pumpkin spice latte, or air conditioning seemed trivial when a person wasn't sure where their next meal was coming from. First-world problems had been replaced by real-world problems. Clean water, food sources, basic sanitation, and security were the focus of the community.

The greatest accomplishments were made by a group of elderly women who had transformed the local flower shop nurseries into food-producing greenhouse gardens. Several farmers decided to pull in closer to town after their own homes had been repeatedly attacked. Those farmers drove their old antique tractors into town and decided to disc up the high school football field and any other available open, flat ground. All those little vegetable sprouts at the flower shops would soon be transplanted in the new community gardens.

The largest community engineering project was to keep the city's waste-water treatment plant operational. What seemed like a fairly simple retrofitting project in theory had, in fact, been problematic in every way possible, using every mechanic, plumber, and electrician in town only to figure out they didn't have the proper parts, which would need to be procured or fabricated by hand.

Victor taught his first weapons handling and marksmanship class to a class of four: two teenagers, the family restaurant owner who was now the designated community chef, and one elderly lady who owned a greenhouse garden. Even with such a disappointingly small group, Victor gave it his all, showing them how to safely operate their firearms, how to load and unload, basic marksmanship fundamentals, and the best way to carry a weapon to access it quickly. He thanked them for coming and asked them to come back for additional training.

Victor signed up for various labor projects when he wasn't involved with Sheriff Bohner. At the moment, he was helping process firewood, Zavier was helping in the gardens, Michael was on a hunting party, and Curtis was on a scavenger team systematically going from empty house to empty house, searching for anything useful. So far, they had been very successful, finding odd working electronics, small caches of canned food, cast-iron cookware, gardening tools, some firearms and hunting knives, fishing equipment, a lot of rowboats, bicycles, and even a couple of old working cars and four wheelers!

As usual, they would all come home dirty and tired. Of course, there were a few lazy individuals inside the city limits who felt they deserved a nightly community meal ration without contributing in any fashion to the labor duties. These loud-mouthed parasites had made enough of a fuss and had all the convenient excuses to still get a meal, but that sort of leaching mentality was contagious and must be snuffed out quickly.

On the south end of town, long stretching shadows cast by the growing mound of firewood signified to the wood-splitting crew—Victor, Bob, Ted, and Victor's next-door neighbor, Ben Cortman—that it was getting late in the day. Sunburned, sweaty, covered in sawdust and filth, all of them with aching muscles, they decided to call it quits and trudged back toward town. One good thing about this new catastrophic lifestyle: Victor was quickly losing his beer gut.

The lumberjacks were casually walking down the center of the road, each with an axe over a shoulder, bragging and joking about how many logs he had split compared to the weakling next to him. They laughed and fantasized longingly about how great a cold beer would taste, which led to another bolstering argument of what beer was best and what was piss water. They all hollered their disparagement when Victor said all IPAs taste like pine sap.

Halfway back to the center of town, their enthusiastic conversation topic of tomorrow's hunting and fishing duties was cut short by a spine-chilling shriek coming from deep inside the neighborhood to their right. Instinctively, they all went from a casual stroll to a defensive squat, clutching their axes with both hands.

"The hell was that?' Bob whispered.

Victor looked around at the obviously nervous group of lumberjacks, "Don't know. Let's go check it out."

"Shit, no. Are you crazy?" Ted asked.

"Someone is either in trouble or that was some sort of large animal. Either way, we should go check it out," Victor replied.

"I have a better idea: let's continue on this here road and go tell the sheriff to check it out! That's his job, not ours!" Ben cried.

Thankfully, Bob spoke up and said, "All right, Victor and I will go scout it out. You two hurry back into town and send help."

Ted and Ben took off at a hurried yet cautious trot toward town. Judging from their speed to find someone at the sheriff's office and then a return trip using a vehicle, Victor estimated about fifteen to twenty minutes until backup arrived. He shared his estimates with Bob, then smiled and pointed in the direction of the shriek and said, "Shall we?"

Bob and Victor marched forward at a hurried pace, each taking an opposite side of the street, carefully using houses, hedges, and abandoned vehicles for concealment. Most of this old and unnervingly quiet neighborhood was now uninhabited because either its residents resettled closer to the city center, cottage owners vacated with the postholiday exodus, or the owners had been out of town when the world went dark.

Bob paused behind an old Cadillac with a torn black canvas top and a strange license plate that read "OTIS." He was just about to cross an intersection when Victor held up his hand in a fist. Fortunately, Bob had seen enough war movies to know that meant to "freeze in place," and they both watched in shock and curiosity as a shirtless, ghostly human-shaped figure sprinted down the road, another following close behind.

After a few moments passed, Victor crossed the road to huddle in close to Bob. "Were those people?" Victor asked.

"I think so, but why did they look like that? That second one wasn't even wearing shoes."

"Did you recognize either of them?"

"Nah, man. Did you notice their hair? It was long and thin like an old person's. I could see most of their filthy scalps. Gross!" Bob turned and spat.

"They're heading that way." Victor nodded, pointing his axe toward town. "Let's try to follow."

Bob and Victor took off in a quick jog, breathing heavily, their bodies already aching from a long day of hard labor. The tall mature trees in the area cast heavy, dreary shadows into the already-dark neighborhood as the sun quickly approached the horizon. Up ahead, they heard shouting and what sounded like growling or barking—then an ear-piercing scream.

They quickly rounded the last house, running recklessly out into the middle of Main Street, and an incomprehensible scene came into view.

The two human-like creatures were circling Ted, who was violently swinging his axe in wild, ridiculous arcs. At Ted's feet was Ben, holding his neck with both hands, curled up in the fetal position on blood-covered pavement, screaming something so pitiful, it made Victor prematurely rush into action without properly assessing the situation.

One of the grayish creatures crouched down into a coil, then sprung at Ted's back with outstretched hands, clawing the air, grasping for purchase. Just as its fingertips found Ted's sweat-stained T-shirt, Victor swung his ax up like a golf club, sinking the double-bladed ax-head deep into the creature's chest cavity. Victor let go of the ax handle as soon as it made contact, spun 180 degrees, pulling Ted in close behind him with one hand and drawing his pistol with the other.

Controlling the direction of Ted's frantic movements with one arm, Victor aimed at the mangled, distorted snarling face only fifteen feet away, aligning the glowing front sight with the rear. His sights followed the creature down as it crouched into attack position. It locked its beady eyes on Victor and let out an inhuman snarl, brandishing stained, blackened, chipped teeth right before Victor placed a 124 grain 9MM Hydra-Shok defensive bullet right through its nose and out the back of its hairless skull, spraying darkened brain matter all over a nearby van.

■■■

"Good evening. This is Elizabeth Corrin bringing you another BBN global news reports. The World Health Organization has declared that the established quarantined areas of northern Mexico have been breached. New traces of the unknown pathogen have been reported as far south as Costa Rica. Brazilian and Columbian governments are sending security forces to assist a UN and WHO-enacted border closure at the Panama Canal.

"The WHO asks anyone in North and South America to report any persons with symptoms of prominent rashes, skin lesions, loss of skin pigmentation, and/or unusual paranoid hostility. Transmission methods are now believed to be bodily fluid transfers and skin-to-skin contact. Investigations are ongoing. Segregation, isolation, and distance of infected persons are the recommended prevention methods.

"In local news, the highly anticipated football game between Barcelona and Manchester United has again been canceled due to recent terrorist activities. Both franchise owners have promised the game will go on despite governmental warning. 'The fans deserve this game. The world needs this game more than ever,' Barcelona head coach stated…"

SHACKING UP

Finding a safe place to crash

Kevin had lost track; he couldn't remember what day of the week it was or how long they had been walking. He estimated three or four weeks of travel. He recalled it had taken about four days to make it up the coast on that small boat. Anny had shown symptoms along the way, then attacked Dan. Six days later, Dan disappeared into the forest. There had been the friendly couple at the farmhouse and the not-so-friendly resident at the next farm a few days later.

After the frightening night in the rainstorm, they had a serious dilemma. If they stayed deep in the woods, they may not find a suitable place to rest at night. If they continued close to the road, there were possibilities of finding human trouble.

Their route progress had become frustratingly slow, hiking at an extremely cautious patrol pace during the day and stopping by midafternoon. Finding appropriate shelter was difficult and time consuming. They needed plenty of time to find a suitable location, observe it for activity to ensure no one was home, then occupy, search for hazards or treasures, and finally fortify against attack.

Kevin had been walking lead for the past couple of hours at a casual stroll. He enjoyed the soft, flat terrain and the pleasant cloud cover, which eased the relentless summer heat. He stopped often to listen to the forest crackling, interpreting natural sounds from possible dangers. A light wind swayed the sentinel pines, casting rippling shadows across the pine needle–blanketed forest floor.

A squirrel darted across the ground to his left, which made him pause and instinctively tighten the grip on his rifle. His muscles relaxed as he watched the squirrel bound across the ground and ascend a tall pine. Just beyond the tree was small clearing. Nestled in the shade of the far wood line sat a small log cabin.

Kevin took a kneeling position and motioned for Stephan to move closer to him. He was looking at what he deemed a very suitable place to lay their heads. "What do you think?" he whispered.

"I don't know. It kind of gives me the creeps for some reason. And look, there's a car in the driveway. Who drives a car like that, anyway?" she asked while scanning the clearing and cabin.

"Are you kidding? That's a Delta 88 Royale. It's a classic!" Kevin said in a hushed excited tone. "Let's do our thing, see if anyone's home. Come on, it'll be fun." he said with a boyish grin.

After a short surveillance and an attempt to communicate with anyone home, they crept around the cabin, peering through the murky, dust-covered windows and checking the doors. A key ring found above the front entrance welcomed them in. Kevin advised that anytime they occupy an abandoned building they adhere to a list of priorities used by the military when establishing a defensive holding position:

SAFE – SOC

S for *Security*. That was first and foremost at all times. After they had confirmed the house was empty of threats, Kevin would watch the exterior of the house while Stephan inspected the structural integrity and scavenged. Their search of the cabin yielded a big stack of blankets, a clean set of men's clothes that were a little too tall for Kevin (but he took the socks and a T-shirt anyway), several cans of beans, some Tylenol, an old filthy chainsaw, and a dirty splitting maul lying by the front door. The interior was clear; exterior security would be maintained at all times.

A for *Avenues* of approach and placement of automatic weapons. If they had any, they would be a great asset, but Kevin's spine didn't like the idea of carrying a heavy machine gun all the way across Michigan. The main avenue of approach was the long, winding gravel driveway leading out to Route 55. If they had a machine gun, it would be pointed down that driveway. In the backyard, some sort of worn two-track path led off into the forest; they would need to keep an eye on that as well.

F for *Fields of Fire*, which are designated left and right shooting lanes. They overlap with each other to ensure full coverage of an area. Having only the two of them, they had decided if anything were to happen during their stay, Kevin was to control the cabin's front and Stephan controlled the rear. Each person was to control their assigned sectors by any means possible to prevent someone—or something—from infiltrating their defenses.

E for *Entrenching* typically meant digging fighting holes (foxholes) while defending a hilltop or some other terrain feature on the battlefield. Here, entrenching meant to make the cabin sturdier, more fortified. They used all the furniture to barricade weak points in the walls, such as the windows and exterior doors. They unhinged a couple of unnecessary interior doors to help cover windows. They placed a book-filled chest under a window of predetermined shooting position to help stop incoming bullets that may penetrate the walls.

S for *Supplemental* fighting positions, or fallback positions, were crucial. In case they could no longer physically defend the barricaded doors or windows, the bedroom at the end of the short and narrow hallway was their Alamo. They had left the bedroom door still attached, staged barricading furniture in the bedroom, and also stored their backpacks with all their essential equipment in there, just in case that room was to be their final stand.

O for building *Obstacles*. If Kevin and Stephan had any barbed wire, it would have been set in the yard at angles designed to channel aggressors into a clear line of fire. They had discussed pushing the old Oldsmobile down the driveway to create an obstruction, but they opted against it in the end. On the living room floor was a broken mirror along with other upended furniture and books from what looked like a struggle took place. They sprinkled the shards of the broken mirror on the front porch, hoping they would hear someone, something, walking on it during the night.

C for *Camouflage*. In the woods, camouflage was a continuous act. As a fighting hole is dug, all that freshly displaced dirt needed to be scattered and hidden. If not, the fighting position would stand out like a sore thumb. Likewise, any concealment vegetation brought in from different areas required refreshing every few hours. Because as it wilted and dried, the color would contrast against the natural living vegetation surrounding it. In the cabin, they avoided using the fireplace during the daylight—the chimney smoke would be a dead giveaway. They closed all the drapes and covered the windows with a secondary layer of blankets to hide any sort of movement or light that may be seen from the outside.

Kevin usually preferred taking first watch. This gave him time to familiarize himself with the portable HAM radio given to them by Harry Cooper. Every night after dusk, he would turn it on for only a few minutes to scan through the stations. Occasionally he'd pick up broken broadcasts on a weak signal, but nothing to get excited about. Not knowing how long the radio batteries would last, he was always searching drawers in these temporary shelters for spares.

They alternated sleeping in the Alamo bedroom and keeping watch. Without a way to keep track of time, they would simply stay awake as long as they could, then wake the other to take over security. It worked quite well, because they'd collapse into a solid sleep state, ensuring a good rest at the end of a shift. The first few nights sleeping indoors, they would frantically wake each other whenever a feral-sounding scream could be heard or when shadows would sweep across moonlit pastures. Now they would only wake each other if the building was being attacked, which hadn't happened.

Sometime long before dawn, Stephan stood up from the chair and quietly moved it out of the way, feeling drowsy. She got down on the floor and started doing push-ups until her arms quivered and gave out, then rolled over onto her back and did crunches until her core was on fire. Reaching into the dark with outstretched hands, she found her chair again and sat down, breathing heavily with a rapid pulse that would keep her awake for a little longer.

Her breath had just begun to calm when she heard a crunching sound. The thought of loose driveway gravel entered her mind; then she remembered the broken mirror they had sprinkled on the front porch. Silently, she retrieved her M4 off the table and crept her way to the living room. She pressed her ear against the cool front door and held her breath.

She jerked back suddenly when she not only heard but also felt fingernails scratch against the door's rustic wood grain. She put the muzzle of her rifle to the door, and she found the safety selector switch with her thumb. The knob rattled menacingly once. Then there was nothing but silence. A deep, foreboding silence.

Moments later, there were more sadistic scratches on the door. The pitch-black void of the night begged her to turn on her flashlight for comfort. After several minutes of not moving an inch, she heard glass crunch again. Then, nothing more until dawn. No more push-ups were needed for the rest of her shift—she was wide awake.

By early dawn, both were awake and starting the daily routine of getting ready. After she reported the earlier occurrence, Kevin seemed as startled as she was. Eager to leave, they quickly rationed the tiny morsels they had to eat, repacked their equipment, and were ready to step out into the early morning sun. When Kevin reached to turn the doorknob, Stephan forcefully put her hand against the heavy door, preventing him from opening it.

Kevin looked at her questioningly.

"*Look*," she mouthed, tilting her chin toward the small window beside the door. He carefully peeked through the curtain as three ghostly gray figures dashed across the long shadowy driveway.

Over the next few hours, they spotted a dozen more—some in packs, some solo. Some sprinting, some were hardly noticeable, hunched over stalking slowly. Two of them camped in the backyard, squatting next to a maltreated shed, not moving except for the occasional violent shudder.

Unsure of what to do, they both agreed to stay another night. This would give them ample time to rest, wash themselves using the tub and bottled water, and clean all their weapons.

Pacing back and forth, fighting boredom, Kevin accidentally found a trapdoor hidden under the living room rug. It led to a musty cellar via a set of rickety homemade stairs. They had hit the jackpot, finding jugs of water and several glass jars full of carrots, green beans, peas, venison, and other mysterious meats. They decided after the sun went down that they would light the wood stove and indulge in a warm meal. They might even stay a third night.

Stephan sat in a chair behind a window with slightly cracked curtains made of a dark floral pattern, observing the things in the backyard with a pair of binoculars. They were motionless, like concrete gargoyle statues, and they brought back terrible memories of the stormy night in the forest. She only found comfort by glancing at the nearby M4 leaning against the window frame.

Setting down another wooden chair, Kevin quietly sat beside her, noticing she had been scribbling notes in her book. "Whatchya got?" he asked in a barely audible whisper.

"I'm trying to hypothesize why they are squatting like that versus sitting or standing. They have been like that for hours."

"Sleeping in a defensive or offensive position?" he whispered back.

"Maybe. With Dan and Anny, the virus made them suffer insomnia, though. They may be resting but not sleeping," she said thoughtfully.

"Maybe they are ambushing? They could be hunting, waiting. I know some hunters who prefer to be on the move when tracking and stalking game. But most of them will sit in a tree stand or deer blind all day waiting for the right trophy to come by."

"That is absolutely frightening. Is this what humans are to become? We could walk directly into them at any point while we are out there. Behind every bush or tree could be one waiting to get us." She shivered.

"Yup," Kevin said, shifting in his chair nervously. "Notice anything else?"

"Physically, yes. Symptom differences must correlate with how long they've been contaminated. The gray ones are mostly bald, but the ones with some flesh pigmentation still have hair." Stephan handed Kevin the binoculars. "I can't tell on all of them, but look out there, at the closest one without a shirt and shoes. At first, I thought it had leaves or dirt stuck to it, but I'm now certain those splotches are large lesions caused by the Leishmania. Some spots look raw and are oozing pus. Others look crusted over with scale-like scabs."

"That is repulsive. And I mean that in the most medical, scientific, professional way possible. Those sores, they are all over them, even on their heads. I think I'm going to be ill," Kevin handed the binos back, his eyes watering, his throat and chest contracting as he fought against dry heaving.

"I agree. In the most scientific way possible. But even worse, those open sores are probably contagious, just like many other skin diseases."

"So now we don't even need to be bitten? They can simply grab ahold of us?" he asked.

"I can't say for sure, but yeah, probably," she replied.

"Great. We should wear gloves and long sleeves from now on, which is going to be awesome in this July—or August—heat. What month is it, anyway? Have you been keeping track?"

■■

There had been four more reports of attacks since Ben had been bitten after chopping wood. He went crazy on a concerned neighbor who'd stopped by for a checkup, then ran off, feral-like, into the forest. It seemed like they were all trapped inside a *Twilight Zone* episode. One day was filled with Independence Day celebrations, then instantaneously the world turned to the dark ages. Now, ravenous creatures were lurking in the bushes. This small community couldn't handle this type of stress and emotional trauma.

A farmer had reported shooting and killing a goat-chasing wild man whom he'd thought was a livestock thief. As he was dragging the bloody corpse out of the goat pen, he noticed the man's horrible rash-covered skin and odd beady eyes with tiny pupils staring up at him. Several days later, in an insomnia-induced hallucination panic attack, farmer Joe attacked his wife and children and had to be put down by his youngest son returning from doing chores.

Reality in this new world was bad enough, but as the news quickly spread, details were grossly exaggerated as they were passed from person to person. Somehow, there had been a rumor started that the Fourth of July EMP was caused by a massive solar flare that had doused the earth with a space disease or cosmic radiation, causing a mutation. Several people committed a ritualistic group suicide from that rumor alone.

The folks on the outskirts of town were either boarding up their houses in preparation of a final standoff or were flocking to the city center in search of protection from the sheriff and the newly deputized Town Defense Force. The high school gymnasium had turned into an overcrowded refugee center as most of the small empty homes in the downtown area were quickly being filled.

Centralizing the town actually had some benefits: organizing work crews had become much easier because there was now a deeper pool of skilled technical talents, and the dissemination of information was far more accurate, which eased a lot of unwarranted fears caused by half truths and rumors. Mr. Art Bell had brought with him a pile of old electronics from his basement. He didn't know if any still worked because he didn't have any power at his home. The next day, with the help of the electricians, some pilfered solar panels, and a large pile of collected boat batteries, Art discovered most of his communications equipment still worked. At that moment, Art unknowingly became one of the most valuable individuals in town.

A new working group with a dual purpose was also located in the high school: the town's veterinarian, two fire department EMTs, a dentist, and the high school biology teacher formed a medical staff. Tasked with normal day-to-day injuries and illnesses, they were also charged with studying and reporting on the new threat that was now terrorizing their once-tranquil little town.

For the safety of every resident and for the protection of the community as a whole, the city council issued a mandatory curfew from sundown to sunup. Everyone was to remain locked inside their homes at night. The Town Defense Force had set up several fortified second-story observation platforms in homes and business rooftops throughout town. Even though they couldn't see well during the nighttime curfew hours, the TDF had orders to "shoot anything that moved."

Tensions were high. Citizens were not trusting any outsiders for fear of catching the mysterious disease. With the exception of a few teachers, a town councilman, and a couple of diehard political activists, almost everyone was permanently armed and kept a polite distance from each other.

The disease wasn't the only threat on people's minds after a deputy was stabbed to death while patrolling the community gardens. His body was found the next morning by a horrified gardening crew, along with several rows of missing produce. This incident added to the cloud of fear, reduced law enforcement resources, and also broke the spirit of all those who diligently maintained the crops in an effort to ease the hunger epidemic.

Work details had to have designated guards. Hunting parties were now searching for the more difficult to find wild game and the increasingly easier to find infected predators. Victor now held full marksmanship classes every other day instead of once a week. On nontraining days, he and a small crew ran rescue missions, helping to relocate folks in town who were too afraid to walk on their own.

Victor was beginning to believe that these rescue missions were a complete waste of time and resources. Instead of being too afraid, most of these people were just too lazy. Some of them only wanted access to the town's only pickup truck to haul unnecessary household goods.

Just over three miles east of town, on the eighth day of running these so-called rescue missions, Victor's temper peaked at max level when he argued nose to nose with a slightly plump older lady who unquestionably had to take her six foot, four hundred pound wooden grandfather clock, which was handmade by her actual grandfather in 1932, and of course her Great-Aunt Margaret's matching china dish collection with 24-carat gold trim, and she unconditionally could not survive a single day without her plush salmon-colored reclining chair!

His face turned a dark red, and a vein swelled in his neck. He was about to say something that would land him in a heap of trouble at the next city council meeting when a pack of six screaming creatures broke through the underbrush on the opposite side of the road.

"Contact!" yelled Curtis, quickly shouldering his newly acquired Mini 14 carbine. He leaned over the hood of the truck, positioning himself properly behind the engine block and front wheel for cover, as Victor had taught him. Curtis didn't wait for instruction or permission—he began to fire, steadily bouncing hot, empty shell casings off the hood and windshield of the old truck. He continued with a slow controlled-shot tempo into the advancing crazed pack, immediately dropping the two lead maniacs who were sprinting directly toward him across an unkempt front lawn.

Victor stiff-armed the annoying lady in the face, pushing her through the open front door hard enough so that she stumbled and fell against the opposite entryway wall. He followed her in without responding to her curses and unslung his rifle, almost muzzle-thumping her as he spun in the entryway. The creatures were closing in fast, but they were still outside his pistol range. For just this reason, Victor's scope magnification always remained on its lowest power-adjustment setting, giving him a wider field of view that enabled him to quickly acquire targets, especially close range and fast-moving ones.

With a released-coil sound, the spring-loaded bipods slapped forward as Victor subconsciously wrapped his arm through the green nylon sling. He spread his feet wide apart, giving him a strong foundation, and paralleled his shoulders to the exterior wall. He brought his rifle up; jammed one of the extended bipod legs into the doorframe, keeping it in place with his nonfiring hand; and leaned forward heavily into the buttstock.

Curtis had taken down three of the monstrous gray creatures before they had split from the pack. He was having difficulty tracking the flanking speed of one that went far left, but he was still sending rounds after it. The one on the far right dodged around nonfunctional minivans that had been parked for well over a month. The middle one jumped into the old truck bed, its beady eyes locked on Curtis.

Victor flicked his rifle off safe. As soon as he found a part of his target, he squeezed the trigger. The sound inside the house was deafening. He could no long hear the screams of the lady cussing behind him.

As the creature dove across the top of the truck toward Curtis, Victor didn't care if it hit center mass or not. A one-shot kill didn't matter; he only needed to alter the attacker's course. With a wet smack, the creature screamed, crumpled, and then rolled off the hood of the truck onto the ground in front of Curtis, who brought the buttstock of his own rifle down onto its head repeatedly.

With so much weight pushing forward, Victor felt little recoil. He worked the bolt without losing sight picture. He held the bipod leg tight against the doorframe and took a step left. To have better situational awareness, he kept both eyes open to avoid tunnel vision inside his scope. He took another step left, swiveling his muzzle to the right toward the minivans. A creature sprinting up the sidewalk leading to the front door startled him and caused him to flinch as its greasy gray form filled his entire ocular lens.

Victor squeezed the trigger, putting a .308 bullet clean through its right lung, spraying blackened bodily fluid all over the shrubbery and several innocent garden gnomes. The thing sprawled out and tumbled, landing directly in front of Victor. Still locked into his shooting stance, his body weight leaning into the rifle against the doorframe, he let go of the rifle's grip, reached down to his hip, and drew his pistol. As soon as it cleared the holster, he tilted the muzzle up slightly toward the creature scrambling to right itself, and he shot from the hip without aiming. Squeezing off round after round, he watched his impacts hitting the target's chest and abdomen until finally the pistol's slide locked to the rear.

With his rifle still pointing toward the sidewalk and locked into place against the doorframe, Victor quickly reloaded his pistol, then holstered it. He worked his rifle bolt, putting a fresh round in the chamber, then put it back on safe, relaxed the tension, and slung it across his back, where it had been only a few seconds before.

The creature withered in front of him, scratching at the concrete doorstep, chipping away its fingernails as it tried to crawl forward. It had one rifle- and sixteen pistol holes in it, and it still had the determination to fight. The pitiful thing hissed and shook fiercely with vehemence until it finally bled out in a pool of nasty fluid.

Victor looked up at Curtis, who only gave him a wide-eyed, understanding nod that suggested he was all right.

"Did you get the one that ran that way?" Victor asked as he visually scanned his son for injuries.

"Yeah. It took me a full magazine, but I got 'em."

"Your buttstock. You need to wash that off. Don't touch it; it could be contagious. Look in her laundry room or under the kitchen sink for some bleach," Victor told him.

Curtis didn't say a word as he entered the front door, stepping over the sobbing lady, who was still sitting on the floor where she had landed. Victor put a calm, understanding hand on his son's shoulder as he passed, which helped ease Curtis's urge to vomit.

Victor looked down at the plump lady with rage in his eyes and a clinched jaw. He pointed his finger in her face. "You, look at me. Look at me! My son right there almost died for your bullshit cups and saucers. You have five minutes—five damn minutes—to gather any clothes, food, and medication you need before we are leaving. With or without you!" he growled.

She crawled to her feet and hustled into her bedroom, still whimpering.

Victor gazed at the creature lying in front of him, amazed at their speed and ability. The thought of Erica struggling to survive wherever she was—finding food, fighting bandits, probably alone and afraid, traveling on foot over two hundred hostile miles filled with these things—suddenly enraged him further.

"And I'm burning that salmon-colored recliner chair!" Victor yelled into the house.

STAGE THREE

ADVERSARIES

Foreign. Domestic. Diseased.

Under a large open gazebo at the public beach, the city council was having an impromptu meeting. It was a nice sunny day with a pleasant breeze drifting off the lake and stirring the smell of roses, with sounds of ducks quacking nearby. In attendance with the mayor were the original city council members, Sheriff Bohner, Victor, and Mrs. Cloud representing the medical research team.

As Victor looked around the long picnic table full of frail and tired faces, his hopes of survival waned. The community's leaders wore the same soiled clothes and malnourished features as everyone else in town. Prioritizing food gathering and security protocols was the basis for this meeting.

The mayor initiated. "Thank you all for coming. Our hunting teams are having difficulty finding rich game areas lately. What they are finding plenty of is danger. We can't say if we've over hunted the surrounding areas, if the diseased people are also consuming animals, or if all the wildlife has been scared away. Or possibly all the above. Either way, our food supply is running dangerously low when we should be investing in a winter reserve."

"Can we send them farther out? To areas that we haven't hunted yet?" asked councilwoman Jessica Holland.

"We must consider that option. But how far out do they go? They could scout out on foot, even preplan to stay overnight in houses known to be abandoned. When they successfully harvest game, they'll need transportation back here."

Victor chimed in, "That could work well for sharing of information with anyone they find in the rural areas as well. The hunting parties could become our ambassadors. Never know—they could find more people wanting to relocate into town or farmers willing to barter."

"Great idea, Victor. If we are all in agreement, I'll talk to the hunter teams to see if any are willing. I can't force anyone to take that kind of risk venturing so far away from town. They'll need some extra supplies too. Victor, could you help make an expedition equipment list for them?" asked the mayor.

Victor nodded. "If the hunters are going farther away from town, that means they'll be exterminating fewer Grays running crazy through our nearby woods. Lately, the hunters have been shooting more of them than they have rabbits and squirrels."

"Can we refrain from saying 'exterminate'?" said the only well-groomed councilman, wearing an almost-clean button-up shirt, at the end of the table. "Those are humans that you all are shooting. Some of them are from this town."

Victor raised an eyebrow. "Sir, have you witnessed any of these sick neighbors of yours in person?"

"No, but that doesn't change the fact that you all are out there sadistically hunting people. I've heard that some of you gun-nut psychos are even keeping score. Is that true?"

Victor gave the sheriff a "please help me" look.

"We are tracking statistics. It's far from a leaderboard for bragging rights. If you care to know, the first week when Ben was attacked, there were four confirmed cases. The following week, there were nine. Last week, there were seventeen. These numbers are attacks on citizens; they do not include engagements by the hunter teams. I'm not the smartest man, Stan, but I can guess next week we'll have around thirty attack reports. Soon, there'll be too many to count," the sheriff said flatly.

"You can call it whatever you want," Victor said. "This disease is spreading and getting worse. We have to do something to secure this town. Not only from the Grays but also from marauders running rampant. I have some ideas that I will run by the engineers. As far as the Grays, I propose we attempt to draw these things away from town and eliminate them at a safe distance."

"Wait. What do you mean by 'draw them away'? Like baiting them or something? You're a maniac! Why are you even here, Victor? You have no authority," the councilman challenged.

Victor gritted his teeth and leaned forward, planting his fist on the green-painted picnic table, about to give this guy an earful when councilwoman Holland intervened.

"Give it a rest, Stan. Victor has been putting himself and his family in danger to ensure residents are relocated safely. He's contributing more than most of us, including you. Now, unless you have solutions to—"

"We should be capturing and treating these sick people, not indiscriminately euthanizing them! It's murder. And by the way, I've heard how Mr. Knight-in-Shining-Armor treats the evacuees!" Stanly interrupted.

"Mrs. Cloud, can we treat them?" asked the mayor, ignoring the councilman's accusations toward Victor.

"Based on the few autopsies we have performed, no. Not yet. We still don't understand the virus; it's unlike anything any of us have seen or studied. In fact, we believe that it is still evolving. We haven't witnessed the worst of it yet. It's quite sophisticated." Mrs. Cloud addressed the table, avoiding the previous intense argument. "Stan may have had a clever idea, though—we should try to capture a couple for testing. We could learn more from live specimens than deceased. Sheriff, if our veterinarian has sedative tranquilizers, could we use your jail to detain a couple?"

"Sure, they are all empty now." Sheriff Bohner confirmed.

Stanly stood abruptly. "Mrs. Cloud, are you now suggesting experimenting on them? Alive? Trapped in cages like lab monkeys?

You're even more cruel than this mercenary!" he shouted, pointing at Victor.

The mayor used his smooth-talking politics to calm the situation. "Mrs. Cloud, see if we have the tranquilizers. Victor, could you bring us back a couple of live ones?"

Stanly scoffed, tossing his hands in the air. Victor simply said, "Yes, sir. It will be risky, but I can manage that with a handful of guys."

"OK. For now, let's focus on capture and detaining. With any luck, we'll learn more about the illness, maybe even a treatment. At a minimum, we'll get a better look at this terror, perhaps discover its weaknesses. In the meantime, hold off on the wholesale slaughtering, but do experiment with drawing them away from town. See what gets their attention."

"Sounds like a plan, sir. Just to be clear: if we encounter hostility with the ability, intent, and opportunity to cause serious bodily harm or death, our first resort for self-defense will be deadly force. That goes for Gray or human. I'm not risking anyone's well-being for this infestation. I'll let Stanly over there kill them with kindness."

■■

Stephan had been walking point, daydreaming about how refreshing a clean set of clothes would be, when a creature baring a mouth full of blackened, jagged teeth leapt through a nearby bush with outstretched hands, caused her to stumble backward. As she fell back, she jabbed the weapon forward towards the vile creature, thumbing her M4 from safe to full auto. She stitched the Gray in a perfect vertical line, putting one round through its abdomen, one to the center of its chest clipping its xiphoid process, one round through its neck, and the last round into its right eye socket at near point-blank range.

As she landed on her back with a thud, her legs lifted, stopping the heavy grotesque corpse from landing on top of her by planting her boots into its chest. Kevin was fast enough to kick it off to the side before any of the contagion could leak on to her.

Both of them were in a state of shock. Kevin reached his hand down to help her up. The weight of her, and her backpack, almost pulled Kevin to the ground. As he assisted her up, the forest came alive with a shudder.

There was a shift in the stagnant air. The birds stopped chirping, clearing the sound waves for dozens of feet, snapping dried sticks and breaking branches. The ground vibrated as a large dead tree landed nearby with a thunder. A chorus of snarls and growls followed.

Stephan looked into Kevin's unbelieving eyes. "Run!" he screamed.

They took off in a sprint in the direction they had been traveling, leaving all tactics behind. Stealth was completely absent. Stephan ran as fast as her legs would pump; she looked for a route between the rapidly advancing trees. She bounded over a chasm and landed heavily, grinding her shoulder into the jagged bark of a mature oak tree.

The weight of her pack was like dragging a boat anchor. Her legs ached as if she had been running on beach sand, and her lungs were on fire, gasping for oxygen like a fish out of water. Salty sweat from her brow streamed into her eyes, stinging and blurring her vision. She could barely see but thought she'd seen movement to her right.

She glanced to the side, where two Grays had flanked them quickly, and the ground suddenly disappeared from under her. She rolled twice before righting herself as she slid down a steep leaf-covered hillside. Coming to a stop at the bottom, she was jolted forward onto her stomach as Kevin tumbled into her from behind, also coming to a quick halt on the slide for life.

Untangling themselves, they helped each other up, stumbled forward, and broke through the forest into a long flat clearing. The sound of growls surrounded them.

"Go!" He pointed. "There, toward that barn."

They tore across the clearing, racing for the safety of the airplane hangar Kevin had first thought to be a large barn. He chanced a glance back toward the forest. The Grays were already in the clearing and closing the distance quickly. He knew they'd never make it to safety before the beasts were all over them. He jockeyed a few steps to the left, stopped, spun around, took a knee, and began to fire into the mass of horrid creatures in rapid succession.

Stephan took several more strides before she heard Kevin's first shots and spun to a halt. She watched two of them fall as she raised her rifle to provide cover fire for Kevin so he could move. In her peripheral, she saw Kevin stand quickly and turn outboard, not wanting to run into her line of fire, scanning hastily to the side, ensuring they were not being flanked.

Stephan put several rounds into each body, but it was only slowing them down, with insignificant effects. Some would fall, then get right back up as if they had only tripped. It reminded her of seeing criminals under the influence of psychotropic drugs getting tazed or shot ineffectively. The pain and shock alone would incapacitate the average person.

Kevin sprinted past her, and at about twenty-five yards to the rear, he stopped and began to fire again. Stephan took the sound of his rifle blast as a cue to get moving. She yelled, "Reloading!" as she sprinted past Kevin, deliberately giving him a wide shooting lane. She reloaded on the move, dropping the nearly empty magazine onto the overgrown grass airstrip. She stopped some distance behind Kevin and began firing again at the quickly advancing pack. As she pulled the trigger, her shoulder absorbed the recoil, and the smell of gun oil and cordite filled her nostrils while the glimmering holographic red dot transitioned from target to target.

Kevin bounded past her, yelling loudly over her rifle fire, "Forget the hangar; we'll never make it. Go for those planes!"

When he began to fire, more rapidly now, she turned and spotted several small planes in a cluster on the near side of the hangar. She darted into the lot to find a small white passenger plane with long blue stripes across its open door. Instead of climbing in, she went prone, lying under the plane, and began shooting into the lower torsos of the half-visible Grays.

A second later, Kevin spotted her under an aircraft marked N688IM taking shots at a cyclic rate. He leapt over her, yelling for her to get in. She did, swiftly, without hesitation. They slammed the door, then sprawled out onto the cabin floor just as the remaining creatures penetrated the cluttered lot of planes.

With both of their white-hot smoking rifle barrels pointed at the door, they were breathing so loudly they thought for sure the snarling Grays would hear them. The small plane tilted suddenly as one of them ran into the wing. From inside the thin-skinned plane, they could hear the muffled, frustrated barks of the creatures frantically searching for them.

After what seemed like several minutes of silence, Kevin cautiously peeked through a window. He let out a long breath as he slid back down the side of the plane, nodding his head to say *all clear*.

Stephan let her head loll back against the floor, her vision blurring. She gulped in air, fully expanding her lungs. With her eyes shut, still trying to catch her breath, she whispered, "So you wouldn't happen to be a pilot, would you?"

Kevin started to chuckle, his shoulders and belly contracting, overcome with an adrenaline-dump giggle fit. "Fat chance. I was hoping that you were a hobbyist. Ever sleep in a grounded plane before? I hope the movie's good. I don't know if I'm in the mood to deboard just yet."

Not knowing if the Grays had moved on or not, they stayed locked up in the plane the rest of the day. They closed all the window shades and used a passenger blanket to cover the cockpit window, then searched the inside for loot but came up empty-handed. Not even single-serving packaged peanuts.

"I dropped four mags out there. I only remember reloading once," Stephan said, examining her vest.

"Same here. I'm down three mags. How did we not kill more of them? They were just absorbing the hits?" he asked.

"They were still taking damage and will likely die sooner or later, but they weren't feeling it. Your headshots put them down quick. The FFI protein must erode the pain processors in the brain. It could be possible that the fungal spore Ophiocordyceps Unilateralis has taken over the nervous system as well. That would also explain why they're so fast. The average person's subconscious will tell the body when to quit for self-preservation. I bet these things would literally run themselves to death to obtain a new host."

"Wonderful," Kevin said with a heavy sigh while reaching into his backpack and pulling out a handful of loaded mags. Luckily they were still carrying Anny and Dan's ammo, but they couldn't sustain many more of these engagements. They debated the need to retrace their steps in the morning to retrieve the empty mags from the grass runway.

They both studied the map that Kevin had unfolded on the floor. "Here, I am pretty sure that we are here. I've been in this city several times, just passing through. The city is called Houghton Lake, but it's known as the Cross Roads of northern Michigan, where Route 55 crosses US 127. It has the largest inland lake in Michigan and a pretty big shopping mall too."

Stephan traced her finger across the map from the coastal town of Tawas, where they had come ashore several weeks ago to the east side of Houghton Lake. "Looks like we've hiked about seventy miles. About another twenty-five to go. We have this pretty big metro area to bypass, or go straight through, or swim across that big-ass lake. I wonder if the infected can swim?"

"I hope not. At least there would be a chance of survival on large boats and places like Mackinac or Plum Island," Kevin said, still gazing down at the map. "You know, when we left work, back in Detroit, this was where I was going to split from our group. I was going to follow the highway north from here to Camp Grayling, the Army National Guard base."

Stephan involuntarily went stiff, suddenly feeling a crushing weight of anxiety. She couldn't do this alone. Even if there were only twenty miles left to go. On a normal day, she could make that walk or jog in only a few hours. Now, it'll take a week or two. If she made it at all. She looked up from the tattered map with misty eyes.

"Not now, though. This plague has changed everything. Most likely, Camp Grayling has been looted, or a rogue group has taken control of its armory and vehicles. Not to mention I would be afraid to death traveling on my own. And what kind of ass would I be to send you out there solo? I'll stick with you, if you don't mind. That little town you are heading to sounds lovely this time of year."

She surprised him when she lunged forward, wrapping her arms around him. "Thank you," she said, sobbing gently into his shoulder. "Of course you can stick with me."

Later, Stephan passed out cold, curled up in a pile of passenger pillows and blankets. Kevin dug into his pack, happy to find that none of the glass food jars had broken. He pulled out the portable HAM radio and scanned the frequencies until a broken and barely readable signal became clear. He reached over and aggressively shook Stephan's shoulder until she woke, sitting up quickly with her rifle in hand, looking around, discombobulated.

■■

Victor, along with Curtis, who had an interest in electronics and engineering, were standing behind Art, patiently waiting for him to go through the power-converting protocol that was way outside Victor's understandings.

A whirling fan from an inverter kicked on, and then small LED lights signaled that twenty-four-volt DC from the battery bank was being inverted to 110 AC for the radio equipment. "Here we go!" Art said enthusiastically, mimicking a child with a recently rediscovered toy.

He started turning frequency dials and flipping tuner switches that neither Victor nor Curtis could keep track of. "Have you picked up any chatter yet? Anything useful?"

Art continued dialing, lifting half his headphones off one ear. "Not really. I have picked up a distress call from a family in Columbus, Ohio, trapped inside a Blaine's Grocery store. No one answered them. That was three days ago."

"Have you broadcasted yet?"

"Negative," Art said. "Town council has forbidden sending, only receiving. They are still using political voodoo to write me up an authorized script. I guess the FCC is governing at the county level now."

"I kind of agree with them on this one. If you announce that we are a thriving community with open doors, we will be attacked and overrun by tomorrow night. It has to be scripted just right so we receive the right type of people."

"Yeah, I understand that," Art said faintly, slapping the headphone back onto his ear and then anxiously spinning a few more dials as if he were fishing for a trophy. He jerked the headphone jack out of the receiver and turned up the volume on the squelch box, reaching for a pad of paper.

"Good evening. This is Elizabeth Corrin bringing you another BBN global news report.

"United Kingdom citizens are reminded to refrain from unnecessary travels in personally owned vehicles. Fuel rations are expected to relax as soon as the British Pound and the Euro have officially integrated into the BRICS currency used on the open oil exchange market.

"Today, the world is at war. NATO forces are reporting substantial casualty rates mirroring World War Two levels. The EU has issued a memorandum to initiate a European-wide military- and civil service draft.

"NATO and allied BRICS forces are stretched thin on many fronts, engaged in bloody conflicts in northern Africa, Yemen, Iran, Syria, and Iraq. We are sad to report that our own local hero, Maj. Henry West of the 42nd Blockade, has been killed in action.

"Taking the entire world by surprise, the government of France has retaliated for last week's Euro terror attacks by detonating a high-yield hydrogen bomb over Mecca, Saudi Arabia. The French president has called the drastic decision 'a last resort crucial to preserving European integrity, historical culture, economic stability, and way of life.'

"India quickly followed suit, detonating a nuclear device in the Pakistani capital of Islamabad, resulting in millions of fatalities. Afghanistan simultaneously launched a military invasion into northern Pakistan, decimating dozens of Taliban strong holds.

"Russian President Putin and Chinese President Xi have strongly condemned Indian and French use of nuclear weapons, calling for an emergency United Nations Security Council meeting to prohibit further nuclear exchanges for the sake of humanity.

"Next, we have an update from the World Health Organization, but first a message from our sponsors…"

■■■

The handheld HAM radio lost the signal during the commercial break, infuriating Stephan, who desperately wanted to hear the WHO report, already knowing deep in her heart that it was about the spreading outbreak. "Get it back!" she cried.

Kevin, who barely knew how to turn the thing on and scan channels, couldn't get the signal back. After several minutes of cursing, he finally turned it off. "If that was a signal from the UK, I'm surprised we got any of it. Especially inside this plane," he said defensively.

"I'm sorry. I didn't mean to snap. It's just…" She trailed off.

"I know," he said reassuringly.

They stayed up later than normal that night, passing a jar of carrots and venison back and forth, stabbing large chunks out with a folding knife. They discussed, dissected, debated, and theorized every piece of information they had just acquired.

By the time they finally passed out, sound asleep inside the locked plane, it seemed like they now had more unanswered questions than before hearing the broadcast.

■■■

Hidden within a dark, damp resale store at the far edge of town, Victor nestled under an improvised bunker constructed of tipped-over shelving units and moldy clothes. A small opening in his hide site allowed him to observe out the store's broken front window while remaining concealed. Across the two-lane road was an adjacent storefront that was illuminated by large dancing flames as thick black smoke plumes rolled off a blazing tire stack.

He was distracted in a daydream, recalling details of the earlier BBN news broadcast they had received. It was a lot of information to process. He may not have believed they were involved in World War III if he hadn't heard it himself. Even though there had been no mention of the United States in the broadcast before Art's battery bank had drained dead, he realized the world was currently too busy with its own problems to send help. America, including this little town, was on its own.

The town council had reacted unexpectedly to the news. A particular councilman, whom Victor was not too fond of, had suggested to suppress the information in fear of causing widespread panic. He had argued that the news had no bearing on their community and would only hinder the work progress being made. Luckily, the mayor had overturned his Orwellian notion of censorship manipulation, contesting that every citizen had the right to know the unfiltered truth.

Victor had been sitting in his hide for hours. The fire was starting to dwindle down, causing darker shadows to stretch farther into the store, submerging him in darkness. He was about to call it quits when he spotted Michael and Zavier lowering down another car tire tethered by a long thick rope, hand over hand, onto the fire below. His sons had been upstairs in that second-level barricaded room for as long as he had been in the thrift store. The boys' tasks were simple: stay quiet, keep the fire lit, and provide covering fire for Dad if shooting started.

This little mission had two objectives: The first, to see if the Grays would be attracted to a fire at night. Testing the "moths to a flame" theory. The community knew next to nothing about these things, other than that they attack on sight, without provocation or hesitation. Which led to the second mission requirement: capture one of them if they came to investigate the fire. Victor hated to admit it, but capturing a couple alive would be beneficial.

He sat up, sitting a little taller, when a familiar menacing growl echoed through the still night air. One of the creatures dashed past the broken storefront display window, startling Victor and causing him to raise the dart gun quickly. Several minutes passed before two more shadowy figures sprinted by.

Even though he'd double-checked that the back door was locked and he'd placed shopping carts in the hallway as an early warning signal, Victor couldn't shake the feeling that they were stalking him from behind. This was the first time he had observed the Grays not sprinting full speed directly at him. He really didn't know what to expect.

It appeared that the creatures were curious of the fire but not drawn directly to it for warmth and comfort, as people would be. They didn't seem interested in the fire itself but more curious of the illumination it provided on the surrounding building, which made him extremely nervous. It wouldn't take long for them to begin exploring.

A creature hesitated in the thrift shop doorway and then squatted, silhouetted against the fire. The black outline of the creature turned its head left and right in jerky motions. Then it gradually looked up toward the second-story window where his boys were hidden. Its body contorted as if it were coughing, producing a series of loud barking sounds. Several of the passing creatures abruptly stopped in their tracks.

Fearing it had spotted his sons and that the Grays were communicating, Victor squeezed the trigger on the dart gun, sending a syringe filled with enough sedative to knock out a horse flying into the creature's back. The creature sprung forward, landed on its feet, and stood upright stiffly in the middle of the road with its neck arced painfully backward. One of its arms was straight out in front, clawing the air as if it were squeezing an invisible stress ball repetitively. It let out a long hiss, then fell over with a thud.

The other creatures vanished quickly, withdrawing into the night without a sound.

Victor let a few minutes pass to see if they'd return. Fearing they would but also hoping to subdue a second creature, he turned on his yellow walkie-talkie and pressed the push-to-talk button. "Seven

Dwarves, this is Bad Apple. Sleeping Beauty ready for a carriage ride, over."

"Bad Apple, this is Seven Dwarves. We'll pull around the block now."

Victor looked up, seeing his boys in the upstairs window, holding a similar walkie-talkie. They looked down at him, giving him two thumbs up. By the time the truck pulled around, Michael and Zavier were coming out of the building.

"Hey, wait over there. Michael, you watch back that way. Zavier, you watch that direction. Shoot anything that moves," Victor directed while walking toward the truck.

The designated hazmat team climbed out of the cab, looking ridiculous. Victor was going to rib them with a joke but decided he wasn't interested in putting his hands on the creature. So instead, he kept his mouth shut and scanned the streets for movement.

The two men wore clear woodshop goggles, ponchos made of black industrial-size trash bags, yellow rubber cleaning gloves, and olive drab fishing waders. They used thick plastic zip ties to secure its arms behind its back, then rolled it into a double-layered floral bed sheet. For safe measure, they put a pillowcase over its head before lifting it into the back of the truck.

Victor whistled for his kids to fall back toward the truck. He opened the passenger door, motioning for them to get in. He jumped in the back with the hazmat team and sat on a wheel well, resting his rifle across his knee, the muzzle inches from the creature's head. With a tap on the side of the truck, they headed toward the county jail.

PAYMENT PLAN

Chronicles of an Apocalyptic Hit Man

His neighbor's house was just over the next large hill. He halted to scan the area using a night-vision device mounted forward of his rifle scope. Stopping to scan every ten steps, he was being overly vigilant in order to avoid stumbling into a squatting hibernating Gray again. The first—and last—time he'd bumped into a crouching Gray in the dark had been a near-death experience. That event awarded him a raging hangover after he'd washed away the experience with an entire bottle of Irish whiskey. Learning from the mistake, he now moved at a more cautious pace. It took him only an hour to make his way to this final waypoint, navigating the thick brush under the cloak of darkness. He planned on being in his hide site before the first signs of dawn.

He was certain of his location, but you could never be too sure. From under his MARPAT shirt, he pulled out a metal compass that was hanging around his neck. Lifting the compass lid, he aligned the radioactive glowing navigation dots, confirming he was still on the correct bearing.

By the time the eastern sky turned pink, Raymond was already secured inside a small hand-dug hide site that he'd used several times before. He'd been working on this, and several like it, for the past month. He'd covertly improved his kill boxes with sandbag-fortified walls and floors made of pallet planks. The ceiling was made of long thick logs that could support the weight of a large man such as himself, then camouflaged with a thick layer of dirt, grass, and leaves. From this hidden spot, halfway up a hill, he could observe his entire neighbor's property with a wide-open field of fire.

Looking out a small gun port, Raymond stared through a pair of range-finding binoculars, scanning the house, looking for signs of activity. It didn't take him long. It appeared that his neighbors had prematurely picked half the green beans and carrots out of their garden; they must have become desperately hungry to have harvested early. The front door of the darkened house opened shortly after, giving birth to a dirty-faced frail man with deep eye sockets. The old man looked left, then right, then quickly ran to the corner of his house, retrieving a rainwater-collecting bucket from under the gutter downspout. The old man waddled back inside the house, sloshing water out of the heavy bucket across the front porch along the way.

Raymond grinned. There were a hundred different ways he could come up with to rid himself of his useless neighbors. The yard around the house was wide open. He could place a time-fused, gas-filled jug on the roof, then sit back and watch the inferno, waiting for fast-moving targets to sprint across the lawn as the family fled their burning residence. That could give him the benefit of decent marksmanship practice, Raymond thought with a swell of sadistic amusement. Maybe the Muldoon family would be worth something after all. In the end, murdering this entire family would be far too easy, not even offering the satisfaction of a small, amusing challenge.

Breaking from his bloodbath fantasy, he focused on what he came here to do. In the window next to the front door, he spied the clearly displayed orange-and-black "Help Wanted" sign. This was his signal that the Muldoon family was in need of his services and had sufficient payment.

Raymond had a special prearranged agreement with all the surrounding neighbors: When abundant amounts of creepy creatures became copiously inconvenient for apocalyptic comfort, the neighbors employed Raymond to cull the herd to a tolerable level. For a nominal fee, of course.

Raymond sat the binos on the ledge of the firing port in his subterranean hide site. Reaching into his backpack, he pulled out a space age–looking air rifle equipped with a huge scope that had probably come off a high-powered sniper rifle. He scanned the house again for movement, hoping the neighbors would be careless enough to cause a commotion, drawing the Grays in on their own. Unfortunately, the Muldoon family was buttoned up tight. He wasn't a fan of animal cruelty, but the second-best bait was the sound of a wounded animal. Like a coyote to a wounded rabbit, the sound made the Grays come running almost as fast as an exposed uninfected human would. He set the sights on the caged raccoon's rear quarter, whispered an apology to the animal, and then pulled the trigger, causing an eruption of pained hisses, growls, and raccoon-laced profanity.

Raymond leaned the air rifle in the corner, trading it for a short-barreled DARPA XM-3 bolt-action rifle equipped with a 3–15X-powered scope and attached suppressor. This rifle originally came with an internal magazine, which he'd kept to collector specification until the day the lights went out, when he then upgraded the bottom metal to accept ten round detachable box magazines for faster reloading of his favorite rifle. He placed ten of those full-box magazines on the ledge in front of him now.

While using the binos to scan the surrounding tree line, waiting for the morning rush, his mind began to analyze what exactly he was doing out here in the great outdoors. Killing for payment. Nothing new, but this was different on many levels. If he had a business card to pass out, what would it read? The title "security" made him cringe. It was borderline mall cop or neighborhood watch, which, in all practicality, is what he was. The security title was insulting to his long professional resume of military service and high-threat diplomatic protection. Besides, neighborhood watch was voluntary; Raymond expected payment.

So maybe it made him a Soldier of Fortune, a mercenary for hire? He was a huge fan of Executive Outcomes, a private South African military company in the early 1990s who'd been hired by the countries of Angola and Sierra Leone. In both cases, Executive Outcomes had come rolling in with Special Forces soldiers, helicopter gunships, and artillery, squashing decades-old civil wars in a matter of days. Even though the outcome was in favor of regional peace, the United Nations quickly realized the risk of armies for hire by the highest bidder and penned the 2001 resolution forbidding the use of paid foreign soldiers, aka mercenaries.

Raymond had been a private security contractor for many years. Many of his coworkers thought of themselves as mercs, but they weren't really, not by the legal definition. As a contractor, Raymond conducted defensive operations, not offensive. Even though he operated in hostile foreign countries, he was employed by his own government to protect US interests—a stark difference from being an old-school "Man Among Men" Rhodesian mercenary.

Assassins typically killed for money; maybe that could be on his business card:

Raymond K. Hessel

Assassination Services

That brought a smile to his green-and-brown-camo-painted face. Even though assassins did kill for coin, they also typically had political or religious motives. Raymond had neither of those.

He continued the time-killing quest of selecting the perfect job title until he spotted a half-naked Gray broke through the shadowed forest edge, sprinting on bare feet straight toward the suspended raccoon cage.

He could wait for the Gray to get directly below the rattling cage, which was suspended twelve feet off the ground from a large branch; that would make for an simple target. But he wanted to plug this hideous creature before more showed up. Taking on one Gray at a time was an easy task, but a larger group of Grays could overwhelm him with ease, even with his impressive arsenal.

He'd figured out weeks ago that if you shoot a Gray in a pack with a silenced weapon, the others would instinctively flee from the unknown danger. But if you introduce a driving mechanism, such as a food source (hurt raccoon) or an untainted human, the Grays would continue to charge forward with no sense of self-preservation.

One technique to shoot moving targets was to locate the target, then watch it through the sights to determine a good time and place to engage. The "tracking" technique was better for open dynamic battlefield situations with room to move and using smaller weapons like carbines or pistols.

He lifted his rifle to his shoulder. Restrained by the miniature size of his hide site, he was forced to protrude the suppressor out of the shooting port slightly. He rested his scope reticle on a clearing halfway between the tree line and the raccoon bait, and he waited for the Gray's image to enter the sight picture.

When using a precision rifle to engage moving targets, Raymond preferred the "ambushing" technique. He was set in a stable, stationary shooting position, waiting for the creature to enter his scope's field of view, offering him a split second to react. Just before the scab-covered rib cage of the muscular nine-mile-per-hour sprinting Gray reached the vertical line of his crosshairs, he squeezed the trigger.

Instead of bisecting the center of the Gray with his reticle, he placed his crosshairs slightly in front of the moving target. This allowed the Gray to travel the additional distance forward the same exact time it took Raymond to pull the trigger, the firing pin to hit the primer, igniting the gun powder, accelerating a copper-jacketed bullet spiraling down and out the barrel, flying six hundred feet though the chilled morning air and into the sprinting Gray's torso.

The lightweight short-barreled .308 rifle recoiled a bit more than modern heavy-target rifles. As he rocked back slightly, absorbing the energy, he slid the rifle bolt knob up and to the rear, then forward again as his body weight returned to his natural point of aim, awarding him with a magnificent view of the Gray rolling on the neighbor's lawn, struggling to get back to its feet. He debated putting another 175-grain hollow point into its cranium to silence the howling creature, but he could easily see blackened fluid spraying from its ribs. It would drown in its own flooded lungs soon enough.

"Sorry, pal, I'm not going to treat that sucking chest wound for you today," Raymond whispered.

One Gray down, many more to go. Looking at the rifle mags displayed before him, he wondered if he had brought enough ammo with him this time. Each week, he was killing more and more of these wild creatures. The Grays' virus was obviously quickly compounding out of control. For the first time in his life, Raymond felt he was losing a battle—one, ironically, against an unarmed opponent.

There was a reason he was doing this work. Payment wasn't it. He could kill these creatures much easier in the comfort of his own home. Killing Grays in his neighboring residences widened his safety circle, keeping the Grays farther away from his own personal sanctuary. And besides, he enjoyed watching his feeble neighbors, who had often stuck up their biased noses at his rough, tattooed appearance, now beg for his help. He made them pay a service fee of food, supplies, tools, anything of value in this new world. He needed none of it, of course, but suffering is the greatest teacher, and these folks needed a tough lesson in survival.

In the rational mind of Raymond, competition winners should never receive a prize, because winning is its own reward. However, losing shouldn't be permissible; losers should be punished as the laws of nature intended. This analogy went double for those who could have succeeded but failed only because of laziness or lack of proper preparation. The final contest had already started when the lights went out and the ill-prepared began turning into gray demons.

Socialites like his neighbors had always been dependent, even demanding lower members of society take care of them while looking down on them at the same time. Members of EMS, fire fighters, law enforcement, military, gardeners, plumbers, electricians, etc. all sacrificed themselves for an ungrateful society of snobs. The tables had finally turned.

To drive that point home, instead of clearing out the surrounding wooded areas at a safer distance, he always baited, then killed the Grays on his neighbors' front yards, piling their corpses as high as he could. A morbid monument of death reminding them all how fragile they were in this new, dangerous world and how much they needed rough men like himself.

At the end of the day, as the evening sun finally faded to the west, he was down to his last rifle magazine sitting on a floor covered in brass shell casings. Each empty shell casing symbolized the death of an American whom he had once sworn to defend.

Although these things were no longer Americans—they were evil mutant Grays. A direct hostile threat to America, which he was determined to fight. Today he had set a new one-day killing record, with absolutely no remorse.

Raymond exited his earthy hide, walked slowly toward the large oak tree, and then lowered the raccoon cage. He released the tormented animal back into the wild, feeling sorry for it as it limped away slowly from being shot several times in the ass with the air rifle throughout the day.

By the time he made his way to the neighbor's house, the sun was completely gone over the horizon leaving just a hint of civil twilight, which signified in about twenty minutes the sky would be completely dark. Raymond stepped onto the porch and reached down to retrieve the bucket that held his service payment. Carrots and green beans. Figures—he should have known that morning. He would have preferred some fresh pork or beef to go with his own produce surplus, but he'd take it because, regardless if he needed the food or not, his services were not free.

■■

Ed and Shaun had been away from town for over a week. They had covered an unknown number of miles looking for any worthy game, which would allow them to make a mercy extraction call to get out of the field. They had depleted their rations in the first few days and were now surviving on foraged roots, edible weeds, bugs, and one tough opossum. They were hungry, but they also knew their town was equally as hungry.

Having little luck hunting, they decided to allocate more time as Lake City Ambassadors in hopes of finding generous citizens or uninhabited houses that could be rummaged through. So far, they had found no houses occupied and zero supplies. Between hunger, exhaustion, and constant fear of the growing Gray threat, they were at their wits' end, ready to quit and call for a ride back into town.

Ed and Shaun had agreed that when they called in tonight's sundown situation report, they'd ask for advice from the town council with hopes of getting pulled out of the field. They'd traveled about another mile without any signs whatsoever—animal, human, or otherwise. The sun was getting closer to the western tree line, signaling that it was time to start looking for a securable shelter.

A change in course was made to get them closer to the main road, where more houses could be found. As they were contemplating crossing a rapidly flowing wide river, Ed spotted their golden ticket. Not wanting to miss the opportunity and without any warning to his hunting partner, Ed quickly unslung his .300 WinMag scoped hunting rifle. With his hands shaking from excitement, he placed the bouncing crosshairs on the large black bear's head. At only 175 yards, there was no need to hold over for bullet drop.

Shaun had been looking in the opposite direction when the deafening blast caused him to jump in surprise, and he fell backward into a thorny bush, screaming expletives. "What the hell was that?" he finally exclaimed.

Ed reached down to rescue his entangled partner with a helping hand and a huge smile. "Look, I got him! Quick, let's cross this river and dress that thing out before dark. We still need to find shelter ASAP!"

They stripped down to their underwear, then placed their dry clothes in a double-layered waterproofing bag inside their backpacks. To add buoyancy to their packs, they quickly drank their water and put the empty bottles inside as well. They used their belts to strap their rifles across the top of their makeshift buoys, which kept the rifles safely out of the water. Ed and Shaun held on tight and kicked themselves across the deep river.

The rapid current took them a few hundred feet downstream from their prize. After reaching the other side, they helped each other out of the river, dried off, quickly got dressed, and then hiked back upstream. The black bear was lying at the base of steep wooded steps leading uphill to a small nearby house. It seemed that their luck had finally taken an upturn.

They took turns keeping watch while the other cleaned, skinned, and quartered the bear. The rifle blast that took down the beast had been loud and attention grabbing. As Shaun stood watch, he expected Grays to stream down the riverbank at any moment and engulf them in gnashing teeth and clawing fingernails. Shaun made the tactical decision to start their house-contact procedure before hauling the meat up the stairs. He wanted to be safe from the encroaching darkness.

They stood a good distance away from the porch, tossing small rocks at the front door. No smoke from the chimney. No movement from the curtains. No signs of recent activity. If anyone was home, surely they'd heard the rifle shot. They expected this house was empty like all the others. They normally would wait at least fifteen minutes before inspecting windows and doors for an easy entry, but it was getting uncomfortably dark fast.

Ed stepped onto the covered porch to look through the windows and try the front door. Shaun went around the side of the small two-story house with attached garage to check the back. As Ed reached to jiggle the front-door handle, he heard *whack* and the sound of something heavy hitting the ground from around the house. "Shaun? Shaun?" he whispered. "Was that you?"

No answer. He unholstered his pistol as he quietly tiptoed up to the corner of the covered porch. Through the darkness, he could barely see Shaun's backpack and rifle on the ground. His heart began to race as he stepped down off the porch, noticing fresh drag marks across the graveled driveway. "Shaun? Where are you, man?" he whispered urgently into the darkness.

Anxiety raced through him. The thick summer humidity had nothing to do with the sweat streams running down his face. The thought of a Gray pouncing on him in the dark was paralyzing. He spun around at the sound of gravel crunching behind him. Something hard struck his outstretched arm, causing him to drop his pistol, and a bag went over his head just as quickly. His legs were kicked out from under him, and then a knockout blow caused him to lose consciousness.

■■■

Ed awoke with a splitting headache and a killer kink in his neck. His mind was swimming in fog, and he was having a difficult time recalling what had happened. It was dark. His eyes were dry. There was a deep smell of dampness and dirt. Something was making his face itch. It was when he reached up to feel what was over his head that he noticed his arms were restrained behind him by cold metallic bracelets.

"Why were you breaking into my house?" a nearby low voice asked, sounding slightly bored and annoyed.

"We're hunters! We're looking for—"

Before Ed could finish his sentence, the chair he was sitting in was kicked over, slamming him backward onto a cold, hard floor. The air flew out of his lungs, his back popped, and his head bounced off the hard floor. He was opening his mouth to curse when the burlap bag that had been over his head became heavy with water, dripping into his eyes and filling his mouth with a foul taste.

He didn't understand what was happening, but the water kept coming. He couldn't cough or spit it out. He was beginning to drown. Panic set it. He thrashed about, trying to escape the water being poured over the burlap bag. He couldn't spit it out fast enough; there was no escape. He was indeed drowning. He was about to die. His back arched, and then he began to convulse. Then it was over, and he was sitting upright again, gasping for air, which burned his lungs, causing him to choke and cough.

"Hunters? There's nothing to hunt inside my house," he said in the same mellow, annoyed tone.

"I'm telling you the truth!" Ed coughed. "We just bagged a black bear down by the river. We were looking for shelter. We knocked on the door for over ten minutes! It's our procedure." He coughed some more water out.

"Procedure for what?"

"For making contact. We have a procedure for making peaceful contact with houses to see if they are inhabited or not. We also act as ambassadors for Lake City—that's who we hunt for."

He could hear footsteps, a door opening and then closing with a locking sound. He was happy to be sitting in the dark alone to catch his breath and thoughts. His mind went from fear for his own survival to fear of the fate of his partner. Where was Shaun?

He lost track of the time he'd been sitting there in the dark. His shoulders were beginning to ache from his arms being restrained behind him, and the smell of wet burlap was stifling. It could have been minutes or maybe hours, but sometime later, the door opened and closed again. The wet burlap bag was forcefully ripped off his head.

He was in a dark room with the classic blinding-bright shop light aimed directly at his face. He squinted, turning his head to the side, trying to protect his eyes from the piercing light turning the inside of eyelids a bright pink. He slowly opened one eye to get a glimpse of his prison or captor.

What he saw made him close his eyes again. Ed began to cry hysterically and mumble incoherent prayers. There was a wide variety of knives and surgical-type saws hanging from a pegboard above a blood-splattered table and pools of coagulated gel on the floor. He was trapped on the real-life set of a sick and twisted slasher movie.

"So you bagged a black bear on my property. You weren't going to walk all that meat miles back into town. What's your plan?" the voice said from behind him.

Ed bowed his head, rocking back and forth in his restraining chair, sobbing uncontrollably.

"If you make me ask you again, you're getting another long drink of water," the man said in a monotone voice.

"We have radios; we call them to come get us if we successfully harvest any big game. I told you, we have protocols! Where's Shaun? Did you kill him? Is he OK?"

Ignoring the question, the voice pressed on. "How do they come get you?"

"We have a couple working vehicles. I call in an address, and they come to get us. The town has become really organized again. People are working together. We found some working vehicles, radios, and other stuff in empty houses around the lake."

"Tell me more about the town," the voice said as the man walked around the side of the room. The dark room shadowed his upper torso, offering only the image of leather suede boots and a weird digital pattern pants.

Ed went on and on and on, spilling every detail about the town's food production, water gathering, shared communal jobs, council projects, the new working radio station, law enforcement and security operations, civilian-firearms training, rescue missions, and he even boasted about the community dinners. Sometimes the voice would ask him about specifics, and sometimes he'd just listen.

"I'm guessing you need to check in every so often?"

"Yes, we give a sitrep every night, as soon as the sun goes down, after we have secured a shelter," Ed said.

"What's your no-comms plan?"

"Our what?" Ed asked.

"Your no-communications plan?" the voice asked, annoyed. "What happens if you don't call to check in?"

"Oh. That happens sometimes the farther we get away from town. They only listen for us at night. That's when Art is listening for the BBN news broadcast on his big radio. If we can't reach them at night, they know we'll try again right before the sun comes up. If that doesn't work, then everyone gets nervous. We try to get to higher ground right away to try again. If we haven't contacted them by noon, we go back to the last place we reported in, and they'll send the truck to pick us up there."

The sound of footsteps walked away, and the door opened and shut again. This time, there was no locking sound. A couple of short minutes later, the door opened again, then the lights came on. Blinded again, Ed squinted his eyes. With his eyes shut, he felt arms wrap around him in an embracing hug.

Opening his eyes again slowly, he could see it was Shaun hugging him, asking him if he was OK. The house-of-horrors room came into full view, and he realized he was in an unfinished basement area used for butchering game, including a fresh deer carcass in the corner next to the bloody table. His numb hands were lifted slightly behind his back, then the handcuffs fell off. His shoulders throbbed, and his arms stung with pin needles as blood rushed back in when he brought his hands in front of him.

A man dressed in a full digital camo uniform with smudged green and brown face paint and a rifle slung across his chest stood in front of him. "It might not seem like it right now, but today is your lucky day. My name is Raymond. This is obviously my house. Come upstairs; I have bear stew cooking, and there's a hot shower and a clean bed for you tonight. I'll give you your weapons back in the morning, and you can call into town for our extraction. Yes, *our* extraction. I'm coming with you."

■■■

Raymond awoke early to fix breakfast for his guests, hoping the gesture would help ease any hard feelings caused by his enhanced information-gathering techniques. He fully understood that his time of battling the Gray demons solo had come to a critical point. Even though he had plenty of weapons, ammo, and supplies, he lacked human resources. As much as he hated modern society, it was time to team up.

The smell of coffee, eggs, and steak must have awoken the hunters, as they came stumbling in with heavy sleep still in their half-open, bloodshot eyes.

"Grab a seat. I hope you're hungry. Coffee's hot; help yourself."

As they ate breakfast, Raymond probed them for more information about the town and about a repeatedly referenced person named Victor, whom they both seemed to have a man-crush on. Ed and Shaun also asked Raymond questions, specifically about his plentiful food stores.

"It's not by luck. I was prepared. Not for a plague but for challenging times in general. Most people rely on someone else to rescue them. Seems that self-reliance is an extinct mindset. Take yourselves for example: you're out here hunting in the woods to feed a community who can't feed themselves."

"Yes, we are out here hunting, but the entire community is providing services that we do not have to do ourselves. It's teamwork. We all work together, and everyone is contributing," Ed said.

"Everyone?" Raymond asked.

"Well, some more than others," Shaun said through a mouthful of eggs.

"Others? You should toss those noncontributors out of town. There've been leaches feeding off hardworking citizens in every society. Maybe by the time we get a handle on this epidemic, those types will have been culled off, making humanity stronger," Raymond said reverently.

"That's pretty harsh," Shaun said, swallowing.

"It's the way nature intended. It's one thing to have protectors of the herd. It's completely different to rely entirely on a safety blanket that others provide. It forms a society of defenseless victims," Raymond countered. "It's time for you to make your extraction call. Here's my address; tell them to pick us up at noon. While we wait, you're my working crew. How big of a truck is coming to pick us up?"

Over the next few hours, Raymond used his new hired hands to fill a twenty-foot covered trailer parked in the driveway. In the back of his garage, behind a hinged cabinet, there was a cleverly hidden stairway that led down to a concealed storage room inside his basement. Raymond had built this room for security, and luckily, the metal cages bolted to the thick concrete floor and walls had protected his sensitive electronic devices from the EMP blast.

To relocate everything in this room, he'd need to make several trips into town. Raymond divided up boxes into piles, then told Ed and Shaun what to grab and how to stack it all in the trailer. While they worked, he stood guard on top of the garage to keep an eye on his guests and to watch for Grays. When they finished one task, he gave them a break while he sorted out the next. This went on for hours until finally the entire trailer was full.

"All right, that'll do it for now. Let's go inside for lunch until your friends get here," Raymond said as he locked and secured the door to the hidden stairway. He turned and looked directly at them. "Listen to me. Hear me. This storage room is mine. Not a word about it leaves your lips, or I'll personally cut out your tongue, tie you to a tree, and then leave you for the infected demons. Do you understand? Not a word—not to your mayor, the sheriff, or this Victor guy that you've been going on about. Nobody." His glare pierced each of them in turn.

Ed and Shaun looked at him wide-eyed, tensely nodding their heads in agreement.

A short time later, Raymond watched an old red truck pull into the driveway. A man and woman stayed in the truck for a few minutes, then got out. The female got out and focused her attention on the wood line in the opposite direction of the house. This gave Raymond a good feeling. They were worried more about threats away from the house, acting defensively instead of offensively toward the house, which the man walked toward, his rifle relaxed at his side in a nonaggressive manner.

Raymond opened the door before the man reached his porch. "We're having lunch; there's plenty for both of you." He waved them in.

The old truck was barely strong enough to pull the trailer's weight, causing their traveling speed to be terrifyingly slow. Raymond, along with Ed, Shaun, and their black bear meat–cargo, rode exposed in the bed of the truck. Raymond could sense at any moment they would be ambushed by road bandits or swarmed by Grays. His favorite DARPA XM-3 bolt-action rifle was slung across his back, while in his hands he held a piston-driven AR15 with a four-powered fixed magnification Rifle Combat Optic with tritium illuminated red chevron and bullet drop compensating reticle for quick multiple target engagements at different distances.

The trip seemed to take forever. The continuous hum of the slow-turning tires on the hot asphalt road was making him anxious. Raymond was constantly rotating, scanning 360 degrees. Observing bends in the roads, deep ditches where bandits could hide in culverts, tree-line shadows, houses close to the roads, abandoned cars, everywhere really. Because he knew from experience—death could be hiding anywhere.

He stood up, observing the road behind them over the top of the trailer to ensure they were not being pursued. He then turned around to see the town coming into view. Ed and Shaun had informed Raymond about their defense wall project, but he had suspected they were exaggerating. It was impressive, to say the least. Before him stood the Great Wall of Shipping. The town had arranged forty-foot shipping containers in a long row, in some cases stacked two high. The wall was truly a modern, albeit postapocalyptic, marvel of engineering. He wondered how they were able to collect and move the giant boxes.

As they approached, there appeared to be multiple disabled cars in the path leading up to a huge vehicle gate. He'd seen this pattern several times before—the cars were purposefully placed in the road in a very specific pattern, forcing any incoming traffic to slow to a crawl and then swerve left and right sharply through the winding obstacle, thus eliminating any attempts to ram the gate at high speeds. Also visible was a sandbagged guard post on top of the second-story shipping container overlooking the vehicle gate. Most impressive. Raymond liked this Victor guy already.

Raymond mentally gave credit to the driver's ability; there was no way he could have maneuvered the truck and trailer on the serpentine road. The driver stopped short of the large gate, got out, and identified himself to the guard, whom he clearly already knew. The heavy gate, made of a school bus paneled with corrugated metal siding, slid to the side, allowing the truck and trailer to enter Main Street in Lake City.

Even though grass was growing knee high and weeds overtook flowerbeds, the rest of the town seemed pretty well kept. Raymond assumed the town had been packed the day the lights went out, but all the disabled vehicles had been removed from the streets. He wondered where they'd taken them and why.

The truck pulled up along the city beach near a large open-air pavilion with a small group of people sitting around a long picnic table. Before the truck came to a complete stop, he surveyed the group. He picked out the mayor, an academic-looking lady he presumed was a doctor or teacher, some people he figured were councilmen—especially a particularly over-groomed man in a clean pink collared shirt—and a well-weathered, stout individual leaning against a wooden support pole with a sense of strong confidence yet possessing a reserved air. *That must be Victor*, Raymond thought.

The group jumped out of the truck, walked toward the pavilion, and began shaking hands with the council. They took turns conducting an informal debrief, talking and answering questions about their journeys. The drivers went first, explaining that everything had gone well, that they had been treated to a gracious lunch, and that the return trip was slow—here they turned to make hand motions toward the long covered trailer—because of the heavy load.

Ed and Shaun went next, going into great detail of all their trials and tribulations up until they killed the black bear. Their story stopped short at the bear harvest; they did not say a word of their activities with Raymond. They stopped talking abruptly, leaving an awkward silence in the air. Raymond was curious whether they were embarrassed that they gotten captured, were scared of repercussions, or if his wonderful cooking had mended any hurt feelings.

He stepped up, extending his hand toward Victor, "I'm Raymond Hessel. I found these two guys breaking into my house last night. After chatting with them, they told me how great of a community you have here."

The man in the clean pink shirt stood up and smiled. "Well, what do you think so far?"

Raymond knew this guy's type: he was quick to take credit for everyone else's hard work without getting his own hands dirty. "It's OK, I guess. I expected more." Watching the councilman's happy expression completely collapse was priceless, and it made Raymond smile inside. But instead of smiling, Raymond simply glanced toward the downtown area as if he was uninterested.

Ignoring the councilman, he turned back to Victor. "I could help you out with your rescue- and security ops. In fact, I have a few neighbors that won't last a week out there without me; they should be relocated here."

The rude comment compounded with Victor receiving all the newcomer's attention, Stanly immediately didn't seem too fond of this new broad-shouldered Raymond guy. Stanly wondered what kind of decent person had so many tattoos and still used hair gel in the apocalypse? "Let me guess: you're also a knight in shining armor looking for an action job?" Stanly sneered.

Raymond looked at him briefly, then turned his back to him completely.

"That's what I thought. We have ourselves another gun-nut cowboy. Mayor, we have enough of these types of people in town already. Do we need another trigger-happy maniac who's quick to kill just to feel good about his manhood? Just like Victor, they go out there looking for a fight so they can justify violence with more violence," Stanly fumed.

Raymond spun around and growled, "You're about to eat your teeth, asshole! You don't know anything about me. I've been protecting and preserving life my entire career. Using myself as a shield to shelter scrawny shits like you for the past twenty years. Sit your pleated pants back down and let the grown-ups talk before I drown you in that lake."

Raymond turned to the person he presumed to be the mayor, who was sitting next to the uniformed sheriff. "I have a trailer full of weapons, ammo, food, and other useful supplies. It's not free, but I'll barter with you fairly for a nice house to live in and my own choice of community duties. I have a special skill set that was not offered cheaply not too long ago."

"Wonderful, an apocalyptic hit man," Stanly mumbled.

This comment made Raymond pause briefly, thinking back to his neighborhood job title quandary. Hit man: paid for killing indiscriminately—a perfect match.

Sheriff Bohner stood up and extended his hand toward Raymond for a strong-gripped handshake. "Follow me. Apartment 408 right up that road is now vacant. It's a small, clean place with good airflow, and you have a cute neighbor in 406 too. If you want, we'll get you a house to live in when one becomes available. After you get settled in, stop by the Town Defense Force building over there. We'd like to hear what kind of goodies you brought for us."

"Will do, Sheriff. Before I forget, you need to talk to your ambassadors about operational security. I made them slightly uncomfortable last night, and they quickly spilled the beans with very specific details about your town, inside and out. In the wrong ears, that information could easily compromise or even destroy this place. They're good-hearted fellows but have loose lips."

INTEL

Gather. Analyze. Distribute.

After wasting many days getting bogged down and then backtracking to avoid impassable infested areas, Kevin and Stephan had decided that Houghton Lake needed to be completely bypassed, which would add several frustrating days—maybe weeks—to their never-ending journey. They were so close to the crossroads of Route 55 and US 127, yet there seemed to be some sort of mystical, apocalyptic barrier keeping them from crossing that final landmark.

The city of Houghton Lake was settled on Michigan's largest inland lake (excluding the mighty Great Lakes). Kevin suggested finding a small rowboat and then paddling across the lake at night, which seemed like a reasonable idea—that is, until they studied the map and were unable to find a single unpopulated area on the far side of the lake. Likewise, there was their physical strength to consider. They had consumed the last of their food days ago, and they were both weak from hunger. They would not have the stamina to oar that far without some nutritional intake.

As much as they were fed up with walking through the woods, the urban areas seemed to be slowing them down a great bit. They agreed to do a very large ninety-degree offset that would put them on a southern heading for about ten miles, turn west for ten miles, then come back north ten miles up US 127, putting them right back on course and completely bypassing the urban area.

Stephan was kneeling down at the corner of a two-story brick building, observing a long desolate street. She had been captivated by the dreary scene before her for several minutes. Loose paper and trash blew down a once well-kept road. Tall grass had sprung up in the cracks of the sidewalk and pavement. Cars that had cruised down this road only months ago now stood abandoned on soft, deflating tires. The few shops that still had windows were now dark and murky. The decaying landscape seemed metaphoric, and it filled her with dread and desperation.

Kevin crept up behind her and knelt down silently, nudging her out of her dreary daydream. "Clear to cross?" he asked.

"Huh? Yeah. Nothing's moving. It's getting late; we should start looking for our nightly shelter," Stephan said with a hint of sadness.

"How about that?" Kevin asked, pointing toward a large, slightly rusted blue LOX Armored Inc. truck parked next to a Gas & Gulp petrol station on the opposite street corner. "Looks like the door's open. We might be able to secure it."

"Sure. Go ahead, I'll cover you."

Kevin bounded across the two-lane street, crouching down next to the giant truck tire. He paused for a long minute, listening and looking around the area to see if anyone or anything had spotted him before waving her over.

"Let's secure this truck, then check out the gas station. Maybe we'll get lucky." He moved to the partially opened back door and put a hand on the handle. Stepping off to the side, he looked at Stephan as she pointed her rifle at the door. When she nodded, he pulled as hard as he could, getting out of her line of fire.

Kevin let go of the door handle as soon as it swung open with a loud squeaking, rusty moan.

"*Ahhhhhhhhhhh*," echoed a terribly loud, high-pitched scream from inside the truck.

Stephan took several involuntary steps backward, taking the rifle's selector switch from safe, past semi, to full auto. Her analytical mind raced to define the close-range target: Gray, human, Gray, human, friendly, hostile… Her eye focused from the shadowy dark movement in the back of the truck to her red-dot sight and back to the target again, her indecisive finger hovering over the curved trigger.

"Please don't hurt me. I'm unarmed!" a frightened female voice pleaded.

Stephan squeezed the pressure switch of the weapon-mounted flashlight, illuminating a frail woman dressed in comparatively clean, newer clothes, cowering against the far back of the armored truck wall, clutching a large backpack.

Kevin took his attention off the women and quickly scanned the street behind them. "Get in. Something was bound to hear that scream!"

As soon as Stephan started to climb in, an eruption of angry howls bellowed through the empty alleyways, vibrating up her spine and causing her to slip on the step, scraping her shin. Right on her tail, Kevin pulled the door shut behind him, finding a locking mechanism near the floor. Once again, they were trapped inside a vehicle with a swarm of pissed-off Grays outside who were hunting them. At least this time it wasn't a thin-skinned plane, and they had a third person for company.

■ ■

At the usual meeting place under the lakeside pavilion, Victor, Raymond, Sheriff Bohner, and a handful of the engineers were discussing ways to expand and improve the town's perimeter wall. Raymond suggested a secondary layer of security—razor wire, a trench, anything to provide the Town Defense Force some standoff distance from outside threats.

"It's only a matter of time before the raiders or worse climb over the wall," Victor said. He was convinced that the metal shipping containers were too easy to scale, that they needed to be double-stacked, with hardened bunkers in strategic spots and overlapping fields of fire.

Stanly walked up nonchalantly with his hands in his pockets to join the scheduled noon meeting. "A wall isn't very inviting, is it? I thought we were bringing people in, not keeping them out. Or are you turning this place into some sort of concentration camp?"

They all turned in unison, giving Stanly "the look"...the look that says *you are stupid as hell.*

"If you haven't noticed, we have been bringing people in—and keeping them safe, I might add—and relocating those who ask and agree to our community work ethics," Victor rebutted.

"Right. Selective entries. Borders cause wars..." Stanly mumbled, turning his back to them and taking his usual seat at the end of the picnic table. The mayor and the rest of the town council, along with the medical staff, rounded the corner, crossing the tall grass to meet them at the pavilion.

A taller bald man with excessive sailor tattoos and sporting a Hawaiian shirt and camo shorts followed them as quickly as he could in his flip-flops, carrying a heavy bag. "Hey, y'all. I've got some good news and some bad news."

"Crazy Chadwick, what did you do this time? I'm really not sure that we want to know," asked the mayor with an uncertain tone and a raised eyebrow.

"Well, the good news is I was able to get my corn whiskey still working again," Crazy Chadwick responded.

To Victor's right, Jessica asked, "Chad, do you think alcohol is a priority in our current state of affairs?"

"Sure it is! Do you know that whiskey means 'water of life' in the old language? My moonshine's pure. Burns blue, even. There's none better. Look, there's a lot of uses for it." He pulled out a gallon-size glass jug of clear liquid. "We can burn it in alcohol engines to make electricity or transportation or manufacturing or whatever. Sterilization of medical and cooking tools. Pain management for your patients, Doc. And, of course, recreational use for special occasions," he said with a smile and a wink while nudging Raymond's shoulder.

"Don't touch me again. Unless you make a triple-distilled malted-barley whiskey, aged in a barrel for about three years, I'll pass," snarled Raymond.

"He does have some good arguments," said Mrs. Cloud.

"What's the bad news?" asked the mayor, leaning forward.

"Oh, nothing really. I kind of burnt down the warehouse behind the hardware store. I saved the still, though!"

"All right, if I forbid you from making more, you'll do it anyway and keep it for yourself. Go ahead and keep at it, but please find a new brick-and-concrete building to do it in, and gather up plenty of fire extinguishers for the next accident that's certain to happen," the mayor instructed.

Raymond eyed Stanly's particularly clean outfit. "Crazy Chad, make some berry flavored. I bet Stanly likes fruity drinks."

"What is that supposed to mean?" Stanly asked defensively.

"Wasn't supposed to mean anything. Just trying to hook you up with the good stuff. I imagine you sitting around with a fruity drink in those well-manicured hands. Intended no harm by it, man. Maybe your boyfriend will like some too?" Raymond smiled.

"You think I'm gay! You have some nerve, pal. I'll see to it that you're back in that shack the ambassadors found you in!" Stanly yelled, getting to his feet.

"Whoa, now, buddy. Look who's talking about selective resident privileges. So you're not gay? Sorry, I misread all the signs: the soft, noncallused hands; the only clean shirt in town—pink shirt, that is. And, of course, the cigarettes in your pocket," Raymond said casually, just egging him on.

"Cigarettes? You're homophobic because someone smokes tobacco?" Stanly asked.

"Ease yourself, Stanly, you're way too sensitive. Maybe it's your low testosterone levels or something, or maybe it's the daily stress of being inside the protected zone. I'm not prejudiced or homophobic. It's a brave new world: you can be whomever you want to be. I only assumed because you smoke feminine cigars. They were originally marketed toward females. It's in the name: cigar...ettes. 'Ette' meaning feminine," Raymond stated with an air of satisfaction.

"All right, all right, that's enough, you two. Mrs. Cloud, do you have a report for us today?" the mayor, asked interrupting Raymond, who was obviously taunting the councilman for entertainment.

"We do have some new information to share. Our studies and experiments conducted at the lab and holding cells—"

"You mean torture?" Stanly grumbled, obviously still angry.

Without acknowledging him, she continued, "We have determined that late-stage infected Grays never slip into an unconscious sleep, yet they will go into a 'power saving' alert-hibernation mode by squatting in place, lowering their resting heart rate to nearly twenty beats per minute. For comparison, the average human has a resting heart rate of sixty to one hundred beats per minute—top athletes average at thirty-five to forty. Bradycardia could be a symptom, or an intended natural mutation caused by the virus. We believe that the lower heart rate, along with their slightly cooler body temperatures, has dramatically decreased their metabolism. They are omnivores, but they do not eat very much or very often."

She continued, "What does that mean for us? Don't plan on them starving or dying of old age anytime soon. In fact, just the opposite, with the recorded ectothermic changes, they'll likely have a lifespan of 125 to 150 years."

There were several grunts and whistles around the table.

"The medical staff had the same reaction. Evidence is inconclusive as of now, but the infection could have a DNA-transforming side effect, turning them into cold-blooded creatures. If so, that could be beneficial to us in the winter season. That's just a hypothesis at this point, with no real data to back it up.

"We've also done several blind tests on their basic senses. To start with, they are positively phototactic—attracted to light. I believe you already knew that, though. We're not sure why. Possibly because the Grays' permanently restricted pupils cause poor light-gathering capabilities or because a nocturnal light source is a curiosity that allows them to hunt. Your guess is as good as ours. Sense of smelling abilities hasn't changed much, although they respond aggressively to perfumes and other unnatural aromas.

"As the hunters and rescue teams have reported, their hearing abilities have unquestionably increased, giving them a wider range of audible wavelength spectrum than the average human. We know this from doing frequency tests in the jail that put them on the same hearing level as bats, and autopsies show decreased thickness of the eardrums, causing more sensitivity. Bats use their supersensitive hearing for echolocation, like sonar, to locate prey. We haven't witnessed this type of ability yet in the Grays."

Stanly got up and started walking toward the beach.

"Where are you going, Stan?" asked Jessica.

"I refuse to be part of this. You're experimenting and cutting sick people open. Not to help or cure them but to give these sadists information on how to kill them more efficiently. You all should be ashamed; I sure am," he said dejectedly.

"Stan, my job is to observe and report. If you feel that you could treat them, I will assist you. But the brain samples we have analyzed show massive amounts of irreversible tissue damage, even in the early stage. In our expert opinion, this infection cannot be cured. Even if you could slow or stop the infection, the patient would never recover or be human again."

Victor took a step away from the group toward Stanly. "Stanly, we're going on a rescue mission tomorrow morning to invite Raymond's neighbors to relocate here. We could use your diplomacy. They've been out there on their own, roughing it since the lights went out, and they might be a little skeptical of what Lake City has to offer."

Stanly eyed him for a moment, then simply turned around and walked away.

"Really?" Raymond scoffed. "He's a liability. I'm not babysitting his ass out there."

"He needs a dose of the real world." Victor explained. "He's yet to embrace what our world has become, because he hasn't witnessed it for himself. His constant skepticism is a threat. He's beginning to get a following of believers that will develop into a much bigger problem than the raider attacks or even the Grays."

■■

The sign language was more like a drunken game of charades, but either way, Stephan and Kevin made it clear to the mystery woman in the armored truck that they were not there to harm her. Stephan occasionally peeked out the fractured side window. Knowing they were safe behind thick bulletproof, tinted glass gave her comfort.

The Grays came rushing in like a shark frenzy. The woman's scream had attracted them like blood in water. The Grays searched everywhere, in and out of buildings. They were so thick that they would push each other out of overcrowded windows. They searched on top of any object they could climb onto or crawl under, including the armored truck.

Stephan could hear them growl and hiss directly above them. The Grays were so thick outside that they pushed into each other, rocking the heavy truck back and forth. Even with the doors locked up tight, the nauseating stench of that many filthy, sickly people made her fight her gag reflex as her eyes watered.

Engrossed by the hive-type activity, Stephan blinked and squinted, bringing her attention back to the immediate area outside the truck. She noticed a nasty-looking Gray that stood out from the swarm. The skin was transparent like the others, with black infected blood giving it a gray pigmentation, and it had thick scabs with oozing sores over every part of its grotesque hairless body. What she noticed that was different was a large softball-size tumorous growth on its neck that seemed to pulsate like a beating heart.

She had seen this before, back in the Detroit lab during the morning brief right before the lights went out. That tumorous bulge was a symptom of the hybrid Nasty, the Ophiocordyceps spore, to be exact. Stephan wondered if this was the next stage of the disease. She watched them until the swarm moved on in their infectious pursuit to find a healthy human.

Kevin, on the other hand, kept a watchful eye on the shivering silent lady, ensuring she didn't make any sudden movements or noise. It was getting dark in the back of the vehicle; outside, the autumn sun had gone down over a glowing orange horizon when Stephan gave him a reassuring "all clear" nod to indicate she hadn't seen any Grays in a while.

"I'm Kevin. This is Stephan. Sorry we scared you earlier. We didn't know this vehicle was occupied," he said in a whisper, reaching over to shake her hand. "Where you coming from?"

Still clutching her backpack like a safety blanket, she said in a barely audible voice, "Nice to meet you. I'm Gaylen Ross. I'm from here in Houghton Lake, but it's become so dangerous, I'm getting out of town and heading south."

"South?" Stephan said in shock. "How far south? Toward metro areas? Most people are heading north to escape them; the cities are war zones now. We were lucky—Kevin had the foresight to get us out of Detroit the day it went dark."

"All the way south. To get as far away from here as I can. I'll go all the way to South America if I can make it. Did you hear the broadcast? They are blocking the infected at the Panama Canal. Besides, life is barely survivable now. Imagine when we have snow on the ground in a couple months," Gaylen said excitedly.

Kevin gave Stephan a sideways glance. "She makes a good point. It's tough living now; going to be tougher when we are freezing to death."

"We'll make it to Lake City way before then," Stephan said.

"You're going to Lake City? Cute town. Haven't heard anything from them lately, although I haven't heard much from anyone..." Gaylen trailed off.

"You're welcome to come with us. Team up, strength in numbers?" Stephan said reassuringly.

"No thank you. I'm heading south. If I were you, I'd bypass the Crossroads Mall area. A small group of friends and I were there when the lights went out. We had everything we really needed, so we stayed put and were quite comfortable until a few days ago. A biker gang led by a madman thought it was a good spot to call home also. They came rolling in, taking the entire mall by force. They looked preposterous, and we actually laughed at first when they crashed through the door. Some were riding classic motorcycles, some rode dirt bikes, four wheelers, and some were even riding some sort of modified monster lawnmowers! We tried to defend the mall, but they had military-grade weaponry. It was horrible. We were no longer laughing. They killed half my friends, captured and tortured the others just for fun. Passed the women around until they got bored, then killed them too," Gaylen said with glazed-over eyes.

"My God," Kevin whispered in disbelief. "Motorheads..."

"Huh?" Stephan asked.

"Motorheads. People who are masterminds with engines and pretty much anything mechanical. Too bad. Would be nice to have a few on the good side," he replied.

"Well, they are definitely not on the good side. This morning, while they were all passed out drunk, I tried sneaking out through a side door. A couple of them spotted me. Luckily, they were still too drunk and unbalanced. I was able to stick a screwdriver into one's neck and groin-kick the other. I ran as fast as I could, not caring about the creatures outside until I was several blocks away and ran into a few around a corner. Then I had to reverse back toward the damn mall. After changing directions a few times, going through buildings, setting fire to one house as a diversion, I lost them and found this armored truck, which seemed sufficient. Sorry I screamed earlier. I thought you were the bikers." She looked at Stephan and Kevin questioningly.

"Don't worry about us hurting you. The offer's open, if you want to tag along with us. We've been on the road awhile; we know what we're doing. We had our own trouble toward the east, so we're bypassing the entire area, we need to find some resupplies first, though. Starting to get a little hungry."

"I could help you out with that. I have a pack full of canned food from a house I was running through earlier. The entire pantry was full! I couldn't fit it all. I could show you were it was at," Gaylen said helpfully.

"Yes, please!" Stephan said as her stomach growled loudly enough for all to hear.

They talked more, sharing stories and information about their experiences while eating cold SMEAT and beef stew. Kevin reached into his backpack to pull out the little HAM radio to scan the channels, hoping to hear anything.

■■■

"Good evening. This is Elizabeth Corrin bringing you today's BBN global news report.

"We are sad to say that Chinese aid workers and Russian security forces in the western United States have met an unsustainable level of hostility, essentially crippling all medical-and supply-relief efforts, forcing Russian forces to reposition offshore. New operational bases are being occupied in southern California on San Clemente Island and San Juan Islands near Seattle, Washington. Officials have reported no deaths at this time, but several casualties are being treated en route to Russia and China.

"The World Health Organization and United Nations security council has filed emergency travel restrictions to and from the entire continent of North America, including Canada, the United States, and Mexico as well as all of Central America as far south as Panama, where government agencies are using any and all resources available to sustain a quarantine. Outbursts of violence and anarchy are being reported throughout the region.

"The world's top scientists are working nonstop to identify the viral strain plaguing the Americas. The World Health Organization's infectious-disease research project, right here in the Cambridge Primate facility, was breached last night. Several monkeys were released by animal rights activists. Cambridge insists that the primates where healthy but asks residents to immediately report any aggressive monkey sightings.

"On a positive note, Allied forces are reporting major victories in the Persian Gulf and northern African regions. EU forces hint that the military- and civil-service draft could come to an end as soon as next spring. BRICS forces are beginning to reposition for stability and reconstruction missions, as well as send reinforcements to the western United States and South America.

"Stay tuned for full coverage of tonight's long-awaited football game between Barcelona and Manchester United. This is the game we've all been waiting for!"

■ ■

Just after the sun came up, Victor and his boys, Raymond, members of the rescue team, the mayor, and Sheriff Bohner gathered around three idling vehicles to go over the plan for the day's rescue mission. The concept of operation was simple: Raymond, in the front vehicle, would lead them to each of his neighbor's houses, where they'd offer their relocation service, give them a couple of hours to pack up their essential belongings, and then come back after spreading the word about giving rides back to town.

They expected a full load on the way back, so only a selected few would go out on the day's mission. After finalizing the plan, they gossiped for a bit about last night's radio broadcast while drinking a pot of wild-berry tea. Just as they were about to load up, Stanly appeared out of nowhere, startling them.

Stanly stepped into the center of the group. "Victor, I know why you asked me to join you today. I will. I need to see what's out there for my own." Stan paused, looking around the group. "I know what you all think of me. I'm not blind to it. I believe that all life is precious, and most of you are willing to kill someone just for looking at you the wrong way. You all seem to think that I am ignorant to the big picture, but it is you who are oblivious.

"I'm not talking about our moral differences. It's simple math. This community is bringing in more and more people, yet the population is steadily decreasing from malnourishment, poor hygiene, lack of medication for the elderly—hell, even the flu killed six people last month. You all don't get it yet. This plague, this curse that is upon us, it's an extinction-level event. If we don't save every single person, humanity will perish. We heard the broadcast last night. Read between the lines. The infection has spread internationally.

"So, Victor, if I can help rescue just one child-producing family, I'll go out there with you. I still refuse to exterminate the very life that we should be desperately trying to save. Mayor, when we get back, can we please revisit the idea of using the radio to broadcast instead of just listening? People need hope. They need to know we are here to help."

The crowd around the councilman was silent. The mayor, humbled by the speech, only nodded at his request. Raymond rolled his eyes.

Victor put a hand on Stan's shoulder. "Hop in my truck. I'll brief you on the way there."

■■■

Gaylen decided to stick with Kevin and Stephan until they reached US 127. They backtracked a couple of blocks to resupply at the stocked pantry Gaylen had found the day before. The home was well organized and tidy, except for a thick blanket of dust covering every surface.

"I don't think Luda's been home in a while." Kevin pointed at the refrigerator to a homemade chalk sign proudly claiming this space to be "Luda's Kitchen."

Just as Gaylen had promised, the pantry still held plenty of food provisions. They dumped a few cans of SMEAT into their packs along with vegetables and crackers. After further inspection of the house, they found a pump-action defensive shotgun, a few boxes of 00 buckshot, and more pistol- and rifle ammo than they could carry. Stephan even found some clean clothes that fit. Quietly saying a quiet thank you to Luda, she discarded the filthy rags she had been wearing. It was shaping up to be a good day.

In good spirits, the three headed south to begin the ninety-degree offset they had previously planned. Along the way, Kevin and Stephan took turns walking point as they normally had. In the thick wooded areas, they walked in single-file line. When the vegetation opened up, they spread out into a large triangle-shaped wedge. Kevin explained they'd have better flank security in that formation. When they stopped often, or came across a unique area, Kevin and Stephan described to Gaylen what they were doing and why.

If Gaylen decided to head off on her own at the highway, she'd have a greater chance of survival knowing some basic patrolling skills. If she decided to stay with them all the way to Lake City, she'd be a greater asset instead of a risk. She caught on quick; Stephan and Kevin never had to tell her or explain a tactic twice. Even though she had never held a firearm in her life, Gaylen didn't shy away from carrying the spare M4 Kevin had been carrying for weeks. When they ran into a small group of Grays a couple of days later, Gaylen didn't hesitate to use it.

After nightly shelters had been secured, they'd share stories of their personal life. Stephan and Kevin had grown to respect and appreciate one another, but having a third member of the team to socialize with was uplifting.

At night, security watch was divided three ways instead of two. They were able to sleep longer shifts, which greatly improved morale, stress levels, muscle recovery, and general well-being.

As they approached US 127, a question lingered on all their minds. Just before noon, a long, flat line appeared through the vegetation. Kevin, on point, held up a flat hand, signaling for them to halt. As he knelt down, so did Gaylen and Stephan, all faced outwardly in direction; looking, smelling, listening. Kevin waved them forward.

"You know, when we escaped Detroit, my goal was to get to this spot right here, then break off from our group and head north to

Camp Grayling. After what I've seen and been through, I think sticking together is the best option. Gaylen, you're a strong, intelligent person, I do not doubt you'll make it to wherever it is that you are going. But our offer still stands: we'd like you to stay with us," Kevin said hopefully.

Stephan looked at her and nodded in agreement. "No peer pressure. You do what you need to do."

"I'm not going to lie. I've always hated Michigan winters, and the next one coming upon us quick will be the worst ever," she told them with her head slightly bowed. "I agree with you, Kevin. After watching you two work together and what you've taught me in just a few short days, sticking together is the best option. I think I was running away from life more than running toward someplace specific. If we get to Lake City and it's anything like what I just left, I'm heading south. Deal?"

"Deal!" they all said together. Kevin reached for a handshake, but Stephan cut him off by giving Gaylen a quick hug.

For the rest of the day, they followed the highway north, using the steep embankment for cover while walking on the flat ground in the tall grass next to the tree line. They covered more distance than any other day so far.

The days were getting shorter as the sun began to set earlier. By late afternoon, they'd just made it to the Route 55 overpass, where they would start to head west again. Kevin suggested they shelter there, but Stephan pleaded for them to make the symbolic crossing of the highway, which would put them on their final leg of the journey. They crossed US 127—not over but under, using a drainage culvert to avoid detection from anyone who might be surveilling the major intersection.

On the other side, parked at the top of the exit ramp, Kevin spotted a woodland camouflage painted soft-top military HMMWV. Rational intellect and instinctive fear told him to not get suckered into the wide-open danger area, but curiosity told him to check it out.

"I shouldn't, but I really want to see what's inside that thing," he told them.

"We just crawled through muck and slime to avoid being caught out in the open, and now you want to stroll right up there? Are you crazy? Come on, it'll be dark soon. We don't have time for this."

He looked around for a moment. "Yeah... It is dangerous. Stay here. If anything happens, make your way to the first house you come to. We'll link up there."

Halfway up the embankment, he turned around to see Stephan and Gaylen right behind him. "What are you doing?"

"Not leaving your ass out in the wind. Hurry up, let's go," Stephan said with some sass.

As the three cautiously got closer, they noticed gobs of black smears and streaks of organic material covering the windshield and side panels of the vehicle. Pausing for a long moment and deciding what to do, Kevin told the girls to stay put. "Stephan, you cover me facing that way. Gaylen, you cover our rear facing that way."

One slow step at a time, he carefully crept forward. He could see enough through the blood- and grime-covered windshield that the front two seats were empty. He began making his way around to the enclosed bed of the vehicle, which was covered with a tall green canvas. Each grinding step he took on the road gravel seemed to announce his presence, which apparently it did, because shots rang out from inside the HMMWV, piercing holes through the thin canvas top.

■■

A couple of hours before dark, the rescue team returned to town with thirteen new people packed into the three vehicles, one of which was towing a trailer full of fresh produce and gardening- and woodworking tools. Only one family chose not to relocate, but they thanked them for the thoughtful offer.

The street was packed with people who were eagerly awaiting a debrief, including the mayor and sheriff and the rest of the city council. They shook hands, greeting the newcomers, then guided them toward the communal dinner and their new homes. Even though the crowd seemed genuinely interested in the newcomers, all eyes were on Stanly, who slowly shut the door to Victor's red pickup truck, looked around sluggishly with an absentminded stare, and then walked away, toward his home, without a word.

The crowd slowly dispersed. Vehicles were returned to the shop for refuel and repairs, and gear and equipment were stowed away. Victor briefed the oncoming guard shift and then finally met up with the town council at the lakeside pavilion.

As he approached, Sheriff Bohner handed him a glass half-full of a light blue–tinted liquid. "I hate to admit it, but Crazy Chad makes a good gin."

Victor took a sip, then swallowed the firewater with a grimace. "You call that good? I'm not sure what to call it."

Sheriff Bohner reached for the glass, but Victor held tight.

"Maybe after a couple more sips it'll be better," he said with a wink. "All went as planned. We were able to relocate three households. One house was ransacked and full of dead, presumably murdered by bandits who left no one alive in sight. And one family refused to leave their third-generation family home. It was a nice home with lots of provisions; can't say I blame them. But Stanly made a solid argument on behalf of the town."

With the mention of the councilman, everyone sat up taller in their seats and leaned forward to hear better.

"We need to keep a close watch on him the next couple of days. He's either had a 'come to Jesus moment' or has completely snapped. The man has a huge heart but a small brain. He means well, he really does. But..." Victor took a longer pull off the gin-filled glass before handing it back to Sheriff Bohner.

"But he almost got himself killed and froze up when a healthy-sized pack of Grays attacked us at the house of death. He was already in shock over the gruesome crime scene; then, at the same time, he watched us dispatch a dozen infected. He didn't try to stop us, and he didn't say a word. I think he was just in shock or in fear. Raymond was on the north side and let a monstrous late-stage Gray slip through, which charged right at Stanly. Stan just watched it rush right at him without moving an inch. Frozen stiff like a statue. I watched it unfold. Many of us watched it. As the creature coiled down, then lunged in the air toward ol' Stan with a rancid mouthful of broken teeth and outstretched claws, Raymond splattered the creature's infected, blackened brain all over the truck. It took us fifteen minutes to rinse the filth off."

Victor motioned for the almost empty gin glass.

"If any of you are close friends with Stan, please check up on him tonight. Everyone handles traumatic events differently. He could probably use a friendly ear," suggested Jessica.

Victor tilted the glass back, finishing off the gin. "Gin's not that bad, I guess. Unless you all have anything else for me, I'm going home to rinse off and see what kind of trouble my kids got into today."

As he sat the glass down on the long picnic table, a rapid series of shots rang out to the north of town. A second later, several more followed.

■■■

Luckily, Kevin was vertically challenged. If he'd been another four inches taller, he'd be lying dead on the pavement next to the HMMWV with an empty cranium. The bullets ripped through the canvas-top cover just above his head, causing him to flatten to the ground and then quickly roll under the vehicle.

"Cease fire! Cease fire! I'm not here to hurt you!" Kevin yelled while drawing his pistol and aiming it straight up into the truck bed floor.

A man coughed and wheezed. "Shit, man, sorry. I thought that you were one of those infected gray creatures again. You're clear to come around. I'm on safe."

"I'm coming around. Don't shoot." Kevin rolled out from underneath the vehicle, keeping his pistol in hand. He slowly peeked around the back edge of the truck, seeing a lengthy pale man lying against a stack of MRE boxes, cocooned among a truck bed full of various equipment. Kevin looked over the sickly man. "Are you hurt? We have a trauma kit." Kevin stepped closer to him, then bent around the HMMWV, waving the girls forward. "He's hurt!" he said, just loud enough for them to hear.

"Yeah, I'm wounded. But your med bag won't fix this," the man said in a raspy voice while lifting his camouflaged sleeve, revealing a vicious bite wound that had already turned black with dark veins branching up his arm. "Happened last night, about five miles up the road."

"You're military?" Gaylen asked over her shoulder while still watching the overpass and highway.

"Yes, ma'am, Lieutenant Murphy, USAF. I stole a plane out of Africa, trying to escape this mess, only to land at the airstrip in Grayling, smack in the middle of it again."

"Wait, you flew all the way here from Africa? The epidemic is there as well?" Stephan asked unbelievingly.

"Yup. From the sounds of it, it's all over South America as well. Not long before it hits Europe and Asia." He grimaced.

"You said you landed at Grayling. Why did you leave?" asked Kevin, wanting to know if he'd made the right choice by not going there.

"Well, I figured it was FUBAR when I called in, requesting to land. Flight LN269 didn't get a response from anyone. Anywhere. I did a couple of circles around the airbase, and it was dark, but I could see some movement, so I lined her up and touched down. I was greeted by some real winners. And by winners, I mean weekend warrior wannabe warlords who happened to be there when World War III had started. I picked up on the mafia-type 'public protection' scheme right away and didn't want to be a part of it. You know the bit: We'll protect the neighborhood for a fee. If not, we'll burn your house down," Lt. Murphy said.

"I played along with them just long enough to acquire some stuff to get me home. Then, last night I snuck off base. Was doing pretty good for a while until I ran into—literally ran into—a herd of infected. Damaged the Hummer pretty bad and got myself bit in the process of trying fix it. I'm better with planes than trucks. I should have just stayed in Africa," he said with a hint of sadness.

"Is there anything we can do for you?" Stephan asked.

Before he could answer, a low, rumbling noise could be heard in the distance.

"Awww, shit, not again." Gaylen spat.

"What is it?" Stephan asked.

"Listen. There. It's getting louder. They're coming this way. We need to move. Now!" Gaylen said, her voice quivering with fear.

"What's going on?" Lieutenant Murphy demanded while trying to sit up.

"Psycho biker gang. Chaos-anarchy type. Not friendly in the least bit." Gaylen bounced on her feet, obviously terrified.

"Does this thing run?" Kevin asked.

"We should just run for it on foot!" Gaylen yelled while having flashbacks of her friends being killed and tortured.

"He can't run. They'll come right to this military vehicle like a kid to an ice-cream truck. Just like we did. We can't let them get the Lieutenant's stuff. Who knows what kind of damage they would cause with it!" Kevin tried to explain.

Stephan was already in the driver's seat, trying to find the ignition key. "Where's the damn keys to this thing?"

The rumbling of the pack of hodgepodge motorcycles was getting closer. "This thing sputtered out on me getting off the highway. It might start, or it might not. It's a military vehicle; it doesn't have keys. Look on the dash, left of the steering wheel, for the engine starter switch," Lt. Murphy said.

The HMMWV engine turned over a few times. "Give it a second. It's a diesel. Now try again!" Kevin said hurriedly.

The engine turned over, then sputtered a few times and died.

The roar of a couple dozen exposed engines closed in on them. Gaylen was ghostly white, screaming for them to run. Lt. Murphy yelled for her to get in or get out of the way, but she couldn't hear over the deafening noise.

The hodgepodge of two-, three-, and four-wheeled motored vehicles came to a slow stop only a hundred yards from them. They revved their engines once, then, in unison all went quiet.

"Well, well, well. Is that our little Gaylen? We meet again, girl. I've got a bone to pick with you, honey. You killed one of my men with a screwdriver. That's just rude," said one of the bikers, presumed to be the leader since he was centered in the front row. He kicked down the stand, dismounted his bike, and then stood next to it.

Stephan tried the engine again with the same results. Cursing loudly. Kevin pulled Gaylen behind him and shouldered his M4. "Sir, I'm going to ask you to stay where you are, and no one will get hurt. We have no problems with you," Kevin yelled back.

"Nor I any problems with you, good sir. But her..." The biker leader pointed a dirty finger at Gaylen. "She'll be coming with me."

From behind Kevin, he heard a metallic slap of a lid slammed shut, and then a familiar mechanical cocking sound. At the same time, the Hummer engine caught. "Move!" Lt. Murphy yelled.

Kevin yanked Gaylen out of the way, pulling her forcibly by the arm. He shoved her toward the passenger-side door, telling her to get in. Kevin brought his rifle up, but before he could acquire a target, Lt. Murphy opened fire with a M249 belt-fed machine gun, sending 5.56mm bullets flying at a cyclic rate of one thousand rounds per minute. Kevin watched as men flew off their rides. Some jumped over the bridge railing, falling to the pavement below.

Kevin was about to start hitting targets when he noticed the Lt. wasn't hitting anyone. He had purposefully aimed high over their heads, then aimed low toward their motorized transportation after all riders jumped out of the way. Within seconds, the entire two hundred round drum was empty. "Reloading!" Kevin took that pause in the chaos to jump into the back of the HMMWV, yelling, "All in! All in! Go, go, go!"

While they were sluggishly gaining speed heading west on Route 55 toward Lake City, Kevin and Lt. Murphy watched out of the back as the trees and bushes along the road swayed and bent over when Grays came pouring out toward the highway overpass.

THE WALL

I walk my post from flank to flank...

Having only ingested one cup of lukewarm instant coffee, Grumpy irritably wrapped his Battle Belt around his waist, looking into the mirror at several new gray beard hairs. Absentmindedly, he did a belt sweep from front to back to ensure the four mags (two Glock and two AR) hadn't gone missing in the last twelve hours. Some days, he would grab a magazine just to be sure the top 5.56 round was stacked on the right side, confirming a twenty-eight round magazine. As his hand automatically swept forward and across the rigid surfaces, he noted that the direction of the mags was still facing bullet-tip forward. He did this every day, just in case Murphy trolled his kit while he slept to impair a split-second life-or-death reload, which would, in all probability, never happen since they hadn't seen a Gray or any raider probes in weeks.

Lifting the heavy daypack off the floor, which was filthy and needed to be cleaned, he sat the burden on the most uncomfortable refurbished folding chair in all of the safe zone. He inspected the pack for extra recharged batteries, spare ammo, a surplus of snacks, appropriate entertainment for surviving a long boring night—be it a loaner book from the library or crossword puzzles—along with a bulky, still-sealed individual first-aid kit. While on the thought of trauma, he reached behind the batbelt to ensure his tourniquet was not lying behind the bed again but in fact was still properly secured in the CAT-T holder and easily accessible for one-handed application in the event of amputation.

As he tossed the single point rifle sling over his neck and shoulder, he slightly tilted the ejection port side of his rifle up toward the candlelight, pulling the charging handle back to see the glint of brass, confirming there was indeed a round in the chamber—just like he did yesterday and the day before that, knowing that the rifle was ready for duty. He would check the gear a few more times on the way, because the monotonous wall-watch days ran together, creating an uncertainty if he had yet to complete the simplest of tasks today...or was that yesterday?

Off to work... One more day closer to getting off the wall. Luckily, his walk to the Town Defense Force building was just two short blocks from his overcrowded dwelling. The TDF building was an old antique furniture store named The Shabby Little Vintage Shop and was flanked by an old barbershop and video-rental store, both of which were now used for TDF supplies and the Quick Response Force. Strategically located right in the middle of town for rapid response to any attacks from any direction and also conveniently located one block from City Hall.

Toward the west end of the building and next to the original storefront window was a large dry-erase board used to assign daily guard duties. Using the natural light coming through the window, he ran his finger down the duty roster until he spotted his name: GRUMPY. He wasn't sure how he got that nickname; he was generally a likable person. Mostly. It could be because he often gave constructive criticism of unnecessary risks and offered unpopular security-upgrade solutions to the not-so-enthusiastic occupants of this town. Maybe he was grumpy at times to certain people, but they could piss off.

It seemed like he was starting at GP4, which was a guard post on the north end of the town's wall. It wasn't a bad spot to start the shift. At that post, there were interesting outlying areas to observe through binoculars, which was an easy way to kill time before twilight faded into complete darkness. If he got lucky, he may spot a deer or other wild game. By reporting that to the forage team, the reward could be fresh protein for tomorrow's community dinner.

At 1745, Victor, the TDF commander, gave a quick brief of any expected incoming or outgoing security patrols, any pertinent information gathered over the past twenty-four hours from outside the town, and any upcoming scheduled training opportunities, several of which caught Grumpy's ear. The advanced training was completely voluntary. Most voluntary off-duty training was ignored by the defense force guards. Grumpy saw the training as an opportunity to expedite getting off the torturously mind-numbing wall duty. After his shift leader gave a quick update of guard post changes or updates, they were released to take over the duties and responsibilities of the town defense.

Right at 1800, he arrived at GP4. One minute later, and the guy being relieved would have been bitching up a storm for him being late. It's not like he had anything else to do, but at the twelfth hour of duty, guards were ready for some personal downtime. The off-going guard reported that all was quiet and he hadn't seen a thing all day as he quickly climbed down and walked back toward town. Grumpy climbed the ladder to the top of the shipping container that composed this section of the wall.

About a month back, someone had had the intellect to build a protective wall around the small downtown area. A large distribution facility located halfway between Lake City and the next town over provided all the shipping containers they could possibly use. Transporting the forty-foot steel boxes and setting them in place had been a real chore.

The mechanics and engineers attempted to mount trailer axles to the boxes and pull them, but after a few failed attempts, they ended up leaving the shipping containers on the semitrucks. Daisy-chained together with straps and rope, a medium-size farm tractor could slowly tow about a dozen semitrucks at once. A large crane and forklifts would have made placing each shipping container in place a cinch. Instead, they struggled to lift, push, and tug each box into position using haybale forks attached to farm-tractor buckets. Over time, the process was refined, and the defensive perimeter wall continued to expand outwardly, offering more and more protected acreage inside the safe zone.

A quick glance around the sandbag-fortified bunker ensured all the standard guard-post supplies were accounted for: an ammo can with extra ammo, binoculars, road flare, whistle, and an old poncho in case it started to rain. He sat his daypack and AR15 in the corner, had a seat on a warped plastic milk crate, lifted the binos to his face, and began surveilling the area. As he was glassing the burnt-out buildings surrounding the perimeter and the dark, shadowy tree line nearby, distracted by the beautiful autumn-tree colors, his mind started calculating the night's guard-shift schedule. Each duty spot was only thirty minutes, which was just enough time to get settled in, give a good look around, and then it was off to the next post. The shortened post time reduced eye fatigue while scanning, reduced complacency, and reduced the possibility of falling asleep on post. A guard who was caught snoozing was usually rewarded with a full week of hard labor.

After this post, he would slowly walk the distance of the wall between here and GP5. After GP5, he'd walk back to the Town Defense Force HQ building, looking for anything suspiciously out of the ordinary on the interior of town. Back at HQ, he would be on the Quick Response Force for two hours, which translated to a nap in the "Ready Room" while waiting for an emergency.

While daydreaming about the schedule, a rattle from below startled him, causing him to jump off his milk-crate stool and drop the binoculars. It took him a second to realize that his thirty-minute post was up already, and now Joe was there to relieve him. A couple of deep breaths calmed his nerves. Joe laughed as he climbed up the ladder, knowing Grumpy nearly soiled himself. At that exact moment, an unseen white-tailed deer in close proximity gave an extraordinarily loud alarm snort that echoed off the shipping containers, causing Joe and Grumpy both to duck while reaching for their weapons.

It wasn't uncommon for deer to be this close to town, which was why they kept an eye out for them. But to have one whistle was a reason to be cautious.

"Something spooked it," Grumpy said while scanning the area using the four-power magnification of the ACOG atop his AR15.

"Us maybe? Being too loud?" asked Joe nervously.

Giving Joe a sideways glance out of the corner of his eye, Grumpy could tell Joe was shaken. "I doubt it, man. Haven't had one haul tail like that lately."

They both sat, crouching in silence for a good five minutes with their guns up, scanning near to far, then back again. Joe covered the left sector, and Grumpy covered the right.

"Well, I don't see anything. Keep your eyes and ears open. I'm going to start my rove down to GP5. I'll go slow; if you need me, blow the whistle, and I will come running back," Grumpy offered.

Joe nodded, relaxing his rifle, then picked up the binoculars that Grumpy had previously dropped.

Grumpy could walk on top of the shipping containers all the way over to GP5, which would give him better visibility of the area, but there was absolutely no cover up there. One of their guards had gotten herself sniped by raiders a few weeks back over by GP2. One time, a kid tripped and then fell off on the wrong side of the wall, then had to stealthily and painfully walk all the way around to the side gate on a busted ankle using his broken rifle as a crutch. *Yeah...no thanks*, he thought.

So, hand over hand, he climbed down the wobbling makeshift ladder that would end up killing someone someday. Planted firmly on the ground, he took a long pull of water out of his canteen, adjusted his rifle sling, did a quick gear check, and then started a nice, slow, stealthy walk eastbound toward GP5.

A patrol every thirty minutes equaled forty-eight patrols a day, carving out a nice foot trail between the guard posts. Even then, as the sun was setting, it was easy for someone to put their head down and daydream while easily walking and getting hypnotized by the passing tan, red, and plum rust colors of the rigid metal siding. But that deer incident had made his Spidey-senses tickle his neck hair.

Almost halfway to GP5, he did a little tactical pause, just as he had every one hundred yards since he'd started his rove from GP4. Grumpy took a knee, caught his breath, closed his eyes for better hearing concentration, and inhaled deeply. That's when he smelled it: a putrid, rank smell of disease and filth that he had almost forgotten existed. The buttstock of his rifle instinctively went into his shoulder pocket, his nonfiring hand slid farther up onto the handguard, and he found the selector switch with his thumb, ready to disengage the safety.

Something heavy hit the opposite side of the wall with a loud *thud*. Then another. And another. And another. Soon followed a frantic scraping sound, comparable to an angry dog clawing its way through a door. The noise resonated, piercing right through him. The vision of a raider clan climbing over the nine-and-half-foot container wall using makeshift devices filled his thoughts, but the smell slapped him quickly back to reality. Grays were outside the wall.

Is it on top of the wall? Grumpy could hear it directly above him. He could smell it deep in his throat. The aroma stung his eyes. He dared not move. The Grays' pinpoint pupils, caused by intracranial pontine hemorrhage of the frontal lobe, could not see well at that time of day, but their hearing was borderline sonar with acute tracking abilities.

The Grays were apex predators hunting the clean souls of the earth with the singular purpose of spreading disease. This one sensed that Grumpy was near. It inhaled deeply, searching for a trace of scent, but the infection in its lungs caused it to bark out a series of spasmodic, demonic coughs. It leapt from the wall and then landed, heavy and disorientated, no more than ten feet in front of Grumpy. For the first time ever, a gigantic late-stage Gray was unrestrained inside the safe zone.

Staring at the massive, grotesque, deformed figure, Grumpy had a hard time concentrating. Even in the fading light, he could easily see the black ink-like fluid pulsating under its clear skin armored with thick, scabby layers. These things closed in quick, tackled, clawed, and bit until its victim passed out, covered in pus and virus, to never wake up sane again. Distance was the best defense, and right then, Grumpy had none. As soon as he moved, the beast would hear him. If he remained still, eventually the Gray would smell him or worse—it could escape into town.

With the wall to Grumpy's back, he could only go left or right. He chose the right, the familiar way which he had just recently traveled, knowing it was free of trip hazards. The barrel of the AR came up smoothly until the buttstock planted in his cheek, acquiring a sight picture of the tritium-illuminated red chevron-shaped reticle center massed on the monster of a Gray, selector switched to semi, and Grumpy started squeezing the trigger in a rapid cadence while simultaneously sidestepping to the right, quickly gaining distance.

About a dozen 5.56 millimeter green-tip NATO ball rounds traveling 2900 feet per second punched into the protruding vertebrae area of the beast's backside before it spun around to zero in on him. The part of the human brain that signals pain did not exist in Grays; they would continue to operate until an ample amount of physical damage was dealt to disrupt biological integrity. It focused in on Grumpy and began its charge.

Grumpy put five more rounds into its upper chest as fast as he could accurately squeeze them off. The thing stumbled and fell to the ground in a heap. His sights tracked it as it fell with three more rounds slapping into the side of its gray, hairless skull at point-blank range. Continuing to back up, gaining distance from the disease splattered everywhere and leaking all over the ground, Grumpy drew his attention toward the top of the wall where the Gray had first appeared.

Nothing was moving. With his ears ringing, he couldn't tell if the other Grays were still attempting to climb over or not. Keeping his muzzle elevated and pointing at the top of the wall using only the death grip of his right hand, Grumpy reached for a full magazine with his shaky left, did a quick reload, then pocketed the almost-empty mag in his back pocket.

Still breathing heavily and with his heart threatening to beat out of his chest, Grumpy sensed a quickly approaching presence behind him…

WOLF PACK

Family. Loyalty. Lethality.

Victor was pleasantly surprised as he sprinted up Main Street and saw that the Quick Reaction Force was already outside the HQ building, frantically doing gear checks.

"On me!" he commanded as he sprinted past them, heading toward the northern section of the defensive wall. He was so eager to find out what had happened that it wasn't until halfway there that he realized he was only armed with his holstered pistol and a couple of spare mags. Luckily he had the QRF team as backup—the team that was quickly falling behind by a good one hundred yards. He wanted to yell at them to hurry up, but they were carrying a heavy equipment load-out while he was stuck carrying only a pistol.

Victor slowed down just a tad to catch his breath and calm his thoughts while QRF closed the gap. If he'd heard just one shot, he would've predicted that a wall watchman had negligently discharged a firearm by accident or maybe shot a deer, but hearing that many shots in rapid succession was an obvious sign of contact.

The only thing worse than incoming enemy fire is incoming friendly fire. For that reason, as the QRF was getting close to Guard Post 4, Victor called out, "Green, green, green," which was their brevity code for incoming friendlies ready to be assigned a task.

"Green here!" was reported back to the QRF as they approached the ladder to the base of the guard post. "That way, about halfway to GP5. Grumpy took contact."

With that report, the QRF changed directions and took off without hesitation.

There had been only one volley of shots fired. So either the watchman was dead or he had successfully suppressed the threat and was now jacked up on adrenaline. Either way, Victor didn't want to run into a bad situation blindly. Victor commanded half the QRF to push out, away from the wall, and provide flank security. He was not running now but walking at an alerted fast pace with his pistol drawn at a low ready position.

A couple of hundred yards down the trail, Victor called out, "Green, green, green."

In the near distance, a "Yellow, yellow, yellow," was shouted back, which eased Victors nerves. Yellow was a caution signal, meaning the person was OK but in an unsecured situation. If "Red" had been the reply, it meant a known active threat was in the immediate area, which would change tactics drastically.

Throughout military history, there had always been some sort of "challenge and password," words that could be rotated daily for a guard to identify friendlies from foes. The problems were that either higher echelon would often not pass down the daily codes to the lower echelon, the sentries would forget the code words six hours into a mind-numbing guard shift, or the turds would straight-out not care enough to learn them. The TDF's unique color-code system was not as secure, which could easily be manipulated by hostile forces, but it was considerably easier to remember and had a dual tactical purpose.

Victor slowed his pace, and about halfway there, he gave the green call again. This was to ease the mind of the link-up person to avoid fratricide and also let Victor know the link-up person's exact location, like playing the game Marco Polo in the dark. This communication also worked very well inside urban areas, when everyone had nervous trigger fingers.

On approach, there was barely enough ambient light left in the evening sky to make out the shapes of Grumpy the watchman and a monstrous Gray lying facedown in the dirt.

"QRF, push out a twenty-five-yard perimeter on this location. Eyes up, guns out," Victor commanded. "Grumpy, what happened here?"

■■

Rolling down Route 55, relieved to be alive and in a moving vehicle for the first time in months, Kevin busted out into another posttraumatic laughing fit in the back of the Hummer. "Holy crap, that was a close one! Great work with that machine gun, Lieutenant. Did you see those thugs diving off the bridge? That was magnificent!"

Kevin's laughter quickly faded as the loud, roaring engine sputtered, rattled, and then went quiet as they quickly decelerated. Stephan had to double-grip the steering wheel, fighting against the lack of power-steering, to force the wheels to turn. She steered toward a down-sloping gravel driveway, rolling to a stop near a dark farmhouse roughly seven miles from the highway's crossroads.

"Shit!" Stephan cried out. "I knew we couldn't be that lucky to make it to town tonight. We need to hurry up and clear that house. It's already dark!"

"Lt., you and Gaylen watch the outside; Stephan and I will clear and prep the house. I wonder if we could push the Hummer around back. It'll draw a lot of attention once the sun comes up."

■■

Victor pulled Grumpy off wall-watch duty for the night. The Lake City town council, mayor, and sheriff were waiting for them as they came walking back into town. Gathering at the pavilion, once again, Victor had Grumpy retell his story, which he did in extraordinary detail. He talked fast and nervously; he was either excited from his near-death encounter or because he was speaking directly to the town's policy makers.

"Did you say that there were multiple Grays and they helped lift one over the wall?" asked Mrs. Cloud.

"I was on the interior, ma'am, so I can't say for sure. But the noises I heard, yeah, it sounded like that's what happened. I don't know if it got over deliberately with help or was just lucky," Grumpy said, nervously ringing his hands.

"Thank you, Grumpy. Take the rest of the night off and get some rest." Victor shook his hand and patted him on his back. The sheriff told him that he had saved many lives tonight. As he was walking away toward the TDF HQ building, Victor continued, "Two concerns to immediately address: One, either the Grays are getting smarter or are starting to work together. Both are scary scenarios. Either way, we need to make border-defense improvements. Two, reports of Gray activity close to town are getting more frequent. It's time to address how to clear them away."

Luckily, Stanly was absent—there was no one there to say anything counterproductive. The rest of the attendees all nodded their heads in agreement.

"Victor, start putting together ideas on how we can lure them away from town," the mayor said. "Raymond, can you start working on low resource–big-impact fortifications for the wall? Our labor power is getting thin. Start with easier, smaller improvements first. And lastly, I think we are ready to transmit. We'll broadcast right after the BBN news report on the same channel and again in the morning right at sunup. With luck, someone besides our little town is also listening to BBN."

"For the record, I still feel it's a bad idea, but you're the boss," Victor said.

"I concur; we should fortify the wall first, because you're going to get a lot more than helpless grandmas at the gate as soon as you announce the location of an organized community," Raymond agreed.

"We've waited long enough. We've relocated all the locals in the area that we could. Nobody else knows of our safe haven or your services," concluded the mayor.

■■

Victor returned home to find his boys in the den, curled up on the couch and rocking chair, reading books around a homemade mason-jar candle fueled by Crazy Chad's corn whiskey. They must have heard the earlier gunshots as well, because they each had their rifles and gear propped up next to the front door ready to go.

"Everything OK?" Michael asked.

"Yeah, a Gray hopped the wall. Luckily, a guard was there to take care of it. But we need to go thin the herd again and draw them away from town. Are you boys up for another black op?" Victor asked and was met with nods all around.

The four snuck out of town through the northern gate, heading for their most successful purging sites. They had been out here killing Grays for the past couple of weeks, yet the security incidents seemed to be getting more frequent. Apparently they were not killing enough Grays, but perhaps after tonight's close call at the wall, the town council would finally sanction these types of culling operations, making them a daily duty. Until then, Victor knew that for security and safety, it had to be done quietly.

Victor certainly wanted to try Raymond's squealing-raccoon bait trick, but tonight he didn't have the time to trap one. Tonight, they were going to attempt a new technique by playing a pulsating, high-frequency tone on a working portable tape player. The tone was outside the human audio frequency range, though Mrs. Cloud reported the Grays could still hear it. To aid in luring them in, Victor sprayed the radio player with a healthy dose of cologne to attract the Grays.

At this hunting site, they used a technique called "wolf packing." Michael was in the hayloft of a towering red barn a couple hundred yards away at the end of the road. Curtis was barricaded in the second-story bedroom of a house a few doors down. Zavier and Victor were camped in a small room that must have previously belonged to a young girl. Zavier seemed more distraught being trapped inside a pink room filled with dolls than by the horde of infectious death they were luring into combat.

Ten minutes was their Standard Operating Procedure. From the time they split to the time Curtis would toss a Molotov cocktail, igniting the tire- and pallet stack and illuminating the bait area. While they waited, their minds began to wander.

Victor still held on to hope that Erica had survived and someday they would meet again. Whenever the kids would ask about her, his heart swelled and ached at the same time. He knew the odds, but he wasn't quite ready to accept the most plausible outcome. With each passing day, the cruel, likely reality was harder to ignore…

Curtis was thinking of better ways to dispatch Grays in bulk. Having bodies out here in the dark pulling triggers was too dangerous and too slow. Last week, they had flooded a small street section with gasoline; the idea was to lure a bunch of Grays into the kill zone, then light them all on fire. Unfortunately, the Grays smelled the fuel and didn't even get close. Someday, Curtis wanted to trap a Gray horde between a couple of shipping containers and then run them over with a steamroller. Yeah…

Michael inspected the rudimentary range card that he'd drawn on the barnwood the first time they'd used this hide site. He checked his ammo placement, confirming his rifle was loaded and his scope elevation was adjusted for two hundred yards. Settling into a comfortable shooting position, he began making plans for tomorrow. Michael was going to tie up a net—that he alone had constructed out of twine—to the soccer goalposts at the community park, then beg the farmers to help him round up the fenced-in goats that grazed on the soccer field. There'd been a few younger boys in town talking trash about having superstar ball-handling skills, which they had yet to demonstrate. It was time for Michael to give them a lesson…

Zavier got situated on the top bunk next to his dad, still cringing over being in a pink princess room. Every touch of the girly bed linen felt like boiling acid to his skin. Soon his thoughts drifted to cookies. Chocolate-chip cookies. Chewy and soft. Warm. Right out of the heat box at the old diner with a cup of fresh milk. If they didn't have chocolate chip, oatmeal raisin would do, or peanut-butter crunch or—

The tire stack in the middle of the street engulfed in flames. The high-frequency recording must have worked, because there was a large group of Grays already gathered. Time to wolf pack.

The concept behind wolf packing was to deliver a constant flow of offensive precision fire from multiple dispersed, concealed positions while maximizing angles to prevent enemy's use of cover. It also prevented the enemy from being able to pinpoint the wolf pack's exact locations for a counterattack—if the technique was performed aggressively enough.

When engaging, only one sniper position would attack at a time. The shooter would empty their magazine as accurately as possible. Then the next position would immediately do the same while the other guns cooled their barrels, reloaded, and gained some situational awareness, avoiding tunnel vision inside their scopes' field of view, fix their shooting positions or if they needed to relocate, they could do so with covering fire.

They were hidden well within the shadows of their hide sites while using suppressors, but if a hide site got compromised, the other two sniper positions could easily give fire support or cause a secondary diversion as the Grays converged. This was a very effective tactic to use on both enemy forces and Grays alike, causing mass amounts of battlefield confusion and enemy casualties.

They all took turns crumpling and stacking lifeless infected bodies around the slowly fading fire; even in the pink princess room, little Zavier, using a Barbie pillow as a front support on a wooden bunkbed railing, removed one diseased threat after another. While Victor spotted targets for Zavier, he studied the swarm's reactions and patterns. The individual Gray acted confused and jittery, wanting to escape from the unknown threat that was killing its companions, yet it was drawn to the mysterious sound and odor.

Victor wished he had some sort of electronic night-vision devices to help him scan the area, preferably mounted to a weapon. But they didn't. Shooting precision rifles at night took some getting used to, but his boys were getting better. Observing wind patterns and spotting bullet trace were nearly impossible. But there were plenty of low-light techniques that allowed standard rifles with daytime scopes to be used at night. The hardest obstacle to overcome was finding the center of the black crosshairs in the dark; having an illuminated reticle helped tremendously. Of course, that reticle illumination needed to be dialed as far down as possible to avoid washing out the eye's natural night-vision sensitivity, which could take up to half an hour to regain.

Having the natural illumination of a full moon could help visibility a great deal—that is, if the cloud cover would cooperate. But even with a full moon, good equipment was needed. Inside a riflescope are several lenses that light bends and refracts before passing through the pupil to the photoreceptors in the back of the eye's retina. Highly polished lenses with an expensive coating would help prevent the loss of light transmission as it passed through each of these lenses. This was one reason why scope clarity came at a huge price tag back when people could go shopping for such things.

Different low-light techniques had different obstacles to overcome. Temporarily lit targets—from a lightning bolt, for example, or flashing lights—were not too bad if the target was stationary. But if it's in motion, the shooter must gauge the target's speed, then estimate where it'll be during the next quick lightning burst, and the sniper has to be quick on the trigger. A backlit target, like the Grays gathered between the roaring tire fire and Victor's hide site, are silhouetted perfectly. The creatures are simple to see and track; the hardest part with backlit targets is centering a black reticle on a darkened shadowy profile.

A front-lit target, like the Grays on the far side of the blaze, for the most part, is no different than shooting in daytime. Although the dancing flames cast wavy shadows over the landscape, making a stationary target appear to sway. An inexperienced shooter may mistakenly lead a motionless target.

Victor's wolf pack would continue the culling until the tire firelight diminished or until they were out of rifle ammo. The carbine and pistol ammo were reserved for the walk home. Even with Raymond's generous stockpile of ammo he'd brought to town, ammo supplies were getting low. Tonight, in their hide sites, they each consciously collected all the empty brass shell casings to be reloaded at a later time.

Late into the night, the four drowsy members of the covert Eradicating Team strolled back through town, not expecting to find anyone but TDF guards. If anyone were to ask what they were doing out past curfew, an "outer perimeter patrol" was their rehearsed cover story. The little wolf pack was almost to the safety of their cozy blue Victorian home, where warm, comfortable beds called for them, when Art came rushing down the street. "You're not going to believe this!" Art said excitedly out of breath. "You have a mission!"

■ ■

Between meeting Gaylen and hearing all her enlightening stories, Lt. Murphy's riveting stories of Africa and Camp Grayling, and then the occasional informative BBN news broadcast, Kevin was becoming addicted to fresh information from the outside world. Secretly Stephan was, too, which was why she subtly got excited when Kevin pulled the portable HAM radio out of his backpack, unwrapped the waterproofing baggy and turned it on.

He fumbled around for a while, scanning through the channels, always coming back to the known BBN frequency. He paced back and forth in the darkened living room of the farmhouse, searching for the perfect spot that would receive a signal better than anywhere else. Eventually, a weak voice broke through the static.

"This is WGON, broadcasting from Lake City, Missaukee County, Michigan. Latitude +44.482147, longitude -85.178525. We are a community that can provide security, shelter, clean water, short-range transportation, and minor medical treatment. We are low on food provisions, but I say again we have ample security. If you would like to be a member of our hardworking and growing community, we can assist you. You do not need to suffer these dark times alone. We will broadcast at sunup and sundown every day, but we are always listening. This is WGON, broadcasting from Lake City. Out."

Without consulting his group, or even asking for opinion, Kevin immediately pushed the talk button while holding the radio high, hoping for a better signal.

"WGON, WGON, this is Leprechaun. I hear you, three by three. You're coming in broken but readable. We are located seven miles west of Houghton Lake. We have four PAX needing immediate assistance, over!"

■■■

"You're kidding," Victor said in shock. "What did they say?"

Art said excitedly, hardly able to control his speech, "That they were about halfway between here and Houghton Lake. There were four of them. The signal transition was weak and distorted, but I think he said two males and two females that had traveled all the way from Detroit!"

Victor's tactical mind went into overdrive, almost losing focus of Art, who was standing directly in front of him. "What else did they say, exactly? Leave nothing out!"

"You weren't around to consult, so I just made a decision. I told them to meet our team on the second morning at Foree Electronics store next to Buff's Pizzeria in the small village of Willamette on Route 55."

Victor looked at Art curiously for a long second. "Why there?"

"Well, it's the first place I thought of, and I figured while you're going that way, you could pick up some electronic parts. I know that's not your job, but we've never sent the scavenger teams out that far yet. If you could get me a few things, I could boost our transmission range, and I could possibly broadcast on several frequencies at once instead of only the BBN frequency."

Even with the long day he had of rescuing Raymond's neighbors, the excitement at the wall, and the covert eradication op that he had just come in from, Victor couldn't sleep. He had doubts about broadcasting, but it had worked, instantly. He wondered how many more would answer their call, and at what distance. First things first, though: it was time to plan a long-range recovery op.

■ ■

The autumn night's temperature had dipped to a cool level, ideal for sleeping comfortably while keeping the summer mosquitoes at bay. Even with the chilled air and exhausted muscles from a long hike, sleep evaded all in the farmhouse that night. Gaylen was excited to put physical distance between herself and her nightmarish past. Lt. Murphy was beginning to suffer from viral insomnia symptoms. Stephan and Kevin were both ecstatic being so close to their destination after hundreds of miles and days, weeks, months of walking, encountering more life-and-death situations than they could count.

Just before sunrise, Kevin and Gaylen took inventory of the HMMWV as Stephan was on the farmhouse roof, providing overwatch. Lt. Murphy rounded the corner, looking pale.

"There you are, sir. We were looking through all your loot here. I don't think the four of us will be able to carry it all. Is there anything in particular you want prioritized or left behind?" Kevin asked.

Lt. Murphy took in a big breath of chilled, crisp morning air while looking up at the pink autumn skies, tracking a flock of Canadian geese migrating south. "You know, I think I'm going to go fishing. There's a little rowboat over by the pond, and I bet some poles are in the garage."

The others looked at each other, puzzled. "But, sir, we should get going soon to make it to the extraction point," Kevin said, unsure of Murphy's infected mental state.

"You all go ahead. I understand how the virus progresses. I've seen enough people turn to comprehend the ugly course it takes. I have about a day, maybe two, left before I lose it altogether. I'm going to spend my last couple days fishing. Take whatever you want out of there; just leave me a box of MREs and a case of water. It's only two or three miles to that little village they spoke of on the radio. You should be able to carry a heavy load that far. Take as much as you can."

Stephan peered down over the roof, sadness written all over her face, and a lone wet tear streaked down Gaylen's cheek. Kevin simply nodded his understanding. "Would you like some help with that boat, sir?"

PREGAME

Drinks, Snacks, and Rally Caps

Victor ran around town the next morning like crazy, gathering key personnel and supplies for tomorrow's recovery mission. He was planning contingencies for every bad scenario that they could possibly encounter.

At the beach, Victor had used a roll of twine and tent stakes to create a large grid pattern in the sand that resembled the north/south and east/west lines on a map. Inside the grid squares, he'd used black spray paint to draw roads, blue paint for lakes and rivers, and piled-up sand to depict elevation changes across the topography. He'd also used Lego blocks to mark all the buildings shown on the map plus additional buildings he recalled from memory. Scattered about the model were little green plastic army men and miniature toy trucks marking strategic locations.

Huddled around the terrain model were Victor, his sons, Raymond, a deputy who would be tagging along as a law enforcement liaison, the town's head mechanic, Mrs. Cloud representing the medical staff, a few TDF guards, and Art the radio operator.

"All right, we are here. The model is oriented north, which is that direction. The situation is we have a handful of refugees about ten miles east of here on Route 55 who have requested our assistance." Victor pointed a stick to the cluster on the terrain model depicting Lake City, drawing a line in the air eastward over Route 55 toward the small village of Willamette.

"Our mission is to retrieve the four of them tomorrow morning and bring them safely back here. We'll do this by utilizing three elements—"

"Are you really giving a full operations order for a simple pickup?" Raymond scoffed.

"Yes," Victor said, glaring back at him.

"Really? Orientation. Situation. Mission. Execution. Admin and Logistics. Command and Signal. All that?"

"Yes," Victor said again, gritting his teeth. "The majority of the players involved have never worked together before in this magnitude. It's imperative everyone is on the same sheet of music, knowing what is expected of them. It's only ten miles away, but it may as well be deep behind enemy lines."

"Yeah, yeah, forward edge of the battle area, got it. But we all know when bullets start flying, this elaborate plan will shit the bed. I prefer 'initiative-based' tactics. The mission is known; I'll make the rest up as I go."

"Well, for everyone else, I'll continue, in long…drawn-out…detail," Victor said slowly.

Raymond rolled his eyes and scoffed, yet he remained with the group huddled around the three-dimensional map for the entire duration of the mission briefing.

An hour later, Victor concluded the meeting, giving hard times for final gear checks and reminding them to get some chow and rest before they rolled out at 0200. He caught up with his sons as they dispersed from the briefing and walked back to their home.

"Dad, that's a lot of information to remember," Michael said.

Zavier agreed, nodding his head.

"Don't worry, most of it doesn't apply to you, and you boys have the easy job. Pretty much the same thing we've been doing on our black ops, but you'll be running the mission without me. The reason I made you sit through that long boring brief is because it's important to know what the other pieces of the chess game are doing. When we get back to the house, I'll go over your part of the game again while we have lunch. Ask any questions you may have. Remember, the most important task you have is to take care of each other and come back safely at any cost. Do you understand?"

■■

The morning sun came over the eastern horizon, warming their faces and threatening another relentlessly hot day. Already missing the crispness of the cool night air, Stephan took one heavy step in front of the other while hunched over, carrying an overstuffed backpack that weighed more than her own body weight.

She looked down often to ensure she was stepping on flat ground to avoid twisting an ankle, which was extremely easy to do while packing this kind of weight. Kevin had suggested doubling up on their socks and using elastic wraps out of the first-aid kits to give them extra ankle support. Ordinarily a twisted or sprained ankle would put you on the couch watching movies for a couple of days; now it could be a death sentence.

Stephan found herself looking down often, not to search for a flat place to step but merely from exhaustion. The arches of her feet ached, sweat dripped in her eyes, and it hurt to stand up straight. She wasn't watching her areas of responsibility; that was dangerous and stupid. She held up her hand to halt the group. "Break time," she said. The break times were becoming more frequent as the landscape inclined slightly to the west.

"Once we crest this hill, we should be able to see the village," Kevin said quietly after chugging a bottle of water. Over the past couple of months, hydration management had been a continuous battle. Due to the lack of clean water, they could only drink just enough to stay healthy, but no more. That morning, while pillaging Lt. Murphy's Hummer, they had found several cases of water, more than they could possibly carry. With water so plentiful now, he had the luxury of slamming an entire bottle of H2O, just because it tasted and felt so good. The simple things in life.

"I'll take point," Stephan said, tightening the backpack shoulder straps. The lead position tended to be the most dangerous spot in a formation, having the highest probability for close-range contact. Any slacking off while walking point not only put herself in danger but her friends as well. For that reason, she tended to be a little more alert compared to when she was in the rear of the pack.

The crest of the hill was a lot farther away than the few hundred yards she had estimated. By the time they finally got there, with sweat-soaked shirts and shaking legs, it was unquestionably break time again. The only concealment options at the crest were a small cluster of bushes and trees or an outcrop of boulders. They picked the comfort of shade provided by the vegetation. All three flopped down on the soft ground, facing outward with their packs touching in the center so that they could lean back into each other while stretching their legs out straight.

"I think I'm getting too old for this," Kevin said and wheezed.

"I think I'm too short for all this," Stephan agreed.

"I think I'm just too soft and out of shape," Gaylen said with a pitiful laugh, knowing she was carrying only half the weight of her new friends.

Kevin wiggled out of his shoulder straps, taking off the pack. He reached into an outside pocket to grab a small pair of binoculars and a bottle of water. "I'm going to see what's on the other side of this hill. You two sit here and keep an eye out."

"Ohhhh, OK. You talked me into it," Stephan teased him while rubbing her sore calves.

"If you hear me yelling, it's probably just leg cramps," Kevin said. He high-crawled away from them, taking advantage of the usable vegetation concealment and because his legs hurt too much to stand up.

About half an hour later, he returned to find them both chowing down on an MRE and chugging water. "Careful eating too many of those things in a row. Military ration meals will bind up your intestines. Next time you take a poo, it'll be like giving birth. You should mix in some of our canned food every other meal to help grease the track." He knew why they were gorging themselves; it wasn't because they were starving and now had plentiful amounts of food after being hungry for months and months—it was because they were reducing their load weight through consumption.

"So the good news is the village is literally right over this hill. The bad news is the village is a little larger than we'd expected, and the electronics store is right smack-dab in the center of it. I didn't see any signs of life, but we'll have to be extremely careful on the final approach. If we get into contact, it'll be difficult for us to evade—not to mention where would we evade to, since this is our extraction point? We'll take it slow and easy. There appears to be a small stream looping around town, flowing right next to this hill we're on. We can use that for cover to get in close to the first row of buildings."

"Are we in a hurry to get down there?" Gaylen asked. "It's only ten o'clock. Should we watch the village some more? I only ask because I am beat. Really tired. I hate to slow you guys down, but I could pass out right now if I closed my eyes."

"I didn't sleep at all last night either," Stephan agreed. "I'm pretty fatigued myself. Kevin, can I get the binos? I'll go watch the town for a while if you want to get some chow while Gaylen takes a nap. Then we can rotate. Wouldn't be a bad time to let your feet air out too."

"If you do, only take one boot off at a time in case we need to move in a hurry. Keep your rifle close by too. We can see the finish line; let's not get sloppy now," Kevin reinforced.

■■■

"Curtis, are you OK being the QRF driver?" Victor asked.

"Sure. Seems simple enough. I'll just be hanging out in the truck once everyone is set into place?" He shrugged.

"Yes, hopefully that is it, if all goes well. It's the alternate scary version that I'm referring to. How about the bait—almost ready?"

"Yup, almost ready. I still need to test a couple components to ensure the entire package works," Curtis replied.

"OK, let me know when it's a hundred percent solid," Victor said.

"Are you feeling well, Dad? You seem really on edge," Curtis asked.

"Me? Yeah. I have an odd feeling about this mission. Something's different from the others. It's probably nothing, but it's eating at me. I'm really tired, I need to find a minute to take a nap. But first, Michael and Zavier need to link up with their rear-security element to brief them. I want to be there for support in case old men don't like taking orders from kids."

■■

Kevin hadn't napped in the middle of the day since he was enlisted in the army. In the infantry, there was plenty of downtime in the field while waiting for orders. Grunts usually killed that time with a quick nap. In fact, they were famous for being able to sleep in the oddest, most unusual positions imaginable. When Stephan nudged him awake, his eyes flew open, and he was fully alert, his heart pounding as he looked around with drool on his cheek.

Stephan knelt next to him with her finger on his lips, quietly shushing him. She took her finger off his lips slowly, pointed her index and middle finger at her eyes, then pointed her M4 in the direction of the village. She flashed both hands open, then closed, then open again in front of the scrunched-up ugly face she was making. She was telling Kevin that she'd spotted twenty Grays toward the village. Kevin nodded that he understood, then quietly put his boot back on.

The Grays were in a pack with no visible leader. The group didn't flow together collectively like a school of fish; it was more like a disorganized gaggle. Yet they all eventually migrated in the same direction, stopping occasionally to sniff the air and bark at each other while searching buildings, open vehicles, or anything that made an interesting sound.

Kevin, Stephan, and Gaylen looked at each other with raised eyebrows and just shrugged, not knowing what to think of it. After watching the pack disappear in the distance, they decided then would be a good time to make their way into town. Using the shrub-lined streambed, they cautiously made their way toward the first building, quietly and unnoticed.

"We have a couple blocks to go. I'd feel better dropping these insanely heavy packs here to clear the way first. We can retrieve them afterward if the coast is clear. I'll take point. Stephan and I will rotate cover at danger areas. Gaylen, we need you to watch our six o'clock. Keep a good eye to the rear, but don't lose us and get left behind. If we get separated, stay where we last saw each other. If we get hostile contact, let's fight our way back to this building where our gear is cached. It'll be our Alamo. Sound like a plan?" Kevin briefed.

With that, they stepped off. Gaylen was amazed at how fluid-like Kevin manipulated his weapon. As he came up to a building corner turning right, he smoothly switched the buttstock into his left shoulder, then seamlessly switched his support- and firing hands as if he'd done it a thousand times before. He went to a knee, then took a quick peek around the corner, exposing only a sliver of shoulder and head.

The first time Gaylen had witnessed this, she had several questions as to why, but after watching the same technique used while rounding corners in different directions, it finally made sense. He wanted to look around a corner while keeping his rifle muzzle up in case there was a threat, yet he didn't want to telegraph his presence by over presenting himself to the unknown area. Always keeping his body near the wall and weapon on the outside. Wall-body-weapon. Very smart. Although Gaylen didn't think she could shoot left-handed very well, so she didn't even try.

They came upon a long, shaded alleyway with a lot of open back doors into dark abandoned businesses. Kevin paused for a brief second to let the others catch up. He made a hand signal with one finger, making the letter *O* in the air in front of him, as he whispered, "Rolling cover. Gaylen, keep covering our rear and watch these upper-level windows. It'd suck to get infected by a falling Gray." Then he stepped off again, with his rifle lifted on his shoulder, pointing in the direction of travel.

He came to the first door and slowed down a tad but did not stop. He turned his light on, illuminating the dark room that they were bypassing, giving respect to the deep corners and cluttered areas that could harbor hidden dangers. He was quickly clearing the room from outside in the alleyway, careful not to over penetrate the threshold with his barrel. While Kevin was momentarily inspecting the unknown space, Stephan stepped around him, then passed him, taking the twelve o'clock lead position.

The moment he'd cleared as much of the room as possible without physically going in, he turned off his light and spun back around, giving full attention to the upper windows and roof. At the next dark opening, Stephan cleared it the same way Kevin had. While she was paying her respects to the creepy dark void, Kevin stepped around, then passed her, taking point again. They were clearing only what absolutely needed to be cleared, completely bypassing closed doors, which kept the group in forward motion toward the electronic store destination like a well-choreographed tactical ballet.

Toward the end of the dark, damp alley, Kevin paused and took a knee next to a filthy green dumpster that smelled of rot and disease.

"I'm pretty sure the next block houses the electronic store. Should we try the front or the back first?"

"Let's try the back door first," Stephan recommended. "Worst case is we'll have to circle around to the front. But at least we'll know what's around us if we get trapped inside."

Kevin nodded. They were so close, they could taste it. By this time tomorrow, they'd make the link up, get extracted, and ride with escorts to the finish line of a very long and treacherous journey. He took a deep breath of enjoyment, then immediately regretted it as a lungful of rotten dumpster odor coated his nostrils.

■ ■

On a very quiet Main Street in the center of Lake City, a crew of nine loaded into the town's two pickup trucks at 0145. The third working vehicle, along with a few members of the TDF, would remain in town as a backup. Everyone shook nervous hands with each other, wishing one another good luck and a speedy return. At 0200, under an expansive blanket of stars shimmering bright in the heavens, Victor signaled his drivers to roll out.

■ ■

The back door of the electronics store had been unlocked and open, but they decided to scout around the area anyway. The village was dead quiet—a spooky, unnerving type of quiet that made a light breeze whistling through an unsealed window casement seem loud. They secured the store, then returned for their backpacks without a problem. Stephan didn't want to jinx them by saying it out loud, but this all seemed way too easy.

That night, they barricaded the doors and set out noise-making trip wires in the back alley. Using a bunch of bizarre "We Stand

United Against The Infection" posters they found piled in the store, they obscured the front window the best they could. A search of the building didn't produce any weapons or food, but they did score half a bottle of vodka and a couple of Maltesers chocolate bars from the manager's desk.

"I could use a drink!" Gaylen begged.

"Let's save this bottle for tomorrow. It'll be our victory toast after we cross the finish line," Kevin suggested.

Stephan nodded her head in agreement, knowing they were still very much in the race.

Before it got dark, Kevin killed some time by going shopping through the store aisles, cramming boxes full of miscellaneous noncircuited electronic items, wiring, and fuses that could be useful later on, then stacked it all carefully at the front door for easy loading. They all took turns on night watch, but nobody really slept.

■■■

Stanly watched the Victor parade leave town while everyone gushed over his self-proclaimed heroics. It was preposterous. Armed taxi drivers were all he and his posse were. Stanly had gone out with them a couple of days ago and witnessed with his own eyes how quick they were to use their murderous death machines. Yeah, the infected showed a heightened level of aggression, but why wouldn't they? Savages like Victor were out there running wild, killing sick people indiscriminately without hesitation. At some point, a desperate population would eventually fight back, completing a perpetual cycle of hate. Violence was never solved with more violence. There must be a different way to reason.

The entire city council had been seduced by Victor and his genocidal peacekeeping. There wasn't much Stanly's political power could do about strategies outside the wall, but he could take better care of his constituents inside the walls, including the sick citizens locked inside the jail like tortured lab rats. An inspection of the testing area was long overdue; he needed to see for himself the extent of inhumanity going on in there. He envisioned shackled, malnourished prisoners suspended from cold concrete walls by heavy chains, probably starving to death in a cage of filth or being cut open while still alive, strapped to a metal table. There was no way that would happen in this town while Stanly possessed even a splinter of control. It was time to examine the jail without the interfering eyes of the other so-called "leaders," who were huddled around Art's radio, hungrily waiting for mercenary updates.

The key ring in Stanly's hand rattled in the moonlight as he nervously searched for the right key to the sheriff's office. What would people say if they found out? What would he say if he was caught snooping around the jail? The idea of having to sneak around his own town to conduct a health and welfare inspection made him angry enough to huff a cloud of vapor out into the chilled night air.

He tiptoed down the hall through an administration office that had been rearranged from the original cubicle layout into some sort of work area filled with black rubber aprons, galoshes, goggles, trash bags, rows of duct tape, yellow rubber gloves, and buckets of bleach. Stanly quietly rounded the corner, heading toward the prisoner-holding facility. In his mind, the jail represented the worst of humanity and always gave him a haunting chill. There was something disturbing about locking people up against their will, which, to him, symbolized modern-day slavery. With each step, he mentally prepared himself for the absolute worst. Stanly lifted his crowbar, ready to break into the dungeon. But when Stanly rounded the final turn, he was surprised to find the holding area's large, heavy steel door was not locked at all. In fact, it was wide open, with strips of thick clear plastic covering the entryway.

He stepped into the cold, dark room, confused by what he saw before him. Large black blankets covered the bars of the four holding cells like curtains. He didn't understand. The medical staff had been observing them during their tests, but how? Stanly twisted around in circles, holding a candle out to lighten the narrow passageway between covered cells. Perplexed, he reached up to scratch his head and spotted large slanted mirrors mounted near the ceiling that allowed him to peer into each of the cells.

Curious, he took a wavering half step toward one of the dark cells, trying to get a better look into the large mirror. He couldn't see anything; it was too dark. He wished that he'd come in earlier in the day, when the jail would have been sun-lit through the barred windows. Intrigued by the curved mirror high above, he lifted the candle up over his head and wondered if anything was still alive in this place. As he stared into the mirror, a pair of hate-filled eyes emerged out of the shadow, penetrating directly into his soul.

His stomach flopped, and his heart began to race, but Stanly held his gaze, examining the bizarre eyes in the mirror. The thing inside the cell let out an animal-sounding growl that caused his knees to buckle, and he stumbled backward into the holding cell–bars directly behind him. Stanly calmed himself, taking several deep, comforting breaths, rationally reassuring himself that these were only sick people that needed his help.

Leaning on a thick blanket that padded the cell bars against his back, he exhaled a long breath. A pair of hands thrust between the bars and grabbed ahold of Stanly like a blanket-wrapped burrito. He let out a frightened scream, clumsily dropped his candle, spilling hot wax all over himself, and then his crowbar clanked across the floor.

"I'm here to help you! Please. I'm here to help!" Stanly pleaded with the creature, who held on so tight that it began to hurt. The louder he pleaded and the more he squirmed, the stronger it held on, digging its claw like bony fingers into his shoulders. He felt his muscles tear from the bone. Terrified, Stanly finally fought back with force, hitting and prying, trying to free himself. Being trapped in the blanket pacified his movements like a straitjacket, giving him no leverage against the claws. The pain of the sharp bony fingers burrowing through the blanket caused his legs to give out. He dropped straight down to the floor, pulling the blanket-curtain with him into a heap. The beast's grasp broke free as its arms raked against the metal cross section, unable to maintain its grip.

The ghoul-like creature materialized out of the darkness before him as the blanket caught fire atop the spilled candle, illuminating the exposed cell. The bald, muscular thing was humanoid in shape only. Thick black veins, pumping ink-like infected blood, road-mapped across its pus-covered translucent skin. Thick, scaly scabs flaked off chunks of crust as it reached its claw-like hands out of the cage. It swiped at the air with bony digits missing the meat around the end of its talon-like fingers.

Stanly was repulsed by the creature before him. He had come here to help sick people and had found only monsters instead. The horrid, deformed beast had a large, bulbous tumor on its neck the size of a melon that pulsated like a black heart. Stanly slowly lifted himself upright again, standing on unsteady legs. The tumor seemed to swell with every heartbeat. Just outside the raging monster's reach, he stood, staring at it in the flickering glow of the blanket fire.

The thing tilted its head back at an unnatural angle and wailed a terrifying yowl. Stanly instinctively inhaled a quick breath, filling his lungs with a startled gasp at the same time the creature's tumor popped, spraying him in a foul-smelling cloud of spores that coated his face. His open mouth captured a revolting taste that made him fall to his knees, gagging and vomiting. In an attempt to flee, he crawled toward the jail exit through a puddle of his own bile. When Stanly's vision went fuzzy, just before he lost consciousness, he fell face-first and smacked his head on the cold concrete as the blanket fire diminished to smoldering ashes.

STAGE FOUR

GAME TIME

Penalty: unnecessary roughing

"Debris in the road, shift left," Raymond commanded the lead vehicle's driver. His night-vision monocular displayed the world through a light-amplified green filter, allowing him to scan the steadily approaching road for obstacles and the passing tree line for nocturnal predators. "Fallen tree, shift right." Briefly, in a moment of similarity, Raymond imagined he was back in Iraq, running low-profile high-threat personal security missions.

Victor rode shotgun in the second vehicle with Curtis at the wheel, who carefully navigated using only the illumination of a high- and bright full moon. Curtis followed at a safe distance to avoid accidentally rear-ending the lead vehicle if they came to a quick stop. After a few minutes out of town, his eyeballs' chemical composition had adjusted slowly, boosting the retinas' photoreceptors' sensitivity, allowing him to better see outlined shapes in the road. Still, he focused on the tiny cat-eye, unpainted slits of the vehicle taillights in front of them.

Even with the headlights turned off to avoid unwanted attention from Grays or other undesirables, the brilliant lunar radiance allowed the two-truck convoy to idle along on Route 55 at twenty miles per hour. To help increase the drivers' sensory perception, Victor had the mechanics unplug the dashboard fuses to completely blacken out the cab interiors. This allowed the drivers to focus better on staying between the moonlit white road lines.

The first couple of familiar miles out of Lake City, they knew the road had been cleared of all broken-down vehicles, making for an easy drive, but this far out was unexplored territory. As they swerved past obstructions, Victor made notes of the locations and types of vehicles for the mechanics to return later to salvage fuel and parts.

It only took them half an hour to reach the village boundary, where forestry and farmland turned into a pattern of man-made structures. Curtis slowed, then turned, following the lead truck down a narrow two-lane city street. The convoy continued to turn left several more times, lapping a specific block twice before coming to a slow stop. Ready for a quick escape, the trucks were left running with doors propped opened as they got out and waited. Waiting for something to happen, ready to react when it did. Auspiciously, nothing happened.

As planned, Raymond and Victor attacked a gift shop, swiftly and aggressively clearing the two-story structure. A low whistle from up above signaled to his boys that the building was clear and safe to bring up the bait bomb. Curtis, with the help of his dad, quickly strung up a tape player rigged to light a road flare using a model-rocket engine igniter at precisely 0700. With the road flare–rigged radio, twin propane tanks hung from the second-story window. The tanks would be remotely opened by his little brothers at the same time the road flare was automatically ignited, making a nice-size boom. Curtis looked at his dad and nodded.

"Do it," Victor confirmed.

When Curtis pressed play on the tape player, there was a five-minute delay of dead air before the music started playing at full volume, which would have any Grays in the area running. They would need to hurry, and they did. Down the dark stairway, they took two steps at a time, ran out the front door of the shop, then jumped in the truck. To ensure everyone was accounted for, Victor did a quick head count before accelerating to the end of the street, circled around a couple of blocks, then stopped again at a Hallowed Grounds coffee shop.

"All right, boys, this is your stop. We'll pick you up here thirty minutes after the kickoff. Good luck. Remember, stick to the plan no matter what."

"OK, Dad, we got this," Michael said, looking more like a young man today than a little boy.

Zavier only nodded, wearing a small pack on his back and carrying a rifle in his hands, looking extremely anxious.

Victor wanted to give them both a big hug but decided to avoid embarrassing them in front of their security team. Instead, he gave each of them a strong fist bump. He watched Michael, Zavier, Grumpy, and Deuce take off toward the bridal shop, where they'd be slaying a pile of Grays in a few hours.

"Curtis, you and Sergeant Dembele take the trucks to the gas station at the edge of town and wait for us to call. If for some reason we lose comms, come rolling in ten minutes after kickoff. Keep buttoned up in the vehicles while you wait; please don't fall asleep," Victor said with a wink, knowing that everyone was at a heightened state of alertness.

Victor and Raymond each shouldered a daypack and grabbed their scoped rifles out of the trucks. "You ready, Darcy?" Victor asked the third member of his team. Fitzwilliam Darcy was a defense-force wall guard who had been volunteering for extra training, showing potential as a valuable asset to the Survivor Rescue Team. Darcy nodded, and the three stepped off in the other direction, toward the opposite side of town.

■■■

"What the hell is that?" Gaylen whispered.

"Is that music?" Kevin asked.

"I don't know if I'd call that 'music'; that noise is far from Mozart," Stephan grumbled, tossing and turning on the floor, sleep evading her.

In the distance, Curtis's cassette tape of dead air had elapsed to his favorite rock band, who was now playing at full volume. Sounds of empty tin cans rattling in the alleyway behind the electronics store alerted them to numerous Grays scurrying past, toward the sound of music.

"Whoever is playing that is really dumb or really smart. Every Gray within hearing distance will be drawn to that," Gaylen said.

"Which will leave this area completely clear. I'd say that they're very smart and clever. I'm looking forward to meeting this Lake City crew; they're impressing me already." Kevin gleamed.

For the next four hours, the visitors of this village were entertained—or tortured, depending on their music taste—by Curtis's teenage playlist as the tape continued to play on repeat, at full volume, until early morning.

■■■

Raymond rolled away from Victor to unzip his dew-soaked pants. Lying on his side, he relieved his bladder, aiming an arcing stream toward a nearby gopher hole.

"Really? Right here?" Victor asked.

"Look at that warm golden-brown flow. It's steaming in midair," Raymond replied.

"That's pretty dark. You need to hydrate more. Don't spray Darcy; he might shoot you in the back," Victor advised.

"This was your plan, remember? Would you prefer I use that tree over there? I could cartwheel all the way if you want me to compromise our OP on this quiet, boring morning."

This wasn't a horrible plan, but Raymond thought it was a bit of an overkill for a simple pickup. Hell, it'd be easy to simply roll in, set up a quick perimeter with overwatch, load up the PAX, then boogie on back to town before breakfast. Raymond was all for erring on the side of caution, but come on…the grass was wet, he was cold, and that appalling music was driving him insane.

"Contact, TRP Three," Victor whispered. "Four armed individuals in formation. Walking east to west. Range me."

"TRP Three is 450 yards at the road sign. No wind. Targets walking diagonally three miles per hour, half value. Aim lead edge. Can you ID them?" Raymond whispered.

"Negative. Appear to be dressed in blue jeans, black leather jackets, and vests. Some hats and do-rags," Victor replied.

"Are they our package?" Raymond asked with doubt.

"Don't know. Looks like a couple ponytails in the group; could be females. Can't tell from here. Darcy, do you have any movement back there?" Victor asked his rear-security man.

"Nothing but birds back here. A few Grays heading toward your boys a few minutes ago," Darcy reported.

"If these are our contacts, they're dumb as fuck. Why are they not at the electronics store already—or are they out for an early morning stroll? Maybe they went to grab the Sunday paper," Raymond commented while tracking them with his reticle. "Coming up on TRP Two. Three hundred yards at the brown-and-tan striped Torual's Taxi van."

■■

Inside the electronics store, Kevin, Stephan, and Gaylen were eager for a signal. They had assumed that the music playing in the distance since 0300 was some sort of diversion and that the Lake City team was already in town for them.

As soon as there was enough ambient light inside the store, they had their gear packed up and staged next to the front door. After an additional half hour of waiting and pacing, Kevin decided to curb his nerves with an MRE snack. Gaylen rinsed her hands and face with a bottle of water, trying to freshen up. Stephan continued to pace back and forth near the front store window.

"What time is it?" she asked again for the third time.

"Almost seven. I'm sure it'll be soon. You should sit down before you wear a hole in the floor."

Stephan ignored the comment and peered out the grime- and poster-covered window, looking for anything that signified the end of their long and painful journey. "Hey! I see people out there!" she shouted.

Right then, a huge explosion shook the entire building, causing hanging lights throughout the store to sway and ceiling tiles to fall, blanketing them in a cloud of dust. Knocked off her feet, Stephan stumbled forward, inadvertently ripping a poster off the window, smearing a clean streak in the grime. Catching her balance and righting herself, she stared out the window into the eyes of four lunatic members of the Houghton Lake biker gang.

Her eyes went wide. Before she could react, the leader raised his rifle and fired, shattering the window around her. She dove over a merchandise counter as the window fell into a million pieces, bullets raking across the shelving around and behind her. She hit the floor with a thud and went dizzy from a vicious pain resonating in her thigh. She tried to roll over and come up to her hands and knees to crawl away, but her leg gave out. Instinctively she reached down to hold the pain and felt a warm stickiness.

■■■

"Shit!" Victor said as his rifle flicked off safe and the trigger was pressed. The third member of the black-clad group had shouldered his rifle and maneuvered behind the lead member, who was shooting wildly into the electronics store. His head was quartered in Victor's reticle until it was split open the same time the rifle recoiled into his shoulder pocket. He absorbed the rifle's energy and slid the bolt back, ejecting a hot piece of brass into the chilled morning air; then he slid the bolt forward again, chambering a new round. He regained his sight picture to see the top of a head canoe'd just above the ponytail, spraying brain matter and pink mist all over the lead shooter.

About to engage his next target, a burst of full-auto gunfire erupted from inside the store. A vicious stream of tracers cut left and right into the bikers, who were diving for cover. Whoever was on the gun inside the store didn't let off the trigger at all, spraying a full two-hundred-round drum at the cyclic rate into the surrounding cars, pavement, and adjacent stores.

Raymond tracked the rear black-clad assailant, who took a protective position behind the tailgate of an abandoned truck that had been rusted out long before the Dark Day. Raymond paused for a split second, debating whether or not to shoot this asshole in the face through the tailgate. A 175-grain bullet could easily punch a hole right through the thin, rusted sheet metal, which would make for an epic headshot worthy of his memoirs. Instead, he aimed for the exposed knee on the pavement under the rear bumper. He preferred to watch his target's face as his soul escaped the physical body into the ether. Unfortunately, with a blown-out kneecap, the man was rolling on the street in pain, not giving Raymond the satisfaction. For the inconvenience, he put the next bullet through his intestines, sentencing this guy to a prolonged, miserable death.

■■■

Kevin slammed the Squad Automatic Weapon on top of the display case and squeezed the trigger. At this range, he didn't bother looking though the sights. He kept his head up with both eyes on the street before him as he traversed the stream of destruction back and forth. He wasn't certain if he'd hit any of the attackers as they dove for cover, but his goal was to give Stephan some cover to retreat to the rear of the store.

The machine gun bounced violently back and forth with a deafening barrage. With his peripheral vision, he watched the belt of ammo quickly getting shorter as hot brass and black links rained down on the filthy industrial carpet. To his right, he could see Stephan lying in a pool of blood. Kevin's mind instantly went from rage to fear. The gun stopped bouncing, and with ringing ears and through a cloud of gun smoke, he tossed the M249 across the floor. It tumbled and rolled to a stop next to the front door, at the same time Kevin reached down to grab Stephan by the arm and dragged her to safety while aiming his pistol out the shattered storefront window.

After a brief lull in the chaos, another firefight flared up in the street.

"Gaylen, grab the med bag!" Kevin shouted, struggling to hear his own voice, temporarily deaf from the machine gunfire in such a confined space. "Stephan, stay with me, girl!" he said, looking into her eyes filled with terror and pain. He went straight to the obvious injury first, cutting away her bloody pant leg as high as he could with trauma sheers.

Gaylen stood over Kevin with the medical bag and a look of complete horror. Kevin had his knee on Stephan's upper thigh, stopping circulation, and one hand pushing down on the wound as he poured a bottle of water over her leg, smearing the blood away. "Gaylen!" Kevin yelled at her. "Help me or get in the fight! I need a tourniquet and the Kerlix gauze out of the bag," he said as he held both hands down on the wound.

She dropped the bag down and unzipped it. "Here!" she said, tossing him a black Velcro strap. "What does the Kerlix look like?"

"It's white, like fine cheesecloth. Either in a roll or folded into squares. Open the package; my hands are wet," he instructed her. "OK, good. If there's any extra in the bag, open a couple more packages of them. Try not to lay them on the dirty floor. After that, try to find a blanket or dry clothes to wrap her in. She's losing blood, and we need to keep her warm."

Gaylen did as instructed, ignoring the gun battle happening just outside the store. Kevin leaned in close to Stephan. "This is going to hurt like a son of a bitch."

"It already does. Just do it!" Stephan said with a shaking whisper.

Gaylen helped him wrap the tourniquet high on Stephan's thigh, then twisted the windlass rod, tightening the strap around her leg until she cried out in pain. He lifted hand pressure off the wound just enough to start packing the thin gauze material into the wound channel. His index finger was too fat, dragging it out of the bullet hole and making a suction sound. Switching to his pinky finger, he stuffed an entire roll of gauze, one little pinch at a time, into the hole while Stephan cursed through gritted teeth.

He didn't let up. He packed another entire roll into the bullet hole until he couldn't pack anymore, then rolled her onto her side and did the same procedure to the exit wound on the back of her thigh. "I've got it packed. Going to wrap it with a pressure dressing to keep it in place. Bleeding's stopped, so I'm pretty sure it missed the artery, and I didn't feel any bone fragments in there. Good news: you'll survive to kick my butt later," he said with a smile and a wink, feeling a lot better about the situation.

He wrapped her leg with a dressing, then loosened the tourniquet windlass rod by one twist. "You've lost some blood. You'll probably be weak and lightheaded for a few days. I'm sure you're good to go for now, but we're treating for shock anyway." Kevin lifted her legs to prop them up on the shelving to reduce the blood flow to her leg and reroute more blood to her organs. Using a coat found in the manager's office, Gaylen wrapped her up, tucking it around her tightly.

While admiring his casualty-care handiwork and about to begin his secondary-patient assessment, he realized he'd failed the first step, which was to ensure the scene was safe. He was so focused on helping Stephan that he forgot about the danger around them. One casualty could have led to two or three—in all actuality, they all would have bled out, ending their journey right there and then.

This realization brought him back to the moment; situational awareness alerted him to the end of the firefight outside, leaving only the ringing in his ears. He grabbed his pistol and stood up at the same time shadowy figures started moving across the street, toward the store.

■■■

"Huh. That wasn't in your mission brief," Raymond said matter of factly.

"Cover us! Darcy, on me!" Victor jumped to his feet, bounding down the small hill, twisting his scope magnification to the lowest power and dialing elevation down to zero. Four men had walked in; he'd killed one, Raymond downed another, and the machine gunner from inside the store stitched one too. Only one more Tango to be dealt with. From the hill, Raymond had a clear line of site to the east. The west was clear for now. The only place for the last Tango to hide was the vehicle cluster between him and the electronics store.

Victor was peeking around the front corner of a purple minivan when the door mirror exploded, showering him with shards of mirror and fiberglass. He gritted his teeth, stepping back to the safety of the engine block as more shots whizzed passed. Victor reached up to his face, pulling a chunk of bloody mirror out of his cheek as Darcy stepped around him.

Darcy knelt low, extending his inward leg toward Victor like a kickstand for stabilization. He leaned out just enough for his rifle to clear the fender of the minivan and began sending rounds at the shooter.

Victor decided to go prone to shoot under the minivan. He spotted movement about five vehicles deep. A shiny steel-toed boot. He centered his reticle on the boot ankle and was about to squeeze the trigger when a volley of incoming bullets impacted the van's tires, dropping the frame by six inches and ruining Victor's shot. He didn't have enough clearance for bipods. He had to roll to his right side, lying on his shoulder on the pavement instead of his chest. Making a fist with his left hand planted on the rough asphalt, he rested his rifle sideways on top of his fist, giving him just enough clearance to make a shot.

Shooting sideways with a scoped rifle canted ninety degrees isn't as easy as lining up the sights and pulling the trigger. When you shoot normally, your reticle's vertical stadia line is aligned with the barrel. When sighted in for one hundred yards, the horizontal stadia line is adjusted for three hundred feet of gravitational bullet drop, plus mechanical offset of the scope height. So when you tilt your rifle sideways to make a tight clearance shot, the shooter must take into account that the crosshair stadia lines are now reversed. The windage turret is now for elevation, and the elevation turret is for windage. To make matters worse, the elevation adjustment needed to sight in your one-hundred-yard shot is no longer accounted for. Ultimately, without making any further adjustments, Victor knew that his shot was going to impact 4.5 inches left and 2.25 inches low.

Victor compensated by aiming high and to the right of the black-laced boot and squeezed the trigger. Not having the rifle properly seated in his shoulder and lack of stable front support allowed the rifle to jump, gouging the scope's ocular lens into his eyebrow and falling to the pavement. He didn't need to look through the scope to see the last Tango rolling around in agony under the line of cars.

Rolling to his back, he looked up at Darcy. "He's hit but very much still alive. Go finish him off, carefully." A moment later, a rapid five-round burst echoed through the automobile graveyard.

"All elements, this is SRT. Half time. I say again, half time. QRF, we need a ride off the field ASAP," Victor said into the yellow walkie-talkie.

"Roger that; QRF en route," Curtis replied.

"ERT, do you copy half time? ERT? Michael, Zavier, do you copy?"

Raymond and Darcy gathered by Victor outside the store. "Want me to go get 'em?" Raymond asked while reloading his rifle.

"No. Stick to the plan. Let's get the PAX loaded first," Victor said, pointing toward the store.

■■

"Detroit, are you in there? Lake City friendlies coming in," Victor shouted.

"Yes, we're in the back. Come quick, we have wounded!"

With his rifle slung over his shoulder and pistol drawn, Victor entered the electronic store prepared to counter an ambush. He spotted a tall blonde-haired woman and a short, stocky man with blood-covered hands near the back. "Sitrep?" he ordered.

He walked quickly toward them, surveying the store layout along the way. The shorter man introduced himself and gave him a situation report. "Stephan took a round to the leg. She lost about two and a half pints. Wound is packed and stable. She's conscious but needs a doctor, ASAP."

Victor rounded the aisle corner to see her lying on blood-covered carpet with feet elevated and an impressive wound dressing. "You did this?" he asked. Kevin nodded. "Great patient care. Did you loosen the tourniquet yet?"

"Yes, only once. No further bleeding."

"Should we change her bandage?" Gaylen asked.

"No!" Kevin, Victor, and Raymond said in unison. "First clot is the best clot. You don't want to risk breaking the clot until it's time to sew it up by a doctor. If it starts to bleed again, retighten the CAT and apply another pressure dressing on top of the first."

Victor stunned the group by handing Kevin his rifle and then kneeling down next to Stephan, placing a soft hand on her forehead. She reached up softly, then pulled another shard of broken mirror out of his cheek, causing a new stream of blood to drip down from his scruffy chin.

She looked up at him with wet eyes. A thick tear dripped down her dirty cheek, splashing onto the blood-soaked carpet. "What did you do to your handsome face?" she asked.

"Was trying to get cleaned up for our big date. I just cut myself shaving, is all."

She giggled a little, almost passing out from blood loss and exhaustion. "I really missed you," she said softly. She'd been waiting to say those words for months.

"I worried for you nonstop, wishing every day to see you come through the gates." Victor leaned down and kissed her heavily, forgetting to breathe. He lifted away with a dizzy head rush, returning the emotional smile. "I missed you too. Let's get you home, shall we?"

"What the hell?" Raymond spat. "We did all this for your girlfriend? Shit, I knew this mission was too extravagant for a simple pickup."

"I didn't know for sure who was out here, but I suspected. And girlfriend or not, she's the most knowledgeable virologist in the world. Kind of designates her as a high-value asset, wouldn't you agree?"

"I can vouch for that. She knows everything about the hybrid pathogen plaguing the world," Kevin added.

"Whatever. Let's wrap this up. I'm hungry." Raymond sneered, turning for the door.

They fashioned a makeshift litter to carry her on, then slid it into the back of Curtis's red pickup truck. Their supplies, the boxes of electronics Kevin had prepared, and their loot of biker-gang weapons were also loaded into the trucks.

Once they had congregated around the trucks, Victor announced, "Change of plans. Curtis, you drive Erica back to the high school; the med-clinic team should already be on standby. Drive fast but safely. Gaylen and Darcy, you go with them. Raymond, you have security in the back of the truck. Do you know how to stick an IV?"

"Yup, used to give them to myself in the field all the time. IV bags hydrate better than water." Raymond grinned, happy to get to practice jabbing veins on live tissue.

"Good. Give Erica one on the way."

"Wait, wait, wait a minute. Who's this Erica person? That's Stephan," Kevin said, confused and looking around at everyone.

"One in the same, Leprechaun. I went by my middle name at the Detroit lab. Stupid alias protocols, remember?" she said with a light smile. "Vic, why are you not coming with us?" she asked as her smile faded into a frown.

"I'm sorry, my love, I hate to kiss and run. But Deputy Dembele, Kevin, and I need to go find the ERT team. Michael and Zavier. They're not answering radios. Something's wrong, but don't worry yourself; we'll be home soon."

"Contact!" Curtis yelled, then began to shoot rapidly over the hood of the truck to the north into a wave of Grays flooding through the streets like an infectious tsunami.

"Go! Go! Go!" Victor said, slapping the side of Curtis's old red pickup truck with one hand and unslinging his rifle with the other.

He began shooting into the wall of Grays while Curtis slammed on the gas, heading west toward Lake City. When the horde was only two blocks away, they jumped in the second truck and hauled ass south, hoping to draw the Grays away from Michael and Zavier's area of operation.

GAME OVER

Would rather be playing video games

Zavier had been out hunting Grays at night with his family several times before, but he'd never seen so many clustered in one area like this. He and Michael had joked around, waging a brotherly bet on who would kill the most, but honestly seeing so many of the decrepit creatures gathered in the street below him was unnerving.

Zavier hoped that in a couple of minutes, Curtis's improvised explosive would kill them all, and he wouldn't have to fire a single shot. He was not going to get laughed at by his brother by saying that out loud, though. If his dad hadn't seemed so adamant about needing him, he would have asked to stay home this time. Killing Grays next to his dad was one thing; this was completely different. He trusted Michael, who was a pretty good shot—almost as good as he was—and they did have the two security guys to watch their backs, but having his dad next to him would make him feel much better.

Michael motioned to Grumpy and Deuce that they were about to kick off the mission. Zavier rearranged his equipment and his shooting position one last time. His rifle sat on bipods, resting near the edge of the flat graveled roof they were perched on. His other rifle—which his dad had called an AR pistol due to its very short barrel—sat next to his pack. Before the world had gone dark, he used to shoot similar guns, but they were smaller, lighter rimfires. Since the dawn of the superbeast with armored skin, his dad upgraded him to 5.56 for both guns. These were a little bit heavier, but the bigger, faster bullets did the trick on the Grays, and having suppressors was pretty cool too.

He watched the road flare sprout a bright-red flame three hundred yards down the street, giving off a long wisp of slowly drifting smoke. To his right, Michael aimed at the propane tanks and fired. Zavier had been ready to start shooting every remaining Gray still standing, starting close and then working his way out. His extra rifle mags were laid out neatly in a row for quick reloads. Pulling his favorite MTC hat down low shaded his scope, giving him a nice crisp sight picture.

What he wasn't ready for was the enormous explosion that brought down half the village block. They could only guess that what happened was three months of rotting and decaying organic materials had gathered in the sewers, fermenting massive methane pockets, creating a subterranean shape charge that had been ignited by Curtis's bait bomb.

As soon as Michael pulled the trigger, the roof heaved violently, then gave way, sending them into a free fall. The front of the two-story bridal store caved in, causing the entire building to collapse forward at an angle. Before Zavier could cry out, he hit the roof as it came crashing to a forty-five-degree angle. Dust and debris filled the air, stinging his eyes, so he squeezed them shut tightly as he rolled and slid on the falling roof gravel until his tumble came to an abrupt painful stop on solid ground.

Remarkably, his gear landed tangled-up on the sidewalk next to him. In a daze, he picked up his dust-covered pack and swatted the dirt off it. Hanging off the pack was his yellow walkie-talkie, completely smashed. Looking down, he saw his rifle snapped in two. *Ohhh, man. I'm going to be in so much trouble,* he thought, holding a broken stock in one hand and a bent barrel in the other. Next to that, his shorty AR pistol looked to be in good shape.

Zavier covered his mouth and coughed, looking around the rubble at his feet and finally coming to the understanding that the building had fallen down. Just like a snow globe, the thick dust cloud surrounding him slowly began to settle. Resembling a horror movie scene, the image of his brother lying facedown in a pile of loose debris came into view, emerging out of dense fog only five feet away.

Zavier pulled and tossed away chunks of brick and rubble until he was finally able to roll his brother over. Michael's eyes were closed, and he wasn't moving. Zavier began to panic, not knowing what to do, trying to remember what his dad had taught him about emergency first aid. *Stop the bleeding with pressure*, his dad had always preached. He looked over his brother; there didn't seem to be any bleeding. What else did Dad always say? Breathing. Thirty and two. Thirty chest compressions and two breaths. Even in this moment, terrified his brother was dying, the thought of locking lips with him made him shiver. Zavier moved his face to Michael's and was happy to feel his warm breath on his cheek. He sighed in relief; he wouldn't have to lock lips with his brother, but why wouldn't he wake up?

An eruption of gunfire echoed in the distance toward the east, and his relief turned to confusion again. Who was shooting and at what? Now he began to worry that his dad was in trouble too. A thousand thoughts and images went through his imaginative mind, and none of them were good.

Zavier's eyes went wide and his stomach flopped when a moan came from behind him. He jumped up with his rifle, suddenly remembering just a moment ago that there were hundreds of Grays in the street. Zavier looked through the thick dusty haze, inspecting the rubble pile composed of half roof, half storefront. The moan was getting louder. Not wanting to leave Michael, he had to wait for the dust to clear. Starting to get nervous again, his heart began to drum. He reached down to shake his brother's shoulder.

"Michael. Michael. Michael," he said in a loud whisper while shaking his shoulder. "Wake up. Michael, wake up."

The moaning behind him was getting louder. Zavier started to get scared. He looked around frantically. The air around the building was clearing. He could start to make out shapes in the rubble. A large metal dented square, maybe an air conditioner or air filtration box of sorts, was in the middle of the pile. Something odd drew Zavier in to give it a closer look. The big metal box was sitting on something familiar. The longer he squinted, the more clearly he could see through the haze, looking at the wreckage until he realized it was a squished human under the big metal box—one of his security guys.

Zavier gasped, pulling in a lungful of dust. He took an unintentional step back, tripping over his brother. The moan was louder now, almost a cry. "Michael, wake up. Michael, I need you," Zavier yelled, shaking his brother. There was a new sound in the air. Not of moaning or crashing bricks settling into position. It was a growl. A low bark. The sound of Grays. Zavier studied the dust-filled street, straining to see past the sidewalk he'd landed on.

A Gray came darting out of the haze. Zavier shouldered his shorty rifle and fired into the creature, putting three rounds into its upper chest and one final round into its ugly face as it landed with a thud beside him. Zavier turned to find the moaning that had turned into a painful cry. It was Grumpy; his legs were pinned under a slab of concrete.

"Help me!" Grumpy pleaded.

But looking at the size of the concrete, Zavier knew he'd never be able to lift it.

Another Gray charged in. Zavier ventilated that one as well. The more Grumpy cried out, the more Grays came. The more Zavier shot, the more they came. "Michael!" Zavier cried, reaching down and slapping his face, trying to wake him up. He knelt over his brother in a protective straddle. In between gunfire bursts, he screamed for Michael to wake up, slapping him harder.

"Shut up!" he yelled at Grumpy. He knew the man was in pain, but the sound of a wounded human was drawing the Grays in faster than he could shoot. Zavier was reaching a level of fear he'd never experienced before: a fear for his brother, a fear of not knowing what to do, and a fear of being bitten by a Gray, not to mention his dad was also in trouble. A sinister thought briefly came to mind as he turned around, pointing his rifle at the wounded man, his uncommitted finger hovering outside the trigger guard. But instead of silencing Grumpy, he climbed up the rubble to him and handed him a rifle that had landed just beyond his reach. "We need to fight them off!" Zavier said, pointing down the street.

The scenery of the village street had changed dramatically from a few minutes ago: Every building on the right side of the street had completely collapsed. Cars had been flipped over and were now on fire, spewing thick black smoke into the sky. Where the storm drains had once been were now huge smoldering craters. The road was completely unidentifiable.

He slid back down to his brother and gripped his shirt, attempting to drag him, but being only eight years old, he didn't have the strength. He was budging him only an inch at a time when two more beasts charged through the dust. Zavier emptied his magazine into one, made the fastest reload of his life, and put five rounds into the second before the empty mag fell, bouncing off Michael's face.

"Ow. That hurt. Get off me, squirt."

"Michael, you're awake!" he cried out with tears streaking down his dirt-covered face. "We need to go. Now. Can you get up?"

Michael slowly rolled over, coming up to his knees, then fell over again, his head swimming with confusion and vertigo. Zavier was in continuous engagement, firing back and forth, shifting left and right, finding one sprinting target after another. Like horde waves on a video game, the Grays kept coming, faster and thicker. This was one game Zavier didn't want to play to the end.

On his hands and knees, Michael dug his own rifle out of the rubble, using it to help himself up. Standing on wobbly legs, his vision cleared as he grasped the severity of the situation they were in. "Zavier, we need to go!" He grabbed his little brother by the backpack and started tugging him backward up the inclined fractured roof.

"Reloading!" Zavier yelled, running up to where Grumpy was pinned.

"Go, kids, get out of here! I'll cover you!"

"What? Wait. No, we have to dig you out!" Zavier said, blasting another Gray.

"You can't. Even if you could free me, my legs are broken," Grumpy yelled. "Give me another mag, and you boys get moving!"

"Z, he's right!" Michael said, shaking his head with wide eyes. "We need to go right now!"

Down the street between the blown-out buildings, Grays were pulling themselves out from beneath the rubble. There were at least a hundred shapes taking form in the dust cloud that floated between the huge wreckage piles.

Grumpy had started shooting into the incoming mass of Grays as Z and Michael quickly climbed up the rubble pile. Michael stood at the edge, rubbed his eyes as he tried to focus through a fog of dizziness, and then leapt across a deep gap, landing on the roof of a one-story building. Right behind his brother, Zavier also made the leap, then turned around to see Grumpy load the last mag into his rifle as the swarm was almost upon him. Zavier's conscience was torn; they couldn't leave him like that. Michael yanked Zavier's arm, pulling him toward the fire escape, and screams of pain echoed off the surrounding buildings as Grumpy was attacked by hundreds of infected teeth.

■■

Sliding down handrails had always been fun, until today. Zavier landed hard in the alley, almost stumbling into a trash can. He looked left, then right. "Let's go!" he yelled to Michael, who was still coming down the fire-escape stairs. He obviously hadn't recovered fully from being unconscious.

Zavier grabbed his hand. "This way, hurry!"

Stealth had always been their best defense, but right now they needed speed and diversions. While running at full speed toward the end of the alley, Zavier reached down, swiping up a couple of loose rocks. His brother, stumbling to catch up, suddenly stopped, quickly looking both ways for a clearing as he spewed into the crossroad. Z took his slingshot out of his back pocket, loaded a rock, and sent it flying high down the alleyway. Just as Michael had caught up to him, Grays began spilling off the rooftops. They had been spotted, but some of them went the opposite direction as the rock projectile bounced off several dumpsters and trash cans.

Michael raised his rifle to shoot, but Zavier pulled him toward the sidewalk. "Come on, we need to run!" At the next alley, they changed direction, hoping to lose the pack, and continued to zigzag through streets and alleyways, changing direction several more times as Zavier continued launching rocks behind them, hoping to hit a window, trash can, or anything that would make a clatter.

Michael kept coughing up dust and blowing snot rockets out his nose, but he must have been feeling better, because he finally began to outpace his little brother. They were exhausted; their lungs were on fire, burning with every gasp of air; their muscles ached and threatened to cramp, yet they kept running as fast as they could. If they hard pointed in a building too soon, they would have been swarmed by Grays. It only takes one nearby creature to spot you sneaking into a hiding spot to ruin it. After several blocks of changing directions, they seemed to have lost the swarm.

Noticing an open front door to a house across the street, Zavier pointed and ran straight for it, bounding up all five porch steps at once. They ran down a musty hall with their rifles up, ready to blast anything that jumped out at them. They rounded a corner into a foul kitchen, then opened a sliding door into the back yard. Michael sprinted across the backyard to the tall wood-plank privacy fence. He squatted down with his back against the fence and clasped his cupped hands in front of him.

"I'll give you a boost. Hurry!" he said.

Zavier put one foot into his brother's cupped hands as he lifted him by standing upright and thrusting his hands upward at the same time. Zavier almost flew over the wall, but he grabbed hold of the top just in time to steady his fall. Michael chicken-winged the top of the fence, flopped a leg over, then rolled, landing on the other side.

"Up there!" Zavier said, pointing toward a backyard tree house. "We'll be off the ground and will be able to see what's coming."

They quickly climbed the rickety wooden ladder—ignoring the "Zeke and Julie's tree house: STAY OUT!" sign—up through a tight hole in the floor, quietly shut the hatch, and then collapsed in the safety of a ten-foot-high tree house. Zavier looked around while lying on the floor, breathing heavily. It was probably the coolest fort he'd ever seen. He felt a sense of security being elevated, and it had a feeling of familiarity that reminded him of his old tree fort back home. But at the moment, he didn't enjoy the tree house. He only wanted to go home.

■■

"We need to figure out were we are," Michael said after a few minutes of catching their breaths.

"What happened back there?"

"I don't know. I shot the propane tanks. Next thing I know, you're on top of me. My face hurts; did you slap me?" Michael asked, holding his jaw.

"I was really scared, Michael. They're dead. They're both dead. And I thought you were dead too," Zavier said, looking down, beginning to sob deeply. "I almost shot Grumpy because he wouldn't be quiet. I tried to drag you, but you're too heavy. I thought we were going to get bit and turn into monsters. They got Grumpy in the end. Maybe I should have shot him."

"Grumpy is a hero. He saved us. And so are you," Michael said, trying to comfort his brother.

Zavier surprised Michael by hugging him. For the first time in their lives, they embraced each other in a heartfelt, emotional hug.

"I was so scared, Michael. And Dad's in trouble too. I heard a firefight over in that direction. Maybe we should go that way to find them. I really want to go home." Zavier sniffled.

"Dad said to stick to the plan no matter what. And what was the most important part of the plan?" Michael asked.

"That we take care of each other and come home safe."

"And that's what you did for me. And we're going to stick to the plan just like he told us to. I lost my stuff, and your radio is busted. That means we initiate Plan B. When Dad doesn't reach us on the radio and we're not at the pick-up point, he'll know we're escaping and evading. We stick to Plan B so we can get home."

"OK. But which way do we go?"

Michael sat up, then slowly raised his head over the windowsill until he could see out. He pulled a small compass out of his cargo pocket, shook it, tapped the lens, and put it away. "OK, if we're not at the coffee shop, we're supposed to go to the gas station, but we know there's a hundred Grays in a hunting frenzy back that way, so I vote we don't do that. That means we need to go all the way to the third pickup point on the west side of town."

"Yeah, it's the first farmhouse on Route 55 with a big yellow barn at the edge of the village," Zavier said helpfully.

"Correct. At the edge of this backyard, there's a stream running toward the west. Looks like we can use the stream bank to sneak most of the way there. What do you think?"

Zavier nodded his head.

"You didn't answer my question: Did you slap me?" Michael asked again.

Zavier wiped the tear streams and snot hanging from his nose away, then looked up with a guilty grin. "Maybe. Maybe a couple times. By the way, I won the bet. I get your dessert tonight."

"Not fair; I was unconscious."

"Doesn't matter. I shot more Grays than you did. A bet is a bet."

■■■

They hid in the tree house for another half an hour, looking out for Grays that could be heard howling through the streets. When Grays caught wind of or set their beady eyes on a human, they whipped themselves into a frenzy. Zavier and Michael had done just that, making this horde extremely dangerous. They took their time eating a couple of snacks that Zavier had brought in his backpack along with a bottle of orange-flavored water.

When it seemed to be clear, they slipped down from the tree house and scurried across the yard into the stream. Water flowed through the stream about shin-deep, making each step slow but quiet. If it had begun to rain, they'd be in trouble, because the steadily flowing stream had cut a head-high crevice into the soft soil, which if flooded, would be terribly hazardous.

For now, the shrub-lined crevice with sporadic clumps of trees provided perfect concealment for their escape. Zavier, with his AR, was walking point, and Michael, with only his bolt action, walked rear. They stopped often, whenever a strange noise was heard or when they crossed a clearing. The original plan had them linking up at the third pickup point right at dusk. Which meant they had all day to get there. No need to hurry.

Even by taking their time and having to low-crawl through the stream at some points where the ravine shallowed, they still made it to Route 55 by noon. The farmhouse was on the other side of the road, so they decided to slither through a slime-filled culvert instead of going over the road. They plopped out of the tube like turds into a toilet bowl, landing in a chest-deep marsh. Zavier's boots sank into the mud, causing him to lose balance and fall over into the nasty-smelling gunk. Michael lifted his foot, losing a shoe to the muck's suction.

On their elbows, they crawled free of the swamp mud onto solid ground. Looking back on Route 55, they could view the still-smoldering village. A simple walk in the park had turned into a nightmare. Zavier decided right then; he never wanted to visit this village again. He turned to face toward the farmhouse with its large yellow barn which had its big wooden doors open. Deep within the shadows was a familiar pickup truck waiting for them.

"Michael, look! They're here. Let's go!"

"Whoa, wait a minute. There could be Grays in the woods over there. Let's not just run out in the open and get ourselves tackled right before the end zone."

They took their time crossing the expansive front yard. Michael would walk slowly toward a tree, then kneel next to it, looking around. Once he established it was safe, Zavier would do the same thing, slowly leapfrogging forward. As they got closer, he noticed their dad in the hayloft covering them with his scoped rifle. When they finally made it inside, Victor came down to greet them. He walked up to them with sad, knowing eyes. He could sense what had happened, and his heart ached. He blamed himself for putting them in danger.

"Grumpy and Deuce?" he asked.

Michael shook his head. Zavier looked down.

Victor's eyes watered at the thought of what they had gone through. "I'm so sorry," he said, kneeling down and pulling them both in tight for a strong, long-lasting hug.

"It was really bad, Dad," Zavier whispered, his voice cracking.

"I know. Tonight, tell me everything that happened. OK?"

Zavier and Michael nodded, looking up at the other men stepping closer.

"We picked up the refugees. This is one of them; his name is Kevin."

"Nice to meet you, young men. You can call me Leprechaun if you'd like," he said shaking their mud-covered hands and not caring about the slimy mud.

"Guess what, boys? The Leprechaun granted us a magical wish. He's brought Erica to us. He's been with her on a very long journey all the way from Detroit!"

All the stress and turmoil of the day's chaotic events washed off their faces, replaced by great big smiles.

Zavier jumped into the back of the pickup truck. "Well, what are we standing around here for? Let's go!"

Баба-Яга

The motherland of milk and honey

Силы Специальных Операций operator Dragan Ilic had watched countless Amerikan broadcasts portraying California as a luxurious paradise of endless beaches, flawless women wearing scandalous bikinis, a variety of convertible sports cars on every street, never-ending sunshine, and warm weather. Even through a Kevlar-lined neoprene dive suit, he was deeply disappointed when he felt the coldness of the ocean around him. The six-man special operations team breached the surface simultaneously into the frigid night air with the same climate shock reaction.

"О, твою мать! Can we swim back down to the warm submarine?"

"Speak English, Potrovsky. Russia put us through years of linguist classes. Use it, you big ox," Captain Vassili chastised his man.

"Not quite the bath water I expected," Ilic agreed. "It's as if we're still in Siberia."

With chattering teeth, the team went to work, pulling each other into the inflatable rubber boat that had also ascended the silent aquatic depths from the P-650 special-purpose midget submarine. Ilic's teammate distributed weapons and night-vision devices from a large dry bag, which was then refilled with their dive fins and masks. Normally they'd take off and stow away the dive suits, too, so they could hit the beach running, but tonight they kept them on for warmth.

Ilic was scanning the horizon in all directions. While pointing off the starboard side, he nudged his team leader with a boot. "Land ho, Kapitán." A quick glance at a compass confirmed that the mountain mass jetting out of the water was their target. A wrist-worn waterproof GPS would be used along the way to guide them to their insertion point. After a nod to the coxswain, the motor purred to life, and they were on their way, propelled across gently rolling swells toward San Clemente Island.

The voyage across the sea during midnight boat raids usually gave way to daydreams while lying on the gunnel tube, bouncing up and down. However, tonight Ilic's mind was processing the magnitude of their mission. The United Nations had labeled it a humanitarian operation, the BBN referred to it as peacekeeping, but everyone knew that was *херня*. For the first time ever, Russian military was on Amerikan soil, uninvited. A *гребаное* invasion.

Dragan Ilic had been training his entire career for this moment. From when he was six months into his eighteen-month universal military obligation, he knew that he wanted something better. The regular army unit ranks of mandatory service conscripts were treated like the slaves they were. Daily degrading work details outweighed the occasional bare minimum of combat training, which none of the conscripted soldiers cared to do. Every excuse was made to leave. Desertion and insubordination had been constant occurrences.

When he had heard rumors of a new special operations command being formed in 2012, Ilic did everything possible to be at the tryouts, including bribing a unit commander with stolen vehicles from a sister battalion. Ilic lacked the commissioned rank and time in military service required by the special operations unit, but with pure determination and performance, he proved himself worthy. By the Spring of 2013, the new CCO unit was officially born, and he was in it. Their first task was to provide antiterrorism security for the Winter Olympic Games in Sochi.

When not deployed, he attended every military training course available, sometimes having to pay his own way. Dive school, airborne school, communications, leadership seminars, western language and culture classes, and then finally the coveted Spetsnaz sniper school.

His six-man team had been on numerous successful classified missions in Europe and along the southern Asian border. But never in a million years had he thought that Mother Russia would take the fight to the Yankees. The seemingly impossible thought made his pink frozen cheeks lift into a smile. Written in the history books thereafter, he would be part of the great reshaping of the world order.

Even though intentions of western domination were obvious, they still had to pretend to be the good guys. United Nations liaison officers were on the ground overseeing hundreds of Chinese relief workers—fake relief workers who were mostly Chinese army regulars awaiting orders, with battle equipment close by. That's why the amphibious midnight mission was covert—not for a surprise assault against the Americans but to avoid United Nations scrutiny.

Politics always slowed down progress, Ilic thought. He wondered why President Putin didn't dissolve the UN altogether; it's not like the UN had power or funding anymore without the west. *All for a show*, he concluded.

His helmet-mounted phosphor night-vision technology displayed the approaching rocky landmass in light shades of gray. The picture clarity was far more advanced than the older light-amplified green-filtered goggles. He hoped to recover working Amerikan military tech to compare and to take home as war trophies. The coxswain turned the boat slightly toward a small crescent-shaped beach now in view.

The team repositioned themselves in the rubber boat quickly while they rechecked gear and weapons. Slung across his back, Ilic had an Orsis T-5000, a bolt-action rifle built in Moscow. He chambered it in NATO 308. He chose to deploy with this rifle with the assumption NATO ammo would be easier to come by in Amerika. In his hands, sweeping the shoreline, he held a Vityaz-SN submachine gun. Ilic had never been so focused and alert.

After a massive swarm of infected crazies had overwhelmed the Russian and Chinese forces in San Francisco, the Fifth Red Banner Army Brigade needed to establish a new foothold. The San Clemente Island US Naval base would be a perfect location for a forward operating- and logistics base. That is if they could clear and hold it. But first, they needed to know who—or what—was occupying it. For forty-eight hours, they would conduct reconnaissance and surveillance around the main airfield, reporting to higher-ups every thirty minutes. They were briefed prior to expect former base workers, maybe some security staff, civilian refugees that fled the mainland to seek refuge, possible an island full of the cursed creatures or worse. The US Navy SEALs also used this base for training, which meant they could face a worthy adversary. It made no difference which they encountered, they would all be dealt with in the same permanent way. Hence the reason they were going in quietly, with no UN liaisons.

■■■

Novikov looked out a port window of the Mi8M transport helicopter. The morning sun had just crested over a mountain range on the mainland to the east, giving fresh light to the quickly approaching island. The squadron pilots did them a favor and lapped the 147-square-kilometer island, giving them a full inflight tour of the old dirt airstrip centered on the island, a fairly large barracks facility, and an urban training area. From the air, nothing seemed to be alive on the surface.

White-capped waves crashed against the rocky western shore. Vegetation seemed sparse, revealing a more arid, rockier terrain than he'd imagined the advertised southern California "paradise" would be. On the island's northern tip was a long paved airstrip flanked by several buildings, some of which were smoldering with tall, thick plumes of blackened smoke.

As the pilot straightened the helicopter out on final approach, the ground around the airfield came into better view. The pilot favored one side of the airstrip, away from the piles of debris, toward a clearing marked by a tired-looking special forces operator. The wheels touched down on the flight line, bounced once, and then the back ramp dropped, inviting them to disembark.

As quickly as the helo's rear ramp dropped, Novikov's platoon jumped out onto the tarmac, avoiding the tail rotor, and formed 360-security around the bird while fighting against the rotor downwash. As their ride lifted off, the thumping of the helo blades fading into the distance, they were left to take in an horrific sight: the piles of debris littering the airfield were mangled human corpses.

The company and platoon commanders stood in a group with one of the CCO operators, who pointed here and there. With a quick salute, the meeting was over and the infantry mission began.

The airfield compound was divided into quadrants; each platoon would do a detailed search of their designated quadrant to look for anyone—or anything—breathing. Afterward, they would rotate to the next to research the quadrant the other platoon had just searched. While looking for survivors, any valuable, useable, or just plain interesting Amerikan equipment was to be logged for further inspection.

After the airfield was searched without finding a living soul, Novikov's platoon began fortifying the airfield and running security patrols. The other platoons took off on foot to search the rest of the island. Nobody went within ten meters of the dead lying piled about in fear of infection. There had been an estimated three hundred personnel on this island, and it appeared that they were all dead and rotting before him. Novikov prayed he wouldn't be on that cleanup detail.

The next wave for transport helos brought another platoon of soldiers, an entire helicopter full of men in white hazmat suits, and a small group of clean-cut, sunglasses-wearing civilians with matching jackets. *GRU intelligence services*, Novikov thought.

Oddly, the spooks didn't meet with the unit commanders. They glanced around to get their bearings, then walked straight toward a large concrete building as if they knew exactly what they were looking for. It wasn't until they found it locked that they talked to the company commander for assistance. After several hours of cutting and grinding, they finally opened the massive metal doors to expose an ammo supply point completely full of every type of ordinance in the US naval inventory, from bullets to cruise missiles. Jackpot.

After that treasure box had been opened, the spooks took aim toward a round metal-roofed building the size of an airplane hangar, with the logo of an eagle holding a trident above the large overhead door. The CCO operators were protecting the entrance. It seemed that they had wanted to loot the Amerikan SEAL team's warehouse more than the spooks did.

■■■

The next morning, Ilic sat overlooking a bluff, staring across the ocean toward the mainland. Several ships were parked off the island coast now: a battleship, an aircraft carrier, a refueling ship, a hospital ship, a couple of cargo ships full of shipping containers, and a submerged submarine he knew was patrolling around the island. By the end of the day, the engineers would have generators running and power grids and waterlines working. Within a couple of days, this place would be fully functioning to support their "peacekeeping" efforts, he thought while scrutinizing a smoldering mass grave at the ocean's edge.

Ilic scratched his scruffy chin, took a swig of coffee, and lit a cigarette. He started daydreaming about the Amerikan tactical dune buggy they had found in the hangar. As soon as he cleaned himself up, he'd take that thing for a joyride around the island—as a security patrol, of course. Ilic was just about to stand up when an army regular sat down next to him with a field ration in hand.

"Morning," the young soldier said, shifting comfortably into position. He peered down the bluff toward the pile of burnt bodies. "Is that your handy work?"

Ilic was used to vaguely blowing off questions about his classified missions, so he just took another swig of coffee, ignoring the soldier.

"Were all of them infected?"

Normally he would tell this kid to отвали, but Ilic liked his demeanor. Army regulars usually have an inferiority complex about themselves around special operators and would immediately begin blabbing, trying to explain how they were going to do spec ops, but didn't because [fill in the blank] with whatever lame-ass excuse. Sad and annoying. That went double for the mandatory service conscripts. But those киски were all deployed to the phony Middle East stabilization effort, where NATO was doing the heavy lifting.

This kid next to him held his head up high and talked straight with him, aggressive almost. He wasn't there by mandatory service. Only volunteers who reenlisted were honored with this campaign. Maybe it was the weight of the mission, a bond all of them could share. Those who could later in life proudly say that they were *there*. They were there, conquering the savage lands of Amerika, reshaping the world.

"Probably most of them were cursed," Ilic answered coldly. "Hard to tell at night, while you're stacking them up by the moonlight."

"That's brutal."

"Needed to be done. Won't be the last time," Ilic answered, but he was thinking more about the missions to come.

"What's next? Where are you off to now that this rock is secured?" asked the soldier.

"We've only been here a day; I wouldn't call it secured," Ilic said, dodging the direct operational-security question the soldier should have known better than to ask. "We'll probably deploy somewhere else on the coast to gain another foothold, then start working our way east toward the Rockies."

The soldier licked his spoon clean, nodding his head, envisioning a long bloody road ahead of them. Even with the cargo freighters full of troops and logistics floating in every day, taming this land would be more difficult than when the English settlers had arrived here a couple hundred years ago. He stuck the empty ration container in his cargo-pant pocket and reached over to shake Ilic's hand. "My name's Novikov. Good luck out there."

Ilic took his hand firmly. "You, too, Novikov. Watch your back."

Before Novikov could get to his feet, a form darted from the bushes like a Баба-Яга, tackling him hard to the ground. A ball of entangled bodies rolled over the edge and onto a ledge five meters below, landing with screams of pain and rage.

Ilic jumped to his feet, unslung his submachine gun, and aimed over the edge. He couldn't shoot without hitting Novikov. Normally he'd casually shoot them both dead without a care, but he liked this kid. He slung his weapon over his shoulder and jumped, landed hard, and punched the attacker in the back of the head with no effect. He punched and punched again, pulled his diving knife from its sheath, then drove the blade up to the hilt through its neck and then pulled back until he scraped against vertebrae.

Breathing heavily, with a moan, Novikov heaved the attacker off him, rolling it to the side. Ilic offered him a gore-covered hand to help him up. Both soaked in dark-grayish blood, they stared into the pinpoint pupils of the twitching attacker, who continued to claw at the ground to get them, even with a ripped-out, gurgling throat.

■■

Two days later, after many heated protests, engaging in hand-to-hand fighting while resisting physical restraints, and then eventually getting knocked unconscious and subdued by GRU spooks, Ilic and Novikov both sat in a grungy locked stateroom aboard a freighter ship heading north up the coast of California.

"This is хуйня! There's a submarine right out there, escorting this ship with my team on it!" Dragan Ilic shouted. "I'm not infected. Are you infected?"

He didn't wait for Novikov to answer as he paced back and forth in the small, cramped living quarters, yelling at the secured heavy metal hatch. He had spent a lot of time on ships, even submarines, without a problem, but the confined dingy stateroom, that smelled of a stale mop bucket, was making him claustrophobic. No porthole to look out of, no television, no books. Same as all sea-bearing vessels, every piece of furniture was secured to the deck or bulkhead to avoid shifting during high seas.

Ilic felt as if he were going mad. There was no way he would allow them to pull him from the historic operation. That particular mission was the climactic reward for weeks, months, and years of pain and suffering. To be yanked from him, after one day on the ground, was insulting; the military may as well end his life and get it over with! He wondered if his team would still getting missions now that it was down a man and not at full strength. Probably only shitty, low-risk overwatch missions, all because of him. He felt disgraceful, a dishonor to the CCO and to his brothers.

Novikov understood his comrade's frustrations. Leaving the battle for an illness was always laughed upon. A sign of weakness. Even if the sick soldier returned to full duty, they were to be made fun of. Something else stirred in Novikov: Not fear of being a coward or weak, but of getting sick. A fear of turning into the cursed. He could feel it in him. Crawling on his skin. Cramping his stomach. Eating away at his memory. He was feeling the exhaustion set in but couldn't fall to sleep. If he was infected, then so was Ilic.

"Maybe if we play nice and show them that we're not infected, they'll let us out of here and return us to duty?" Novikov offered, in an attempt to calm his roommate.

Ilic's mind slipped for a moment, forgetting why he was locked in the stateroom to begin with. The comment brought him back to the moment. A sliver of paranoid skepticism crept in. "They suspect that we're infected," he agreed. "So why didn't they kill us on the spot? Why lock us in here?"

"I'm infantry. Besides the airborne training, my position is easily replaceable. But you? How much time, money, and resources did Russia spend on you? They want to make sure you're infected before discarding a valuable resource. I'm just lucky to be your acquaintance," Novikov acknowledged.

"You're a pretty bright kid. When we get out of here, you should find a better job in this military," Ilic complimented, yet in his foggy mind, he envisioned scalpels and needles puncturing his skin while he was tied down on a cold metal table being experimented on. He needed a plan to get out of the stateroom and then off the freighter so he could get back to his team.

■■■

Novikov's mind was swimming, trying to remember details of his home and family. Even recent memories were fragmented. "Were you at the San Francisco port?" he asked Ilic, receiving only a negative headshake. Trying to hold onto a thought, Novikov began to talk out loud, attempting to piece together what had happened.

"My company replaced a unit who first secured the seaport. The war planners in Moscow picked San Francisco as the first Amerikan landing zone because of the political climate. We know that Yankees love their guns and would fight against any foreigners, but California had strict laws prohibiting personal ownership, and the population of San Francisco had been completely unarmed by choice. Headquarters expected little resistance, only the typical food riots and sporadic disorderly misconduct from the indigenous, but nothing that would require deadly force.

"The aid workers, attached to armed security patrols, ventured into the urban and industrialized areas around the docks. They had found an entire warehouse full of people—sick, dying, and some already dead from disease and malnutrition. The warehouse had been divided up by blankets and cardboard-like indoor slum shanties. There was some sort of whacked-out zealous leader that kept them all locked up inside using fear as control. The aid workers attempted to get some of the sick to come back to the hospital ship for treatment, but none of them would leave the security of the warehouse in fear of monsters.

"A day later, we encountered some of the psychotic crazies the warehouse people feared. We employed riot gear, tear gas, rubber bullets, the usual. Soon after that, the local regulars who crowded the port entrance every day no longer seem interested in medical care or rations. Mobs became more and more aggressive, even attacking each other.

"A week into it, our barricades couldn't hold them back any longer. Chain-link fences toppled over from the mass. The people didn't look right—not like malnutrition but savage looking. Tear gas and batons had no effect, but they weren't armed, so the rules of engagement prohibited us from doing much more. A directional-sound cannon was used, but it only made the crowd more aggressive. They swarmed toward us, pushing us back down the pier toward the ships. More and more kept coming; the streets were packed with them, shoulder to shoulder, sidewalk to sidewalk. Without provocation, they charged at us. Stampeding. Trampling their own.

"The yelling and screaming was so loud I couldn't think. One of our younger soldiers got scared and let an AK burst rip into the crowd. Fear and confusion set in, thinking that the crowd was shooting at us. And then it happened. Carnage. We slaughtered hundreds, and they kept pouring down through the city streets toward us. The commanders didn't call cease-fire. Just the opposite. They ordered the machine guns on the ship to cover our retreat. A dozen PKM machine guns swept back and forth, into the unarmed mob that continued to charge forward in a barrage of death.

"I don't know if I was afraid or sick to my stomach watching a massacre of thousands right before my eyes…" Novikov trailed off. "I was prepared to fight the mighty Amerikan army, but I was not prepared for that. Nobody was. The UN liaisons were as afraid as we were. They didn't say a word during the massacre."

Novikov continued, "I think that you might be right. They know we're infected, and we're going to be lab rats to be experimented on to figure out what this cursed disease is. Knowing the GRU intelligence services, they'll weaponize it against the Persians."

"Well, if we're going to get out of here, we need to do it quick. Once we reach Washington, this freighter is heading west into open waters without the rest," Ilic said.

"What? Why? How do you know that?"

"This freighter we are on is empty. It's returning to Russia to pick up another infantry battalion. The submarine that is escorting us right now is stopping in Seattle. Whidbey Island, Naval Air Station was my team's next objective to secure. Whidbey Island is the next foothold. We need to be off this freighter before then," Ilic instructed.

Later that day—evening time, they presumed—the heavy metal hatch cracked open slightly, just enough to slide in a couple of field rations and bottles of water. Instead of attacking the door, which Ilic knew was chained to prevent them from escaping, he simply took the items provided. "Thanks, comrades. Could you let us know how much longer we're to be quarantined? It's *гребаное* boring in here."

A muffled voice replied, "The doctor will examine you tomorrow for symptoms. Sit tight." A man in a white hazmat suit peered through the narrow opening.

Ilic nodded his thanks as the door shut and the locking mechanism engaged. Hidden next to the door, Novikov held the jagged metal leg of a broken chair, ready to stab and slash his way to freedom. Ilic looked into his beady eyes and shook his head. "Next time, friend. Next time we're getting out of here before they dissect us for science."

They tore open the field rations, looking for anything usable to enable an escape. As sleep and hunger avoided them, neither of them ate or slept.

■ ■

Ilic could hear them coming. Whatever damage his eardrums had suffered from years of gunfights and explosions had been repaired by the virus. Rubber soles of the Hazmat suit squeaked against the linoleum-tiled floor, and the soldier's boots thumped heavily as they approached through the long passageway.

The locking mechanism on the outside disengaged with a *clank*, and the heavy metal hatch cracked open with a groan. Their morning rations and water bottles slid into the stateroom as they had the day before.

"Comrade. Comrade," Ilic whispered through the crack. "We have a plumbing problem. The toilet's broke, and I can't seem to fix it. Could you ask your boss to move us to a different room, please?"

A hazmat mask peered through the crack. Ilic turned his face to prohibit the man from seeing his constricting pupils. He motioned with a hand toward water on the deck.

"Turn on the lights," the man ordered.

"I would, but my friend is sleeping," Ilic said in a hushed tone, motioning toward the bunkbed, where a lump was covered in a thick gray wool blanket. Ilic fought the urge to reach through the door to choke this guy.

The man in the hazmat suit shifted his head to inspect the bed, then slid out of view.

"Step back, away from the door. Turn around and put your forehead against the wall," the soldier commanded. Ilic complied.

The chain was lifted, and the steel hatch opened fully. Ilic sucked in a silent, excited breath through his teeth. The soldier stepped in and placed the muzzle of an AK47 into Ilic's back. "Do not move."

The light bleeding into the darkened stateroom from the passageway shifted as the man in the hazmat suit entered to inspect the restroom. Sloshing through the puddled water, he peered down into the overflowing toilet to see plastic ration packaging clogging the drain. Before he could comprehend the problem, Novikov, hidden in the shower stall, hit the man across the back of his head with the broken chair leg. The sound made a sickening crunch, and his limp body fell backward into the stateroom.

The escort soldier tensed, shifted his eyes briefly from Ilic to the fallen white suit. Before the soldier could react, Ilic spun 180 degrees, palm struck the AK47 to the side with his left hand, and punched the guard in the face with so much force it lifted him off his feet. Ilic was on him again before he landed. With two hands, he lifted the soldier's head, then slammed it against the deck, knocking him unconscious.

Ilic didn't want to kill the soldier, with whom he felt a military brotherhood bond. He felt sorry for injuring the man, but he had stood in his way to freedom. An alien command took control over him. He took the soldier's arm, lifted the sleeve, and sank his teeth into the flesh until he tasted blood. Confused by his own actions, he turned to find Novikov doing the same thing through the hazmat suit.

They locked the two men inside the stateroom before fleeing down the passageway. They didn't know where they were, but they knew where they wanted to be: topside.

Ilic looked above a broom-closet door at a small metal plate that read "03-20-4." Every compartment on a ship is marked with a coordinate designator. The first set of numbers lets you know what deck level you are on. The second set was a reference to the frame location in relation to the front of the ship. And the third, depending on whether it was even or odd, referred to either port- or starboard side of the vessel.

"Come on," Ilic whispered as he descended down a set of steep stairs. They needed to go down two more decks before reaching the main level. Just before they rounded a corner at the end of a narrow passageway, Novikov grabbed Ilic, stopping him and pulling him pack against the bulkhead. "Get ready," Novikov whispered, right before three ship workers rounded the corner and walked right into them.

Ilic couldn't recall his mother's name, the school he attended as a child, or even what year it currently was, but his Systema martial arts training flowed through him with perfect clarity. His own speed and strength surprised him as he punched, grabbed, gouged, applied pressure to joints, and bit into flesh in a whirlwind of combat. He didn't feel the pain of the blow that slipped through, his muscles didn't feel fatigued. Maybe the disease in them wasn't a curse, but a blessing. Ilic felt more lethal than ever before.

Novikov had never been taught or practiced advanced hand-to-hand combat, yet he parried and countered punches with ease. His blocks and strikes flowed like wind through branches in a tree. Barely breathing heavily, with a face covered in blood, he glanced behind him to Ilic, who held an unconscious man in a standing choke hold with his teeth buried in his victim's collar.

The two-man team of terror continued toward the main deck, pacifying eight more ship workers and armed soldiers along the way. The thought of arming themselves with the dropped weapons never entered their minds. They charged through the last hatch into blinding sunlight that warmed their pale, sticky skin and fresh air that filled their nostrils with the smell of the salty sea. The lack of shipping containers piled high across the deck verified that Ilic had been correct in assuming this freighter was empty. Off the starboard side to the east, the Amerikan coastline was close enough to make out details of beaches and small buildings. Off the portside was the vast open sea, all the way to the horizon.

Novikov found a few orange life preservers, offering Ilic a couple. But Ilic gazed out into the open, empty sea, searching for something invisible. Ilic was supposed to do something. Go somewhere? Meet with someone? But he couldn't remember.

"There's an inflatable life raft; let's go!" Novikov insisted while he tugged on his stationary friend.

As Ilic stared out at the open sea, he heard and felt a deep muffled drum, followed by a shockwave that rippled across the water's surface until it hit the freighter, causing them both to take an involuntary step back to catch their balance on the nonskid deck. Not too far off the portside, a massive bubble of fire, smoke, steam, and spray erupted that shot a hundred meter geyser into the air.

The freighter sirens blared. Red lights flashed. The captain began to steer away from the subsurface explosion with evasive maneuvering. Watching the fireball rise and roll up from the ocean surface, Ilic remembered. He remembered his CCO special operations force team in a P-650 special-purpose midget submarine. Had they just been destroyed? Ilic couldn't comprehend what had happened.

He turned and ran to catch up with Novikov, who had just tossed a life-raft pod over the edge and was preparing to jump. Ilic leapt over the railing past him, crossed his arms over his chest, and tilted his head back, waiting for the twenty-meter freefall to come to a swift, watery stop.

By the time Ilic resurfaced to find Novikov and a small bright-orange rubber raft, the thoughts of his prior teammates and a blown-up submarine had been erased from his memory as the prion continued to deteriorate his brain.

They both looked upward at the massive gray-colored shipping freighter named "Amherst Islander" passing by, as huge wakes threatened to tip over the tiny raft. They were relieved to have escaped the pending torture of being lab rats, pleased to realize that, by the time the freighter reached Russia, most of—if not all—the crew would be cursed.

Novikov handed him an oar, and they both began to paddle toward the mainland, to a place where they could be predators once again and continue their conquering mission.

HOMECOMING

A time for gathering and celebration

The muffled sound of gunfire woke Erica in a panic. She sat upright quickly, inducing a rush of dizziness that made her stomach queasy. Her vision came into focus, and she could then see Victor sitting in a chair next to her bed. At the foot of her bed, sitting on the clean, tiled floor, were Zavier, Michael, and Curtis, playing a card game. The small room had a hospital-type feel to it, but she couldn't remember Lake City having a hospital or even a doctor's office.

"Were those gunshots?" she said, a little woozy, laying her head back down and wincing at the sharp pain from her leg wound.

"Yes, don't worry about it, though. The guards on the wall are taking care of a small group of Grays. How are you feeling?" Victor asked concerned

The children dropped their cards on the floor, jumping up to see Erica. Curtis and Michael kept a comfortable distance, knowing that she had been injured, but Zavier dove right in and gave her a big strong hug, which she accepted and returned.

"It's so good to see you boys. I feel like I am dreaming. Where are we?" she asked after Zavier finally released her from his clutches.

"High school nurses' station. We've transformed the adjacent rooms into our designated infirmary. Mostly for elderly patients. Some cuts and bruises to fix periodically, but you're our first trauma patient." Victor explained.

"How long have I been out?" Erica winced, attempting to sit up.

"A couple of days. You lost a lot of blood," Victor said, glancing toward her leg bandage. "You'll be interested in the other wing of the school that is being used for biological research."

"Really?" she said, not quite believing him or the capacities of a small town to conduct any sort of substantial research.

"Really; our medical team has made some extraordinary discoveries. With your help, maybe all the pieces can be put together to paint us a clearer picture of what this disease is. But that all can wait until after you've healed up. The boys and I want to hear all about your journey over the past few months."

"'Few months'? What month is it, anyway?"

"Mid-October. You've been on the road for a while."

"I *wish* we had been on the road. It was more like a cross-country hike through hell." Erica went on to tell her captivated audience about her dangerous adventure, starting on the day the lights went out until their linkup. Victor wrote in a notebook, occasionally asking questions about specific occurrences he felt needed to be retold to the Town Defense Force. "We had to leave behind an extraordinary man near Houghton Lake. He had a military vehicle full of supplies. If possible, we should go back for it."

"Already did. Kevin told me about it. After we rendezvoused with the boys, we brought it back to town with us using the winch as a tow cable. We off-loaded the hardware, and the mechanics are working on the radiator problem right now. They think it'll be an easy fix if you all didn't overheat the engine too bad." Victor shrugged.

"Lt. Murphy?" Erica asked with sadness in her eyes.

Victor only shook his head. When they had retrieved the Hummer, a small rowboat was anchored in the middle of the pond. With no signs of him, they assumed he'd taken his own life after spending his last day doing what he loved most.

After she concluded with her retrospective account of their bloody linkup story, Victor quickly highlighted their most noteworthy experiences. Knowing she was tired, he cut his stories short so she could rest.

"Please don't leave me," she pleaded, her eyes slowly opening and closing from exhaustion.

"Get some rest, my love. I need to go check on a few projects. You're in a safe place here; don't worry. I'll come by later with dinner. As soon as Doc says your stitches are stable, we'll get you home. You'll love the house we picked out for you." He kissed her forehead softly.

"Can I stay here with Erica?" Zavier asked.

"I would love that," she said as her heart swelled with warmth, healthy and full of love again.

"OK, little man, but please let her rest," Victor said, tousling Zavier's hair on the way out.

■■■

Victor decided to walk back to the TDF building to grab his gear before heading out to check on the perimeter improvement projects Raymond was managing. Glancing toward the choppy lake and thinking that the fishermen in small boats were probably having a difficult day, he noticed something different: three tall antenna-type towers had been erected and secured to the park pavilion. Attached to the top of these towers were large rotating fan blades of various sizes.

Intrigued, he walked in that direction to get a closer look. One of the town's mechanics and an electrician were running wires and tightening bolts when Victor reached the base of the tower. "What do you think, boss? We're using alternators pulled from a semi, a pickup truck, and a small sedan. The windmill blades were made of different materials as an experiment. We built the different models to test our theories. If any of these actually produce electricity, we can easily replicate the best windmill with all the spare parts lying around."

"That's quite impressive. Any conclusions yet?"

"Well, you're here just in time," the mechanic said, reaching to the picnic table to retrieve a head-light assembly, which probably came off a cannibalized scrap vehicle that had been stripped down to make the windmills. The electrician carefully held the stripped ends of the descending wire. When they touched the wire to the headlight, it flickered, then came to life. With high fives and back slaps, they congratulated each other. After successfully testing all three windmills, the two men began debating again on which design was better and how to best use the energy.

Victor left them to enjoy their creation. Walking down the street were a couple of older gentlemen he recognized as farm tractor operators. "Hi, guys. What's happening?" Victor asked the joyous men.

"We have some fantastic news for the council. You're not going to believe our luck. Earlier at the distribution center, we were prepping more shipping containers to pull into town for the wall when we found a couple too heavy to lift. Canned goods! Packed full of food that was in transit to a grocery store somewhere. We spent all morning dispersing the pallets into a manageable transportation weight. Our container-wagon train is parked out by the south gate right now with enough supplies to last us at least a few weeks, if not months!"

Victor couldn't believe it. The undernourished citizens had been rationing food for so long that there was not a single overweight person in this small town. Starving to death during the winter was their biggest fear, even more so than Grays or marauder attacks. The container could be full of cat food and he'd still have been happy. Lost for words and almost becoming emotional, Victor could only shake their hands in triumph for the magnificent find.

Lost in a euphoric daydream, Victor strolled toward the wall. He climbed up to the elevated GP9 position, greeted the guard, and then started walking along the shipping-container tops to where the improvement work was being conducted. He was surprised to see Curtis on top of the wall. "What brings you out here?" Victor asked.

"I have an idea to help with defensive fortifications. I came to ask Raymond his opinion before I begin implementation."

"Oh, yeah?" Victor said, raising an eyebrow. "Care to share?"

"It's a surprise. You'll have to wait until it's done," Curtis teased.

"Huh. You know I hate waiting and can't stand not knowing a secret. Speaking of which, my birthday is coming up. Did you get me a present?" Victor poked his son.

"I wouldn't tell you if I did."

"You're no fun," Victor said, joking with his son. "Are you staying up here? I'm going to go down to give those guys a hand for a while. Could you cover us while you are contemplating my birthday present?"

Victor swung a leg over the edge of the wall and spider-dropped only a couple of feet to the soft ground below. He picked up a lonely machete and began helping the working party by chopping down tall thin poplar-tree saplings.

"It's about time you showed up and did some work," Raymond commented deprecatingly.

"Oh, please!" Victor rebutted. "I don't see a tool in your hand. Not a sweat stain on you."

"Someone has to wear the white hat. Keep these slackers on track," Raymond argued back. There weren't too many people brave enough to argue back with the rugged Raymond. After several years of likeminded military service, Victor understood Raymond's dry sense of humor. Most of the time, when Raymond made a rude or derogatory remark, Victor knew he was secretly hoping someone would fire insults right back at him.

"Where are you placing all these punji sticks?" Victor asked, swinging his machete.

"Anywhere around the wall that doesn't offer substantial standoff distance. If I were to attack this place, I'd use those abandoned buildings and thick vegetation to mask my movement, to get as close as possible, without being detected. I'm guessing the Grays do the same. That is where we're placing the impaling stakes. At night, the beasts and raiders will run right into them."

"It should definitely help," Victor agreed.

"We'll see," Raymond said, unconvincingly. "It can't hurt to try."

■■

"Hi, handsome. I thought that you were bringing me some dinner?" Erica asked with a rumbling belly as Victor entered her makeshift hospital room.

"I brought you something better. This fancy, shiny wheelchair that matches those beautiful sparkling eyes of yours," Victor said with a wink.

"Diarrhea! You two are gross," Zavier said, making a fake gagging motion.

Victor smiled at them both. "Doc said that your stitches are looking good, with no signs of infection. So you can get out of here, but only if you behave and don't try standing on it. He prescribed

Trioxin 2-4-5 to fight infection and some mild pain-management meds. Would you care to join me at the community dinner?"

The diner parking lot had a few new shipping containers, side by side, which Victor assumed held their new food supplies. Along with the town's miniscule winter surplus, these food containers would need to be carefully guarded at all times. He pushed Erica in her wheelchair to the end of a picnic table where Curtis and Michael had saved them a seat. They ate a light meal made up of diluted vegetable-beef stew and a cornmeal-type of bread while casually talking. Glancing up from his bowl, Victor sensed something was wrong.

Erica felt odd. She felt like she didn't belong there. After being alone in the woods with only Kevin for so long, the large crowd of people was overwhelming. She felt guilty for being clean, in new clothes, and eating a warm meal that she didn't have to forage for herself. Her back felt light without her backpack, but she felt comfort when feeling the cold metal of the pistol on her thigh. She didn't feel safe, and she glanced over her shoulder occasionally to check her six.

Victor startled her when he placed his hand on hers, looking into her uneasy eyes. "You are safe here. Tomorrow, I'll show you the security measures we have put in place. We all play a part here, and so will you. All these people need you and your knowledge." Victor comforted her, seeing right through her anxiety. He'd returned home from countless deployments overseas, feeling the same apprehension.

Mrs. Cloud, sitting at the next table, was describing to Sheriff Bohner a bizarre scene they had found at the jail a couple of days prior. Victor and Erica turned their heads to better hear the conversation.

Someone had been in the holding area. A crowbar was found on the floor along with a pile of ashes, which they had assumed to be from the missing blackout curtain. In the exposed holding cell was a deceased Gray. What happened, exactly, was unclear. However it was quite obvious that an unauthorized person had snuck into the jail and was now potentially infected inside the town. They needed to brief the council at tonight's meeting.

Erica looked to Victor as if she wanted to say something, but instead, she quietly took in and analyzed the information. She'd get more answers soon enough.

Afterward, as the sun began to set, Victor wheeled Erica across the street to Art's new communication station that had been gradually upgraded to offer soft LED lighting, cozy paintings on the wall, and several chairs. The entire town council was seated, plus essential department heads.

The low murmur in the room quieted immediately when Art unplugged his headphones from the tabletop HAM Radio and turned up the speaker box.

■■

"Good evening. This is Elizabeth Corrin bringing you another BBN global news report.

"Parliament has announced that fuel rationing will be discontinued after this weekend. The energy crisis has been thwarted while middle eastern regions begin to stabilize as Russian military focus on providing security for OPEC production. The league of Arabs is rumored to be drafting a multinational cease-fire declaration of surrender.

"Simultaneously, the IMF and World Bank declared BRICS currency has stabilized, as eighty-five percent of the world's nations are currently invested in the BRICS monetary system with gold reserves or natural resources.

"Humanity is ending one historic atrocity only to face another. The viral pathogen plaguing the Americas has crossed the Panamanian-quarantine barricade, forcing Brazil to evacuate continuity of government officials to Cuba. Likewise, South Africa is rumored to follow suit, as the World Health Organization is reporting major outbreaks quickly spreading throughout Sudan, Ethiopia, Kenya, and Tanzania. The WHO and BRICS alliances have requested EU military forces to reposition across North Africa and to increase Mediterranean naval patrols to enforce the largest quarantine in human history.

"On the West Coast of the United States, Russian security forces now outnumber Chinese aid workers three to one, provoking questions from the United Nations security council regarding the BRICS peacekeeping strategies.

"Unofficial civilian reports from North America are describing unfathomable, hellish conditions, a complete social and government collapse, which beg the questions: where are the American Atlantic and Pacific naval fleets? And the unsolved mystery of US military forces disappearances in Japan, Afghanistan, Iraq, and Germany?

"Strategists suggest that some American military units disbanded, then blended into the local populations. There are reports from the Middle-East of rogue US special forces units fighting a guerrilla war against terrorists. Some American service members pledged their service to British and French commanders, while others suggest small pockets of deployed American military units are making their way home by any means possible.

"Now for some good news: Barcelona has agreed to challenge Chelsea Football Club at Wembley Stadium next week. Manchester United has demanded a rematch after a brutal loss."

■■

Jessica was quickly scribbling notes of the BBN broadcast so information could accurately be disseminated to the rest of the town. While the BBN news report was coming to an end, Art was preparing to broadcast the nightly Lake City beacon. Before he could begin, a faint voice broke through the static.

"Hello. Hello. Is anyone out there?"

Art tried to respond, then determined they did not have the transmitting power to reach whomever they were hearing.

"Hello. Hello. My name is Chase Carter. I'm hiding out in the broadcast room at the University of Oregon School of Journalism."

Another undecipherable voice seemed to respond to the first. Art continued to twist nobs, trying to tune them in.

"Listen, if you can hear me. I'm heading southeast toward someplace less populated. I left Seattle a few days ago, just in time too. The foreign-aid missions they speak of on the news are a complete fabrication. Russian planes are firebombing the city and those so-called Chinese humanitarians are mowing down infected crowds with machine guns. It's complete genocide there! Nowhere is safe; there is nobody to help us."

There was another unreadable, scrambled voice.

"Wyoming? Yeah, I could probably make that. Anywhere has to be better than here."

The transmission reception became worse, then eventually faded into static. Art pushed the talk button and began his daily script, notifying everyone of the town's defense, security, and ability to aid. For the first time, he also reported minor scientific findings of the pathogen and defensive strategies against the Grays. Immediately after signing out, a reply came through loud, clear, and feminine.

"Hey, neighbors. This is Mayor Madeleine Short, just north of your location. Listen, we're not interested in relocation or joining your community, but we'd like to set up a trade agreement with you. We don't have much, as I'm sure you don't either, but we are in need of a doctor to visit once in a while. We have elderly folks here that could use a checkup. What do you say?"

Art looked back at the council for advice. They all looked back and forth at each other, not knowing what to say. Even the mayor seemed taken aback.

Victor stood up and talked into the microphone. "Mayor Short, thank you for the opportunity to trade. Let us consult our council and get back with you tomorrow."

"You're welcome, neighbors. Also, be advised, the surrounding areas have become less friendly than usual. And I'm not referring to the damn zombies running around, if you catch my drift. Careful on the roads. The trouble could be spreading out toward your area."

"Thanks for the warning. We'll contact you this time tomorrow. WGON, out," Art concluded.

■■

Half the town had gathered around the lakeside pavilion to hear of the BBN news report from Jessica. She wondered if Art could wire up speakers from his radio receiver to the street so the population could hear the broadcast for themselves. At this time of year, the sun went down early, but with the windmill-powered battery bank, the LED lights around the pavilion offered a soothing glow that represented a hint of a rebound into modern civilization.

After the crowd dispersed, the nightly town council came to order. "Any idea who our neighbor on the radio is?" Victor asked.

"Madeleine Short is the mayor of Kalkaska." The mayor answered, then continued. "She's a good person. The town's about thirty miles north of here. I say that we hear what they have to trade; it can't hurt to form an alliance. I can't force anyone to go with me, though. It might be worth going to get more information on that threat she didn't want to elaborate more on."

"I agree. I will go with you, Mayor," said Sheriff Bohner. "Speaking of trading, some local Amish trotted up to the gate today in a horse and buggy. They also wanted to trade."

Everyone gave the sheriff an odd glance. "What did they want?"

"Strangely enough, guns. They wanted guns," said the sheriff.

"For what? I thought that they were a nonviolent society? Forbidden to do violence, even for self-protection?" Victor asked.

"Well, that's what I thought too. So I asked them, just out of curiosity. They have always kept rifles around their farms—not for protection but to shoot critters and pests in their crops. Apparently they no longer see late-stage Grays as human and now consider them pests who are killing their goats, cows, and even a horse. They're requesting more modern firepower in trade of produce and livestock."

Several eyes drifted toward Stanly, expecting him to say something condescending regarding the killing of the infected. Everyone under the pavilion all wanted to say, *See? Even the Amish have figured it out.*

But Stanly only sat quietly in the shadows, looking extremely pale and clammy, his eyes staring straight ahead.

Sheriff Bohner continued, "I told them to come back tomorrow."

Raymond stepped forward, posturing. "So whose guns are you going to trade? The only extra rifles you have lying around are the ones that I brought. Those are for town defense, and they happen to defend me while I sleep peacefully. They're not for religious nut-job farmers who barely know that we're in the apocalypse."

"Maybe instead of bartering with firepower, we trade the copious amounts of hair gel you obviously have a generous supply of?" Victor grinned.

"Let's not get carried away, now. And don't be envious that I can still look this good during Armageddon." Raymond rolled his shoulders and crossed his tattooed arms, noticeably flexing.

"We thank you for the supplies, which you negotiated fairly for the community use. This would be good for our town. The Amish are not a threat, and having livestock could mean more eggs, milk, butter, fresh meat if we're forced to slaughter, or breeding and trading young calves next year." The mayor argued.

"Yeah, whatever," Raymond said, stepping back to lean against a wooden pole, knowing the mayor had made a good argument. And besides, he had more firepower stashed away at his house in the woods by the river. His gaze lingered over Gaylen, who had cleaned up well since she had been rescued. She was dressed in a pair of jeans and a fluffy white winter coat, wearing a ponytail of sandy-blonde hair pulled through the back of a camouflaged baseball hat. He gave her a little wink that was returned with a flirty smile. "If you want their animals, we should just go take them. Those black-hat loonies will be dead or infected by spring anyway."

The mayor rolled his eyes, knowing that Raymond was only talking a big game because he wanted everyone to remember who provided the supply. "I say we make the guns-for-livestock trade. But limit the ammunition allotment to force them to come back for more trading. Any other objections?"

Breaking the long silence, Jessica asked those gathered around the table, "What's your take on the reports of the West Coast?"

"Troubling, Mrs. Holland." Victor paused. "Most troubling, indeed."

"Not much we can do about it from here," said the sheriff.

"Until the Russians and Chinese reach the Midwest, anyway; then we'll be needing those guns back from the Amish," Raymond said under his breath.

"Just another reason to reach out to the surrounding communities. If it's true, that the federal government—and most likely state governments have collapsed—that means this town and villages like ours need to band together quickly to avoid power vacuums. The absence of legally elected government has always given birth to brutal tyrants throughout history," the mayor lectured. "You never know. Maybe we could rebuild our society without a central government through free trade and open communication. That wouldn't be a horrible scenario."

"That's a good idea, Mayor," Victor agreed. "The communications part. When you go off to make trade agreements, take Art with you to look at their communication equipment. If more and more communities could pass information freely back and forth using HAM radios, improved antennas with repeaters, the rebuilding process would become much easier and faster."

■■■

"Wait, there are zombies in Kalkaska?" Zavier asked while curled up on the couch, snuggled into Erica's side under a thick quilted blanket.

"No, idiot, they meant the Grays." Sitting close to the fireplace, Michael made fun of his younger brother.

"You're the idiot. They said zombies, not Grays," Zavier argued back.

"Children, please! Out of everything we have just learned from the radio broadcast, you want to focus on what our neighbors called the infected?" Victor pleaded.

Ignoring their father, the debate continued. "Zombies are undead. Risen from the grave, and they shamble around moaning a lot with outstretched hands. Brain-dead souls, in search of living brains," Zavier explained.

"How about those movies that had sprinting infected crazy people who attacked everyone? Those were the best kinds of zombie movies," Curtis interjected.

"I hate that kind of zombie; they're scary and harder to shoot," Zavier said.

"Ophiocordyceps unilateralis, also known as the zombie spore, is part of the infectious hybrid pathogen in the Grays. So, technically, they are zombies. Just not in the traditional rotting undead sci-fi sense." Erica winked at Zavier.

"Zombie snipers of the apocalypse." Victor said jokingly.

"ZNIPERS" Zavier said grinning.

"Heck yeah!" Victor cheered, leaning over to fist bump with Zavier.

"You know, there were a lot of brain-dead zombies walking around before the Dark Day. Stumbling around with their face buried in a mobile phone, paying no attention to the world around them," Victor preached. "Or how about the brainwashed zombies that couldn't form a coherent original thought, the zombies who took emotional commands from mainstream propaganda on TV?"

"I miss my phone," Michael said sadly, missing the meaning to his dad's rant.

"I miss cartoons on TV," Zavier added.

"And I missed all of you, and I'm so very happy to be here. In this wonderful home. Listening to you bicker back and forth again. Just like old times," Erica said, smiling.

SILK ROAD

Trading of goods and services

Victor had just brought in an armload of chilled wood from the front porch and was carefully organizing logs into a perfect pattern inside the fireplace to reawaken the smoldering ambers when he heard a gentle knock on the door.

"Good morning, Victor. Is Erica awake yet?" Mrs. Cloud asked in a hushed tone as he slightly opened the door, keeping out the frigid morning air.

"Yes. Please come on in and out of the cold," Erica said from behind Victor.

"You're not supposed to be standing," Lawrence, the town's veterinarian, scolded Erica, then gave a sharp look to Victor, who only shrugged his shoulders, silently refusing responsibility of her stubbornness.

"Oh, please! I'm not completely crippled. I can hobble from bed to couch. But I could do it better if you brought me some of those pain relievers," she said with a subtle plea in her voice. "It's nice of you to come by for a house visit."

"Well, we wouldn't make you hobble yourself all the way up to the infirmary. Seriously, though, if you are not going to use the wheelchair, I'll splint your leg and give you crutches. Your damaged muscle tissue needs time to repair," Lawrence warned her.

Erica exaggerated an eye roll as she turned away from the veterinarian to find a younger Hispanic man. "Hello, I don't think we've met yet."

"Pleasure to meet you, ma'am. I'm Jake. I was an EMT on the Fire Department when the lights went out." The young man stepped forward, politely shaking Erica's hand.

"Well, as nice as it is to have company, I don't think your entire gang needed to come for a simple checkup?" Victor quizzed them.

Mrs. Cloud took a seat in the rocking chair next to the couch Erica had planted herself in. "If you are feeling up to it, could we discuss what you know of the outbreak?"

"Sure, I can tell you in great detail about the strain, as well as observations I have made in the field. But from what Victor has told me, you all have gathered some substantial materials yourself."

As the medical research group began discussing the hybrid pathogen, possible origins, and early symptoms to late stages with Erica, Victor hung a kettle in the fireplace to boil water and made tea for his guests. Most of their dialogue was outside his realm of understanding, but he stayed to listen, catching bits and pieces he could use for survival while outside the wall.

"So, in your opinion, a parasite, fungus, and prion are working as a singular unit?" Jake asked.

"Yes," Erica confirmed.

"But the Cordyceps fungi prefers insects with low immune systems. It doesn't target warm-blooded species," Lawrence argued.

Erica rebutted, "Each piece of the hybrid produces a specific symptom that is easily noticeable. But the Grays are a product of the combined effects. The prion destroys the human psychological and social part of the brain; the parasite alters the host for favorable conditions, including lowering the body temperature and protection; and the fungus takes control of the nervous system. Whether Ophiocordyceps unilateralis is supposed to attach to mammals or not doesn't change the fact that it is happening now."

"Yes, yes," Mrs. Cloud agreed. "Compared to a normal, healthy patient, all of our subjects have exhibited dangerously low core temperatures with extremely low resting heart rates."

Jake and Lawrence nodded their heads in agreement.

"There have been other physical changes to the infecteds' anatomies," Lawrence added. "Leishmania has eaten the flesh from around the first and second knuckle of each digit, enabling them to use sharp, bony fingers to grasp, claw, and scratch. Additionally, the tendons in their hands have become semipermanently restricted."

"Interesting observation," Erica noted. "Any theories on why this is happening?"

"I have a theory," Lawrence continued. "It was after we noticed their hands tightly curled into balls that we first thought they were in a fighting or defensive posture. But that was wrong. Instead, their fingers are now naturally clinched into fists, much like an owl's talons. With restricted ligaments, it takes physical effort for them to open their hands wide. After they clasp onto whatever it is they are grabbing, they relax their hands and will have a death grip on their prey with no effort or energy spent."

"That is terrifying!" Victor said from the doorway, truly shaken yet impressed by the lethality of the Grays.

"I would love a tour of your observation facility," Erica stated enthusiastically.

"Have you seen the tumors on their necks and heads?" Mrs. Cloud asked.

"At the lab in Detroit, we were shown pictures of a late-stage victim with a cantaloupe-size growth on the neck area. Then, just a few days ago, while I was in Houghton Lake, I observed a Gray within a horde with a large tumor. Maybe it was a week ago; I'm sorry, it was difficult to keep track of time out there."

"That's OK. We think the tumors are spore pods. Would you agree?" Lawrence asked.

"That would be a strong assumption," Erica agreed. "The early infectious stage spreads through bodily fluid, then it mutated to skin-to-skin contact. Spreading via airborne spores would be the next logical evolution mutation."

"In our observation area at the jail, inside a locked cell, we found a deceased subject with a neck wound. Our best guess is that an unauthorized person was in there, probably a junkie looking for meds. The intruder got too close, and the Gray's spore-tumor popped, infecting the victim through the bars. If they are infected with the same spore that controls—then kills—ants, it makes sense." Mrs. Cloud added.

"If the Gray died after releasing its spores, just like in the ants, then could the bursting tumor be the end of the lifecycle? Maybe these things will die off sooner than we originally thought?" Victor asked.

"We can't say." Erica looked down. "If we were dealing with any of the three elements separately, I could give an absolute answer. But this hybrid is far different from anything we have seen before. As soon as a host is contaminated with any virus, the strain goes to work, altering and adding genes to the human DNA sequence. That's not uncommon. Turning humans into those things out there…yeah, this hybrid is something far more advanced."

"Speaking of altering DNA and evolving, we have another question—a hypothesis," Lawrence said.

Mrs. Cloud glanced at him with a look of warning. Jake straightened in his chair anticipating the question to come. Even Victor picked up on their shifts in body language.

Lawrence went on: "With bodily deformities and the thickness of scabbed crustaceans, it is difficult to observe them in the wild, and admittedly, we mostly only cataloged infected killed at the wall or the few live subjects that Victor has captured...but we haven't seen an infected female in months."

Erica's eyes widened as she understood the implication of the statement. Her mind slipped, rewinding, remembering every encounter with a Gray over the past couple of months. How did she miss that detail? She was trained to study, catalog, and report the slightest of abnormalities.

She shook her head slowly. "Neither have I. They have all been males." Her mind began to hypothesize the meaning: *Is the lifecycle of females shorter than males? Are there packs of females, and if so, where are they? Is there a gender hierarchy among the Grays? Did the males kill the females, or are the females being protected?*

■■■

The conversation in Victor's living room went into overdrive. He could no longer keep up with the scientific terminology, chemical formulas, or the medical journal articles being referenced.

Victor attempted to intervene, suggesting that Erica should get some rest. The outcome was just the opposite. She demanded someone wheel her down to the lab so they could get to work immediately. He wanted to object, but he was happy to see the spark of life returned to her hardened eyes. She needed to be back in her element, to help the traumatic recovery of being in the field for months.

Stepping out onto the porch to go find the sheriff, Victor spotted Kevin walking up the sidewalk. He climbed down the stairs to shake his hand.

"I was just coming by to say hi and check in on Stephan—I mean, Erica. How's her leg?" Kevin asked, genuinely concerned.

"Oh, she's doing just fine. Keeping her off of the leg will be the hard part. You mentioned that you were in high-risk security before the lights went out?"

"Security at the lab wasn't all that high risk—not like running diplomatic missions in Kabul or anything," Kevin corrected.

"True, but you were a Cav Scout in the army, and you do know about physical security measures and emergency action plans. This town has an important position for you. That is, if you're willing to accept. How would you like to be in charge of our Town Defense Force?" Victor asked, putting a hand on Kevin's shoulder.

■■

The old red pickup truck slowly rolled around the corner and onto Main Street. Victor and Kevin burst into laughter at the sight of goats standing in the truck bed, looking over the roof, and Sheriff Bohner trying to steer with a dozen frenzied chickens inside the cab while a tethered cow trotted behind.

"Keep laughing, a-holes!" Sheriff Bohner yelled out the window as he passed.

Kevin slapped Victor on the shoulder, still laughing, "I guess he made a deal with the Amish folks. Looks like he made out fanta-a-a-astic," Kevin said, mimicking a goat.

They caught up with the truck at the TDF building, where farmers had relieved the sheriff of the animals being herded toward the fenced-in soccer field. Sheriff Bohner was swiping chicken feathers off his coat when he pointed a finger at Victor and Kevin. "Not a word, or I'll lock you both up," he said with a scowl.

"Congratulations on making the deal. You know that there are some dairy farms out near that Amish community. There's no way that they could manage that many cattle without modern equipment.

Maybe we could barter for a few milkers? Cheap even, I bet," Victor offered.

"Sure, fine. But you get livestock-transportation duty next time," the sheriff said with a grin.

"While you're here, I have news: Kevin agreed to take over as TDF commander, so I can go out on the rescue missions that are farther away. We had three new requests for relocation assistance come in yesterday."

"Good. Glad to have you on board, Kevin. Anyone that can survive out there as long as you did deserves the position. It's an important task, keeping the entire town safe." Sheriff Bohner shook Kevin's hand. "Speaking of the defense force, I'm going to borrow a few of the finest later. The council has decided to open up trade with Kalkaska to the north. See what they have to offer. The mayor and I will go on horseback, with escorts, up the railroad to avoid road bandits."

Victor approved. "Smart plan. Whatever was troubling the Kalkaska mayor, it must be serious. Let us know if we can help."

■■■

Victor spent a couple of hours showing Kevin around the TDF headquarters building, showing off the TDF armory and its capabilities, pointing out the location of all the guard posts, and describing their basic reactionary plan, which needed to be updated as the town expanded. Victor confessed that he hadn't been conducting as many security drills as they should have due to workloads and missions.

Afterward, Victor, Raymond, and a couple of recovery team members prepared to move out, using the two pickup trucks. As they checked weapons, gear, and radios, the diplomatic excursion trotted by on horseback. A pair of hunters went with them as guides, joined by a few protection team TDF guards; Sheriff Bohner was the authority figure, and the mayor served as the emissary.

Reaching into his saddlebag, the sheriff pulled out a couple of mason jars of Chad's corn whiskey. "We should be able to trade something for these." He smiled.

"If you don't drink it all on the way there," Raymond sniped as the caravan trotted by.

"All right, gents, of the three addresses for us to visit today, the family farthest away has children. I say we go there first. The closest family can wait till tomorrow if we don't get to them today." Victor eyed his crew. "Any bitches, moans, or complaints? Good, I didn't want to hear them anyway. Let's roll out."

The two-truck convoy headed out the town's south gate. As the gate slid open and they slowly rolled through, Victor spotted the town's newest security measure: three small cottages that had been rentals earlier in the summer. Structures that close to the perimeter wall had been a security risk and were almost burnt down by Raymond to provide a clear field of fire. But instead of burning down the little cozy cottages, they stacked more shipping containers around each house, creating individual quarantine zones for newcomers. The engineers argued that a chain-link fence would be far easier to build than shipping container emplacement, but Victor countered that it was the town's responsibility to protect and care for anyone placed in quarantine. Chain link was not a proper barrier from the occasional raider harassment.

The convoy turned west on Route 55 and then slowly traveled toward their first objective. As the sun peaked in the sky, the morning frost layer melted away, giving way to an unusually warm day. Taking advantage of the sun's warmth, Victor turned off the truck heater and opened the passenger window for some fresh air, catching a faint whiff of chimney smoke.

"They call it an Indian summer," Victor's driver, Roger, said. "You know, the last blast of warm air, right before we get slammed with snow?"

Looking out the open window at the windswept fields of dead, brown grass and the gray leafless trees that held fat squirrels, Victor agreed. Winter was almost upon them, which would bring new hardships and challenges with it.

The lead truck slowed, stopped, and then reversed into the driveway of a cobblestone farmhouse. Victor's truck did the same, parking side by side, both truck engines running, with the drivers' doors open for a quick getaway if needed.

Raymond flanked left around the house; his driver, Doug, flanked right out of sight. Roger stayed with the vehicles, watching the road as Victor casually stood fifty feet in front of the house with his rifle slung across his back, nonthreatening. This is the part Victor hated most. He stood there, completely vulnerable. His fate lay in the intentions of whoever occupied the house. Victor would rather fight off a horde of Grays than face nervous uncertainty.

The pickup trucks, still idling with rusted mufflers in the driveway, were not quiet by any means. If anyone was home, they were immediately aware of Victor and company's arrival. But they had yet to come out. Which meant that the occupants were deathly scared or deadly sly.

"Hello. Hello, we are from Lake City. You requested relocation assistance. You may come out; we have the area secured. There are no infected in sight," Victor yelled toward the house through cupped hands.

He spotted a window drape pull back briefly. His pulse accelerated. He fought the instinct to reach for his weapon and dive for cover. *Here it comes*, he thought. At that moment, he could be perceived as a heroic rescuer, then greeted with hugs and gifts. Or he could be easily gunned down for two running vehicles, weapons, and whatever supplies the ambushers assumed their victims had brought them. If Victor didn't get shot within the first five seconds, he took that as a sign of good luck.

The front door cracked open. A tall, skinny man wearing khakis, a flannel shirt, and eyeglasses poked his head out and looked around skittishly. Victor waved to him.

"Hello, sir, I'm Victor. I have perimeter security set around your house. How many travelers do you have today, and do you need assistance carrying luggage?" he asked, staring authoritatively into the man's eyes to establish the fact that Victor was in charge, and to surreptitiously inspect the man for constricting pupils.

"Hi, I'm Don. Thank you so much for coming. We had doubts. We lost our faith in humanity after our gardens were plucked clean last month by neighbors who we thought to be close friends. Then raiders tried to break in a couple weeks ago; they didn't care if we were home or not. They shot up the place, but luckily, cobblestone is mostly bulletproof. After that, they set fire to our car, just for fun." He pointed to a charred, gray four-door Volvo, the "S604OEW" on its license plate barely readable. "We were so relieved to hear your broadcast on the radio. Last week finally broke us; a tribe of crazed cannibals circled the house and demanded that we send out 'the young, tender children.' We refused, of course, but we had to eventually fight them off with steak knives, because we ran out of ammo months ago."

"'Tender children'? You mean they were for-real cannibals?" Victor asked, shocked. He'd heard story after story about raiders, some pillaging for supplies, others taking slaves. But this was the first report of cannibals! "Do you think that they really wanted your kids?'

"I thought it was just a scare tactic at first. But on the fourth day of siege, they strung a man up from that tree right there," he said, pointing toward a tall maple tree in his front yard. "They hung him by his feet, cut his throat, bled him out, and quartered him as if he were a deer. Some cooked limbs over a fire, others ate him raw. Listen, when I bring out my wife, Alice, she's still traumatized by it. She hasn't spoken a word since then. Bless you for coming for us."

Victor didn't know what to say. He stared at the maple tree, noticing a frayed yellow nylon rope swaying in the breeze. It gave him chills. "Get what you need from the house. Let's get you out of here."

"My kids, Tammy and Andy, don't have winter coats. Can they ride up front?" Don asked.

"Yeah, sure. Whatever. Let's make this quick." Victor couldn't imagine what the city council was going to say about cannibals. The thought of what the poor family had been through made him appreciate the security and safety of Lake City even more.

■■■

Sheriff Bohner and the mayor talked casually about town projects and the coming winter weather while rocking side to side in the saddle. "It's been many years since I've ridden a horse. My crotch is going to be sore tonight." The mayor winced.

"Don't expect me to rub that for you," Sheriff Bohner mocked him jokingly while scanning farther up the railroad tracks, where he knew the two hunters were scouting forward. "Look there, they must have found something." He motioned to the scouts riding toward them without haste.

When they finally regrouped and paused to hear what the hunter scouts had found, the TDF guards naturally pushed out security farther into the tree line in all directions.

"There's a house up there, just past the bend in the tracks. The owner would like to chat with you, sir. He didn't say if he wanted to trade or move into town, but he has beehives. Rows and rows of buzzing beehives!" the scout reported with a big smile.

The mayor immediately fantasized of all the uses for honey and honeycomb wax. An image appeared in his mind of getting his head stuck in a honeypot like Winnie the Pooh. The chefs at the town diner would be praised if they had sweetener to cook with. Morale in town would increase, which meant people would work harder on the long—and growing—list of priority work projects that needed to be completed before snowfall. He wouldn't admit to it, but he wondered if Crazy Chad could make mead, which would taste a whole lot better than his now-famous rocket-fuel whiskey.

■■■

"We're almost to our next stop," Victor told the young boy and girl sandwiched between him and Roger. "When we stop, I want you to stay in the vehicle. Do not get out. No matter what. If any shooting starts, get as low to the floor as possible. Roger here will drive you away to safety. OK?"

The big-brown-eyed dirty-faced kid nodded his head nervously.

"Don't worry. We don't find danger very often. You'll like it in Lake city; it's safe there. On Sundays, we have scavenger hunts and play short cartoon movies on the outside movie screen before dinner. Do you like cartoons?"

"Yes, sir," the girl, Tammy, said sheepishly.

"I have a son, just a little older than you. His name is Zavier. You and he can be friends. He likes to play cards and board games. Reads a lot, too, when he's not out hustling for cookies." Victor grinned.

Half an hour into their drive back to Lake City, turning down county roads riddled with potholes that had sprouted weeds, the lead truck finally slowed, stopped, and then reversed into another driveway. This time, Victor told Roger to park his truck closer to the road, away from the house.

As the truck stopped, Victor got out and circled around the back. "Stay in the bed of the truck. Don't get out," he told Alice and Don. Alice caught his eye, then quickly looked down, frightened. "We don't expect trouble, but you never know these days. If we start shooting, Roger is going to speed away, straight toward Lake City. I'll catch a ride in the second vehicle, OK?"

Victor's casual tone and composed demeanor, along with a selfless plan to safeguard her family, gave the mother confidence in her family's decision to relocate. She looked up with watery eyes and nodded a *thank you*, as Victor interpreted it.

Raymond and Doug flanked the small ranch-style house, as they had on previous rescues. For reasons unknown, Victor was hesitant to sling his rifle behind his back like he normally did when introducing himself to refugees. He shifted his gaze from the dirt-covered front porch, across the overgrown grass, to a small wooden shed with a leaning door hanging from a broken hinge. The nearby silent tree line was slowly scanned for movement. His eyes shifted back to the dormant house, then to Raymond, who looked back with a tilted head and pinched-together eyebrows. Raymond positioned himself for a better view of the entire backyard while stepping in closer to a large tree for cover. Something was off; they both felt it.

Instead of stepping into the open, Victor remained behind the truck for cover. "Hello. Hello, we are from Lake City. You requested relocation assistance. You may come out; we have the area secured. There are no infected in sight," Victor yelled toward the house through cupped hands as he had done so many times before.

The front door creaked open immediately, swinging all the way open, exposing a woman of average height with strong, full features. Her light-brown hair fell over her shoulders, and her clothes were relatively clean, an M4 strapped across her back. She walked toward Victor with confidence, without so much as a quick scan for Grays, when exiting the house.

Victor found it odd that the male of the group didn't present himself first. Instinctively, he took his eyes off the approaching woman to scan the tree line again.

"Hello, we've been expecting you. Thanks for coming," the woman said, shaking Victor's hand with a firm grip.

"Not a problem at all," Victor said, holding her hand. Looking past her toward the open front door, watching for movement. "How many PAX today?"

"Just two. I'll grab our stuff, if there's no special instruction for us?" she asked Victor, still gripping his hand and staring into his questioning eyes.

Victor released her hand, his analytical mind putting the pieces together. "How long have you been living here?" Victor pointed with his chin toward the house that had no signs of being lived in. Even lazy people these days would sweep their front porch off to avoid tracking in dirt that could no longer be vacuumed. Their flower beds, where most people planted vegetables, were overgrown, and there was not a family garden plot in sight.

"Oh, for a while," she said, seeming to avoid a specific answer. "We came across it while foraging, after the initial attack."

She stood straight, shoulders back, with a commanding presence. Mirroring Victor, her eyes glanced behind him, surveying their vehicles, the civilians in the truck, the man smartly providing security near the road. The woman was fit, not skinny or malnourished like so many of the other refugees. This woman was not defenseless, nor was she without supplies.

When she turned toward the house, Victor commanded her, "Tell your man to take his sights off me and come out of hiding, or I'll shoot you in the back before you reach the door."

She paused, turning slowly to face him again with a grin. "It was only a precaution. We don't know you."

"And I don't know you. Nor do I enjoy having guns pointed at me. We're not the bad guys here. You called us. Remember?"

She waved a signal toward the shed where her overwatch was hidden. The limp door pushed open, casting light into the shadows and revealing a stocky, bearded man in blue jeans and a green flannel shirt. In his gloved hands, gripped tight to his chest, he carried an M4 with an advanced-combat optic gunsight and attached suppressor. The burly man swung the door shut behind him softly.

With hardened, critical eyes, he also surveyed the rescue group. He gave a nod toward the woman. The big man strolled across the brown grass with an arrogant swagger. Almost to the truck, the bearded man's eyes went wide with rage when Victor raised his rifle at him.

"Contact!" Raymond yelled, right before he unloaded a full magazine into four Grays who had broken through a wall of thick pine trees.

"Move!" the flannel-wearing man yelled as he took a knee behind and offset to Raymond.

Raymond, already running past the newcomer toward the truck, loaded a new mag, thumbed the bolt release, pocketed the empty mag, and spun around to engage again. As soon as Raymond began firing into the next wave of Grays, the newcomer stood and took off in a sprint as well. Instead of running toward the truck, he darted off in the direction of the house.

Victor's truck, carrying the family of four, peeled out near the end of the driveway, creating a cloud of dust and road gravel. Victor noticed and smiled, pleased that Roger hadn't hesitated to follow procedure.

"They're leaving us!" the woman yelled over the gunfire.

"My driver's following SOP. Getting civilians to safety," Victor yelled in between a controlled burst.

Raymond's driver, Doug, was already behind the steering wheel. He gave three quick horn blast. "Get in, get in, get in!" Doug yelled out the window.

Gunfire and truck horns tended to attract Grays like bears to honey. Bearded flannel man burst through the front door of the house, carrying a large, overstuffed hiking backpack in each hand. Victor and the woman were already kneeling in the truck bed. Victor covered the left side of the house, she covered the right. Her shot tempo was smooth and controlled as she rested her rifle on the edge of the truck bed for stability.

"We're rolling; move your ass!" Raymond yelled, slamming the passenger door. The big man's thick legs landed heavily as he sprinted across the front yard with a swarm of infected closing in on him. He tossed the backpacks in, just missing Victor. The woman's rifle went empty, so she rolled to the front to get out of the way. The truck began rolling forward. Victor increased his shot tempo, hammer-pairing two rounds into the torso of each snarling Gray, attempting to slow down the advancement of horror. It was difficult to miss at that close of a range.

Hearing the deep gurgling growls, the big man turned and fired into the swarm on full auto, dumping an entire mag in less than two seconds, swatting back the first couple of rows of outstretched, scab-covered arms with talon-like digits that were lusting for healthy human flesh. He lowered his M4 to his side, controlling it with his left hand, while smoothly reaching for his pistol with his right. Before he could draw his pistol, Victor grabbed him by the shirt collar, jerking him onto the tailgate as the truck pitched forward.

Gaining speed up the driveway, they turned sharply onto the road, tossing them into the truck bedside wall. Still, the big man rolled onto his back, lifted into a crunch, and fired his pistol between his knees into the swarm of Grays spilling out of the driveway onto the road in pursuit.

"We're clear!" Victor yelled at the man who continued to shoot. "We're clear, save your damn ammo!" he yelled again, until the man's pistol slide locked to the rear on an empty magazine.

"Every one of those fuckers that we kill now will be one less that can attack us later on. We should go back there and exterminate all of them!" the bearded man said through gritted teeth and with fire in his eyes. He took the hand Victor offered to help pull him into a seated position.

Victor eyed both of them and their government-issued full-auto weapons. "Nice shooting. So if I had to guess, I'd say you're Army SF. Who are you with?" he yelled over the wind-weathered muffler and tire noise, staring at them coldly.

The two refugees looked at each other, then back to Victor. They each shrugged, refusing the question. "I'm Stacy Thomas. This big guy is Pete Cunningham. Thanks again for picking us up."

"Yeah, well, don't thank me yet. You get to sit in our quarantine for a few days before you're allowed into town. It's boring as hell in there. Maybe after a couple days of isolation, you'll tell me who you are and why you're really here." Victor glared at them, but he doubted the newcomers would give up information. These two had clearly been government trained, and Lake City's quarantine was far cozier than any SERE training.

■■

Days ago, Stanly had gotten himself infected. It was all Victor's fault. Victor, his mercenary goons, and the conspiring council's fault. They had never liked him, and he knew they been plotting against him since he'd been elected councilman three years ago. Stanly shook his head, trying to clear the fog of paranoia surrounding him. But, the longer he thought about it, the clearer it became. They'd tricked him into going into the jail that night. They had set him up, hoping the monsters would kill him without a witness.

He didn't know how much time he had left before turning into one of the horrid, ghoulish creatures he'd seen in the jailhouse, but he knew he didn't have long. His pupils were constricting, his skin was pale and clammy, black veins raced across his chest, and the only comprehensible memory he held tight was one of revenge.

The evening after he broke into the jail, Stanly's friends had come over for tea and gossip as they did every Sunday. It was then that he had begun building his army. A few drops of his saliva in the teapot and a few drops of blood mixed into the strawberry preserves would do the trick. Before his guests left for the evening, he made them promise to come back Wednesday for a special treat.

Three days gave him time for preparations. Time to put his plan in motion.

"Good evening, Stan. It's dark out here, may I go in? Oh my, you don't look so good. Are you feeling all right? Should I get a doc?"

Stanly greeted each of his returning guests on the front porch of his overtly modern home. The contemporary house had blocky architecture and drab colors that didn't fit the woodland theme of the northern town. As his guests stepped through the threshold, they fell through a spring-loaded trapdoor hidden under the entry throw rug and into a basement holding cell he'd built over the past couple of days. Stanly needed them together, secured in one place. He knew his enemy; he had witnessed how fast Victor and company would kill without conscious. Stanly couldn't beat them one on one, but collectively, his army had a chance for a successful coup.

The lustful thought of sinking his teeth into Victor made him twitch and tremor with pleasure. His fantasy expanded with visions of his obedient friends standing over bloody bodies of the entire wretched town council assembly. The time had come for Stanly to lead this town. The people would follow him, the council would follow him, the worthless mayor and soulless sheriff would follow him—they just didn't know it yet.

He'd give himself two more days until his evolving army would be ready to strike. Hoping to speed up the infection metamorphosis, Stanly went to the kitchen to prepare his imprisoned guests another tainted meal.

■■

Raymond leaned out the passenger-side window, his long black hair blowing over his face. "Are we going for the third objective?" he yelled back.

Victor waved forward. "Head back to town. We need to regroup and top off ammo," he yelled into the wind.

Raymond gave a thumbs-up, then tucked himself back inside the truck's cab, motioning to his driver to take the next left toward Lake City. A few minutes later, the southern vehicle entrance gate came into view. They stopped short, then pulled to the side where Roger had parked the other truck, waiting for them.

Victor gave the newcomers the in-brief. "If you want to join our community, you're to stay in quarantine for five days. You may keep your weapons if it makes you feel better. You'll receive clean water, food, and medical care while under protection. You may voluntarily leave at any time, but if you leave, you may never come back. Ever."

Both groups agreed and entered the individual isolated homes voluntarily. Locking the heavy quarantine gate behind them, Victor pushed the talk button on his radio. "TDF HQ, this is Victor. We have six PAX in quarantine bays alpha and bravo. How copy? Over."

"I'm glad that you're back early," Kevin's agitated voice came over the radio speaker loudly. "Make your way to the north gate ASAP. We have a major situation here."

COTERIE

Small groups. Big ideologies.

"Mayor Short, it's very nice to see you again," Sheriff Bohner said reaching down from atop his horse to shake her hand.

"Same to you, Sheriff, but please call me Madeline. Welcome to Kalkaska. Let's refuel your rides. There's a water tank and hay for them right over there by the old grain store." She pointed.

While the scouts tied up and tended to the horses, the rest were taken on a quick walking tour of downtown that ended at City Hall for tea and a warm cup of thick stew. The two mayors talked casually while Sheriff Bohner took mental notes of the town's layout and security—or lack of it.

They continued talking casually, but both were holding back strategic details about their towns' capabilities. Eventually, Sheriff Bohner opened up his bag and took out a clear jar of Crazy Chad's alcohol. "Give this a try, Madeline. It'll warm you right up on the coldest of nights. And by warm you up, I mean that you can burn it or drink it if you dare. We have a guy that makes it by the barrel. We mostly use it for fuel and medical sterilization. This is all we brought with us; it's yours, but we have a lot more to trade. We also have a medic who could come routinely for check-ups, a skilled radio operator who can boost your transmitting capabilities, and mechanics who are building windmills."

The simple statement must have broken through the trust levee, because the hours that followed were a flood of information and resource sharing. They learned a great deal, including that a similar trade route had been established already between Kalkaska and the great lakes peninsula urban area of Traverse City, which had an abundance of wine, cherries, and fresh-water fish.

They also learned that Kalkaska had turned their school gymnasium into the largest hydroponics and indoor fish farm they had ever seen. With the use of steam engines, they could grow and harvest fresh fish and vegetables all winter long. They had a strong chance of surviving the winter, if they could endure the region's newest deadly menace that was headed toward Lake City.

The Lake City emissaries would stay the night in Kalkaska, and begin their journey home in the morning.

■■■

Victor and Raymond drove through town at top speed. The old red truck came to a screeching halt at the northern gate, where they spotted Kevin in the overwatch guard post.

As they quickly jumped out of the truck, Kevin descended the ladder. "I think we have a problem here, boss," Kevin explained. "There's some guys out there dressed in army uniforms, with four up-armored HMMWVs and an eight-wheeled light-armored Stryker. They say that they are representing the US government with orders to stabilize the northern Michigan region. They asked to come in and speak to our mayor or whoever is in charge."

"Well, that sounds like great news. So what's the problem?" Raymond asked.

"Well, when Stephan—I mean, Erica—and I met Lieutenant Murphy near Houghton Lake, he informed us of a group of rogue Guardsmen at Camp Grayling who were exploiting small towns. Offering their protection services, for a fee of course. They'd make life difficult if a town refused," Kevin explained. "The group out there shows a lack of discipline. I'd bet these are the same goons."

"Wonderful. Just what we need right now." Victor scowled. He wondered if the two spooks that they had just brought into quarantine were related to this in any way. "Raymond, jump up in the guard tower and cover us. Kevin and I will go out to talk to them."

■ ■

"Good evening. This is Elizabeth Corrin bringing you another BBN global news report.

"The world celebrates. There is hope and promise that the war has finally come to an end, as the League of Arab Nations calls for an immediate cease-fire. European Union and BRICS are scrambling to draft a terms-of-surrender agreement. We will be bring you further updates as this story unfolds.

"In other news, the World Health Organization reports that the new viral strain, which is believed to have originated in North America, has spread all throughout Africa. The international refugee organization Hope 4 U has evacuated continental Africa and has relocated their headquarters to the Spanish Canary Islands. The WHO would not comment on rumored reports of infection in Germany."

■ ■

The next morning, Victor and Raymond relocated, without incident, the third couple who had requested their assistance. Victor was looking up, admiring the clear blue autumn sky while waiting for the mayor's group to return from their diplomatic mission. Victor caught a reflecting glint off something high in the sky. Curious as to what he was looking at, Raymond and Kevin looked up, shielding their eyes with cupped hands.

"It's circling. A plane maybe?" Kevin guessed.

"Hold on." Victor ran into the TDF building and ran right back out with his rifle. In the middle of the street, he laid on his back, pointing the rifle straight up at the UFO. "Yeah, it's definitely a plane of sorts." He zoomed in by turning the power adjustment near the ocular lens.

"Do Russians or Chinese have drones? It almost looks like a Predator or Reaper. Why is it circling Lake City?" Victor asked, puzzled.

"Maybe our radio broadcast has brought us some unwanted attention?" Raymond speculated.

"Does Camp Grayling have drones?" Kevin asked, looking a little troubled. "That group we sent away yesterday is probably planning their attack on us."

Victor shook his head. "I don't think Camp Grayling is a drone base, but they do have a runway. Did Lt. Murphy mention seeing any drones there?"

Kevin shook his head. "Nope, but he did say that he was the only pilot they had."

The sound of horse hooves broke their concentration.

"Assemble the council. We have much to address," the mayor said while trotting up Main Street. "We have good and bad news. There's an armed nuisance headed our way."

"Too late, Mayor. We already met them yesterday."

■■■

"Is this everyone?" the mayor looked around the picnic table under the pavilion. "Where's Stanly?"

"Who cares?" Raymond said with a yawn.

"All right, then, someone fill him in later. First, the good news: We have successfully opened trade with Kalkaska. In doing so, we now have access to trade with Traverse City, which is rich with cherries, grapes, wine, and fish." The mayor smiled. "The question is what do we have to barter with? Both Traverse City and Kalkaska desperately need ammo. Ammunition has become a precious metal, a new currency, if you will."

"Absolutely not!" Raymond roared. "Our ammo supplies are running low as it is. The couple reload presses that we have can't keep up with the ammo that's being expended defending the wall against the Grays, and we only have a limited amount of powder, primers, and bullets left."

"Surely we can find something else to trade with," Victor agreed. "How about Crazy Chad's whiskey or our windmill technology?"

"On our journey, we located a working apiary with more honey than they know what to do with," the mayor reported. "We found an abandoned home not too far away with an entire roof covered in solar panels. And we also found a loaded freight train on the KTX rail line. Surprisingly the conductor, Jung Suk-yong, was still on board, holding onto hope that someone was coming to fix his train."

"We brought him back with us, but he wasn't starving by any means if you catch my drift. There's a lot of food in those train cars, according to his manifest," Sheriff Bohner added.

"Surely we can barter with honey, solar panels, or whatever is on that train. We need to send a couple horse-and-wagon carts up there to start transporting goods back here before the snow falls," Jessica suggested.

"Now for that bad news: Kalkaska briefed us on a band of misfits with a bunch of military weapons and vehicles from Camp Grayling that are traveling from town to town, demanding taxes in form of supplies," Sheriff Bohner said. "Victor, you said that you met them yesterday?"

"Yup. Right outside the gate, and where their presumed leader, Sergeant Eddie Parks, pretty much implied the same thing. Protection of our city for a fee. I told them that we are already well defended against raiders and Grays, but the decision would be up to the council."

"What did they say?" Erica asked.

"Said they would be back in a week for a decision. But they got themselves a good look at our wall and defense. They know we don't need them. I'd expect a heavy attack within the next couple of days."

"What? Why would they do that?"

"A show of force and to instill fear. They have the weapons and vehicles to punch right though our wall. They'll show how vulnerable we are, then demand a tribute to avoid further attacks."

"I hope that's not the case. Let's hope that they come back next week peacefully," the mayor suggested.

"These are not peaceful people, Mayor. They're thugs doing thug shit in the absent of law and order. Them showing up at our gate at the same time as the spies and surveillance drone wasn't a coincidence."

"What spies?" asked Sheriff Bohner.

"A male and female we rescued yesterday. Although they didn't really need rescuing at all. They're both special operations of some sorts looking to get inside our town. Neither are talking, though," Victor said, pacing back and forth. "We need to deal with this Grayling group. It's not a situation that will just go away by ignoring it."

■ ■

The constant complaining and crying in Stanly's basement had finally subsided a day ago. His imprisoned guests squatted in the dark silently, aside from the occasional cough that sounded like a demonic bark. A platter of tainted food he had provided them several days ago now sat stale and soggy in the center of the holding cell. Their appetites waned, along with personal memories buried under a blanket of fog.

The pressure building behind Stanly's eyes felt like the worst sinus pressure he had ever had, yet the discomfort didn't hold his attention. He couldn't remember why he was down there in a cold, dark basement. An overwhelming sense of rage caused his muscles spasm and twitch, but the rage wasn't reserved for the unfamiliar souls caged before him. Stanly couldn't comprehend why he was tethered to the gate by a long string. He squatted in the dark, he rocked back on his heels watching the slack string go taut, then relax again as he rocked forward again. The string went taut each time he rocked back, the cage door-locking mechanism turned slightly.

Was he supposed to remain here to watch the cage? Was he supposed to open the gate? And if so, when? Was he waiting for a specific time? Maybe the memory would return. He should stay here a little bit longer, Stanly thought.

KILL OR BE KILLED

The best defense is a good offense.

The idea of a preemptive strike against an American military unit exploded into a fiery debate that did not end well. It seemed every person at the table had a difference in opinion and stormed off in a different direction. As Victor turned to leave the park pavilion, only Erica and the medical staff remained to discuss population statistics.

"Michigan has a population of ten million people. Of that, how many are still alive and healthy?" asked Mrs. Cloud.

"Doomsday preppers estimated only a ten percent survival rate after the first year of an EMP," Victor chimed in.

"But our situation is slightly different. Not only are we struggling against the crash of modern society but we are also facing a rapidly spreading virus," Erica stated.

"So would you estimate the survival rate to be lower than ten percent?" asked Mrs. Cloud.

"I would. Probably closer to three to five percent, which only leaves three- to five-hundred thousand healthy people in Michigan after the first year."

"To fight off nine and a half million Grays?" Victor asked as if the number was unfathomable.

Erica shook her head. "No. The majority of humans are still going to die off from the same hardships before being exposed to the virus. But the questions still remain: How many will survive the first year, how many will perish, and how many will get infected? I don't think we can accurately predict that."

"Any possibilities that humans have an innate immunity?" Mrs. Cloud asked.

"Anything is possible, but very improbable. Even with very contagious strains of Ebola, there is still a micropopulation that has a natural immunity. But this is an unknown hybrid. Alone, Leishmania is difficult to treat. The FFI has a one hundred percent mortality rate. And we have absolutely no idea of what the Ophiocordyceps spore is doing to us."

"So, in other words, we are screwed." Victor scoffed and then headed toward his house. After the hectic events over the past few days, on top of the preparation for the soon-to-come snowfall, he was beyond stressed and needed to sit on the couch for a minute and rest his eyes.

He walked slowly, enviously watching a flock of Canadian geese flying south for the winter. Victor rounded the corner to find Curtis on the front porch with an empty fuel can.

"Where are you going with that?" Victor asked, puzzled.

"Glad that you are here, Dad. Can you come with me? I need to go outside the wall to check on something. I'll go inside to grab my gear."

"Ahhh, OK. Can I ask where we are going and what for?"

"Nope. Top secret. Grab your rifle and gear too," Curtis instructed his questioning father.

"Should I get the truck?" Victor asked, hoping to make this a quick trip to get back for his much-needed nap.

Curtis tilted his head a little. "Nah, we should do this on foot the first time."

Victor hung his head. "OK, let me grab my gear," he said with a heavy sigh, secretly longing for the couch pillows.

The two strolled through town, then out the southern gate. They chatted softly about different activities, gossip around town, chores that needed to be done, and what they had planned for the upcoming relax day on Sunday.

Victor let Curtis lead the way while he kept rear security. Every few steps, Victor would look behind him to ensure they weren't being followed. Outside the wall, suburbs quickly thinned into rural farmland and thick forest. Without saying a word, Curtis lifted an open hand in the air to signal a halt, then patted the air beside him, signaling to Victor to take a knee.

His son lifted a compass to his cheek and looked through the lens to check his azimuth and then through the site wire before retuning it to his coat pocket. Curtis waved forward, telling Victor that he had regained their bearings and they were on their way again.

His children were rapidly growing up in this new dark age. Not too long ago, his sons were enjoying sports, video games, and hanging out with friends. Victor's eyes welled up with tears; his kids were becoming skilled survivalists, and Victor hated it.

Curtis pushed away a thick pine branch, opening the forest curtain and revealing an overgrown wheat field. The rural area they were heading toward was familiar; it was one of their best culling locations when they had snuck outside the perimeter at night on their black ops.

"I found this spot last time we were out here with Michael and Zavier, hunting Grays," Curtis said as they rounded an old yellow farmhouse. In the backyard, near another overgrown fenced-in field that at one time held cattle and horses, were the ghostly remains of an old wooden barn that had since burnt away, leaving only a skeletal structure on top of a cobblestone foundation.

Victor reached forward and grabbed his son by the shoulder. "Stop. There are Grays close by. I can smell them," Victor hissed, looking around frantically and waiting to be ambushed. He shouldered his rifle and looked just over the sights, clinching the pistol grip, finding the safety switch with his thumb.

Curtis put his hand on his dad's arm casually and waved him forward. "I rigged up a small solar panel to charge a battery so it can stay out here permanently. I used the high-pitch recording on a loop again, but I was able to use a photosensor to make it play only at night."

Victor was confused by what Curtis was saying. He kept looking back nervously while following close behind his son.

They stepped up to the old barn foundation, and the overpowering stench stung their eyes, instantly making them water. Victor turned his head and almost vomited, forcing him to cover his face with his coat sleeve.

"The bait only works at night when the Grays can't see well," Curtis explained. "They come rushing in and fall right into the pit, immediately impaling themselves."

Victor looked down into what would have been hay storage under the barn back when it was originally built. The cobblestone-foundation walls were twelve feet high all the way around. Protruding from the hard, compact floor were dozens of sharpened rebar rods and metal fence posts cut at sharp angles.

"I used a hacksaw to cut apart a chain-link fence for the spikes. I figured metal would last longer and would withstand the fire needed to sanitize this cesspool. There's a big drum of diesel near the house that we can fill up the gas can with."

Victor didn't know if he was impressed or appalled by the display of death before him. There must have been a couple hundred vile, retched creatures twisted and piled below him in a pool of black, infected sludge. Three, sometime four, Grays were skewered onto spears like a disgusting shish kebab.

The brisk late-autumn air was welcome, because the summer heat would have made the stench completely unbearable. As much as Victor wanted to look away, he couldn't help but admire how effective Curtis's trap had had been in killing so many Grays without using a single bullet or putting human life in danger.

Curtis walked up behind him, carrying a sloshing can full of diesel fuel.

"How long have you been doing this?" Victor asked, still staring at the sickening pit of death.

"I got the idea when Raymond was putting punji sticks near the wall. I began working on it then. I got the radio to turn on, then off again with a photosensor switch a couple days ago; then I placed it up there on that pole in the center. Today's the first time I've been able to check on it. Seemed to work OK," Curtis said nonchalantly.

"I'd say it worked just fine! This is a major game changer! No more need for midnight wolf packing." Victor reached over to put a rewarding arm around his son. "Any chance you could build more of these?"

■ ■

"Good evening. This is Elizabeth Corrin bringing you another BBN global news report.

"The ceasefire peace agreement with the League of Arab Nations came to an abrupt halt this morning as Europe was rocked again with another wave of terror attacks. Fire brigades throughout the EU are now battling to extinguish several oil refinery fires.

"We will continue to follow this story as damage assessments are reported. This attack will certainly have an impact on fuel rations for all of us.

"All NATO countries have pledged to send the maximum amount of resources to support BRICS in the war with Persia. Military units are being mobilized at this moment.

"France has threatened another nuclear strike on multiple targets, which has drawn severe criticism from the United Nations security council.

"To the far east, South Korean Crown Prince Yi Chang claims the city of Hanyang has been attacked by Chinese terrorists. Chang is demanding immediate and harsh actions be taken by the UN security council. China denies the claims, calling the accusations absurd.

"Stay tuned for another World Health Organization report after this commercial break."

■■

After the evening's news broadcast, the town council sat around the picnic table under the pavilion, which had become a respected ceremonial centerpiece for the entire town. In fact, the park around the pavilion was the only landscaped area in town, with grass and hedges trimmed by an unknown volunteer. Those who sat at the picnic table were treated with a high level of respect by the townsfolk, which made Victor feel incredibly awkward.

"Sounds like Europe is having a hell of a time," the mayor said, opening the dialogue.

"Not much we can do about it. Would be nice if they could send some of that support our way, though," Victor added.

"At least they still have electricity. And food," Erica said quietly with a rumble in her hungry stomach.

"Speaking of food, the dairy farm out by the Amish community would like to give us some milk and beef cattle. Even offered to let us borrow his cattle trailer," Sheriff Bohner mentioned.

"What's the catch?" Raymond asked flatly, as if he knew his guns and ammo were about to be bartered away.

"We have to transport the cattle trailer. His modern tractor is inoperable, and he's asked if our mechanics could fix it for him in trade of the cows," the sheriff explained.

"Seems fair enough," the mayor said with a favorable nod. "On the subject of food production, are the underground gardens still producing?"

"The what?" Victor asked, confused by the mention of underground gardens.

"Yes, they are. We planted late-season vegetables like celery, broccoli, cauliflower, cabbage, and Brussels sprouts, but I fear that we're going to have to harvest before they're full grown. We have simply run out of time. Winter is coming," Jessica explained to the mayor, then shifted in her seat to look at Victor. "We dug a trench about eight feet deep and the width of the bulldozer blade, then we put our hoop house roof on it at ground level. Between the natural subterranean ground temperature and the greenhouse effect of the plastic roof, we can grow produce longer into the season. The trench needed to be dug in a specific direction to maximize the sunlight."

"And it works?" Victor asked with a suspicious raised eyebrow.

"Yup, warmest place in town." Jessica smiled. "Speaking of, we have begun relocating families to homes with wood fireplaces. During the winter, I fear that living conditions will be cramped with two or three families living in—"

Victor's attention was broken by a distant *thump* sound.

Victor waved his hands. "Quiet. Shush yourselves."

"What was that? It sounded like a car door slamming," the mayor asked, puzzled by Victor's sudden change in demeanor.

"Quiet, damn you!" Victor cursed.

Another *thump, thump, thump* could be heard. Victor looked at Raymond.

"Incoming!" Raymond shouted.

Victor dove over the picnic table, tackling Erica to the ground, spreading himself over her. Raymond tackled the mayor next to him at the same time the abandoned and boarded-up ice-cream shop, which had previously offered the largest cones in the north, exploded into a ball of fire, smoke, and debris.

Another explosion erupted inside the town out of Victor's immediate view. Then another quickly followed. An earsplitting thunder and blinding flash of light exploded on the beach near the pavilion, violently shaking the ground, spraying boiling-hot water and sand all over the picnic table. He laid on Erica for a moment longer to ensure the attack was over before helping her up.

Kevin was already running for the TDF HQ building. He would have the reactionary forces ready to deploy in a moment. If the fight was over, they'd be tasked to put out fires.

"What was that?" the mayor screamed with deaf ears, visibly shaking to the point he couldn't stand upright by himself.

"Mortars! Who has the capability and motive to bomb your town? I'll give you one guess!" Victor glared at him, holding onto Erica's hand tightly.

He looked past the mayor toward his house to ensure that his children were safe and caught movement down the street. A dozen shadows whipped back and forth. Victor guessed that frightened townspeople were rushing toward the pavilion for answers or to help. But the shadowy people were erratic, jetting in and out of sight.

As the group raced closer, Victor finally made out details of the lead person sprinting toward him. There was only one person in town who wore a pink buttoned-up shirt and pleated khaki pants.

"Damn it, Stanly, we don't have time for your crap right now!" Victor yelled. "We're in a bit of an emergency here!"

But Stanly kept sprinting faster than Victor would have given someone with his physique credit for. He assumed the people behind Stanley where his friends coming with him to help, but why were they acting so weird?

The LED lighting on the pavilion, which was powered by the windmill-charged batteries, cast a ghostly glow over the park lawn. Stanly's pink shirt had stains and was untucked. It was the first time Victor had seen the councilman in an unclean, unpressed shirt.

Victor was about to chastise Stanly with a comment about his unkempt appearance when the wind shifted, bringing a rancid scent of feces and sickness. Then Victor heard the growling from the pack rushing toward him. By instinct, he protectively pulled Erica behind him as he reached for his pistol, but she had hers out first.

He had just cleared his holster, drawing his pistol, when an eruption of gunfire opened around him. Stanly's beady eyes locked in on Victor. His pale-gray face contorted into an expression of pure hatred and lust. Stanly's arms reached out, displaying black veins through his pale skin. He sidestepped back and forth, then went low, preparing for his final lunge toward his victim.

Victor's pistol light came on as he drew his weapon. He fired a hammer a hammered pair from his hip, as the light on his pistol found Stanly's chest. His left hand found the pistol as it was thrust forward toward his target's head. When Victor's arms fully extended, his weapon light shone right into Stanly's face, illuminating every diseased detail.

Victor fired in fast succession. The first round entered Stanly's wide-open mouth, missing his jagged teeth, clipping a blackened tongue, and exiting out the back of his throat. The second round was absorbed by the bone tissue behind Stanly's wrinkled nose. The third popped Stanly's hate-filled right eyeball, showering Victor's coat with vile bodily fluid and brain matter as Stanly landed on him forcefully, knocking him backward into Erica, all three landing heavily on the concrete.

Victor grabbed Stanly and rolled off Erica, raising his fist, ready for hand-to-hand combat, but Stanly was already limp. The gunfire around him came to an end, and Victor brought himself back to his feet. Every member of the council had a weapon in their hand: Victor. Erica. Kevin, with the QRF. Jessica. Sheriff Bohner. The mayor. Even Mrs. Cloud. Gaylen held a lever-action rifle with a smoking barrel next to Raymond, who was reloading his pistol with a slightly annoyed and bored expression on his face.

Kevin briefed them. "Post eight is reporting headlights heading eastbound on Route 55. I think the attack is over."

Raymond tilted his chin toward Victor's gore-covered coat. "Are you good, man? Looks like you have bits of ol' Stan on you."

Victor nodded.

"Good; grab your stuff. Pick me up with the truck at my place in thirty. We have business to conduct," Raymond said as he patted Gaylen on the butt and grabbed her accepting hand, walking toward his apartment.

Victor pulled Erica in close to him and kissed her fiercely until he began to see stars from lack of oxygen. She held him tight, pressing herself into him, ignoring the contaminant on them both. "I'll be back in a few days. This needs to end," he whispered into her ear.

She was shaken by the violence that had ended as a near-death experience. Erica looked down sadly, not wanting to be apart from him again, but she understood what needed to be done.

"Where are you going?" the mayor demanded.

Victor studied the faces of the dead and dying creatures who had been friends of Stanly's and fellow townsfolk, brutally discarded on the manicured park lawn. He shifted his gaze from the blaze engulfing his favorite ice-cream shop to the rising smoke plumes of the various destroyed homes, wondering how many innocents had been killed or wounded.

"To cut the head off the snake," Victor said flatly. "If the Grayling group returns, stall them. Agree to their terms. Give them some minor supplies, maybe a cow or goat. Do not give them weapons or ammo. Got it?"

SNAKE EATERS

Decapitate and Devour

After a quick rinse to clean the bits and pieces of Stanly off him and donning a fresh set of clothes, Victor hugged his children goodbye. Michael almost begged to come with him, commenting several times that he could provide security. Victor reluctantly stepped out the door with an overstuffed backpack on his back and a rifle in his cold hands. Making his way to the motor-pool garage, he ensured the old red truck was topped off and put two extra gas cans in the truck bed.

Raymond exited his apartment, carrying the same equipment, as soon as Victor pulled up to the curb. "Mind if I drive? I want to stop by the old house to pick up a few things on the way," Raymond said. "You think we should take a couple TDF guards with us for security?"

"Nope, I'd prefer we do this alone," Victor stated matter of factly, thinking about how Michael had begged to come along. Victor didn't want a bunch of questions or witnesses to the immoral acts which would be conducted in the days soon to follow. Blasting a charging Gray in terror shook most people. Killing a fellow human in self-defense would leave traumatic scars on most survivors for life. Hunting and premeditatively killing a human being, as if on an elk hunt, was reserved for a very select few who were morally flexible.

Outside the gate, Raymond slowly negotiated the roadway serpentine obstacle turning the wheels sharply back and forth, then came to a stop in the middle of the road. "Going dark," Raymond said, turning off the headlights, then holding up a night-vision monocle to his left eye while steering with his right hand.

The old truck picked up speed, cruising at forty miles per hour, slowing occasionally while steering to the left or right to avoid debris on the road. Without night vision, Victor peered out the passenger window into darkness, watching the moon appear in and out through barren trees. Even after several months since the dark day, he still hadn't become used to how many stars were visible stars in the clear night sky without manmade light pollution. The enormous star-filled sky made him feel lonely, and he wished that they could rewind time to when they shared the road with other motorists.

Victor wondered how many people were still alive out here, isolated in the wild. The hardships those people faced out here alone simplified the complaints of his life inside the protective walls. His mind came back to the moment as Raymond slowed the truck and turned slowly onto a winding dirt road. He came to a stop, then backed into the driveway next to a house with an attached garage.

Raymond put the truck in park and turned off the truck, submerging them in silence. They waited and listened for several minutes, anticipating Grays to appear. Finally, Raymond broke the quiet: "May I suggest we stay the night here…it's safe, and we both need some rest. I have some chow here for breakfast, and we can repack our kit. We should do a little map recon of the best route between here and Grayling and discuss our course of action."

Victor hadn't realized it, but his eyes were quite heavy from an extraordinarily long and stressful day. As much as he wanted to get this job done and get back to his family, a bed sounded heavenly.

■■

The sound of a clatter woke Victor. Beams of bright morning sunlight pierced through the single boarded-up window. His bare feet hit cold tile, causing a chill to run up his spine. With a pistol in hand, he slowly scanned the hallway as far as he could see from inside his bedroom. About to cross the threshold into the hallway, he caught the long-forgotten aroma of coffee.

Victor lowered his pistol and poked his head out the bedroom door and into the hallway, seeing Raymond rummaging through the kitchen. He got himself dressed and chased the luring smell.

"Omelet with ham or beef frankfurters?" Raymond asked, tossing two military rations on the counter.

"Damn, how old are these? They don't make this kind of MRE anymore." Victor acted repulsed by the options, albeit with a hungry stomach.

"Fine, you get the omelet. Even warmed up, I can't choke that one down. Don't mind the expiration date; I assure you they have been stored in a cool, dark place, which prolongs the shelf life. I brought these home with me after I left the corps. That was a day or two ago."

Victor scowled at the long-passed expiration date of six years ago but opened the meal anyway. The accessory pack was opened first as he searched for the single serving of instant coffee. While he combed through the meal pack, he found the once-treasured jalapeño cheese spread and squeezed the entire package into the omelet sleeve. While doing so, Raymond casually placed two M-67 fragmentation grenades, one M18 Claymore mine satchel, and another weapon-mountable night-vision optic device on the table. "Other souvenirs I brought home, courtesy of Uncle Sam."

Victor dropped his breakfast on the countertop, raising his hands in the air. "Are you kidding me right now? You've had this stuff all this time? We could've used this for town defense months ago!"

"This is my gear, and the people of Lake City are lucky I gave them what I did. I wasn't going to put all my faith in a pair of hunters who broke into my house all those months ago. I didn't know you, and I wasn't going to show all my cards on the flop. Besides, the council probably would have given this stuff to the Amish for chicken eggs or something stupid," Raymond said through a mouthful of brutally dry crackers and peanut butter.

He handed Victor the hot-water kettle and a clean coffee cup. "How do you want to get there?"

Victor thought about it for a minute. "We'll drive at night on the way there for stealth. Backroads only. Nice and slow. Afterward, we can drive during the day, if need be for speed."

Raymond opened a road map of northern Michigan and began marking a couple of routes. "These are probably dirt roads with little to no population. That'll be our primary route." He jabbed a finger at the map. "These improved roads here may have trouble lurking, but they appear to be rural enough. That will be our alternate route."

"Looks about thirty-five miles? Even idling along quietly, we should make it in about three hours. We'll infiltrate tonight, set up a hide, and conduct surveillance all day tomorrow," Victor added.

"What's our objective? Eliminate their leadership only or complete chaos?" Raymond stopped chewing to ask, attentively eyeing Victor for his answer.

"Complete chaos," Victor said, slurping his cup of coffee. "This group is no longer US Military or acting on behalf of America. In fact, they are a direct threat to not only our town but also all citizens of northern Michigan."

Raymond smirked. "I'll bring the Barrett."

■■

After a long nap, Raymond rolled off the couch and onto the hardwood floor. After a quick look around, he found Victor on his front porch in a rocking chair with another cup of coffee.

"You're kind of brave sitting out here, all by your lonesome." Raymond eyed the overgrown grass in his front yard. "There were a lot of Grays in this area when I lived here. There are surely even more now."

Victor reached down on the opposite side of the rocking chair and lifted a short-barreled AR pistol with a folding stock that he had borrowed from Zavier for this trip. He showed it to Raymond with a smile, then leaned it back against the wall.

"Did you rat fuck all the chows for that coffee?" Raymond asked with a sneer, wondering how many ransacked MREs he'd find in the kitchen.

"Just the few you gave me. I had to field strip them to fit in my pack anyway, and we won't be able to drink this good stuff out there—the smell would compromise us." Victor said casually while holding his arm outstretched in front of him with two fingers extended horizontally.

"What are you measuring?" Raymond asked.

"The sun is two fingers from the horizon, which means thirty minutes till sundown. It'll be plenty dark enough for us to move out at the end of nautical twilight, which is ninety minutes from now," Victor stated. "It sure is quiet out here. I'm glad that the mechanics gave the ol' truck a new muffler."

"I'll load up the truck and pull the dash fuses. We'll ride completely blacked out tonight," Raymond told him as he stepped off the porch.

"You do know that pulling the fuses will kill the heater, too, right?" Victor shivered in the cool evening air. "We better dress warm."

■■

Victor drove that night with Raymond as navigator. He cupped the night-vision device to his eye with one hand; he steered with the other. Even though they were creeping down the road at barely an idling speed, the purr of the engine, the muffle from a mostly fixed exhaust, and the vibration of the tire treads beating against road gravel seemed alarmingly loud.

The single lens night optical device that Victor held to his eye displayed the road in a bright green picture, with a limited narrow field of view reminding him of looking through a paper towel tube. Depth perception with dual lens NODs were bad, and single-lens devices were even worse. The benefit to this device was that it could easily be attached to a rifle. Not knowing how deep the potholes were or how big the branches lying in the road actually were, he swerved the truck slightly to skirt around the shadows, avoiding damage to the truck.

Thinking back to his wolf-packing black ops with his boys and to the mess of a recovery mission to retrieve Erica, Kevin, and Gaylen, he began to get annoyed with Raymond's selfishness to withhold this equipment from them. Night vision was a force multiplier, but Victor let it go and changed his focus to the mission at hand.

The truck slowed down to a crawl and then stopped after Victor put his foot on the brake. Reaching up to the ocular lens on the night-vision device, he adjusted the focus to read the trip meter under the speedometer. "We've gone almost three miles from the last turn. The next road should be coming up soon," he reported as he refocused back on the road and began driving at an idling pace again.

Hidden in the passenger seat, Raymond was hunched over with a large winter coat over him. Tucked underneath, he read the road map with a small red LED light. "Turn left at the intersection of Washington and Square."

"Nothing but forest, farmland, opossums, and raccoons out here. I haven't seen a driveway for a while," Victor observed. "It looks like that crossroad is coming up."

"Go ahead and stop. I'll confirm the road sign. And I have to take a leak," Raymond said, pulling the coat over his head, stuffing it behind him, picking up his AR, and putting the sling around his neck.

The truck slowed to a stop as Victor turned the wheel left at the intersection. They both scanned the area for a minute before Raymond opened the door and got out, walking toward the road signs to confirm their location. "This is it. We're still en route. Must be my superior navigational skills…What the hell is that?"

The sound of nearby brush cracking and road gravel scuffling overpowered the truck engine sound. The tranquil night air was split open by an ear-piercing, echoing screech. Victor scanned the trees on his side of the vehicle for movement and then toward the front, where he saw Raymond sprinting for the truck.

"Go, go, go!" Raymond said, reaching for the open truck door.

Victor put the gas pedal to the floor before Raymond was fully in. The truck tires fought for traction, spinning on the loose gravel. The truck pitched forward, shifting to the right; Victor counter steered to straighten it out, fishtailing slightly. Something impacted the tailgate from behind with a loud *thud*.

"What was that! I've never heard a Gray make a sound like that before!" Victor yelled, trying to gain speed, keeping the truck in the middle of the road.

Raymond was facing backward, sitting on his knees in the seat, but he couldn't see a thing out the back window. "The hell if I know! It was like an effing stampede out there as soon as we stopped. Something was swarming us, but I couldn't see a thing!"

Moonlight illuminated the dust cloud following the accelerating truck, clouding any visibility behind them. Frustrated, Raymond turned around so he was facing forward again. "Great, now I really have to piss."

To be safe, the assumption was made that the Grayling group had full military capabilities, including thermal- and night vision. So the decision was made to cache the truck a good distance away from the base on the opposite side of a neighboring lake. They would patrol on foot from there.

Victor briefed his partner: "If we get separated, we meet back here at the truck. If the other person doesn't show for twenty-four hours, head back to Lake City."

"Roger that. Let's go find us a good hide before the sun comes up," Raymond acknowledged in a whisper, turning toward the tree line and taking point on their patrol.

Oversize backpacks bore down on their shoulders. Victor's carried with him a change of clothes, poncho, four meals, two gallons of water, HAM radio with spare batteries, navigation gear, pistol with two spare mags, six mags of 5.56mm for his shorty AR, three mags of .308 caliber for his long gun, a ghillie suit, and the lower receiver of a Barrett M107 50 cal, which slowed him down.

The weight of all their equipment and weapons wasn't the only thing that slowed them down. It was caution and fear. They were both frightened of shadowy predators that could be lurking in the bushes. Getting in a firefight was the least of their worries, for Victor and Raymond both had experience in conventional warfare.

Wild animals, Grays, and whatever had swarmed the road intersection earlier were a completely different story. Raymond paused their patrol often to stop, look, listen, and smell. He knelt and faced to the left; Victor knelt next to him, shoulder to shoulder, facing to the right. Before standing up to continue the patrol, he reached over to give his partner a squeeze on the shoulder.

They continued to patrol slowly through the cold, dark coppice, circling a small lake that threatened to freeze and coming to a tall chain-link fence around an airfield perimeter. Destruction of the rogue group's leadership, capability, and willingness to fight was their primary mission. But Victor also wanted to learn more about this base. He wondered if Raymond and Victor could locate the armory, munitions bunker, or gear-supply building, or maybe seize some military vehicles to take back home. They also needed to answer a troublesome question: Were surveillance drones on this airbase?

The final checkpoint was drawing near, but with little time to spare. A disciplined infantry unit would "stand to" the hour before sunup and after sundown, because that is the most common time for enemies to attack. Victor highly doubted that this merry band of thieves had enough discipline to be a hundred percent alert during the early morning hour. But it was better to be safe than sorry.

Camp Grayling was a decent-size base. Finding a small group of individuals would be difficult. To make matters worse, it was divided into two major sections: combat training and logistics to the south and the army airfield to the north. The logical place to look would have been near the barracks, but surprisingly, they found evidence of activity near an airplane hangar on the north side. After Victor gave it some thought, lacking water and electricity, the barracks wouldn't have been the best apocalyptic place to live.

Parked in front of the hangar were a single tan HMMWV, a fuel-transfer tanker truck, and the same eight-wheeled Stryker vehicle that had visited Lake City. Not a single sentry or guard patrol in sight. Victor suspected that they were all sleeping, secure inside the locked doors of the hangar.

He nudged Raymond. "Do you know how to drive one of those?" He tilted his head toward the light armored vehicle.

"Negative, but how hard could it be?" Raymond shrugged.

"It's probably grunt-proof easy, but we won't have time to figure it out once the boogaloo starts," Victor concluded, then looked behind them. "What are you thinking for a hide site: That tree line across the airstrip or those admin buildings over there?"

"The tree line would give us more flexibility and easier escape. Although the building would give us more cover and shelter. The second story would give us a great field of view for observation." Raymond quickly calculated the distance from the admin building to the hangar. "I'm feeling a little exposed out here in the elements. Let's get inside."

The long two-story concrete admin building was unlocked. Victor and Raymond dropped their packs and long guns near the back door, then cleared the building room by room, swift and silent. The lower level had been ransacked and vandalized, presumably by the young soldiers across the airstrip. Coffee pots were smashed, computer screens and keyboards thrown against doors, unit logos spray-painted on walls.

Boots crunching on broken glass, they carefully negotiated the mess and secured each exit door's locking mechanism. Victor chose a large upstairs windowed office with adjacent rooms for their hide site. According to the numerus awards and citations decorating the dark wood-paneled wall, the office had belonged to base commander General Carter. The connecting interior office was assigned to the general's adjunct. A fire escape across the hallway gave them multiple exit options if needed. The office chairs piled up down the hall, along with trip-wire booby traps, would provide an early warning of unwanted guests, human or otherwise. Raymond lowered the window blinds, leaving only small slits to observe through.

They sat in the dark, motionless, for almost an hour, carefully observing and listening for any sort of activity. The place was a ghost town, and they began to second-guess if they'd chosen the right location to hide.

"Well, nothing is moving, I'm pretty sure we're secure here. We may have to relocate tomorrow night. I'm wide awake if you want to get some rest. It's going to be a long day," Raymond suggested.

As a hint of color rose in the eastern sky, Victor took advantage of the darkness to close his eyes for a bit. With his gear and rifle placed by the door for quick use, he curled up on the secretary's small office couch, using his ghillie suit as a blanket, and closed his eyes, feeling knots begin to form in his tired legs.

■■■

A nudge woke Victor out of a heavy slumber. He could hear birds chirping, and his eyelids were heavy with sleep. Lifting the ghillie suit off his face, Raymond nodded toward the adjacent room. "We have movement outside."

Victor rolled off the couch and crawled around a drab metal desk toward the doorway. The general's office was not used to observe from, because even with the blinds down, the enemy could easily see movement through the window. Instead, they used the general's office as a buffer, keeping it as dark as possible to create a mirror effect to anyone outside looking in. If the line-of-sight angle had been better, they would have preferred to stack two rooms deep for standoff. "What do we have?"

Raymond handed him a small pair of binos. "We're in the right spot. They just now opened the hangar doors, and from the appearance, they just woke up too."

Victor lifted the glasses to his eyes and watched several men lingering around the building, stretching and yawning. *At least they parked their other vehicles inside for protection and quick response*, he thought. He lowered the binos, estimating the morning sun already four fingers above the horizon.

"An hour after sunup. They are a lazy bunch, aren't they?" Victor noted. "Uniforms are a mess too. Boots are unlaced. None of them shaved. Some in civilian shirts. Completely unsat. They are a disgrace to the uniform. I wonder if all of them were enlisted when the lights went out, or if civilians have been recruited to their renegade ranks."

"Hard to say, but there is still not a single person on watch," Raymond added. "They think they're untouchable and are not expecting someone to bring the fight to them. These guys are just a bunch of bandits. Worse than that, because they should be using their training and resources to help people instead of this strong-armed mafia persona."

On the wall hung a dry-erase board, on which Raymond had artistically drawn a detailed sketch of the nearby base, with distances to several prominent features. Apache helicopters to the right were seven hundred yards. Farther down the L-shaped runway to the right were Blackhawk helos at nine hundred seventy-five yards. A pair of radar towers directly adjacent to them on the left sat at two hundred yards. It was five hundred fifty yards to the hangar across a crumbling road and overgrown grassy area.

"No sign of drones?" Victor asked, studying the range card sketch.

"Negative. And by the looks of the flight line, I don't think any of those birds are flying either," Raymond whispered.

Through magnification of the binoculars, Victor surveilled the littered and overgrown runway. When this base was fully active, troops were made to walk the length of the strip, every single morning, picking up any loose trash that could be sucked into an airplane or helicopter engine. Even in the apocalypse, a pilot would demand the same flight-line cleanliness before lifting off. A thick layer of dust on the helicopter's cockpit windows confirmed the suspicion.

"Well, we don't have to worry about aerial threats," Victor said nodding his head happily before he eyed Raymond questioningly. "So who was flying the drone over Lake City?"

Raymond shrugged. "Not these clowns. But that doesn't really matter at the moment, does it? They don't need drone surveillance to drop 81mm mortars into our homes. Hell, that means they launched them blindly without a care where they landed. They could have killed your entire family." Raymond spat with fire in his eyes.

Any reservation Victor had about assassinating US military members had just washed away. Raymond was absolutely correct. Victor thought of all the helpless people he had aided over the past few months on such limited resources. The men loitering around the hanger could have done the same or better, but they chose to oppress the less fortunate instead. Disasters can bring out the best—and worst—in people. They weren't just a band of menacing road pirates—they were an extremely dangerous enemy bound by values of greed and lawlessness. Their blaze of terror was about to get snuffed.

■■■

Victor nudged Raymond awake. "Our boys are back."

Raymond squinted and rubbed the sleep from his eyes. "How long were they gone?"

"About four hours. Looks like they pillaged another town. Hummers are full of vegetables and random tools. I'm guessing that they're tired of eating MREs," Victor said.

Raymond used Victor's rifle, sitting securely on top of a tripod, to scan the returning group. "How many do you count?"

"Twelve in the group that just returned, including the proclaimed leader, Sergeant Eddie Parks. Look for the only guy wearing a black beret. He split them evenly in the four Hummers; driver, truck commander, and a gunner up top," Victor reported, tapping Raymond's shoulder and motioning toward the dry-erase board. "He kept eight behind for working party, which locked the hangar without guard, and took four more hummers to the southern side of base. They returned a couple hours ago full of ammo cans, wooden crates, and more MRE boxes. I'm guessing they have keys to the ammo-supply point and all the other logistics buildings on the base."

"Hmmm, those keys would be nice to have. It would have been a good time to jack that Stryker LAV," Raymond mentioned in a whisper.

"The thought crossed my mind, too, but it would have ruined our element of surprise," Victor added. "Where are the Grays? That's what I don't understand. I mean, these yahoos aren't the quietest bunch."

"Well, there is the ten-foot-high fence topped with concertina wire surrounding the strip. I doubt it will keep out a large horde for long though," Raymond noted. "I wish we could raid their ASP. Imagine what we could do with some 105 artillery shells?"

Victor eyed Raymond curiously as his partner put on an expression of concentration. "Are you an artilleryman?"

"Nah, man, I'm thinking back to the postsurge insurgency in Iraq. We could plant IEDs all along Lake City's outer perimeter. Next time these idiots—or idiots like them—come around with demands, we could simply push a button. Problem solved. Problem staying solved," Raymond said with an evil grin.

"I always said that there's no problem in the world big enough that a small amount of C4 explosive can't fix," Victor agreed.

"Exactly." Raymond nodded. "Grab the lower receiver to the Barrett, would you?" Raymond asked, unstrapping the upper receiver and barrel from his pack and handing it to Victor. He dug into the bottom of his pack, pulling out a large box of ammo, lifting the lid and exposing massive 50 caliber bullets with a gray tip.

"M8 API rounds!" Victor whistled. "Very nice! Those will do some damage to the engine blocks of their HMMWVs."

Raymond almost seemed giddy to bring the hate. "Yeah, buddy. 662 grains of steel-core fun and excitement, followed by an incendiary composition. Screw these guys. So what's our plan, anyway?"

Victor watched through the binoculars as the men laughed and joked while offloading the loot they had pillaged from already-starving villagers. A couple of guys pushed out a large grill, lighting a fire of timber to cook their pilfered feast. Several bottles of whiskey were passed around as they appeared to celebrate another successful day of thuggery. He wondered how long it would take before simple rations would satisfy their lust of power. Soon, if not put into check, enslaved young women could be among their stolen treasures.

"Hit 'em hard right at dawn; use the chaos to escape and evade. We can move faster during the day than at night. Drive like hell back to town."

■■

Two hours before sunrise, they were packed and ready to go. Victor's pack hung from a hook on his tripod, which the weight helped to stabilize. The windows to the general's office had been cracked open and the blinds raised slightly, permitting a clear trajectory path without obstructions.

Victor and Raymond had spent the night putting the pieces into place. Victor had wanted to attach the Claymore mine to the fuel tanker truck to create a VBIED, but with only one hundred feet of wire, it was way too close to detonate without any suitable cover. So an alternate plan to utilize the tanker was hatched.

Several holes had been cut in the fence surrounding the airstrip, with tin cans tied to the fence by a string acting as a noisemaker. They hoped to lure in Grays as a strategic weapon or to at least help mask their escape. Their goal was to create the most damage, chaos, and casualties in the shortest amount of time.

Victor looked at his watch; in about an hour and a half, the time would be right. Even with suppressors, the muzzle flash inside the building would be like a neon arrow pointing directly to their location. They would wait until there was an ample amount of civil twilight illuminating the morning sky in shades of orange and pink.

Their anxiety and nerves made them both fidget. They both scanned the area, watching for movement. Victor took northern sector, Raymond the south.

"See anything?" Victor asked, wanting conversation.

"Nah. Looks like a bunch of critters or small dogs roaming around out there. Quite a few of them, actually. They're pretty quiet; normally you'd hear them yapping all night long," Raymond said calmly. "Whoa, check this out! A target of opportunity," he hissed.

Victor looked through his riflescope, illuminated by the attached night-vision device. A man pulled open the large hangar door, which moaned in the silence of night. He stumbled outside with a red lens flashlight, presumably still drunk from the festivities, staggered to the far side of the hangar, and relieved himself in the grass.

"He left the door open, man," Raymond reported. "Shit, is he wearing a beret?"

"That's ol' Eddie Parks. I'm going hot," Victor said, spinning his elevation turret to compensate for 550 yards of bullet drop. His rifle had been sighted in and scope zeroed out during ninety-degree weather back in July. The cold late-autumn night air would be far denser, creating additional drag on the bullet. Victor added a half minute of angle to his elevation to compensate. He checked for parallax by slightly shaking his head while looking through the scope. The sling was wrapped around the tripod, stiffening his stance and lessening the wobble zone. Calm night air with zero wind deflection. *This is going to be a chip shot*, Victor thought.

"On scope, send it," Raymond demanded.

The reticle centered on the back of the militia leader, who was holding himself up with one arm by leaning against the hangar wall. Headshots from this far away were only for movie theatrics. Completely achievable, even off a tripod, but why risk a miss? Aiming center mass is an almost-guaranteed hit.

Victor flicked off the safety, a cloud of fog slowly escaping his lips, and touched the trigger with a gentle squeeze. The recoil rocked him back slightly. A suppresser on a 308 rifle is nowhere near movie-quiet, but it does take the bite off the bark. Having the general's windows open only enough for a clear trajectory trapped most of the remaining sound inside the large office space.

He lifted the cold bolt nob and slid it back in one smooth motion, ignoring the smoking brass ejecting into the cold morning air, and then smoothly slid the bolt forward with his thumb, chambering a fresh round into the chamber. "Center mass," Victor called his shot.

"Good hit. He's down, but stand by to reengage. Looks like Parks has a bathroom buddy coming out," Raymond informed him. "Get ready; he's strolling over to his dead partner."

A staccato of screeches, hisses, and growls erupted from all around them, echoing off the buildings, rippling through the still morning air. The man walking in front of the hangar stopped suddenly, just short of the corner where his dead leader lay facedown in the dirt with his manhood still in hand. Tiny shadows scurried across the flight line and out of the tall grass, rushing toward the hangar.

The militiaman turned in a hurry toward the safety of the open hangar door but only made it halfway to the HMMWV before being overtaken by a swarm of hungry animals.

"What the fuuuu..." Raymond watched in horror as the man was ripped apart next the military vehicle. His screams could be heard over the rhythmic course of snaps and snarls. Two of the critters tugged and pulled on the soldier's arm until it pulled free from the torso. Three more took interest in a flailing leg. "Those things are spilling into the hangar."

Muffled yelling and shouts could be heard from inside the partly open metal doors. Gunfire soon followed. Victor had witnessed the brutality of war, but what entered his ear canals now were the most haunting sounds he'd ever heard. He almost felt sorry for the men being ripped apart alive.

Two men ran out of the hangar, barefoot and shirtless, with rifles in hand, shooting wildly into the night before being taken down and feasted upon. One soldier sprinted toward the airstrip, and a glistening, blood-covered little demon caught up to him, leapt onto his back, and clawed its way up to his head before the soldier was taken down in a fury of blood, his cries of agony filling the night. Victor could barely watch the grotesque scene, but he needed better visibility of the battlefield.

"Light the candle," Victor ordered.

"Roger. Remember, this will only work if it's not completely full of fuel," Raymond reminded him as he leveled his reticle on the fuel tanker. Even with a 50 caliber armor piercing incendiary round, diesel fuel wouldn't ignite, but maybe the fuel vapors would. He came down a quarter way from the tanker's top and squeezed the trigger. The recoil nearly slid the huge twenty-eight-pound rifle off the smooth desktop being used as an elevated platform. The muzzle blast turned the secretary's office into an instantaneous whirlwind, kicking up papers and dust and knocking the dry-erase board off the wall.

Recovering from a near concussion, shaking the stars from his vision, Victor could see a huge fiery blaze where the fuel tanker had been. Orange dancing light and swaying shadows flooded the immediate vicinity. The hangar sidewall had been dented in and covered with burning diesel fuel, but it had not been breached. Down the flight line to the right, near the Apache helicopters, was a massive horde of ghostly apparitions racing toward the flaming hangar, guiding the Grays in like a lighthouse on a foggy night.

Tiny, glistening, blood-covered creatures could be spotted darting back and forth like vicious sewer rats, from one half-eaten victim to another. Victor couldn't differentiate between bodies and body parts. Even from 550 yards away, Victor could see the pool of blood seeping out from the hangar's bay door. Muzzle flashes and gunfire blasts quickly dwindle into an eerie silence.

"Not exactly how we planned it, but I'd say our work here is done." Raymond looked at Victor nervously.

"I concur. I don't know what just happened, or what those things are out there, but I don't want to find out," Victor said, wide-eyed. "Tear down, pack up, and be ready to move out in five."

STAGE FIVE

VISITING NEIGHBORS

It's never how you imagine it.

The only words spoken while traveling away from Grayling were navigational instructions: *Slow down. Sharp turn left here. Speed up. Three miles until next intersection. Shift right, debris in the road.*

Victor pushed the old red truck harder than he should have, putting distance between them and Grayling. The trip, which had taken over three hours the night prior, now only took thirty minutes. "Go back to my place before heading to town. I have more ammo and supplies to take back for the Town Defense Force," Raymond requested.

Victor nodded his approval, staring blankly over the steering wheel. "You remember that family near your house that didn't want to relocate a few months back?"

"Yeah, the Riddell family. Clayton, Sharon, and little Johnny. They're good people. I wonder how they are holding up." Raymond also stared absently out the passenger window at an obsolete cell antenna towering above the quickly passing landscape.

"Let's go visit them while we are out this way. See if they need anything or to at least pass some information along." Victor said, hoping to distract his mind from the slaughter they had just witnessed. "We'll stop there first since it's on the way to your place."

"All right, then, turn up here at this next dirt road," Raymond directed.

Victor backed the truck into the driveway per standard operating procedure. Leaving the truck running, they slowly got out, and left the doors open.

The large house was dark, with no signs of recent activity. Victor stayed near the truck, in view of the front door, as he typically did on survivor rescue missions. Raymond flanked right to get a view of the back yard.

"Hello," Victor yelled toward the house. "Hello. We are ambassadors from Lake City. Do you need any supplies or assistance?"

He waited for a window curtain to flutter or door to open. Only stillness and silence followed. Raymond waved him over.

"Tracks beat a path through the grass over here, from the tree line to the back door. Looks like bare feet," Raymond said, raising his AR to a high-ready position. "Let's check inside."

Victor nodded, tightening the grip on his shorty AR. Raymond took point, stacking on a partially opened doorway. Victor slid beside him and squeezed his shoulder.

Raymond burst through the door, button-hooking into the room. Victor, right on his heels, crossed the threshold to the opposite side. Both had weapon lights on, sweeping back and forth, careful not to aim their muzzle at each other. Raymond looked at Victor, scrunching up his nose.

Victor smelled it too. Grays. Victor let out a light whistle, hoping to draw the threat to them. Nothing stirred. Another whistle followed, slightly louder. Still nothing stirred.

Raymond and Victor cleared the main level systematically and then the upstairs, not finding a soul. They were making their way back down to the main level toward the kitchen, hoping to find something useful in the cabinets, when Victor caught the smell again.

He waved at Raymond to get his attention, then pointed to his nose and at the door near an empty pantry. Raymond nodded and walked gently across the tiled kitchen floor. When he swung open the basement door, the smell was overpowering. It was a pungent combination of feces, urine, sickness, rot, and death.

Raymond gagged, almost vomiting. Victor's eyes watered, and he reached for a dishtowel to cover his mouth and nose. He put a foot down onto a creaking stair step, expecting to engage a Gray at any moment. His weapon light shone into the black void, offering only a small circle of the unknown.

One creaking step at a time took him deeper and deeper into the darkness until finally he spotted a familiar human shape lying facedown on the cold basement floor. Except it wasn't human at all, a pale hairless scalp, its body covered in dark thick scaly scabs in a painfully contorted form.

Victor hesitated, then squatted halfway down the stairs, shining his light back and forth, exposing several twisted lifeless forms. Victor whistled again, but nothing stirred before him. He took the rest of the stairs one creaky step at a time.

The cold, damp room was swept, checking each of the dozen motionless mangled bodies for life. Shining his weapon light over the spiderweb-filled room, they tried to make sense of it all.

"This place is a tomb," Raymond whispered in a raspy voice, trying to overcome the stench.

Victor shook his head slowly. "Nah, man, it's worse than a tomb. It's a den," he said, studying the Gray corpses before him.

The floor and walls were smeared with dried black, infected blood. The abdomen had been ripped apart on all of them, their dried and decomposing internal organs piled beside their corpses. Some of the Grays were half-eaten. Skeletons—either Gray or human, it couldn't be determined—were all that remained of a few.

"Animals?" Raymond questioned, knowing he had never seen an animal hungry enough to eat a diseased human.

Victor only shrugged, not able to answer the question. "I don't think your neighbors are home," he said, hoping the Riddell family was not among the den of the dead. He tilted his head toward the stairs, and they both tiptoed out carefully, trying not to step in the contaminant.

COMMAND AND CONTROL

Who's in charge here?

Victor drove to Raymond's house to grab the supplies he had mentioned. The task took longer than expected, since they had to take several trips down the hidden stairs into a secret basement storage room to fill the entire truck bed with more weapons, ammo, MRE boxes, and other miscellaneous survival gear. While there, they both cleaned themselves up and changed their clothes, knowing they wouldn't be given a chance when they returned to Lake City.

Moments later, they drove through the northern vehicle gate into town. Victor parked the truck in front of the TDF building and let the guards unload. Grabbing his pack, he headed straight home to see his family. He knew the council would be eagerly waiting for them at the pavilion for a thorough report.

He had just climbed the steps to his front porch when the door flew open, and Curtis, Michael, and Zavier piled, out attacking him with strong hugs before he could finish the climb.

"We missed you, Dad. We were so worried." Curtis said sincerely.

"'Worried?' For what? You know I am unstoppable!" Victor teased his kids, tousling their long, matted hair. "Have you boys ever had a lemon pound cake?"

He tossed them each a green package that he had picked out of an MRE box. The kids ran inside hysterically, almost knocking over Erica, who was standing in the doorway with a big smile and open arms. They met on the porch and embraced until she noticed a group forming near the park.

"I missed you so much. I was worried. I don't want to let you go, but you still have work to do, my love," she said, nodding toward the beach.

Victor let out a moan and rolled his eyes. "I don't wanna. Can't we just curl up on the couch together and stare into each other's eyes?" he said with a wink.

"Afterward, we can get in our PJs and snuggle all night by the fireplace. Come on, I'll walk you there. We can't wait to hear what happened."

They lazily walked hand in hand toward the pavilion, where the entire council was already waiting. Evidence of Stanly's attack could be seen in black stains on the surrounding groomed lawn, but the bodies had been removed. He didn't ask about the cleanup details.

They were nearly to the picnic table when Victor spotted a familiar couple standing across the street. He stopped in his tracks and pointed at them with a knife-hand. "Can someone please explain to me why they are not in a holding cell?"

"Quarantine time was up, and they demanded to be released," the mayor informed him, countering Victor's irritated tone.

"And?" Victor questioned. "We were just attacked, and you let two spies walk through town freely? Who's in charge here, you or them?"

"And they requested to speak to you about some sort of important information," Sheriff Bohner spoke, defending the mayor's actions. He waved the male and female over, each of them carrying their oversize backpacks and military-issued weapons that Victor had seen them use during his last rescue mission.

As the pair walked across Main Street toward the pavilion with a confident swagger, they paused at the distorted sound of a faint helicopter, which grew louder and louder. As the sound drew closer, Victor deciphered a dual set of heavy rotor blades, thumping through the air.

Victor brandished his pistol, pointing it at the ground between him and the couple. "Yours?" he yelled at them, pointing a finger toward the sound of helicopters in the sky.

"Yes," the taller, broad-shouldered man in a flannel shirt said flatly.

"Are you with the Grayling bunch?" Victor demanded.

"Negative," the woman said quickly.

"Then who?" Victor was getting annoyed with having to play the twenty questions game.

"Friends. You'll know soon enough," she said again, putting her hand to her forehead and shielding the sunlight, looking for the inbound helicopters.

The beating sound quickly grew louder until a UH-1 Huey and an escort Cobra attack helicopter flew over them at treetop level, startling everyone. The pair of helos flew out over the lake, banked sharply, circling back around, and then landed softly on the beach, kicking up a windstorm of sand and water mist, forcing everyone to shield their faces and turn away.

Victor watched the questionable couple he remembered as Stacy and Pete as they walked over to the Huey, then helped out an older gray-haired man wearing inspection-ready US Army multicam fatigues. Next, was a civilian in a suit and sunglasses, who Victor thought to be an intelligence spook. Finally, a casually but respectably dressed male and female stepped out of the helicopter with a helpful hand from big-man Pete.

The group strolled toward the pavilion as the rotor blades of the helos behind them slowly came to a stop. Stacy and Pete flanked the group in a protective posture.

No one at the picnic table spoke. They all stared in disbelief as if an alien UFO had just landed—except for Victor and Raymond, who clutched their holstered pistols.

"Hello, I am General Lyons," the older man established.

Victor cut him off before he could continue. "Is this about Camp Grayling? Do you know General Carter?"

General Lyons looked at Victor, confused. "I'm sorry, I don't know a General Carter. What of Camp Grayling?"

"Disregard. Grayling is no longer important to us." Victor looked at his peers with a hardened face, confirming their suspicions. That was the extent of his debrief to the council. "Why are you here, General?"

"May we sit?" the general asked in a polite manner, implying he had much to discuss.

"Of course," the mayor said, offering him his seat at the head of the table.

General Lyons took the seat and clasped his hands, resting them on the long picnic table. He began, "No doubt you all want to know why I'm here. But first, let me bring you up to speed on the current state of the world. The perpetual political chess game of influence and power took a major turn. An eastern alliance of Brazil, Russia, India, China, and South Africa, also known as BRICS, has nearly put the western nations in checkmate."

"But we heard on the radio that the Persians were behind this," the mayor inquired.

"On July fourth, the United States of America was attacked by several high-altitude electromagnetic-pulse weapons that completely crippled our nation and most of Canada. It was being reported that the Persians were responsible, because that is what Russian intelligence is feeding MI5 and NATO. I am almost certain that was part of the chess game: to let one enemy fight another. That being Europe against the Persians.

"To help persuade NATO into their chess game, Russian CCO clandestine operatives staged massive terror attacks across the EU, which manipulatively convinced Europe to plunge into World War Three. With the help of BRICS, NATO nearly conquered the entire Persian Gulf and surrounding regions. When the League of Arabs were about to submit, another wave of fake terror attacks hit Europe. NATO was so angry and desperate to end this war, they sent every single deployable unit surging back into battle."

Jessica couldn't comprehend the drastic differences in stories. "But the news said... How can you be so certain?"

"When was the last BBN news report you heard?" General Lyons paused to look around the table. "BRICS moved their final chess piece two days ago. Europe is now dark, just like the United States. BRICS hit them with EMPs after they mobilized the remaining military forces out of Europe. I'm afraid there will be no more BBN news reports. After the dust settles, Russia and China will be the economic, technologic, and military world superpower, with no means to dispute it. BRICS will have total control of Europe by springtime."

Erica covered her mouth, trying not to cry. Murmurs and questions erupted. Any hope of European aid that was had was now absent. They truly were on their own, except for the general sitting before them.

"So, General, what's your role in all of this?" Victor asked, still wondering why he and his clean-clothed associates had landed in the small town of Lake City.

"Before July fourth, I was with Northern Command. Now, I'm the commanding officer of Special Operations Command and the entire US Atlantic Fleet. My primary mission is much like yours, Victor," the general said, looking at the many awestruck faces, who wondered how he knew Victor's name. "We're sending out SEAL and MarSOC teams to recover key figures to help with reconstruction."

Victor nodded, imagining the missions they must be conducting in densely infected cities. Probably for high-level politicians and heads of federal departments—those were typically the first to be saved.

Sheriff Bohner had the same judgments as Victor. He leaned in to look down the table. "Are you under orders of the president? Is the federal government still intact?"

General Lyons took a deep breath, then paused, arranging his thoughts. "There has been no contact from the presidential bunker or from Camp David. If he's still alive, I don't know where he is. It has been confirmed that Vice President Bentley died in a helicopter crash while being extracted from a campaign rally in Baton Rouge on July fourth.

"There are several lower-level cabinet members who are fighting each other for control in DC. Not just political bickering but real, tactical skirmishes in a minifractional war taking place in the national mall." The general leaned back slightly. "To be honest, I wouldn't take orders from any of them at the moment. We have bigger concerns and don't have time for politics."

"Like the Russians and Chinese invaders on the West Coast? What's your game plan for that situation, General?" Raymond asked, angry that a high-ranking commanding officer was allowing such a thing to happen.

"My primary mission is stabilization and reconstruction, starting here on the East Coast. Although we have limited communication with the still-intact Pacific fleet, which is currently engaged in a guerilla war with BRICS, they are sinking troop transports disguised as freighter ships coming from Russian and China. They have destroyed a battleship, a refueling ship, and one midget submarine known to be carrying a special operations team. They are making life extraordinarily difficult for our enemy, but the Pacific fleet is running low on munitions. Nukes are an option being discussed, but we don't want America to be permanently radiated if we escalate to full-ballistic warfare.

"A Delta team, along with a company of infantry Marines extracted out of Afghanistan, is presently deployed behind enemy lines, near Seattle, Washington, and San Clemente, California, conducting harassment and sabotage missions to supply chains." The general smiled at Raymond.

"Hell, yeah!" Raymond shouted. "That's what I'm talking about!"

"It's an extremely high-risk mission. Not only are the teams fighting unconventionally against a conventional army but they're also being betrayed by collaborators in exchange for special favors, all on top of fighting Hemocytes at the same time," the general stated, noticing a table full of confused faces.

"Hemocytes?" Kevin asked. "Do you mean the Grays?"

"Grays, yes, that is a good name for the infected," General Lyons confirmed.

"Are they related, General?" Erica asked softly. "The timing was very suspicious. Did they release this plague as part of their world-domination chess game?"

"No. We don't think so." He shook his head, then looked at the spook to his right. "They were very careless about it, if they did. The same as any military technology; we wouldn't deploy a weapon until we can counter it first. Following the same protocols for biological warfare, an attacker would have first made safeguarding precautions, like a vaccine or an antidote. The pathogen has spread worldwide, now unconstrained inside Russia and China as well. It won't be long until they have also succumbed to its ravenous nature."

"General Lyons, thank you for sharing this intel that we desperately needed to hear. As you know, fresh and accurate information can be lifesaving and can also build morale. But now for the million-dollar question." Victor raised his eyebrows. "Why are you here?"

■ ■

"As I have stated, my mission is stabilization and reconstruction. Recruiting the right people for the job is crucial. We have been monitoring your progress since you first transmitted. Using the power of the Atlantic fleet, we want to use your town as a model, but bigger. Much, much bigger."

"Was that your drone overhead?" Victor pointed up.

"It was. Along with my advance party." The general paused to motion toward Stacy and Pete. "I wanted to confirm your broadcast claims before spending precious fuel to get here.

"Recruiting. That is why I am here. I would like your mayor to be our liaison. I have a nuclear-powered aircraft carrier plugged into Kent Island at the northern part of the Chesapeake Bay. It's a great location to hide the ship, and the island, which is mostly farmland, is now isolated after we destroyed one of the two connecting bridges. We have resources, but we need organizers like your mayor to help put it all together."

"Wow. I am truly honored, sir," the mayor said with flushed cheeks. "But this town needs me here."

"If you agree, it would only be temporary. Just long enough for you to brief our civil engineers. With you, we would like to recruit Victor and his team," the general said firmly. "We have very talented special operators in our fleet who've done covert operations all over the world. The kind of missions that shape foreign policy but will never be told in history books. They are the best, but they don't have your experience with the Hemocytes. The Grays."

Erica squeezed Victor's hand hard. Helping people in need was a value deeply embedded in him. Having the resources of an entire naval fleet, there was no limit to how many refugees could be rescued from the darkness covering the globe. He would help anyone in need, and they could really help turn this apocalypse around. Three to five percent survival rate is what they had predicted after the first year. Stanly had been right about one thing: this could easily be an extinction-level event. An irresistible sense of duty pulled at him. He needed to help the general. He should go. He *had* to go.

He turned to look at Erica, who had red, puffy eyes and a single tear rolling down her cheek. He remembered the heartache when her whereabouts were unknown. Unknown if she was even alive or dead, when she'd fought through actual hell to find him. How could he possibly leave her now? And his children. Would he dare take them across country to an unfamiliar area? He couldn't go without them; he couldn't separate from them, not in these dangerous times. Looking past Erica, he could see Main Street packed with the townsfolk who came to see who the helicopters had brought. Many of the people in the crowd Victor recognized as people who had called on the radio for his assistance.

General Lyons read the hesitation in Victor's face. "You must understand the gravity of our situation. We're not only talking about the fall of America as all we know it but also as an entire species."

"I do, General. Yet I cannot separate from my family and the people of this community," Victor proclaimed. "You said it yourself: that stabilization and reconstruction is crucial for America's survival, but it's crucial right here in northern Michigan as well. Many people depend on us, and many more need our help. I'm sorry, sir, but I have to sit this one out."

General Lyons's face melted with sadness and disappointment. Evidence of a considerable amount of planning and preparation to achieve hopes and dreams came crashing down. With his defeated palms placed on the table, he was about to stand and plead his case more firmly when a well-dressed civilian woman, who was part of the entourage, stepped up next to the general.

"That's fine. You all can stay here and maybe survive the winter," she said harshly. "We really only traveled here for her, anyway." The woman admitted, pointing a long finger directly at Erica.

The end, for now

EPILOGUE

The birth of a new era

A cold wind blew across the lake, lifting dried dead leaves off the grass. The chill of winter was in the air, along with the smell of wood-burning fireplaces. But it wasn't the chill that raised the goose bumps on Erica's arms.

A second civilian stepped up next to the audacious female who was pointing a long, demanding finger at Erica. "That's not entirely true. But, yes, we are also here for you, Erica. My name is Dr. Russell Barnaby, and this is my colleague, Dr. Diane Blackburne. We are associated with GENUTEK."

"Oh!" Erica said, shocked, stirring a flood of emotions and memories. She had seen neither of these two at her Detroit lab over the years, which added to the mystery of who she had truly worked for. It seemed like an eternity has passed since her escape from Detroit. So much had happened. So many people had been lost. She leaned in closer. "Associated with…"

"You may or may not have known, but GENUTEK was part of a vast research network. General Lyons has viral research at the top of his priority list. He's already rescued dozens of specialists from the Virginia area, a few from New York, and even one of your coworkers from Detroit."

That revelation surprised Victor. Safeguarding politicians and policy makers would have been priority, typically. The general had said he had bigger concerns than politics at the moment; Victor had assumed he only needed help on community planning. He also leaned in closer to hear what they had to say.

Dr. Diane Blackburne took over the conversation, exasperated with their lack of cooperation. "Look, General Lyons didn't parked the fleet in the Chesapeake bay by accident. Yeah, he has a good sanctuary location for civilians, and there's the symbolism of reconstructing America where our nation began hundreds of years ago. That's all fine too. But the real reason is that we're practically next door to USAMRIID."

"USAMRIID. What is that?" Victor asked.

Erica, still holding his hand tightly, answered, "The United States Army Medical Research Institute of Infectious Diseases, which is collocated with the National Institute of Allergy and Infectious Diseases."

"It's a level-four biosafety-biocontainment lab," Dr. Russell Barnaby added. "Which has already been secure, by the General."

"The best bio research lab in the world," Dr. Diane Blackburne concluded, looking at everyone at the table.

"It's operational?" Erica enquired with an eyebrow raised.

"Yes, with live specimens. But right now, we don't know if we should be wasting time with the first-gens," Dr. Diane Blackburne said, flustered.

"Wait," said Mrs. Cloud. "What do you mean by 'first-gens'?"

Dr. Diane Blackburne looked at Dr. Russell Barnaby. "The plague started in the south; it would make sense why they haven't been exposed to the second generation yet," she theorized with her partner.

"Second generation? You mean a mutation of the original strain?" Erica asked, demanding an answer.

"Hemocytes' offspring," both scientists said in unison. "They're breeding," Dr. Russell Barnaby concluded, dropping the biggest information bomb of the evening.

"The mysterious absence of females," Mrs. Cloud said out loud, finally understanding why they had only been seeing males locally.

Erica leaned back, putting her hands on her head as if she needed help breathing.

"If you think your Grays are bad, wait till you meet their vicious little offspring," the general added. "First-gens only want to spread the disease, never wanting to kill a perfectly good host. The second generation is a completely different story; they want to exterminate every clean human, and even Grays."

"They're killing their own?" Kevin asked.

"Yes, to make them the dominant species." Dr. Diane Blackburne answered. "But sometimes for food. When a second-gen is born, it kills its mother in the process, then consumes her until it rapidly grows and develops enough to join a pack."

"Oh, shit!" Raymond blurted out, looking at Victor and coming to the realization of what the horror scene in the neighbor's basement had been. The ripped-open abdomens and half-eaten Grays, it all made sense now.

"Yeah, we can confirm this to be true," Victor said. "We came across evidence of a den of mutilated deceased females this morning. Right after watching a platoon of soldiers get ripped apart by a swarm of little critters, we thought to be a feral dog pack."

■■

Erica snuggled in close to Victor, trapping their heat under the thick heavy blankets, pinning her permanently frigid toes against Victor and triggering a violent shiver to run up the length of his body, which caused her to giggle.

"What do you think?" she whispered, scootching in closer and wrapping an arm around his. "Want to go for a helicopter ride?"

"I still don't know. A lot has changed today. It's a lot of information to take in, analyze, and make an intelligent decision that'll affect a lot of people with, even outside this house." He exhaled heavily.

"They're flying south in the morning. We need to give them an answer by then."

"If we stay here or go with them, we do it together. You, me, Curtis, Michael, and Zavier—together. No exceptions," Victor answered, kissing her gently on her cheek.

AFTER PARTY

A word from the author, the complete zombie pop culture Easter egg hunt, full inspirational acknowledgments and Z Fighter sample pistol, carbine and precision rifle training drills.

Please take time to rate and review ZNIPER!

From the Author

I've always been a huge fan of zombie and doomsday dystopia genres. Every time I hear an emergency broadcast system test, I am deeply disappointed when they do not announce the Zombie Apocalypse. Another day of work, paying bills, and general grown-up responsibilities. I'm sure you can relate.

While deployed overseas, I get a lot of downtime, which is generally filled with older and newer Z pop culture–type movies and TV shows. Most of the time, I'm searching for a new book series that I have yet to read. One day, after not finding anything new from my favorite authors, the dumb idea popped in my mind to draft an outline for a story that I would like to read. So it began.

Authors who give comprehensive details how their creatures came to be really grab my attention, pulling me into the reality they have created, making me think, *Yeah, that could happen...* I figured using a fictitious hybrid of factual real-world diseases would have the same effect. Feel free to googleweb each of the components of my Nasty. It will make your skin crawl.

Typically, I enjoy authors who use ordinary characters describing how they overcome extraordinary circumstances. I do enjoy military-ish heroes if the authors know what the hell they are talking about. Nothing ruins a great story more than Delta operator calling magazines a clip or an M4 unrealistically popping moving zombie heads at 500 yards. Ugh...

Which brings me to my career. My goal was to not only have a decent storyline but to also be somewhat informational at a basic level. I hope that I was able to inject just enough of the technical knowledge I've learned over the years for the average person to get a few nuggets of warfighting wisdom and for the tacticians to say, "Hell yeah!"

Lastly, The Hunt. Here, you'll see full acknowledgment for all the movies, TV shows, and book references that inspired this story. As I said, I am huge fan of this genre, and I know that you are too. Adding in references to this story was in no way intended to plagiarize the genius creativity of others; the references are solely intended to add an extra layer of entertainment and appreciation of the entire Z culture.

Thank you for being a part of my adventure. Someday the story of Victor will continue. Until then, please feel free to follow my other escapades at:

www.MarksmanshipTrainingCenter.com

www.GunfighterSeries.com

Z Fighter Drill Book

Fundamental Pistol Drill Book

Advanced Pistol Drill Book

Fundamental Carbine Drill Book

Advanced Carbine Drill Book

Precision Rifle Drill Book

THE HUNT

ZNIPER Easter Egg Hunt

Pop cultural and historical references hidden in the story:
Anesidora (aka Anny): Pandora's other name, meaning "she who sends up gifts."

Pandora: The first woman, bestowed upon humankind as a punishment for Prometheus's theft of fire.

Pandora's Pithos: In Greek mythology, Pandora opened a jar (pithos), releasing all the evils of humanity, leaving only Hope inside. Often mistakenly referred as Pandora's Box.

Ploutonion: The Ploutonion at Hierapolis is also known as Pluto's Gate or Hell's Gate, where a temple was built on top of a cave that emits toxic gases.

- Prelude KICK OFF
  - *Zombieland* (film, 2009)—Three Sisters Bridal & Occasion and The Other Side of the Moon stores were featured behind the minivan Tallahassee smashed to release stress.
  - *Dawn of the Dead* (film, 2004)—"Propane tanks with road flares" were used to create IEDs detonated by gunshots.
- Chapter PANDORA
  - *Dawn of the Dead* (film, 2004)—News reports of civil unrest at the "Milwaukee Riverwalk" at the beginning of the movie.
  - *Deadheads* (film, 2011)—"GENUTEK" was the biotech corporation responsible for a zombie outbreak.
- Chapter PANDORA'S PITHOS
  - Fear the Walking Dead (TV Series, S5:E1)—Anny's access code "3-8-6-9" is the gate combination to the denim factory where survivors took shelter.
- Chapter PANDORA'S EVIL
  - *I Am Legend* (film, 2007)—"Dr. Alice Krippin" is the doctor who cures cancer using a measles virus.
  - The Walking Dead (TV Series, S1:E6)—"CDC Dr. Edwin Jenner" is the CDC scientist who shares vital information about the virus.

- *Last Man On Earth* (film, 1964)—"Dr. Mercer" was Robert Neville's supervisor.
- Chapter PLOUTONION OPENED
  - *I Am Legend* (book, 1954)—"Dr. Neville" is the main character.
  - *I Am Legend* (film, 2007)— Watch closely as the manikin's head turns slightly to face the main character who asks, "What are you doing out here Fred?"
- Chapter THE ROAD NOT TAKEN
  - *Dawn of the Dead* (film, 2004)—*Subtle Wave* was a boat in the marina at the end of the movie.
- Chapter MONSTERS
  - *28 Days Later* (film, 2002)—"Budgens'" was the UK grocery store chain where the main characters went shopping.
  - *Zombies Have Fallen* (film, 2007)—The evil villain, Raven, was the owner of Raven Health Care.
- Chapter UMBRA
  - *Night of the Living Dead* (film, 1968)—"Harry and Helen Cooper" was a couple hiding in the farmhouse cellar with their sick daughter.
  - *Dawn of the Dead* (film, 2004)—One of the invoices in Andy's Gun Works is made out to Nicholas Gazda, who is the first-assistant art director of this movie.
- Chapter UNWANTED GUEST
  - *I Am Legend* (book, 1954)—"Ben Cortman" was Robert Neville's friendly neighbor turned nemesis vampire.
  - *Night of the Living Deb* (film, 2015)—The main character had old an Cadillac named "OTIS."
- Chapter SHACKING UP
  - *The Evil Dead*:
    - *Evil Dead* (film, 1981)—Takes place in a small cabin in the woods with a trapdoor to a cellar. The key was hidden above the front door.
    - *Evil Dead II* (film, 1987)—Also takes place in a small cabin in the woods, where Ash has odd experiences with old "chainsaw."
    - *Evil Dead III: Army of Darkness* (film, 1992)—Ash has odd experiences with a "broken mirror."

- The same 1973 "Oldsmobile Delta 88 Royal" owned by the director was featured in all three films and several later films.
  o *Night of the Living Dead* (film, 1968)—"Space disease or cosmic radiation" from a deep-space Venus probe caused the zombies.
  o "Mr. Art Bell" was the original creator and host of my all-time favorite late-night AM radio talk show Coast To Coast AM, later turning the show over to George Noory.
- Chapter: ADVERSARIES
  o *I Walked With A Zombie* (film, 1943)—Jessica Holland, wife of sugar plantation owner Paul Mill, was stuck in a zombielike trance.
  o *Dawn of the Dead* (film, 1978)—Small junk airplane at airport, white with blue stripes, with "N688IM" on the side.
  o *Survival of the Dead* (2009, Film)—"Plum Island" was the setting for the movie and also advertised as a safe zone.
  o *Zombieland* (film, 2009) Referencing "Columbus, Ohio" as the lead character's parents. Blaine's Grocery Store is where Tallahassee sought Twinkies and found their new female "friends."
  o *28 Days Later* (film, 2002)—Maj. Henry West of the 42nd Blockade oversaw the military sanctuary.
- Chapter: PAYMENT PLAN
  o *Survival of the Dead* (film, 2009)—Muldoon family on Plum Island refused to kill the zombies.
  o *Fight Club* (film, 1999) Raymond K. Hessel is the convenience store worker.
  o *Shaun of the Dead* (film, 2004)—Shaun and Ed are the main characters.
  o *Zombieland* (film, 2009)—Columbus lives in apartment 408, cute neighbor girl in 406.
- Chapter: INTEL
  o *Survival of the Dead* (2009, Film)—"LOX Armored Inc." blue armored truck with a side window smashed was used for transportation.
  o *Zombieland* (film, 2009)—Gas N' Gulp (patient zero got infected and ring scam later in the movie)
  o *Dawn of the Dead* (film, 2004)

- A store shown in the "Crossroads Mall" is called Gaylen Ross, an obvious tribute to actress Gaylen Ross, who played Francine in the original 1978 film.
- Visible in Luda's room is a round can of something called "SMEAT"—a takeoff on Spam.
  - *28 Days Later* (film, 2002)—Primates escape from Cambridge University, causing the outbreak of Rage.
  - *The Dead* (film, 2010)—Main character is Lieutenant Brian Murphy USAF Flight Engineer. Survivor of plane crash flight LN260 in Africa.
- Chapter: THE WALL
  - *Black Summer* (TV Series, S1:E4)—A character sought shelter in a locked antique furniture store called The Shabby Little Vintage Shop.
- Chapter: WOLF PACK
  - *Dawn of the Dead* (film, 1978)—WGON was the TV news station.
  - *Shaun of the Dead* (film, 2004)—Shaun worked at the Foree Electronics store next to Buff's Pizzeria.
  - *Dead Rising* (video game, 2006)—The game centers a fictional town of Willamette (also in *Dead Rising 4* released ten years later in 2016).
- Chapter: PREGAME
  - *Zombieland* (film, 2009)—"We stand united against the infection' posters displayed in store window of "Three Sisters Bridal & Occasion" when Tallahassee relieves stress on the minivan.
  - *28 Days Later* (film, 2002)—Characters ate "Maltesers" chocolate candies while trapped in a gas station.
- Chapter: GAME TIME
  - *Pride and Prejudice and Zombies* (film, 2016)—Colonel Fitzwilliam J. Darcy, is a main character and exceptionally well-trained zombie killer.
  - *Dawn of the Dead* (film, 2004)—The fictitious stores in the mall include a coffee shop called Hallowed Grounds.
  - *The Dead* (film, 2010)—Sergeant Daniel Dembele is an African soldier who helps the American pilot survive.
  - *Ibiza Undead* (film, 2016)—Brown-and-tan-striped Torual's Taxi van was used in the movie.
- Chapter: GAME OVER

- *Zombies Ate My Neighbors* (video game, 1993)—A one- or two-player arcade-style game takes control of protagonists Zeke and Julie in order to rescue the titular neighbors.

- Chapter: BABA YAGA
  - *Zombie Massacre* (film, 2013—Dragan Illac was the Russian mercenary sniper.
  - *Outpost: Rise of the Spetsnaz* (film, 2013)—Potrovsky was the Russian SOF sniper.
  - *Frankenstein's Army* (film, 2013)—Novikov and Vassili were Russian soldier characters.
  - *Survival of the Dead* (film, 2009)—*Amherst Islander* is the large gray vehicle-hauler ferry boat.

- Chapter: HOMECOMING
  - *Return of the Living Dead* (film, 1985)—"2-4-5 Trioxin" has been mentioned in several zombie movies and documentaries, *Return of the Living Dead* being the first. 2-4-5 Trioxin is a spinoff of one of the two chemicals used to produce Agent Orange, called 2,4,5-Trichlorophenoxyacetic acid.
  - *Dead Rising: Watchtower* (film based on video game, 2015)—Chase Carter is the protagonist of the film. Based in a fictional town in Oregon. The character is also a journalist.
  - *White Zombie* (film, 1932)—Bride-to-be Madeleine Short is cursed by voodoo, turning her into a zombie.

- Chapter: SILK ROAD
  - *Quarantine* (film, 2008)—A fireman named Jake and a veterinarian named Lawrence get trapped inside a zombie-filled apartment building.
  - *Dead Heat* (film, 1988)—Detectives Roger Mortis and Doug Bigelow investigate a pharma company attempting immortality.
  - *28 Weeks Later* (film, 2007)—Tammy and Andy leave their father, Don, while they journey into a zombie-infested region to look for their mother, Alice. A gray four-door Volvo with fire-charred back hatch license plate S604OEW was seen in the movie under a bridge.
  - *Navy SEALS vs. Zombies* (film, 2015)—Lt. Pete Cunningham commanded the rescue team with intelligence provided by CIA agent Stacy Thomas.

- Chapter: COTERIE

- o   *The REZORT* (film, 2015)—Hope 4 U refugee-relocation organization turned refugees into zombies for the Rezort.
- o   *Train to Busan* (film, 2016)—Takes place onboard the KTX, a fast train from Seoul to Busan. Jung Suk-yong plays the train conductor.
- o   *The Girl With All The Gifts* (film, 2016)—The infected children were imprisoned by a group of soldiers led by Sergeant Eddie Parks.

- Chapter: KILL OR BE KILLED
  - o   *Kingdom* (TV series, 2019)—Main character, Crown Prince Yi Chang, fights through ancient Korea to return to his home capital of Hanyang.
  - o   *A Song of Ice and Fire* (novel series, 1996)—"Winter is coming" is a saying often used in reference to the pending frozen undead attack upon the living.

- Chapter: SNAKE EATERS
  - o   *I Am Legend* (film, 2007)—Main character's home address was 11 Washington and Square.
  - o   *Zombie Massacre* (film, 2013)—Mercs in the movie on mission under orders of General Carter.

- Chapter: VISITING NEIGHBORS
  - o   *Cell* (film, 2016)—Movie based around the unification of Clayton "Clay" Riddell, Sharon, and son, Johnny. Cellphone towers playing a key role.

- Chapter: COMMAND AND CONTROL
  - o   *Dead Rising: Endgame* (film, 2016, based on video game)—General Lyons is the military bad guy in cahoots with Phenotrans pharmaceuticals.
  - o   *Navy SEALS vs. Zombies* (film, 2015)—After a deadly outbreak occurs in Baton Rouge, Vice President Bentley dies in a helicopter crash while being extracted from a campaign rally.
  - o   *I Am Legend* (film, 2007)—The "Dark Seekers" are labeled "Hemocytes" in the DVD subtitles.

- Chapter: EPILOGUE
  - o   *Dead Rising* (video game, 2006)—Dr. Russell Barnaby, the main scientist behind the zombie outbreak in Santa Cabeza.
  - o   *Dead Rising 4* (video game, 2016)—Dr. Diane Blackburne is an Obscuris scientist who is working under Fontana during the Willamette outbreak.

Full Acknowledgments:

- *28 Days Later* (film, 2002)
    - Directed by: Danny Boyle
    - Produced by: Andrew Macdonald
    - Written by: Alex Garland
- *28 Weeks Later* (film, 2007)
    - Directed by: Juan Carlos Fresnadillo
    - Produced by: Enrique López-Lavigne, Andrew Macdonald, and Allon Reich
    - Written by: Rowan Joffé, Juan Carlos Fresnadillo, EL Lavigne, and Jesus Olmo
- A Song of Ice and Fire (novel series, 1996)
    - Author: George R. R. Martin
    - Publisher: Bantam Books
- *Black Summer* (TV series, 2019)
    - Created by: Karl Schaefer and John Hyams
    - Produced by: Jodi Binstock
    - Original network: Netflix
- *Cell* (film, 2016)
    - Directed by: Tod Williams
    - Produced by: Richard Saperstein, Michael Benaroya, Brian Witten, and Shara Kay
    - Screenplay by: Stephen King and Adam Alleca
- Coast To Coast AM (radio show)
    - Created by: Art Bell
    - Distributed by: Premiere Networks
- *Dawn of the Dead* (film, 1978)
    - Directed by: George A. Romero
    - Produced by: Richard P. Rubinstein
    - Written by: George A. Romero
- *Dawn of the Dead* (film, 2004)
    - Directed by: Zack Snyder
    - Produced by: Richard P. Rubinstein, Mark Abraham, and Eric Newman
    - Written by: James Gunn
- *Deadheads* (film, 2011)
    - Directed by: Brett and Drew T. Pierce
    - Produced by: Andy Drummond, Brett Pierce, Drew Pierce, and Kevin Van Hagaen
    - Written by: Brett and Drew T. Pierce

- *Dead Heat* (film, 1988)
  - o   Directed by: Mark Goldblatt
  - o   Produced by: David Helpern and Michael L. Meltzer
  - o   Written by: Terry Black
- *Dead Rising* (video game, 2006)
  - o   Developer: Capcom
  - o   Creator: Keiji Inafune
- *Dead Rising 4* (video game, 2016)
  - o   Developer: Capcom
  - o   Directed by: Joe Nickolls
  - o   Produced by: Eduardo Agostini, David McAnerin, and Peter Sobczak
- *Dead Rising: Endgame* (film, 2016, based on video game)
  - o   Directed by: Pat Williams
  - o   Produced by: Tim Carter and Chris Foss
  - o   Written by: Tim Carter and Michael Ferris
- *Dead Rising: Watchtower* (film, 2015, based on video game)
  - o   Directed by: Zach Lipovsky
  - o   Produced by: Tim Carter and Tomas Harlan
  - o   Written by: Tim Carter
- *Evil Dead, The* (film, 1981)
  - o   Directed by: Sam Raimi
  - o   Produced by: Robert Tapert
  - o   Written by: Sam Raimi
- *Evil Dead II: Dead By Dawn* (film, 1987)
  - o   Directed by: Sam Raimi
  - o   Produced by: Robert Tapert, Alex De Benedetti, and Irvin Shapiro
  - o   Written by: Sam Raimi and Scott Spiegel
- *Evil Dead III: Army of Darkness* (film, 1992)
  - o   Directed by: Sam Raimi
  - o   Produced by: Robert Tapert
  - o   Written by: Sam Raimi and Ivan Raimi
- *Fear the Walking Dead* (TV Series)
  - o   Created by: Robert Kirkman and Dave Erickson
  - o   Based on comic book written by: Robert Kirkman, Tony Moore, and Charlie Adlard
  - o   Distributed by: AMC
- *Fight Club* (film, 1999)
  - o   Directed by: David Fincher
  - o   Produced by: Art Linson, Ceán Chaffin, and Ross Grayson Bell
  - o   Screenplay by: Jim Uhls
- *Frankenstein's Army* (film, 2013)
  - o   Directed by: Richard Raaphorst

- o Produced by: Nick Jongerius, Daniel Koefoed, Todd Brown, and Greg Newman
- o Screenplay by: Chris W. Mitchell and Miguel Tejada-Flores
- *I Am Legend* (film, 2007)
  - o Directed by: Francis Lawrence
  - o Produced by: Akiva Goldsman, James Lassiter, David Heyman and Neal H. Moritz
  - o Written by: Mark Protosevich and Akiva Goldsman
- *I Am Legend* (novel, 1954)
  - o Author: Richard Matheson
  - o Publisher: Gold Medal Books
- *Ibiza Undead* (film, 2016)
  - o Directed by: Andy Edwards
  - o Produced by: Templeheart Films
  - o Written by: Andy Edwards
- *I Walked With A Zombie* (film, 1943)
  - o Directed by: Jacques Tourneur
  - o Produced by: Val Lewton
  - o Written by: Curt Siodmak and Ardel Wray
  - o Based on: novel of the same name written by Inez Wallace
- *Kingdom* (TV series, 2019)
  - o Written by: Kim Eun-hee
  - o Directed by: Kim Seong-hun
  - o Original network: Netflix
- *Navy SEALS vs. Zombies* (film, 2015)
  - o Directed by: Stanton Barrett
  - o Written by: A.K. Waters
  - o Screenplay by: Mathew Carpenter
- *Night of the Living Dead* (film, 1968)
  - o Directed by: George A. Romero
  - o Produced by: Russell Streiner and Karl Hardman
  - o Written by: John Russo and George A. Romero
- *Night of the Living Deb* (film, 2015)
  - o Directed by: Kyle Rankin
  - o Produced by: Michael Cassidy, Kyle Rankin, and Chad Nicholson
  - o Written by: Andy Selsor
- *Outpost: Rise of the Spetsnaz* (film, 2013)
  - o Directed by: Kieran Parker
  - o Produced by: Kieran Parker
  - o Written by: Rae Brunton
- *Pride and Prejudice and Zombies* (film, 2016)
  - o Directed by: Burr Steers

- o   Produced by: Sean McKittrick, Allison Shearmur, Natalie Portman, Annette Savitch, Brian Oliver, Tyler Thompson, and Marc Butan
- o   Screenplay by: Burr Steers
- *Quarantine* (film, 2008)
  - o   Directed by: John Erick Dowdle
  - o   Produced by: Sergio Aguero, Doug Davison, Roy Lee
  - o   Screenplay by: John Erick Dowdle and Drew Dowdle
  - o   Based on: *REC* (film, 2007)
- *Return of the Living Dead* (film, 1985)
  - o   Directed by: Dan O'Bannon
  - o   Produced by: Tom Fox and Graham Henderson
  - o   Written by: Dan O'Bannon
- *Shaun of the Dead* (film, 2004)
  - o   Directed by: Edgar Wright
  - o   Produced by: Nira Park
  - o   Written by: Edgar Wright and Simon Pegg
- *Survival of the Dead* (film, 2009)
  - o   Directed by: George A. Romero
  - o   Produced by: Paula Devonshire and Peter Grunwald
  - o   Written by: George A. Romero
- *The Dead* (film, 2010)
  - o   Directed by: Howard J. Ford and Jon Ford
  - o   Produced by: Howard J. Ford and Amir S. Moallemi
  - o   Written by: Howard J. Ford and Jon Ford
- *The Girl With All The Gifts* (film, 2016)
  - o   Directed by: Colm McCarthy
  - o   Produced by: Will Clarke, Camille Gatin, and Angus Lamont
  - o   Written by: Mike Cary, based on his book with same name
- *The Last Man On Earth* (film, 1964)
  - o   Directed by: Ubaldo Ragona (Italian prints) and Sidney Salkow
  - o   Produced by: Robert Lipper and associate Harold Knox
  - o   Written by: Furio M. Monetti, Ubaldo Ragona, William Leicester
- *The REZORT* (film, 2015)
  - o   Directed by: Steve Parker
  - o   Produced by: Nick Gillott, Karl Richards, Charlotte Walls
  - o   Written by: Paul Gerstenberger
- *Train to Busan* (film, 2016)
  - o   Directed by: Sang-ho Yeon
  - o   Produced by: Dong-ha Lee
  - o   Written by: Joo-suk Park
- *Walking Dead* (TV series)
  - o   Developed by: Frank Darabont

- o   Based on comic book written by: Robert Kirkman, Tony Moore, and Charlie Adlard
- o   Distributed by: AMC
- *White Zombie* (film, 1932)
  - o   Directed by: Victor Halperin
  - o   Produced by: Edward Halperin
  - o   Written by: Garnett Weston
  - o   Inspired by: *The Magic Island* (novel, 1929, William Seabrook)
- *Zombieland* (film, 2009)
  - o   Directed by: Ruben Fleischer
  - o   Produced by: Gavin Polone
  - o   Written by: Rhett Reese and Paul Wernick
- *Zombies Ate My Neighbors* (video game, 1993)
  - o   Developer: LucasArts
  - o   Publishers: Konami and LucasArts (Wii Virtual Console)
  - o   Designer: Mike Ebert
  - o   Programmer: Dean Sharpe
- *Zombies Have Fallen* (film, 2007)
  - o   Directed by: Sam Fountayne
  - o   Written by: Sam Fountayne
- *Zombie Massacre* (film, 2013)
  - o   Directed by: Luca Boni and Marco Ristori
  - o   Produced by: Uwe Boll, Luca Boni, Marco Ristori, and Benjamin Krotin
  - o   Written by: Luca Boni, Marco Ristori, and Russell Romick

Z FIGHTER

Sample Z Fighter Gun Drills and Log Sheets

PISTOL DRILL: MY SAFE SPACE

Purpose: Establishing your life saving pistol fighting comfort zone.

Distance: 3 Yards to ?

Target: ZIPSC (Undead) with hostage target. *To make a ZIPSC, simply attach an MTC Z-1 target (free on the Gunfighter Series website) to an ordinary carboard IPSC.

Total Rounds Fired: ? Rounds

Starting Position & Condition: Standing - Surrender / Interview position. Condition 1 holstered pistol.

Description: Stating at 3 yards, draw and fire 1 round into the head ocular Z box. Holster pistol then walk to the target to inspect your shot placement. Return to the firing line and then add 1 yard from you previous successful shot. Continue this drill until you miss the ocular Z box. Then continue this drill further until you miss the head entirely or hit the hostage. Record your maximum accurate lifesaving zombie killing distance.

Goals:

- Meat Bag: 7 Yards.
- Survivor: 15 Yards.
- Z Fighter: 25 Yards.

Variations:

- Infected Humans: Add a 2 second par time restraint for each draw. Run, instead of walk, to check your target then run back to the firing line.
- Mutants: Do not holster between shots and continue to fire while walking backwards.

www.GunfighterSeries.com

MY SAFE SPACE - Data record sheet

Date:	Pistol:	Sights:	Notes:
Undead / Infected Human / Mutant			Max Distance:

Date:	Pistol:	Sights:	Notes:
Undead / Infected Human / Mutant			Max Distance:

Date:	Pistol:	Sights:	Notes:
Undead / Infected Human / Mutant			Max Distance:

Date:	Pistol:	Sights:	Notes:
Undead / Infected Human / Mutant			Max Distance:

Date:	Pistol:	Sights:	Notes:
Undead / Infected Human / Mutant			Max Distance:

Date:	Pistol:	Sights:	Notes:
Undead / Infected Human / Mutant			Max Distance:

Date:	Pistol:	Sights:	Notes:
Undead / Infected Human / Mutant			Max Distance:

Date:	Pistol:	Sights:	Notes:
Undead / Infected Human / Mutant			Max Distance:

CARBINE DRILL: THREE'S A CROWD

Purpose: Increase carbine accuracy, speed and recoil management with multiple targets.

Distance: 15 Yards.

Target: ZIPSC X 3. 3 Targets set up 5 feet apart at 15 yards. *To make a ZIPSC, simply attach an MTC Z-1 target (free on the Gunfighter Series website) to an ordinary carboard IPSC.

Extra Equipment Needed: Shot timer.

Total Rounds Fired: 27 Rounds.

Rounds Fired per Rep: 9 Rounds.

Point Penalty: Live or Die

Repetitions: 3 Reps

Starting Position & Condition: Standing - Low ready. Condition 1.

Description: At the beep of the timer, fire 2 rounds into the A zone body box, then 1 round to the ocular Z box, transition to next target with the same shot pattern and then transition to the last target with the same shot pattern. Goal is to fire all rounds within goal par time, and inside the A and Z zone boxes. If you fail goal par time or have rounds out of designated zone boxes during a repetition, the repetition is a failure.

Goals:

- Meat Bag: 9 Seconds.
- Survivor: 8 Seconds.
- Z Fighter: 6 Seconds.

Variations:

- Infected Humans: Engage from 20 yards.
- Mutants: Engage from 20 yards with 4 shots to the body A box and 1 shot to the ocular Z box of each target while on the move walking left or right. 15 rounds per rep.

www.GunfighterSeries.com

A Sniper's Journey Through The Apocalypse.

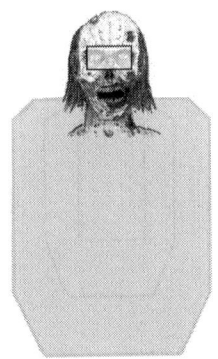 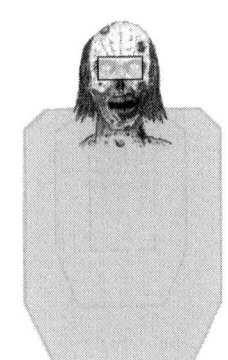 

THREE'S A CROWD - Data record sheet

Date:	Carbine:	Sights:
Rep 1 Time:	Rep 2 Time:	Rep 3 Time:
Go / No Go	Go / No Go	Go / No Go
Undead / Infected Human / Mutant		
Left to Right / Right to Left		

Date:	Carbine:	Sights:
Rep 1 Time:	Rep 2 Time:	Rep 3 Time:
Go / No Go	Go / No Go	Go / No Go
Undead / Infected Human / Mutant		
Left to Right / Right to Left		

Date:	Carbine:	Sights:
Rep 1 Time:	Rep 2 Time:	Rep 3 Time:
Go / No Go	Go / No Go	Go / No Go
Undead / Infected Human / Mutant		
Left to Right / Right to Left		

Date:	Carbine:	Sights:
Rep 1 Time:	Rep 2 Time:	Rep 3 Time:
Go / No Go	Go / No Go	Go / No Go
Undead / Infected Human / Mutant		
Left to Right / Right to Left		

PRECISION RIFLE DRILL: FUNDAMENTALLY AWESOME

Purpose: To reinforce solid shooting position, Natural Point of Aim and follow through.

Distance: 100 Yards

Target: GF-2 (Undead). *Free on the Gunfighter Series website.

Par Time: 25 Seconds

Extra Equipment Needed: Shot timer.

Total Rounds Fired: 5 Rounds.

Point Penalty: Per target score.

Starting Position & Condition: See description.

Description (DRY): Assume a good prone position with a condition 4 rifle. Conduct a set of 10 dry fires as fast as possible while maintaining perfect sight alignment and sight picture.

Description (LIVE): Assume a good prone position with a condition 1 rifle. At the timer beep, fire 5 rounds at the target. For tightest groups; take a little extra time to ensure your body position and N.P.A. are correct.

Goals:

- Novice: 45 points under par.
- Expert: 50 points under par.
- Gunfighter: 50 points with 5 X's under par.

Variations:

- Infected Humans: Start standing behind your rifle. Immediately before the start of the drill, run 50 yards and do 10 push-ups or jumping jacks to get your heart hate up.
- Mutants: From 200 yards. Start standing behind your rifle. Immediately before the start of the drill, run 50 yards and do 10 push-ups or jumping jacks to get your heart hate up.

www.GunfighterSeries.com

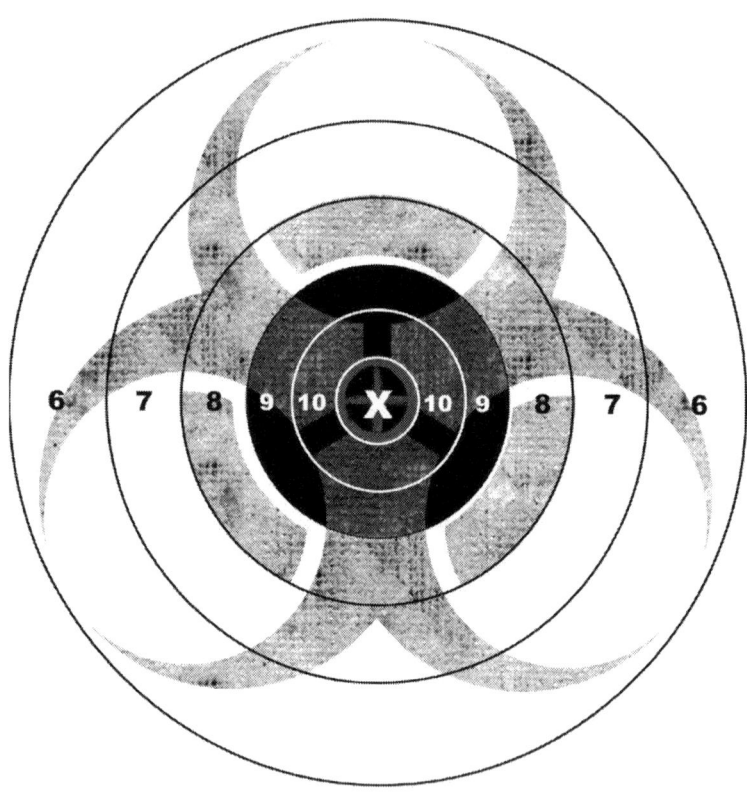

ZF-2

FUNDAMENTALLY AWESOME - Data record sheet

Date:	Rifle:	Scope:
Elev: Wind:	Drill Time:	**Score: # of X's**:
Dry Fire X 10: Y / N	Undead / Infected Human / Mutant	
Notes:		

Date:	Rifle:	Scope:
Elev: Wind:	Drill Time:	**Score: # of X's**:
Dry Fire X 10: Y / N	Undead / Infected Human / Mutant	
Notes:		

Date:	Rifle:	Scope:
Elev: Wind:	Drill Time:	**Score: # of X's**:
Dry Fire X 10: Y / N	Undead / Infected Human / Mutant	
Notes:		

Date:	Rifle:	Scope:
Elev: Wind:	Drill Time:	**Score: # of X's**:
Dry Fire X 10: Y / N	Undead / Infected Human / Mutant	
Notes:		

Date:	Rifle:	Scope:
Elev: Wind:	Drill Time:	**Score: # of X's**:
Dry Fire X 10: Y / N	Undead / Infected Human / Mutant	
Notes:		

Made in the USA
Columbia, SC
19 February 2020